RENEGADE RED

BOOK TWO of THE LIGHT TRILOGY

LAUREN BIRD HOROWITZ

RENEGADE RED

BOOK TWO OF **THE LIGHT TRILOGY**

Published by Papaloa Press, California
Papaloa Press trademark design by Tara French Johnson

Cover photography by Gil Cope
Cover design by Zoe Cope, Zoe Cope Creative
Additional cover photography for "Traveler" edition by Michelle Craig
Interior illustrations by Maren Gunderson

Library of Congress Control Number: 2016913847

e-book: ISBN-10: 0-9745956-6-7
             ISBN-13: 978-0-9745956-6-5

Hardcover: ISBN-10: 0-9745956-7-5
             ISBN-13: 978-0-9745956-7-2

Paperback: ISBN-10: 0-9745956-5-9
             ISBN-13: 978-0-9745956-5-8

Printed in Canada

CONNECT

www.LaurenBirdHorowitz.com

@birdaileen

@birdaileen

 Lauren "Birdaileen" Horowitz

AWARDS & PRAISE FOR
SHATTERED BLUE

Silver Medalist
INDEPENDENT PUBLISHING BOOK AWARD
BEST YOUNG ADULT FICTION 2015

Finalist
USA BOOK AWARD, BEST NEW FICTION 2015
USA BOOK AWARD, BEST FANTASY 2015
INTERNATIONAL BOOK AWARD, BEST FANTASY 2015
NEXT GENERATION INDIE BOOK AWARD,
BEST YOUNG ADULT FICTION 2015

"Anyone who's ever fantasized about kissing a Fae will enjoy Noa and Callum's first, sexy kiss. ...Hip ... fast-moving ... lyrically concise."
—KIRKUS REVIEWS

"I guarantee you'll be hooked
and anxiously awaiting the next book in the series."
—USA TODAY, Must-read Romances of 2015

"A fantastical tale of love and betrayal
...more than enough emotion and angst to keep any romance-
loving teenager glued to the pages, and the promise of a trilogy
will keep them eagerly anticipating the next book."
—SCHOOL LIBRARY JOURNAL

"A book to fall for"
—BUZZFEED

"Not your average fairy tale ... will have you clamoring for more
of a story that you didn't see coming ... new and surprising."
—HYPABLE

for T,
my fellow Renegade

… and Ninj,
still wagging with each word
(especially when it's Frisbee)

TABLE OF CONTENTS

Awards & Praise for *Shattered Blue* vii

The Story So Far xvii

The Fae Colorlines. xviii

Family Trees xix

Epigraph xxi

Preface. xxiii

Part I. 1

Part II 71

Part III 177

Part IV 251

Part V . . . .   , , , , ...383

Join Fae Nation. 391

Poetry Appendix 395

Acknowledgments. 401

About the Author 405

THE STORY SO FAR

STILL REELING FROM the tragic death of her older sister, Isla, fifteen-year-old Noa Sullivan met and fell for Callum Forsythe, a mysterious transfer student at her elite Monterey boarding school. As they grew closer, Noa discovered Callum's secret: he was *Fae*, a magical exile banished to her world from his realm of Aurora—and in terrible danger. To save him, Noa made a dangerous alliance with Judah, Callum's rebellious, deceptive brother—all while trying to help her own family, and especially her beloved little sister, Sasha, survive its own loss. But during Noa and Judah's desperate rescue mission, Sasha herself disappeared into a collapsing Portal between worlds, and Noa leapt in after her, Forsythe brothers in tow, with no idea where they—or Sasha—were headed.

THE FAE COLORLINES

BLUE FAE
Fae with the power to control the elements and manipulate the physical world.

GREEN FAE
Fae with the power to control feelings and manipulate emotions.

RED FAE
Fae with the power to control thoughts and manipulate the mind.

CLEAR FAE
Fae with no intrinsic powers of their own, but with the ability to Channel
Colored Fae's gifts through physical contact.

THE FAMILIES

SULLIVAN

Hannah ┬ Christopher

Isla (dec.)   Noa   Sasha

FORSYTHE

Darius ┬ Lorelai

Lily (dec.)   Callum   Judah

Faeries, come take me out of this dull world,
For I would ride with you upon the wind,
Run on the top of the dishevelled tide,
And dance upon the mountains like a flame.

W.B. Yeats

PREFACE

Aurora
(before)

WHEN JUDAH FINALLY stopped struggling, when they were beaten, bloody brother-mirrors, Callum let him rise. The darker, slighter boy levered himself up against the bars. This cell had somehow caged it all: Callum's lies, Judah's anger, and guilt enough for Lily's loss to drown them both. Judah bled from a gash above his eye; Callum wiped a smear from his broken nose.

"You'll be the first Banished there, since Kells," Judah said.

Callum smiled a little. "Always first."

Judah scowled.

"You stay," Callum warned him again. "For Lorelei."

Judah's jaw clenched, but he didn't argue. When he spoke, his voice trembled, like it had when they were young: "Do you go right through, or…" He turned, afraid.

"The Gatekeeper's supposed to make sure I don't get caught between."

"But what's it like? The In Between?"

Callum stayed tall, and still. "Lorelei once said it's the place where you find out."

"Find out?"

Callum met his little brother's eyes. "What you truly want. What you'll truly give. And if, in the end, it's enough to save your life."

PART I: HARLOW

"YOUR SISTER IS DEAD."

Hard and sharp, discrete and precise: Noa Sullivan blinked painfully as she wakened to the grim words. She struggled through tangled blankets, squinted into the gray morning light. A black shape loomed ominously.

And laughed.

"Did you hear me? Isla is dead meat if she doesn't get her ass to class on time. Three tardies she might get sent for Review."

Noa rubbed an open palm over her left eye. The hovering shape sharpened into her best friend, Olivia Lee, its looming teeth merely the pink-hued points of Olivia's trademark half-buzzed hair. Olivia was wearing her Harlow uniform properly enough—pants ironed and pleated, blouse buttoned three buttons high—but no amount of regulation could tame her rebellious punk-chick eyes, rolling sardonically on top. And of course, her perfectly pressed short blouse sleeves only better showcased the concentric-circle tattoos spiraling down her arms.

But to Noa, no one was less intimidating.

1

Noa groaned and pulled her pillow over her head, muffling her voice. "Isla's not back *again*?"

Olivia laughed. "You two really were born in the wrong order. *She* should be the baby of the family, not you. The wild-child gene must've gotten confused."

"Tell me about it. She'd better not abandon me this weekend—" Noa broke off, too late, as Olivia snatched her pillow away.

"*O!*"

"Up and at 'em, Noser! I sure as hell don't want a tardy too. Review is the only experience I am *not* willing to try once."

Noa sat up grudgingly, wincing. She didn't know why, but the last few weeks she hadn't been feeling rested. It was as if her body never recharged—probably because of the thinner-by-the-year boarding school mattress. Harlow, her Monterey prep school, prided itself on being just as rigorous and elite as the East Coast name-brand schools like Exeter and Andover, but creature comforts were lacking.

Noa stretched, trying to convince her aching back to forget its troubles, and her tablet screensaver flashed a picture of her with her sister Isla, the one who was evidently still out partying and apparently never needed sleep. Isla was two years older, but she and Noa had almost identical features and were often mistaken for twins.

This was something Noa never understood: Isla was regal, with imperial silver eyes and iridescent blond hair. On Noa, those same eyes were drab and gray, that same hair a mish-mash tangle of dirty blond. In pictures like this one, where she and Isla stood side by side, Noa thought they barely looked related, let alone identical.

Noa frowned at the photo taken this past winter break. Isla was grinning, arm slung over Noa's uncertain, anxious shoulders; they stood in front of an abandoned cabin they'd secretly explored in some woods in Maine. It was supposed to be haunted but had really just been derelict, and they'd been lucky the whole floor hadn't just caved in under them. Noa hadn't wanted to go, but Isla had made it a *test*. Her little sister, she said, couldn't live her *whole* life as a coward.

Noa had never been good at telling Isla no.

"Have you checked yet?" Noa asked Olivia, looking away from the picture. There were other, more pressing things to worry about today.

For once, Olivia sounded nervous. "Not yet. I waited for you."

"Well ... I guess we should look," Noa said uneasily. "Since we're both up."

"Yeah, so let's look."

Neither of them moved.

"This is so silly," Noa said. "I mean, who even cares?"

Olivia raised a pierced eyebrow. "You're right. The Beautiful Little Fools are only the most exclusive and powerful female secret society at Harlow, and we're only about to see if we got the nod into the world of social stardom beyond our wildest dreams—or if we've been denied, chucked aside, fated to be nobodies for the rest of our boarding-school lives. No big deal."

Noa frowned. "Okay, fine. It's a big deal."

"At least *you're* a legacy."

"Just because Isla's in the Little Fools doesn't mean I got tapped. In fact, knowing her, it probably means I *didn't*."

"She *is* willing to be your roommate," Olivia pointed out.

"Rooming with me to appease Mom and Dad is one thing. She knows I can't stop her from doing anything, no matter what they hope. I'm just her lame baby sister."

Olivia nodded seriously. "Now that I think of it, I hope your rep doesn't rub off on me. Isla knows I'm a rebel, right? I mean, check the hair. And the skin art? Seriously."

Noa grinned, used to Olivia's deadpan brand of teasing. "It's not exactly rebellious if your parents support your choices, O. Your mom *took* you to get those circle tattoos."

"I *know.*" Olivia sighed dramatically, lifting her tatted arms. "I can do no wrong. How infuriating."

"High-class problems, O." Noa ran a hand over her chest, where the long diagonal scar sliced down beneath her collarbone. "I wish my parents would let me turn this thing into a tattoo or something." For some reason, Noa had been obsessing about her mysterious scar a lot lately. She knew she'd had it forever—her parents, Isla, had grown tired of assuring her she'd probably been born with it—but she couldn't shake the feeling that there was something else about it, a memory or a dream that sublimated the moment she tried to grasp it.

Olivia laughed. "Somehow I don't see Hannah and Christopher Sullivan going for a tattoo. But I think you should leave it anyway. Nothing like a huge scar to fierce up your image."

Noa looked skeptical. "Even when no one remembers how you got it?"

"Especially then! You could be a sleeper bad-ass spy vixen! Code name: Girl Beast."

Noa got to her feet. "Well, if that's the case, I can't be afraid to open the door. So come on. We'll open it together, and either we see signets or we don't."

Olivia squinted shrewdly. "You know, these girls are *pretty* arrogant, just doling out rings without even waiting to hear if the person accepts."

"Have *you* ever heard of a tap from the Beautiful Little Fools being refused?"

They walked to the front door. "Okay, O, on three. One, two…"

• • •

"I HAVE BROUGHT shame to the Sullivan name," Noa moped, as she and Olivia walked to Dr. Chandler's classroom, signet-less.

"Only *half* the name," Olivia pointed out. "Isla's still a Fool, so fifty percent of Sullivan is still respectable."

"You didn't get tapped either!" Noa reminded her with a laugh. She was disappointed, but she wasn't as overwhelmingly upset as she'd thought she'd be. Maybe because, deep down, she knew she was no Isla. The wildness, the adventuring, that was Isla's turf; Noa lived in a quieter realm. Not that it wouldn't have been cool to get to feel like Isla, even if just for a little while. Olivia was at full snark, but Noa knew, without question, that Olivia would have joined only if they'd both been tapped anyway. Fiercely loyal like Isla, she was not afraid to make history and turn down even the most elite Harlites imaginable.

Annabelle Leighton, another classmate, walked up to join them in the imposing hallway. When she'd been a freshman, Harlow's stone-walled corridors had seemed infinitely daunting to Noa, with their soaring ceilings and echoing marble. Now she hardly noticed them. The same could not be said, however, for the howling wildness around the school, visible through massive windows and glass-paned double doors. Inside, Harlow was strict and sharp, but outside, the creeping Salinas wilderness ruled, as if the school itself were caught in the claw of a mythical beast, soaring through some wild, wailing unknown.

Annabelle was wearing the skirt version of the Harlow uni, which clashed angrily with her freckled, flaming red cheeks. Her cross-ties looked agonized, as if she had tortured the knot into submission.

Olivia hid a laugh. "No signet for you either, huh?"

"*Technically* I can say nothing, of course, giving respect to the secrecy of the process," Annabelle seethed, "but let's just say I won't be letting any known Little Fool rent out my room anytime soon." Noa raised her eyebrows. If Annabelle meant it, it wasn't an idle threat: Annabelle made a boarding-school fortune renting out her dorm room for … illicit … activities and selling forbidden contraband. For this alone, Noa had been sure Annabelle would be tapped; you couldn't get more indispensible when it came to debauchery.

"What's the status on everyone else? What do we know?"

Annabelle scowled. "Well, no one's talking, of course. You know, just in *case* the snobs change their mind—"

"But…," Noa prodded.

"It's what you'd expect. Carly Ann, Ansley, Leticia, Mary Jane are all in," Annabelle said, listing Harlow's most popular juniors. Noa looked down the hall, where pretty Carly Ann was beaming with pride, watched by a gaggle of impressed underclassmen. Noa wasn't surprised: Carly Ann was the most beloved and outgoing girl Noa knew. She even dimmed Isla. Her coterie of girl-cadets—Ansley, Leticia, Mary Jane—looked like dim impressionist paintings when they stood next to her exquisite, elaborate beauty.

Noa, Olivia, and Annabelle couldn't help but be mesmerized as Carly Ann strode victoriously past the row of lonely lockers lining one wall—so-called "commuter lockers," for those rare students who attended Harlow but didn't board on campus. Noa felt a little shiver creep down her spine as her eyes fell on them. Strange, since she'd never even met a commuter, half-believed they were a myth.

Noa turned back to Annabelle and Olivia, who was scowling. "Where are Ansley, Leticia, and MJ? Shouldn't they be making their victory lap, too?"

Annabelle shrugged. "Probably out celebrating."

Noa's eyes lingered on those creepy commuter lockers. She had that feeling again, that feeling of something sublimating out of her grasp—

"Yo! Noa!" Annabelle snapped her fingers an inch from Noa's eye. "You should be most pissed of all, a legacy and everything!"

Noa tried to look more disappointed.

Olivia laughed. "Pitiful. But I *guess* we forgive you. People lose all sense of priorities when they're in *lurrrrrve...."*

Noa blushed furiously, tried to fight the immediate grin. It was true: it was hard for her to feel too depressed about not making Isla's girl squad, not when she had ... *him.* The boy who had transferred in ... and changed everything.

Annabelle threw up her hands at Noa's sappy look. "That's what I need to make me feel better! A transfer student—"

"Correction: a *super-hot* transfer student," Olivia interrupted.

"Right, a super-hot transfer student to come in, sweep me off my feet, and be my boyfriend-in-shining-armor. Then I won't care about the Pitiful Little Fools either!"

Noa let her smile shine. It was true. Not even Isla had a boyfriend like him. She looked down the hall, almost as if she could feel him approaching, as if she could sense him, as if she carried a piece of his soul in her heart. She saw him in her mind before he even turned the corner: that coronet of curls, those dark, gorgeous eyes...

Judah.

"My, my, Judah Smith, showing your face in the halls?" Noa teased, as she half-walked, half-pranced up to her boy. She wanted to run but knew better than to fly so publicly to him. Judah was like an unbroken colt; he spooked easily.

One side of Judah's mouth quirked up, the way Noa loved. "You're doing terrible things for my rep," he agreed. "People might start thinking I'm actually studious. It's positively *shameful*." He whispered the last word in her ear, leaning in close, his warm breath brushing her hair from her shoulder. A tingle raced down Noa's neck. His hand slipped smoothly into hers, like a secret, and she sneaked a tiny glance back at Olivia and Annabelle. Olivia wiggled her brows, amused; Annabelle tried to cover her envious expression.

Judah followed Noa's gaze and chuckled softly. "Your friends need better poker faces. I can practically read their minds."

Noa smiled. "You wish. Besides, they know better than to play cards with the likes of you."

"What? I am a *paragon* of virtue!" Judah pulled Noa close and pinned her back against the wall. His face hovered a centimeter from hers, eyes glinting. "Who else could be this close to you...," he whispered, his lips closing in...

And then pulled back, smirking. "Only an angel could resist."

Noa's blood raced, but she managed a mischievous smile. "Dark magic," she agreed. He looked smug, leaned in to collect his kiss—but this time *she* pulled away. "A magic I share," she teased, as he growled a little.

"Noa! Cut the PDA and move your *a-s-s*!" Olivia called from down the hall, interrupting their game. Noa looked at her watch and jumped. "I have Chandler. You better move to get to—"

"Yeah, not going." Judah's hand held her fast. He lifted a brow. "How about you not-go with me?"

Noa bit her lip. Before she'd met Judah, she would never even have considered cutting History. It was such an *Isla* thing to do. But Judah somehow brought that out in her.

"I wish I could...," she began. Judah scowled, not even really listening as she finished: "But with Parents' Weekend tomorrow, I can't risk probation. Isla was totally MIA this morning. I can't let my parents come and have both their daughters be disciplinary no-shows."

"You are always covering for Isla!"

"You don't have siblings. You don't understand," Noa flared, immediately wishing she hadn't.

Judah darkened and dropped her hand. "It's not my fault I don't have a family."

"I'm sorry. I didn't mean..." She reached out to touch his arm, but his body caved inward, away from her. Noa knew how sensitive he was about being a foster kid, especially since nothing was known about his birth family. Smith wasn't even his real last name.

"You'd better go, or you'll be late anyway," Judah mumbled, turning away. Noa didn't try to stop him; she knew better. But surprisingly, he didn't immediately stalk off. He lingered, scowling hard.

"Judah?"

"I also … I mean … I wanted…" He fumbled, pulled at his hair with annoyance when the words didn't come easily. Finally he looked up, somewhere between fury and accusation. "Olivia told me there's some stupid Alumni Ball coming up and said I should ask you." He looked so angry, Noa had to press her lips together to keep from laughing.

Judah was watching her closely, as if trying and failing to read her mind. Finally he burst: "So … we should go?"

Noa laughed happily, leaned forward and kissed him. "You'll look great in white tails." Judah scowled again, but Noa saw the happy smile dancing in his eyes. She kissed him again, spun on her heel, and danced to Dr. Chandler's room, not worried at all this time if he saw it.

• • •

WHEN NOA TWIRLED into the classroom, she was nearly knocked over by Miles Keenan, crashing adorably by her in a mess of sandy hair and sun-kissed freckles.

"Oh! Sorry, Noa!" Miles flashed her his trademark winning grin, the one that had led the lacrosse team to back-to-back championships. Miles was a living Harlow legend, the prized, heroic all-state superstar goalie who'd made them champions every year since his freshman year.

Noa blushed involuntarily by his proximity, temporarily

starstruck. Part of what made Miles so popular was that he was a genuinely *nice* guy. If Harlow had secret societies for guys, Miles would definitely be their king—but then again, he'd probably invite everyone to join. He was just that way.

Now Miles turned back to make sure Noa was okay while trying to simultaneously look frantically over his shoulder. "Did I miss it? Did he do it?"

Noa followed Miles' gaze to his best friend, resident class clown Jeremy Robsen. Unlike Miles, Jeremy fit the boarding-school ass-hat cliché to a T.

Noa scolded herself: she had promised to try to think more nicely about Olivia's boyfriend. It was a tall order, especially now, when Jeremy was wearing a stupid trucker hat, tilted askew, like he was above caring about the wardrobe infraction he would undoubtedly receive. Enough wardrobe infractions could mean Review. A moronic trucker hat seemed like a pretty stupid reason to risk upsetting the Man with White Hands.

Seeing Miles, Jeremy winked and cleared his throat. Miles hurriedly grabbed Noa's arm—sending a little shock through her system, as if a celebrity had touched her—and pulled her with him to the two open seats. "*Watch,*" he whispered excitedly, like it was a secret between them, like they really were equals or good friends.

Jeremy turned to Olivia, whose pink hair was bent over her notebook, copying the day's list of dates from the board. He cleared his throat. She looked over, and Jeremy jumped onto his desk, did an elaborate, ridiculous bow, and whipped off his stupid hat. Two long white rabbit ears popped up from a headband the hat had been concealing, and Jeremy jumped into a silly tap dance, turning to wiggle what appeared to be a cotton bunny tail. He was even wearing tap shoes.

"Olivia Lee," Jeremy crowed with gusto, "you make me wanna wear white tails. Go to the ball with me?"

The class erupted into whoops and hollers, led by Miles, and Olivia's cheeks turned a shade of pink that rivaled her hair. She nodded happily, even her trademark snark forgotten for a moment.

Noa couldn't help but smile and silently apologize to Jeremy for her earlier critical thoughts. She didn't *love* Jeremy, but she did love the way he made her bestie all atwitter, and the hat, the tap shoes, the dance—pretty gallant of him to risk all those Harlow strict no-no's just for Olivia's amusement. It was Harlow tradition to ask a girl in an unexpected, extravagant way. Judah's nervous, private offer to go—because he wanted to make *Noa* happy, even though it was not a place he would feel comfortable—was special and rebellious in its own way.

"All right, settle down," Dr. Chandler said with a laughing smile as he got up from his desk. Noa liked that he had allowed Jeremy to have his moment—even *dance*—without reporting him to Ms. Jaycee, and even though it cut into class time, when they had tons of lists of dates to memorize and recite. Dr. Chandler was a *real* teacher, down to the patches on his tweed elbows and ink stains on his fingers, and he never forgot teaching meant *liking* kids.

Miss Jaycee, Harlow's vice headmistress, could stand to remember that, Noa thought with a shiver. Ms. Jaycee always smiled, sweet and polite, but no one scared Noa more. And not just because she could send you to Review with the headmaster, the Otec, whom the students whisperingly called the Man with White Hands. Most students like Noa had never seen the Otec, but Ms. Jaycee never let them forget that they all owed him their obedience and their gratitude for keeping them safe. It was *very important* not to upset him.

Luckily, good students had nothing to fear. Only the worst troublemakers ended up in Review and met him face-to-face.

Dr. Chandler began leading the class in their daily recitation: "1914, 1919, 1920…" Noa had long ago stopped wondering what actually happened on those dates. Classes always went like this: lessons involved writing down, memorizing, and repeating lists of numbers or names.

Noa's pencil tip broke. Miles leaned across the aisle, handed her his spare. She took it gratefully—and froze when another shiver tingled down her back.

Miles looked at her quizzically. "You okay?" he whispered.

Noa shook her head minutely, tried to smile. "Nothing. A little déjà vu."

"Me handing you a pen?"

"Sort of. More like you and me in class, you giving me something I'm not supposed to have…."

Miles smiled, whispered: "That's me, pure rebel."

Noa turned back to the front, trying to find her place in the recitation, but Miles leaned over to whisper again. "You get your signet today?" When Noa shook her head, he blushed. "Oh, man, sorry. I just thought, with Isla—"

Noa shrugged. "She sucks. I'm over it."

Miles smiled in a lopsided way that for some reason made Noa think of a golden retriever. "Maybe she thought she was looking out for you." Noa looked skeptical. He grinned. "You wouldn't understand. You don't have a little sister."

"Mr. Kessler, Ms. Sullivan? I don't hear dates," Dr. Chandler interrupted. Noa and Miles immediately faced front guiltily, joined in with the class.

But though Noa mouthed the dates in rhythm, her heart beat with different words, pumping icy shivers down her spine:

You don't have a little sister.

• • •

NOA WAS STILL feeling shivery when she met up with Judah later in Lamont, Harlow's smallest, most hidden library. Lamont had become their special place to be alone—rarely used by students and, even better, minimally staffed by monitors itching to report infractions. This afternoon was a perfect example: the solitary librarian stayed in her office in the corner, so unnoticeable and unnoticing as to fade into a background blur. Noa and Judah had slipped easily into a private alley in the stacks, completely out of sight from prying eyes.

Sitting together on the floor, backs to senior dissertations from decades past, Judah ran his fingers intently through Noa's hair. He was trying determinedly to braid it, a challenge Olivia had given him.

Judah huffed in frustration for the twentieth time as Noa's many blond strands slipped again through his fingers. "This *cannot* be this hard."

Noa chuckled. "Game point Olivia."

Judah sighed. "Maybe you're right."

"Oh, can I get that on tape?" Noa gloated instantly, spinning

to face him. "I've been looking for a new voice mail greeting...."
Judah made a grab for Noa's hands, but she deftly slipped his grip,
pinning him back instead.

"Okay, I give up! I failed! It's true!" Noa beamed as Judah
laughed, loving to catch him in a rare carefree moment. But, as
usual, it quickly disappeared. His shoulders knotted and his eyes
fell. "Okay, so ... I realize I didn't do the whole big ball-proposal
thing right."

"Judah—"

He looked around, sharp-eyed, to make sure they were alone,
then lowered his voice to a barely audible whisper. "I kind of...
made this for you." He avoided her eyes, embarrassed, as he gently took out a little pile of small paper shapes from his pocket,
each with a careful, intricate pattern on one side. He shrugged.
"It's kind of stupid, just—"

"*A puzzle*," Noa breathed.

Judah pulled back, cheeks flushing. "You hate it."

"I love it," Noa whispered, taking his hand. "But Judah—"

"I know, it's against regulation to make stuff like this. But no
one can see us here, and for some reason I felt like..."

"You were right," Noa assured him, a strange and frightening
warmth growing in her chest, odd yet so familiar, as from some
long-forgotten place. "It's perfect."

Noa's fingers shivered as she slid the homemade pieces to
their places. The lines came together to ask, "Go to the ball with
me?" beside an exquisite sketching of their faces.

It thrilled her.

Noa picked up an edge piece, the one that held his eyes,
his curls, and then it happened again—that wave, that frisson,

spinning through her cells. Like déjà vu but different, like the ground was upside down. But of course Noa had never had a puzzle of her own. She'd never even seen one. She gasped and dropped the piece.

Judah grabbed the pieces immediately, crumpling them in anger. "I'm sorry, I never should have … I knew it was wrong.…"

Noa gasped again, shut her eyes tight, but put out a hand to touch him. "No, Judah," she managed. "It's like … it's like something I *remember*.…" She struggled for the words, opened her gray eyes to find his—

That's when she saw her, just for a moment.

"Judah, *look*," Noa whispered unsteadily, pointing behind him. Judah turned sharply—but it was clear he could see nothing.

Noa lowered her arm sadly, shook her head. The face—the small, fierce face—was no longer there. "I thought I saw … but no…" Noa brought her hand to the scar that fell across her chest. "There's no one there."

• • •

"WHAT DO YOU mean, you're not going tonight? I need you!" Olivia cried in outrage, flinging up her arms in exasperation. Even the precise mathematic shapes of her tattoos looked disappointed. Noa's eyes lingered on those concentric circles; they did not make her feel the same way as Judah's secret puzzle sketches. Perhaps that's why they were permitted, where 'art' like his was not. "Nose! Are you listening to me?"

"I'm sorry. I started feeling weird with Judah earlier…"

Olivia smiled dryly. "Your moody-meter finally break?"

"No." Noa eyed her. "It had nothing to do with Judah at all. And he's not moody. He's just—"

"The poster boy for brooding?"

"O."

"Just *come* tonight." She picked up a tiny silver bracelet from the floor. "And hello? Wear this. Why haven't I seen it before?"

Noa leaned forward. The chain was fragile, delicate, and there was a small charm shaped like a treasure chest hanging from the links, faintly glowing blue.

Noa furrowed her brow. It looked familiar, but she couldn't think from where. "Must be Isla's."

Olivia shrugged, fastened it onto Noa's wrist. "Finders, keepers. It's yours now. And now that I've showered you with gifts, you must do my bidding and *come*. The Pre-Parents'-Weekend-Blow-Off-Steam-Bash only comes once a year!"

"Your parents are in love with you. You don't *need* to blow off steam. Plus, you have Jeremy!"

"But that's precisely why I *need* you. He's been acting … a little weird. Jumpy. I can't figure it out. I need your girl-dar."

"He just asked you to the ball—"

"I know, but trust me. He has these moments lately, I don't know if he's been toking too much or what. It's like he … thinks he's somewhere else. He, like, zones out, or randomly shivers. It's weird."

Noa bit her lip. *He's not the only one.*

"*All* right," Olivia finally sighed dramatically, realizing she wouldn't win. "I guess I'll go see if Annabelle wants to be my wing-woman. I simply cannot face Carly Ann and the new Fools alone."

"See how resourceful you are? Good for you!" Noa teased.

"*Please.* I'm gonna get enough butt kissing tomorrow when my adult fan club arrives for Parents' Weekend." Olivia huffed from the room, the door shutting behind her.

Noa froze. For the briefest fraction of a second, had the door just … flickered? Noa reached out to touch the wood. Solid and smooth.

Noa pressed her palms flat on her desk, counted deep breaths in and out. She needed to calm herself, refind her center, which was the real reason she hadn't wanted to go to the party with Olivia. Something had begun uncurling in her rib cage, an urge she knew she had to fight—something awakened in the library. She'd felt this urge before, an animal rising in her stomach, prowling up into her chest—but it had frightened her so much she'd never talked about it, not even to Olivia. She'd tried to smother it, lock it away.

It was getting harder.

Especially today.

Almost not of its own accord, Noa's body got up, went to kneel beside her bed. She'd bought something once from Annabelle, just in case, the first time she'd felt this inner-beast. She'd hidden her purchase immediately, tried desperately to forget it was there—but now it drew her to it, a fiery magnet. Noa's back bent parallel to the floor; her arms reached beneath the bed and her hands pulled up the loose floorboard. Her fingers dipped into the secret vacancy—and pulled out the crisp, cream journal.

Hands trembling, Noa lifted the little book to her face, fanned the pages, breathed in the scent of paper waiting to be filled.

Stop! her brain screamed. *It is forbidden!*

But Noa didn't stop. The smell, the feel, intoxicated; she was drunk with pages white, thirsting for ink. She ran her fingers down the journal's open spine, across its faces, felt the currents humming beneath the leaves. Then somehow she was on her feet, at her desk, deep-black pen leaping up into her hand. Its body burned against her fingers, tip humming hotly to meet the page.

Noa swept onto her bed, opened the journal, creased down the inside cover, relishing the hiss and whisper as it bent. She lifted the pen, black star tip poised above the white—

—and Noa began to write.

• • •

NOA HAD NEVER read a poem. She knew what a poem was because it was forbidden, part of the list of things they had all memorized, of things they must never, ever make or even see. The Otec had forbidden these things—these "arts"—for their own safety. Arts invited *imagination*, a force that could destroy them all.

But even though Noa had never read a poem, had never even seen one, somehow she knew, from the very soles of her feet up through the tip of every blond hair, that a poem was what she was about to write.

A poem. A message. To the one Noa felt but could not see, the one Noa knew but did not know. The one Noa remembered, but in no memory.

Girl, she called it, in mind, in ink. My poem to the *Girl*.

Nib touched paper, and words spilled from Noa's veins, giving blood and flesh to what was too wet for mind to hold. Noa wrote, rewrote, wrote anew, tried to form skins and eyes and bones to shape the figment—and finally stopped, panting. An hour had passed; sweat beaded at her neck. Her fingertips traced her cheeks and found them wet. She realized she'd been crying.

That's when the suite door opened.

"Jeremy got super freaked-out when he was drunk, I had to take him home—" Olivia broke off immediately, turned and slammed the door. She ran to Noa's side, knelt beside her. "Are you okay? What's wrong? Are you hurt?" She frantically scanned Noa's face and neck—then saw the open journal in Noa's lap.

Her fear turned instantly to panic.

"*What have you done?*" Olivia cried, ripping the journal from Noa's hands and flinging it onto the floor. It slid, still open, to the corner, fresh ink still exposed. Olivia grabbed Noa's ink-stained hands, as if to heal them with her own. *But that's absurd,* Noa thought. *No one can heal through touch.*

"Noa, please, we have to hide this!" Olivia was pleading. "Where did you get it? What were you thinking? They'll send you to him for this, to the Man with White Hands!"

Noa tried to focus, but she still felt outside her body. She pulled her hands free, dug her nails as hard as she could into her forearms, wanting pain to force herself back inside her limbs.

"Something's not right," she told Olivia helplessly.

"Writing is forbidden! The Otec—"

"*Praise Otec,*" they both said automatically.

"Olivia, I know, I just—" Noa shook her head.

Olivia jumped and clutched Noa hard. "You have to stop, you have to stop! Promise me!" She clutched so tightly Noa finally felt it; she could barely get a breath.

"Okay," Noa wheezed. "Okay, I promise."

Olivia pulled back, but did not release Noa's arms. Her eyes were fierce. *"Swear."*

For the briefest moment, Olivia's terrified face shimmered into the Girl, the Girl Noa could not quite see—

"Swear," Olivia pleaded, shaking Noa desperately. Noa grunted, body aching.

"I swear."

• • •

NOA LAY AWAKE in her bed that night, staring up at the ceiling. Olivia had waited, worried, until Noa had done an impressive fake sleep for a good forty-five minutes. Noa wanted nothing more than to actually fall asleep, forget the Girl, and keep her promise to Olivia, but the Girl and a growing blur of new mirages now ran in an endless ribbon through her mind. Curls like Judah's—but not Judah's—a downiness against her hand. Something small and precious, but incomplete, a puzzle piece from someplace long ago.

Noa turned over, saw Isla's empty bed. A sudden, violent panic made her snap up, brace herself on the wall. *Isla!* Desperation, urgency, fear—irrational, inexplicable, but suffocating, drowning, strangling—Noa wanted Isla *now*, had to see her *now.* Suddenly she was sure she'd never see Isla, not ever again—

But Isla's only out with her friends, like always, Noa told herself. *She'll sneak back in the way she always does.* She tried to count out steady breaths. Nothing was going to happen to Noa's big sister. Isla couldn't be caught, she'd never be pinned; nothing could ever, ever break her. That was what made her Isla.

Isla's tablet had been tossed carelessly across her empty bed, of course left on, and another photo of the sisters flashed on its screensaver slideshow. This one showed Isla laughing wildly over mac 'n' cheese, her favorite, while Noa sat with her at their family's round kitchen table. But the shot was wide, oddly wide, the pair of them off-center. As if something else had once been included in the frame.

Someone.

Noa shut her eyes tight, stomach twisting. Was she actually losing her mind? Was this why the Man with White Hands had banned creative things like Judah's puzzle and her journal— because art really drove you mad?

Noa heard a rustle at the suite door, and relief flooded over her. Her sister was back. Isla would have all the answers, the way she always did. She would laugh askance and roll her eyes, tell Noa she was a worrywart, and Noa would realize how silly she'd been—

"Noa, honey?"

Noa's body seized in horror. It wasn't Isla. The voice was sweet, *too* sweet.

Ms. Jaycee.

Noa could only watch, paralyzed, as Ms. Jaycee walked into the Sullivan sisters' dorm room, bright in her candy-pink silk pajamas. The vice headmistress wore her fat, bright smile, but her hawkish eyes raked every nook and corner—and like magnets, flew to Noa's journal, still open in the dust.

Ms. Jaycee's whole face rounded, eyes to cheeks to chin, and drained white. She turned to Noa, stricken.

"Ms. Jaycee please, it was an accident—"

"Where's your sister?" the vice headmistress spluttered.

"Uh, bathroom—"

"You'd better come with me, Noa."

"It's not what you think—it's old! I ... I found it!"

Ms. Jaycee reached into the pockets of her matching pink silk robe, slipped out a pair of latex rubber gloves. She rolled them delicately down over her narrow, manicure-tipped fingers; they made a polite little snap against her wrists. Then she moved slowly to the corner, reached gingerly to pick up the journal as if it were diseased. She turned to Noa, smiled a terrible, pitying smile, blinking rapidly in sympathy.

"I'm sure we can sort this out," she said in a tone that mimicked comfort. But as she turned, Noa saw her eyes.

They were black and hard, like knives.

• • •

NOA SAT UNEASILY in the vice headmistress's office, fighting panic and the desperate urge to flee. She tried to focus on the words curlicued across the Japanese screen behind Ms. Jaycee's desk: *Alone we can do so little! Together we can do so much! Let the Otec guide you!* Noa immediately shut her eyes. The Otec. The Man with White Hands. The savior she had betrayed.

Ms. Jaycee cocked her head at Noa from behind her desk, furrowed her brow with delicate precision. "Noa, what are we going to do?"

"I ... I found it. I was going to report it..." Noa tried, trailing off as her pitiful lie echoed into silence. Ms. Jaycee just stared, simpering with that saccharine sympathy that didn't reach her eyes.

"I'm so sorry," Noa dissolved tearfully. "Please don't send me to the Man with White Hands—"

Ms. Jaycee frowned. "The Otec—"

"*Praise Otec,*" they both said.

"—keeps us safe. You know that."

"I know," Noa whispered, staring at the floor.

"You're safe here, and happy, aren't you? With your sister, your friends, even this new boy." Noa looked up. Ms. Jaycee nodded. "The Otec—"

"*Praise Otec.*"

"—wants me to notice everything, so I can help keep everything running smoothly. You want everything to keep going smoothly, don't you?"

Noa nodded numbly.

"I'm on your side, Noa. You need to know that. There is nothing so important to me as my students. Look behind you. Look at my Wall of Pride."

Noa turned slowly to the wall behind her, which showcased a collage of students, all posed in uniform, smiling the same smile, oriented in just the same way.

"Those are my success stories, Noa. Students here who forgot the Otec's grace—"

"*Praise Otec,*" Noa mumbled.

"—and who lost their way, but I helped them back onto the right path of obedience. Many of them became class presidents, honor-roll students, a credit to this school."

Noa looked over the pictured faces, recognizing some here and there, but not others, who must have graduated. She turned back, cheeks aflame.

Ms. Jaycee seemed to have relaxed a little. "Since this is your very first offense, I think Probation is in order, not Review." Noa closed her eyes in relief.

Ms. Jaycee smiled beatifically. "But no Parents' Weekend. I'm sorry."

Noa knew she should be feeling only gratitude, should take this punishment and sing its praises, but she fought the urge to cry anyway. What she wanted, *needed* more than anything right now, was to run into her mother's arms, to have Hannah stroke her hair, whisper the ghosts away. She needed the four of them— she, Hannah, Christopher, and Isla—to pull tight their family knot, leave no end loose, weave up every strand.

Noa got up shakily, told herself just to get out the door quickly without crying, but her body paused. She heard her own voice, small, turning and speaking back.

"Ms. Jaycee? What happens when you see the Otec?"

Ms. Jaycee said nothing for a moment. She eyed Noa carefully. "*Praise Otec*, Noa," she prompted quietly.

Noa flushed, nodded quickly. "*Praise Otec*."

Ms. Jaycee smiled. "You may go now, Noa."

Her tone was sweet, but Noa flinched. Again the vice headmistress's pupils shone glinted like knives.

• • •

NOA WOULD HAVE preferred to stay in her room during Parents' Weekend since she was not allowed to see her own, but Ms. Jaycee's punishment included making her watch her classmates' reunions through the floor-to-ceiling windows of Harlow's new Probation room. The room itself was an oddity at Harlow, a glass cube suspended above the central auditorium. The students had named it the Birdcage.

Noa was one of three offenders, but the other two students—Leticia Jones and Avery Hunter—sat in the far opposite corner, blending into the background and out of Noa's particular notice. She doubted they'd want to commiserate anyway, since they weren't her friends. Noa was relieved, however, that Dr. Chandler was supervising. Something about his casual, awkward posture—leaned back on his chair legs, scuffed loafers up, glasses in his mouth, book open on his lap—made Noa feel warmer. He wasn't at all like her father, Christopher, who lived in neat corners and careful lines, but he was better than Ms. Jaycee all the same.

The probees were supposed to study, but Noa couldn't help looking down at the excited family reunions below. Everyone always complained about Parents' Weekend—especially Isla, who always whined for a solid month about the imminent landing of the "colonizers"—but invariably, Noa knew, almost every classmate's eyes shone and footsteps quickened when parents actually appeared.

Noa couldn't see details, but she easily picked out Olivia's shock of pink hair and the two black-haired, ant-like figures hugging all over her. Noa didn't need to see their faces to know the Lees' boundless adoration: it shimmered brightly over their reunion like colored light from falling fireworks. Noa could only partially see Olivia's posture, but she knew her friend's smile was half-sincere and half-ironic, with the tiniest little curl that reminded Noa so much of Judah. But Judah of course was not among the happy ants. He had no family to visit him.

The Lee reunion was rivaled only by the Keenans', where two tall and lanky parents gesticulated wildly over their superstar son, Miles. Miles was bent backward, laughing loudly at some adventure of his father's in a way that made Noa almost want to cry. It was strange—she and Miles were friendly but not exactly *friends*, yet she was overcome with relief that Miles was so easily beloved, his life so smooth, that he didn't have to know loneliness, or despair. It was the future he deserved, Noa's heart somehow knew with every beat, no one deserved it more.

Noa's parents suddenly walked in, and all thoughts of Miles were swallowed by a paralysis of longing. Noa watched as Isla danced toward them across the room, a pixie under shining, starlit hair, and pirouetted into their father's arms. Christopher startled to hug her, only to find he grasped at nothing, as just as quickly Isla flitted from his hands.

Noa's rib cage felt pulled inward, as if it housed a black hole and not a heart. She saw Hannah looking around, knew she was wondering where Noa could be. The anxiety in Hannah's posture made Noa sick: her traveler-mother had always been the sun, shining into every shadow; not this profile in searching curves, waning moonlike to the tide.

Thank Otec at least Isla was there.

A scream split the air, so loud it traveled even into the Birdcage. Noa found herself on her feet, Dr. Chandler at her side, pressed against the wall closest to the sound. It had come from Jeremy Robsen, who was being visited by two older women figures—his aunt Celia and their housekeeper, Noa guessed, who lived on the Sullivans' street. Jeremy had lurched away from them and was screaming unintelligibly in the corner of the room. His aunt hurried over, making him scream more loudly; he spun, pounded frantically against the wall as if to break it down, as if he needed to escape.

Noa pressed her ear to the glass, and Jeremy's shrieks contorted into sonic shapes: "Don't! I don't want to go! Don't throw me in there!"

"Don't throw him where?" Dr. Chandler murmured, forehead wrinkled intently as he pressed his own ear against the glass. Noa surveyed his face, and it happened again—the windows behind Dr. Chandler seemed to flicker, turn blurry—almost, Noa realized, like a digital hiccup in an image. Noa immediately touched the window, but just like her door the previous night, found it once again quite solid.

Below, two aides corralled the struggling Jeremy away, and Ms. Jaycee gestured to the shell-shocked parents, inciting hurried hugs. Apparently, visiting weekend was over.

As the room below quickly emptied, Noa turned to Dr. Chandler. She could tell his mind was whirling. Not really knowing why, but suddenly desperate to know, Noa lowered her voice to ask, "Dr. Chandler, why do our books only have lists of dates and names? Don't you ever … wonder … what they stand for?"

Dr. Chandler was still intent on the window. "I never have," he murmured, sounding worried. "I never have before."

• • •

NOA NEARLY TRIPPED over Judah as she descended from the Birdcage. He had been sitting hunched against the door to the stairs, and when she opened it, he leapt to his feet, agile and tense, ready for a fight.

Judah's posture eased when he realized it was Noa. "They wouldn't let me come in," he said, dark eyes stormy.

Noa leaned into his shoulder, let the feel of his muscles' knots loosen hers. "I'm glad you're here."

She felt him nod curtly, but his hand was gentle as it slid into hers. They moved swiftly together in silence, as if in some unspoken agreement to talk only when in their own, safe space.

Judah knew that for Noa, the safest place would always be her tree. The large one out on the grounds near the groundskeeper's shack, the tree where she said she always felt protected. She'd thought they would immediately discuss Jeremy, but when her mouth opened beneath the safety of the tangled branches, she whispered something else: "It was hard to see my parents disappointed. My mom. It somehow made me miss them more."

Judah's hand tightened on hers, tension rippling down his fingers. "Sometimes I think I have it easier, not having a family."

Noa exhaled softly, leaned into him and against the trunk's smooth bark. For some reason, her free hand was tracing her scar. "Yes," she murmured, "I guess you can't miss what isn't there."

• • •

JEREMY STILL WASN'T back in Chandler's class on Monday, and Olivia was uncharacteristically disheveled. Her worry about her boyfriend radiated from her frizzy tumbleweed of former Mohawk, from the wrinkles in her pants and blouse. Noa knew she'd dressed from a pile on the floor.

Noa had tried to comfort her, had even enlisted Judah to ensure Olivia would never be alone, but Olivia remained nearly catatonic. Noa knew she was afraid to say aloud what might have happened: Review, the Man with White Hands. Students who met the Otec rarely came back.

Noa wished she had listened to Olivia earlier about Jeremy's acting strangely. But what could Noa have done?

What Noa did *not* share was how, since Jeremy's disappearance, she herself had been feeling ... more strangely ... herself. The figment Girl haunted her constantly now; walls flickered and blurred with ever-growing frequency. Noa had tried to tell Judah, but after days without Jeremy's return, he'd shut down, closed off. His body screamed the words he wouldn't say: *Don't, don't name it, I can't have you vanish too.*

In Chandler's class, Noa closed her eyes against the smooth olive skin, the flutter-kiss from a little mouth shaped like a bow. Judah was right: she couldn't risk losing everything—Judah, Olivia, Isla too—by allowing herself to lose her mind.

"Okay, everyone," Dr. Chandler announced to begin the class. Noa opened her eyes and gasped at how haggard he suddenly looked, as if he'd aged forty years since Parents' Weekend. His teacherly messiness was gone, replaced by something far more worrisome.

Shakily, but with a deep breath as if to muster up some courage, Dr. Chandler held up a hand. "No, don't take out your textbooks. We're going to try something ... new."

Noa, Olivia, and Miles—who had chosen again, for some reason, to shine his star on Noa and sit beside her—all froze identically in surprise. Dr. Chandler's hands had curled into little, shaking fists.

"These dates and names are points in history. But we never think about what they mean." His eyes fell briefly on Noa's.

Olivia turned to Noa, perplexed; Noa tried not to react. "I want you to"—Chandler took a bracing breath—"*imagine* what these events and people may have been like." Shocked gasps rippled through the classroom. "Imagine them as parents, children, brothers, *sisters...*"

Noa's head suddenly spun, her body swayed; the Girl smashed into her mind. She heard herself cry out, felt her cheek against the cool, cool floor.

From somewhere above her, Noa heard Miles: "Get the nurse!" His words sounded strange and far away; she looked up at him, at his face hovering over hers where she must have fallen, but somehow it wasn't his. The sandy hair, the freckles turned to chocolate ringlets soft as silk; his hands on her shoulders became small and sticky, warm—and there was something wrapped up with Noa's legs: warm, round legs, tangled in shared sheets, an unzipped sleeping bag. Everything was upside down and backside up, mismatching puzzle pieces from her mind, her memory, her heart.

Noa tried to reach to touch them, fit the pieces together into an image that made sense—and they shimmered through her fingers. Clear sensations took their place: Olivia's hands and spiky, frizzy hair; Miles' blue eyes and hanging forelock. And that sound—the *click-clack* of heels through the doorway, followed by a high, shrill voice.

"What happened here?" Ms. Jaycee, somewhere to Noa's left.

"We were imagining ... She fainted..." Carly Ann, words fading into buzz. Dr. Chandler's lower tones, Ms. Jaycee's answering shrill vibrato, then sharp talons pulling Noa up, nails piercing Noa's shoulders.

Noa wasn't sure what was happening, but her survival instincts went on high alert. *Cover!* a voice screamed inside her head, conjuring Judah, catlike, ready to fight. *Focus and cover!*

"Oh, Ms. Jaycee!" Noa trilled, anchoring herself as best she could to the plane of here and now. Her swimming eyes found Ms. Jaycee's sharp ones; she stretched her mouth into what she hoped looked like an embarrassed smile. "They didn't need to call you, I just didn't have enough for lunch. Total low-blood-sugar spell."

Ms. Jaycee's hawk-eyes narrowed.

"Used to happen all the time when I was little!" Noa insisted, smiling more widely.

Ms. Jaycee studied her, seeming unconvinced; Noa felt sweat sliding down her back, felt her head begin to sway—

"It's true," Miles suddenly said, drawing Ms. Jaycee's stare. "I was right next to her. She fainted before class even began." Olivia quietly helped steady Noa's wobbling as Ms. Jaycee sized Miles up, then decided to believe him. Noa said a silent prayer of thanks to Miles' unexpected kindness. No one had more credibility to gamble—his lie was taking quite a risk. And they weren't even friends.

So why?

Noa didn't have time to wonder as Ms. Jaycee turned full-force to Dr. Chandler. She cocked her head, gave him that sad, sympathetic smile.

Noa's stomach dropped. Miles' lie couldn't save them both.

"The Otec will need to see you."

"*Praise Otec,*" the class chorused in hushed unison.

Ms. Jaycee held out and fluttered her peach-polished tips. "Come along."

Dr. Chandler, pale as paper, began to follow, then suddenly whipped back to the class. "Don't forget your last assignment," he urged, looking straight at Noa. Then Ms. Jaycee's peach talons closed on his arm, yanked him forward and away.

Too late, Noa realized she should have said goodbye.

• • •

NOA RAN TO Judah's room, cheeks flushed even as her whole body shivered. Panic had sharpened her senses, but her mind whirled so fast she could barely process what she saw and almost collided with the Residential Supervisor making his rounds through the Boys' Annex. At the last possible moment, a hand pulled Noa into a hidden doorway, saving her from being caught in violation of the rules of coed visitation—an instant sentence of Review.

Noa looked up; her savior, again, was Miles.

She began to thank him, but Miles quickly put his hand over her mouth, his palm warm against her lips, smelling faintly of peanuts. After a moment, they heard a door open and shut, and Miles peeked around the corner, then let her go.

"Coast is clear."

Noa sighed shakily. "Why, why do you keep saving me?"

Miles shook his head, brow furrowed. "To be honest, I don't know. Looking out for you just … feels right."

They locked eyes a moment, and Noa bit her lip. For a moment, she almost thought she saw a flash of distant yearning in his eyes….

But Miles stepped back, flashed that golden-retriever, friendly grin. "Hurry up and get to Judah's. I need to rest up before rescuing you next."

• • •

NOA FLEW INSIDE Judah's door. He was instantly wary.

"It was terrible, Judah," Noa breathed, afraid even to speak too loud. She sank onto his futon, the black one where she'd so often lain safe inside his arms. She nestled backward, desperate to feel that safety again, and he lay at her side—but for some reason it felt uncomfortable, mismatched, just like everything else these days. Even Judah's messy clothes, strewn about the room, looked somehow out of place.

Almost like the room belonged to someone else.

Noa took a shaky breath, pressed her palms downward on the futon and sat up again, trying to ground herself. "Ms. Jaycee took Dr. Chandler. To see the Otec."

Judah sat up to face her, and she watched him nervously. Too late, he said, "*Praise Otec.*"

Noa barely breathed. *"You too?"*

Judah scowled sharply, turned away. "You need to forget about this. Dr. Chandler is not your problem. Jeremy and Olivia are not your problem."

"It's not just them, Judah, you know that—"

"Stop, Noa!" Judah interrupted. "Don't you get it? If we talk about this stuff, if we even *think* about it, *we* could be next. We could lose each other!"

"I'm not going anywhere—"

"*It won't be your choice*," Judah hissed. "Do you want to leave me? And Olivia? And Isla? Your own sister?"

Noa pressed her hands against her temples, shut her eyes. "Judah I can't help it! Something is *wrong*. They're our friends. Even Dr. Chandler in a weird way is a friend. I can't ignore it—"

"I'm not saying ignore it! I'm saying…" Judah threw up his hands, scowled harder, steeling himself. "I don't know. Just don't *look*."

"How?" Noa asked. He snorted, but she insisted, "No, I'm really asking, Judah! *How? Tell* me how we can go back!"

Judah tensed so much he became a knot that broke. His body sagged, then trembled. Noa realized he was … afraid.

He shook himself as if to shake away the weakness, took her hands hard, looked firmly into her eyes. "We don't think about them, we don't think anything but us, here, together."

"But Judah … *she's haunting me*," Noa wailed softly.

Judah shuddered, dropped her hands, curled backward and covered his face. Noa waited for him to ask who she meant, what she was talking about, but he didn't. Instead, he said something else: "Noa, please," he pleaded, voice small, and breaking, "She's not real. *Forget her*."

It was the smallness that undid her. She leapt up, angry, pulled the napkin she'd stolen from the Dining Hall from her pocket. The words were messy, the pen having often pressed holes right through the grain. She tried to make him take it; he refused; so instead she read it to him:

Girl
my lids close and your eyes open:
silt-rich and promise-thick,
chocolate pools for wildflowers
if I could only
stay
and
watch.
I blink—you ringlet up,
snail-curled inside your shell. A spiral
I can't pick from
endless, shapeless sands.

But when I write—I *feel* you,
fingers small and fat in mine,
we ink each word together
we make sticky prints in sap.

Who are we, are we starfish?
Hand-cups sucked together fast?
I taste your salt
I smell your tang
Why
do
you
never
last?

"Who is she, Judah? Who is she?" Noa begged, crying now.

"Noa…" His voice was ragged, but she saw him glance reflexively toward his bed—and the way he instantly tore his gaze back.

But Noa knew his body, knew its words. She was fluent in his smallest movements. She flew to his bed, to the spot beneath, pried up his floorboard—a trick he had learned from her. There, in the secret space, she saw it: the sketchbook, hidden like the journal had been in hers.

Judah cried out in protest—not words but noise—but Noa didn't listen. She flipped open the cover, rapidly turned page after page after page. They were filled, all filled, with hundreds of sketches, all of the same face. A small, impish face with chocolate curls, drawn with exactness from every angle.

The Girl.

• • •

"JUDAH?" NOA HELD the pages in shaking hands. Judah shook his head, ran his hands roughly through his hair. "This is her, Judah! You see her too?"

Judah nodded miserably. "Everywhere, every time I close my eyes. Just like in your poem."

Noa flew to his side, knelt beside him. "Who is she, Judah?" she cried. "Why is she never here?"

"I don't *know*. I've looked everywhere, I've driven myself insane—"

"You should have told me—"

"No!" He spat angrily. "Look around us, Noa! Look what happens to people who question, who see what they're not supposed to see!"

"But don't you feel it?" she demanded. They were face-to-face and breathing hard; blood pounded in his cheeks. They had never fought before, not really, but somehow it felt so familiar—together, eye-locked, full of heat—as if their bond were forged in conflict, always had been from the start.

Noa tried to steady her voice, calm her fury. "She's important, Judah. That's the only thing I know for sure. That she's important, and—"

"Somewhere else," Judah finished helplessly, deflating. Noa felt it too; without the rage, only emptiness was left. She leaned her forehead against his, steepled—but Judah still would not give in. "She's somewhere else, but *we're here*, Noa. We're here, and we're together. That's what we need to protect."

• • •

AT LUNCH, NOA couldn't stop thinking about her fight with Judah. She turned it over and over in her head as she chewed her chicken salad without tasting it. Judah didn't even try to eat; he just stared at her, frowning intently, as if to change her mind with the fierceness of his thoughts alone.

Annabelle looked from one to the other in their silence, curious about this strange, unspoken war. Olivia, however, didn't seem to notice, lost in her own anxiety.

Annabelle finally noticed him first. "Oh my God." Her fork hit the table with a clatter, startling them all to look.

Jeremy Robsen had just entered the Dining Hall.

Olivia became a blur, on her feet and over to Jeremy before Noa could even exhale. She crashed into him in a fevered hug—a display she would have considered far too simpering only days before—not caring who looked or saw. Jeremy actually looked a bit confused. He stood motionless for a moment before slowly lifting his arms around her too.

"I bet you did all this just to get out of wearing tails," Olivia teased, tearful with joy. She hugged him again, then pulled him indelicately to their table.

Before Jeremy had even taken his seat, Olivia was grilling him. "What the hell happened to you? Do you know how freaked we've been? And what's with the choirboy hair?" Noa was so relieved to see a glimmer of Olivia's signature brashness that for a moment, she was sure everything was going to be okay.

Noa gave Judah a tiny smile, wanting him to share in this moment; she knew he would read her thoughts just from her face, the way they often spoke without words. But he wasn't looking back at her; he was watching Jeremy, frowning. Noa noticed for the first time that Jeremy looked a little … different. Not in an obvious way, but his uniform was immaculate, hair neatly combed, eyes free of mischief. He didn't tease Olivia for her interrogation, either, as Noa would have expected him to; he merely took it calmly.

Really calmly.

"I feel much better now," Jeremy said simply. Noa noticed he was also sitting particularly still in his chair, not draping on it backward or tilting it on two legs and fidgeting, per usual Jeremy style.

"Gee, don't overwhelm us with the deets," Olivia laughed, eyes bright. Or was it, Noa wondered now, that Jeremy's eyes seemed flat? His whole self actually seemed a little dimmer now that his annoying, smug little glint was gone.

Jeremy just shrugged. "I was feeling out of sorts—"

Judah glanced at Noa. '*Out of sorts?*'

"—so I went to the Otec for Review—"

"*Praise Otec*," Annabelle, Jeremy, and Olivia chorused, Judah stumbling in a little late. He looked warningly at Noa, who had missed the recitation entirely. She bit her lip, but no one else had seemed to notice.

Annabelle leaned toward Jeremy with huge eyes. "You met the Man with White Hands?"

Jeremy smiled blandly. "I was Reviewed, and now I feel much calmer. I was having these terrible dreams before, even when I was awake. The Otec helped me."

"*Praise Otec*," Noa mumbled with the others, glancing at Judah. But Judah's eyes were on Jeremy, wary.

Even Olivia was starting to look uncertain. "You feel … better, Jer?"

Jeremy nodded calmly. "I had forgotten to focus on what's here right now. The Man with White Hands reminded me that's all we need to worry about." Jeremy smiled blandly at Olivia. "Going to the ball, doing our homework. The Otec—"

"*Praise Otec.*"

"—worries about the rest, that's how he keeps us safe. And it's so much easier this way." Jeremy sighed, content. "I'm glad he sent me back here for a while. So I could remind you guys, too."

"What do you mean, 'a while'?" Noa replied quickly.

Jeremy just smiled serenely at Olivia. "Can't wait to take my lady to the big dance."

• • •

JUDAH DIDN'T SAY a word until he'd pulled her into his room and closed the door. Immediately after lunch, he'd grabbed Noa's tray, bussed it with his, and pulled her from the Dining Hall, tight with tension.

"Judah—" Noa began.

Judah held up his hand, jaw set. His eyes began to fill; he shook them clear angrily. "I just have this feeling…" He shook his head again, steeled himself. "Like I'm going to lose you. Like somehow … we're only together when we're *here*—"

"Judah, no." Noa pulled his hand over her heart, pressed hard so she could feel it beat. "*This* doesn't change." She held his eyes, his distrusting, frightened eyes, tried to beam her certainty into his mind. "But—"

"Something's wrong here," he nodded, dropping his eyes. "And we can't ignore it because we're scared."

"Yeah."

Judah wrapped her hands in his, clinging to her as if she might disappear. His brow furrowed as he noticed the delicate bracelet on her wrist. "What's that?"

"Olivia found it my room the other day. I think it might be Isla's."

Judah reached over, fingered the small treasure chest. The crease on his brow deepened, almost darkened.

"What?" Noa pressed.

Judah shook it off, got up. "I need to show you something." He walked to the secret floorboard where she'd found his sketchbook, then reached behind it to a second floorboard, farther back. A second hiding place, one Noa hadn't found. He pulled out a second sketchbook, even thicker than the first. "It's not just the Girl for me."

He handed her the book. She took it carefully, sat against the futon with it on her lap. He paced. Noa opened the cover and gasped—three faces stared at her: a man's, a woman's, and a boy's.

Noa swallowed, recognizing the line of a jaw, the curve of a cheek. She didn't know these faces, not exactly, but somehow she still knew the strokes by heart.

Noa turned the page: two figures stood, arms slung around each other. It was Judah and the boy, as if posing for an old photograph. Noa ran her hand over the pair of them. The other boy was a little taller, a little broader, maybe a little older. "You have a brother…."

Judah nodded; she didn't see him, but didn't need to. Noa turned the page. An older man stared back, his face and eyes like Judah's, like the brother's—but the angles sharper, somehow regal … and chillingly severe.

"Your father."

Judah seemed to shiver; it passed to Noa, to her hand as she turned more pages. The figure didn't change—Judah's father stared at her from every angle, sketched in every size. From corner to corner, harsh eyes pierced each panorama; pages squeezed between the tense muscles of his mouth. Judah's jawline, Judah's hair—but frightening, sharper, hardened to the bone. As if Judah was his echo, or he was Judah amplified, a reverberation that destroyed Judah's fragile, hidden harmonies.

Finally, on the last page of the sketchbook, the woman figure reappeared, just once, like a gasp of air and light. Instantly the chill was gone. Noa had never seen a face so beautiful and ethereal, yet somehow safe—alabaster pale but with long black hair, so black it was almost blue. Hair that could fall around you, a chrysalis against the world.

Then Noa saw her eyes. Her eyes were filled with stories: each iris held a map of sadness, but also love. Every experience, every memory written like a poem in her eyes.

"I think…" Judah swallowed softly. "She's my mother."

Noa closed the book and closed her eyes. "You have a family."

Judah sat beside her. "Or had."

"You mean…"

Judah shrugged painfully. "Sometimes people see the Otec and they don't come back."

"You think that's what happened to them?"

Judah shook his head. "My brother … how could I forget my brother?"

Noa thought of Isla, how much it would hurt to lose her. "Maybe you were made to, because forgetting was easier."

"Like Jeremy now, forgetting who he is?" Judah asked.

Noa frowned helplessly. "I don't know."

"The thing is, Noa…" Judah looked down, struggling for the words. "I think, somehow I know. I *feel* something, something else…." He forced himself to look her in the eyes. "In my father."

Noa's chest tightened.

Judah nodded sadly; she clearly felt it too. He took a folded page from his pocket, a page she realized he had torn from one of his sketchbooks, kept with him, afraid to leave it unattended, even hidden. He unfolded it: his father's face, overwritten, time after time, with a single, repeated word:

Otec.

"I hear it, over and over, in my dreams," Judah whispered, fighting desperation. "I see his face and hear it. It's him. I know it is."

"Your dad … is the Man with White Hands?" Noa breathed.

Judah nodded miserably. "I'm the reason, Noa, don't you see? If my father's the Otec, this—everything—it's my fault. The reason Jeremy … and the Girl! Something must have happened to the Girl, Noa. You feel it too—"

Noa grabbed his hands, forced him to look at her. "No, Judah," she said, soft but firm. "This has nothing to do with you. Even if he is your father, which *we don't know*—"

"I wanted so badly to ignore it, Noa," Judah said harshly, turning his anger inward in the way that broke her heart. "To think that there was something good—"

"There *is* something good, Judah. You and me, and Olivia and Jeremy … Miles, Isla! People are happy all around us! Their lives are great!"

Judah shook his head violently. "You feel it too! Don't lie!"

Noa clutched his hands tight. "If he is your father, Judah, then we don't have anything to worry about. Don't you see? Because if he is, then he made *you*."

Judah looked at her, doubting and desperate, wanting so much to believe. She kept her eyes firm on his, her hands strong.

She told herself, over and over, that it wasn't necessarily a lie.

• • •

OLIVIA YANKED NOA into her room the moment she reentered the Girls' Pavilion.

"I've decided I have to do something," Olivia informed her as she quickly shut the door. Annabelle was inside, unpacking something at Olivia's desk.

"Do something?" Noa asked cautiously as she slowly lowered herself onto Olivia's orange inflatable couch.

Olivia seemed anxious, frantic. "I'm not sure," she said, chewing the side of her mouth. She sat next to Noa, drumming her fingers, tapping her foot up and down in a blur. "I'm happy Jeremy is back, I am, and I'm grateful the Otec helped him—"

"*Praise Otec*," chimed Annabelle.

"But…" Olivia shook her head. "For some reason, the whole thing makes me want to … *do* something. For myself."

Noa met her friend's manic eyes, and her scar suddenly flashed hot. She recognized something in Olivia's look—it was Noa's look when she'd written her poem.

"What are you going to do?" Noa breathed.

Before Olivia could answer, a soft but insistent rapping shook the door. Olivia's brow furrowed as she jumped up to answer it, hesitating before turning the knob. Noa cursed, for what felt like the millionth time, Harlow doors' lack of peepholes.

She caught herself—she hadn't needed peepholes before. Had she?

Olivia opened her door a sliver and yelped in surprise. She turned sideways to let the visitor slip in: Miles Keenan. Noa was surprised—but at the same time somehow not surprised at all.

What was happening?

Annabelle, at least, still seemed sane. "Miles? What are you doing here?" she asked in shocked disbelief.

Miles shrugged, looked uneasy himself. "I don't know. I just wanted to see how you guys were. Now that Jeremy's back, I guess?"

Olivia didn't seem to care one way or another why Miles was there, just hurried him in. "If you stay, you can't tell anyone what we do or say here. Room rules."

Miles smiled his golden-retriever smile. "Never." He plopped down easily next to Noa. She fought the feeling of familiarity, ignored the way her body automatically prepared for and adjusted to his weight beside her on the inflatable couch.

"Okay, O," Annabelle said from Olivia's desk, where she had finished unpacking a tattoo kit.

"Your plan is to get new ink?" Noa asked.

Olivia's mouth twitched. "Well, Jeremy's always loved my tattoos, too. But"—she paused, struggling to explain—"but I don't want any more mathematical shapes. I want something…"

"Forbidden," Miles finished for her. Noa looked at him, and then she saw it in his eyes, too. That *thing*. Her heart pounded.

Olivia frowned. "I just don't know what tattoo to get."

The words were out of Noa's mouth before she even knew she was speaking them.

"A poem," Noa whispered. "It should be a poem."

• • •

NOA WAITED ANXIOUSLY outside her sister's Mandarin class. Even though she and Isla shared a room, she felt as if she hadn't actually seen Isla face-to-face in what seemed like forever. Isla had always been a night owl, but now their relationship seemed to exist only in the traces Isla left behind: her bracelet, dirty clothes, crumbs from late-night snacks attracting ants on their shared floor.

And Noa needed Isla, not her leavings. She needed to confide how everything felt like it was unraveling, how she was certain she was supposed to find a girl who did not exist, how people were disappearing or changing strangely and even Judah was haunted by faces he'd never seen. Isla would know what was real and what was not; she would make some flippant quip that dismissed all

Noa's nightmares, brushed off her fears. Isla could do that. She didn't worry. She laughed.

Noa needed her big sister.

But as Noa waited in the hall, trying every so often to peek in through the Language Center's cloudy, opaque glass, she felt only rising panic. Usually, just knowing she would soon have Isla's refuge put Noa at ease. But now, each second that passed felt more frantic. Instead of feeling closer to seeing her sister, she had the insane feeling that she was closer to never seeing Isla again.

Slowly, Noa turned to face the hall, looking at the shapes of clustered students. A fog of paranoia crept and wove its way around her, and she suddenly wondered, with startling clarity, when she'd last seen anyone up close—not from a distance— besides Judah, Olivia, Jeremy, or Annabelle. Carly Ann, Noa remembered, but who else? Noa looked now at Ansley, Leticia, and Mary Jane, holding court with their backs to her a little distance down the hall. They'd been inducted to the Fools, but Noa hadn't actually heard them brag or seen them strut.

That was strange.

With a careful breath, Noa walked slowly toward them, trying to ignore the urge to turn and flee in fear. When she came up behind Ansley, Mary Jane, and Leticia, she paused—no giggles or voices floated her way. She reached out a shaking hand to tap Ansley on her shoulder.

Ansley didn't turn.

Cringing, Noa touched her shoulder again. When Ansley still didn't turn, Noa walked around to face them, and screamed.

The three of them—Ansley, Leticia, and Mary Jane—had no faces.

. . .

NOA FLED, RUNNING as fast as she could away from the face-less girls. She didn't know where her body was taking her; she thought feebly to herself to go to Judah but wasn't sure her legs could respond. Suddenly, she was in the hallway in front of Dr. Chandler's History class, which was about to start. Olivia was there, and Annabelle, and Miles. And Jeremy, staring serenely at the door.

"Word is, we're gonna get Jaycee as a sub," Annabelle was saying gloomily as Noa sped around the corner.

Miles saw her first. "Noa?" he asked, instantly worried. "What's wrong? Why are you so late?"

Noa shook her head, words completely failing her.

"Get Judah," Olivia told Miles urgently. "Go!"

Noa stood stock-still, shaking, unable to explain what she had seen.

"It's going to be okay, Noa," Olivia said, voice high and forced. She took Noa by the shoulders, tried to look into her eyes. Noa tried to focus, but her heart was pounding, vision swimming black and white. The whole hall behind Olivia flashed and blurred and jarred—that static again, but now unending, until *she* was there, the Girl, small mouth moving, wide eyes huge.

"I can't hear you!" Noa cried to the ghost.

"Noa, it's *me*, Olivia—" Olivia tried, frantic. "Please, it's going to be okay—"

Olivia was suddenly jerked backward, yelping under sharp, peach talons.

"It is most certainly *not* going to be okay." Ms. Jaycee's voice was shrill and harsh, simpering smile nowhere to be found. Noa's eyes finally focused as Ms. Jaycee yanked down the back collar of Olivia's blouse.

Noa's words, in black script, spun down Olivia's neck.

Olivia's eyes filled with tears as she looked at the only one who could have been Jaycee's informant. "Jeremy," she whimpered, "are you even in there at all?"

"You should be thanking him," Ms. Jaycee snapped. "Explain yourself!"

Olivia looked ready to collapse—but then, all of a sudden, she ripped herself from Ms. Jaycee's grasp like a wild Amazon, her collar tearing off in Jaycee's hand. She clawed off her blouse entirely, threw it to the floor, stood defiant in her hot-pink bra. With her back ramrod-straight and proud, she yelled right into Ms. Jaycee's face, "*Read it for yourself!*"

Ms. Jaycee froze—shock and disbelief magnified almost comically across her face. When the vice headmistress finally spoke, each word was separate, seething. "I. Would. Never."

That's when Noa found her voice. Or rather, heard it, speaking the words she'd found in her own heart:

"Girl-Beast wake and wail with me
Pack your wounds with rocks and mud
Let growls rip betwixt your teeth
Be killer, hunter, fighter, thief,
Give no mercy, no relief,
Spill truth with flesh and blood!"

Ms. Jaycee whirled. Annabelle cowered into the wall, whimpering, but Noa stood her ground—not because she was frozen, but because she felt electrified, heat and certainty spinning out from the scar across her chest.

"I should have known this was you," Ms. Jaycee said, her sad, cold smile finally making its reappearance. "I thought we had an understanding."

"Noa may have written the poem, but Annabelle is the one with the contraband," Jeremy pointed out blandly, as if he wasn't betraying every one of them. Even Annabelle's terrified yelp provoked no reaction.

"Well, I have no choice. Review for you *all*." Before any of them could think to run, Ms. Jaycee had Noa and Olivia in her razor clutches, and Jeremy had Annabelle pinned by her hands. Noa and Olivia struggled, but it was useless; Ms. Jaycee was fueled by righteous indignation, by zealotry and a sense of duty. She and Jeremy pulled them roughly around the corner—just as Noa thought she glimpsed Miles and Judah, heading the wrong way, past the windows in the hall.

"Jud—" Noa tried to cry, feeling one last spark of hope—if only they turned, if only they saw—but Ms. Jaycee yanked her hard through a door before the word was out.

There was no earthly way he could have heard her.

• • •

MS. JAYCEE LOCKED her office door after they'd been bound to chairs, their hands tied behind them in plastic circlets, their mouths taped shut. Now in control, she became calm, collected.

She looked at them with her most compassionate, kind smile—
their teacher once again.

"You know, I think of you kids as my children, truly," she
confided, in that faux-intimate way Noa loathed. "There is
nothing that I treasure more than knowing that I help to shelter
and to guide you. It's my purpose. My calling." She walked to
her Wall of Wonder, those photos of so many students, just like
them, whom she had straightened out, had 'saved.' She sighed,
gently touched a face or two.

Ms. Jaycee turned to Olivia, whose nakedness she had swad-
dled in her own powder-peach designer blazer. Olivia was scowling in a way that would have made Judah proud, but as Ms.
Jaycee tenderly tucked back a wisp of hot-pink hair, Noa saw
fear crowd out the defiance in Olivia's eyes.

"I know you feel betrayed," Ms. Jaycee told her softly. "But
Jeremy reported you because he loves you." Olivia looked down,
blinked back tears. Noa knew Olivia would rather kill herself
than cry in front of Ms. Jaycee.

Ms. Jaycee murmured, as if in understanding. "You already
see that, don't you. That's why I'm going to give you two a little
time, let him explain his side. So you can sort things out before
you see the Utec, praise him." Ms. Jaycee nodded to Jeremy,
who stepped forward to lift Olivia's lassoed hands from her chair
back, then began to guide her out. Olivia's eyes darted wildly; she
looked in panic at Noa, who tried her hardest to look reassuring.

Once the door had closed, Ms. Jaycee turned to Noa and
Annabelle. She walked first to Annabelle, who looked paralyzed
with terror.

Ms. Jaycee sighed deeply. "Oh, Annabelle," she began sadly, "You've been here the longest, you know." Noa looked between them, wondering what that meant, but Annabelle looked too freaked out to care. Ms. Jaycee continued, as if wanting to explain, to unburden herself for some terrible decision. "The danger of what you've been doing, Annabelle, is that you help others to act out, even if you yourself are merely a facilitator and not a practitioner." She touched Annabelle's wet cheek, slick with silent tears. "Don't worry, Annabelle, you'll see him first. He will make everything so much easier."

At that, Annabelle's tears turned to awkward, clumsy sobs, partially muffled into tortured sounds by the silencing tape. "Oh, sweetie!" Ms. Jaycee cried, embracing her. "There is nothing to be afraid of! The Otec, praise him, is your protector! We all must do our part!"

Ms. Jaycee helped Annabelle up and guided her to a hidden sliding door behind the Japanese screen—the one that showcased Ms. Jaycee's quote *Alone we can do so little! Together we can do so much! Let the Otec guide you!* Ms. Jaycee pulled Annabelle, sobbing, stumbling, behind her, as two hands reached through to help them across the threshold. Strong, male hands in latex gloves of blinding white.

Judah's father.

Noa tried to rush to the door, succeeding only in crashing over in her chair as the door shut. Her shoulder slammed into the marble floor, but at least her head hadn't collided with the sharp corner of Ms. Jaycee's desk.

Now on her side, her arms still lassoing her to the chair back, Noa bicycle-kicked her legs to slide herself, and the chair, backward toward Ms. Jaycee's filing cabinet. She rocked her weight as much as she could toward the ceiling until she rocked herself onto her knees, chair now over her like some terrible tortoise shell. Noa shoved backward at the filing cabinet, trying to jam two of the chair legs under the lip between stubby legs and floor. She shoved once, twice, three times, sweat dripping down her face, shoulder still screaming with every contraction of every muscle, until she finally hit home and wedged two chair legs into the crevice. Then, with an almighty lurch, she tore her body forward, away from the trapped chair. The chair shuddered but stayed wedged as she dragged and twisted off it, the lasso of her arms finally ripping from the chair back.

Free of the chair, Noa collapsed forward on her stomach, her arms still bound behind her. She panted against the tape on her mouth, tasted the tang of sweat seeping through the tackiness. Her shoulder burned and pulsed so much she was sure she'd broken something, but there was no time to worry about that now, or to try to catch her breath—all that mattered was getting to that door where Annabelle had disappeared. Without hands, Noa slithered forward on her belly like a snake until her forehead hit the wall. She flipped herself onto her back, shoved the back of her head and neck into the wall, and slowly, painfully, pushed herself upward with her legs until she could stand.

Exhausted, Noa let herself lean against the wall for a moment, completely drenched and drained from the mere act of getting to her feet. But she couldn't stop. Hands still pinned, she stumbled forward and ran clumsily to the secret door behind Ms. Jaycee's still-open sliding screen. It was shut tight, of course, not that Noa could actually have turned a knob without her hands, but there was, in keeping with Harlow's architectural style, a long sliver of a window in the door's face.

Finally, Noa thought, a purpose to Harlow's numbing uniformity.

Noa pressed her frantic eye against the transparent sliver, its narrow ribbon of visibility. She saw Annabelle's back and shoulder, guided by Ms. Jaycee's peachy nails, and the disembodied hand—gloved in white—of the Otec.

Noa shuddered as Ms. Jaycee's profile leaned into visibility, her eyes gazing reverently out of frame, presumably at Judah's father. She nodded, then began to position Annabelle in front of what looked something like an enormous, life-size picture frame. Noa could see only her friend's left side, shoulder to foot, and the wisps of her side-ponytail, which Ms. Jaycee lined up perfectly inside the frame's border.

Noa could only watch Annabelle's left arm: it was trembling, then began to squirm violently. Ms. Jaycee's face flashed across and back, obviously trying to soothe Annabelle's panic, just as obviously to no avail. Then the white hands of Judah's father appeared, reached to hold Annabelle down firmly by the shoulders—

—and a blinding, punishing green light exploded in the room. It was so bright, so sickening, that Noa fell backward, landing hard on her bound hands and tailbone. She wailed against the silencing tape, but any sound she made was lost to the harrowing, endless scream that came through the secret door. Annabelle's scream, too strong for any tape, for any earthly thing, to block.

Noa scrabbled to her feet again, stumbled back against the window, forced herself to watch. Her tailbone and shoulder throbbed, and it was almost impossible to keep her eye open against the green explosion. She smashed her body into the door itself to remain upright, slid her eyelid against the window to pin it open.

Noa had never seen anything like this virulent, shattering green light before—at least she had no memory of it in her mind—but her *body* seemed to know it, fear it, a muscle memory, primal and deep. Noa fought her body, forced herself to stay. Whatever was happening to Annabelle, Noa did not want her to endure it alone.

Eye forcibly peeled, Noa forced herself to watch, her scar exploding in pain like wildfire. Inside the vortex, Annabelle's entire body flashed—and then, in a shattering blast that threw Noa backward like a bomb, the body that was Annabelle completely disintegrated, skeleton to stars, a spray of a million shards of light.

Noa heard and felt bones crack—her own bones, she knew—but she half-crawled, half-lurched herself back to the door, to the bottom of the window. Her cheekbone crashed against it, tears blurring her eyes, but Annabelle's legs and feet were gone. The bottom of the picture frame was empty, the light extinguished. Noa forced herself to her feet, pressed her face up and down the window—

But Annabelle was gone.

• • •

NOA STUMBLED BACKWARD, numb, fell against Ms. Jaycee's desk. Before she could think, process, regroup, the door—that horrible door—opened, and Ms. Jaycee appeared, smiling her toothpaste smile, which faltered only slightly as she took in the scene.

"Oh, dear, you do like to make things harder." She leaned over Noa, and Noa felt the sharp pinch of a needle in her shoulder.

"A calming serum, just to keep you from being ... difficult," Ms. Jaycee explained kindly.

Noa breathed out harshly through her nose as any last physical energy hissed away like air from a dying balloon. Her heart and head remained frantic, alert, but physically she could not move, much less struggle.

Ms. Jaycee looked at her sympathetically. "I'm sorry you had to see that. I'm sure it seemed a little scary. But Annabelle had been here almost the longest, Noa. There just wasn't enough left after Review for the Otec to send back to school. Now, I don't think we need this anymore."

Ms. Jaycee leaned over and pulled the tape from Noa's mouth. Noa gulped in air, but even that was painful, difficult with the serum; she knew immediately it would be impossible to scream.

But Noa would not allow herself to die in silence.

"You killed her," she whispered thickly, voice hoarse and sluggish, every word a giant boulder to expel.

"Heavens, no!" Ms. Jaycee replied sunnily. "She's simply done her duty. The Otec cannot keep us safe alone, after all; we all must contribute in turn."

"What ... does that...," Noa gasped. It was too hard to speak; the serum had grown too strong.

"Now, now, Noa, don't exhaust yourself. Besides, there's no point in burdening anyone with too much knowledge, is there? Better to keep things running smoothly."

Ms. Jaycee lifted her toward the terrible door. Noa's mind spun wildly, but she couldn't move or protest. She resolved at least to keep her eyes open, no matter what it took—if she had to face Judah's father, she would face him with open eyes. A warrior. A girl-beast.

Ms. Jaycee opened the door, and Noa looked fully into the room. It was white, immaculate white, the only furniture a metal table and the empty picture frame; it smelled and felt hospital-sterile but worse, the kind of sterile of cleaning up after terrible, terrible things. Noa's body constricted of its own accord, fueled by a fear too bone-deep for serum. *Hospitals*, every sinew screamed. *Hospitals; run far!*

Before she could think to try, serum or no serum, he came in, and her body froze.

The Otec.

Tall, so tall. White hands gloved. Head crowned with Judah's curls, body drawn with Judah's lines.

But he wasn't Judah's father.

He was Judah's brother.

· · ·

NOA KNEW HIM instantly from Judah's drawings: slightly taller, broader, older than the boy she knew so well. In the flesh, Noa now saw that he was lighter too—his hair and eyes a shade less dark, his body traced in fuller, softer lines. It was strange, actually: this boy looked the more angelic, the more ethereal of the two. But how could that be, given who he was and what he'd done?

The Boy with the White Hands—for Judah's brother was a boy, not really a man at all—looked at her oddly for a moment, searching every feature of her face. He looked lost, confused, then shook his head minutely, pushed some question away. He walked to her—graceful, liquid—and gently took Noa from Ms. Jaycee's hands.

Noa shivered—this was the time to try to fight—but she couldn't make her body obey. Even through white gloves, his touch felt warm, even safe; her muscles instinctively relaxed, tingling. As if her body trusted him.

He guided her to the metal examination table, and she did not protest.

The serum, Noa rationalized, as she sat on the table bolted to the wall. *It must be the effect of the serum.* But then why was breathing suddenly easier now, not harder? Why, from the moment she had seen him, *felt* him, had she felt herself come *back* into her body, reconnect to every tissue, as if he'd reconnected what had been displaced? And why, when he now brushed a wayward strand of blond hair from her eyes, tucked it behind her ear, did heat spiral in her cheeks—not the heat of fear, but something else?

Their eyes met. He seemed as unnerved as she.

The boy, the Otec, Judah's brother with White Hands, spoke to Ms. Jaycee without looking away from Noa: "You may go." Ms. Jaycee murmured something, but Noa heard her footsteps obey, retreat; she heard the door click shut.

Noa and the boy stared at each other, brown eyes on gray, until he finally tore away. Noa felt herself exhale—relieved but also, somehow, bereft. The boy steadied himself on the wall. "So, you've caused a little stir," he said, clearing his throat when his voice began to waver. He turned back to her but filled hands, his gaze, with a clipboard: "Noa Sullivan." His brow furrowed as he read her name—then again, he shook it off.

She watched his shoulders draw themselves erect. When he turned to her again, his face was grim, set, though his soft brown eyes betrayed him. "Well, Noa," he said, clearing his throat over her name again, "I hear you've been having a hard time." He said it kindly, sadly, and Noa was struck by how his sympathy was so different from Ms. Jaycee's. It felt *true*, sincere. Noa could feel the truth of his regret, beating inside her own heart.

It scared her.

"I only wrote poems," Noa whispered.

"Which is dangerous," he told her painfully. "For everyone."

"But … why?" Noa knew she shouldn't ask, or wasn't supposed to. But somehow she also knew she had to.

The boy stayed quiet at first, studying her with those gentle eyes. "Not knowing is easier, better—"

"I want to know." On impulse, she touched his shoulder. His body jumped a little; he looked at her warily—but then he began to answer:

"There are things in the world. Messy, dark things. Questions without answers, feelings that don't fit and never will…." He was grappling to explain, to find just the right words. "They bring pain. And loss. Confusion with no remedy." He met her eyes.

"And poetry, and art," Noa murmured, beginning to understand.

He nodded. "Tap into that. Bring up what needs to be left buried. Confuse what can be clear."

Noa thought of the Girl, of how writing the Girl's poem had made her cry; she thought of Judah, how his drawings had tormented him with figments, questions, losses he couldn't grasp or fully see—

"My job," the boy continued, standing taller as he spoke, "my *privilege*, is to keep that messiness away from here, keep you, all of you, safe and clean. I handle that—the murk, the dark—so you don't have to. I keep it pacified, and away, to protect you. Do you see?"

The thing was, Noa did see, or *wanted* to. She had expected the Man with White Hands to be so many things: a tyrant, an oppressor, a worse version of Ms. Jaycee. But this boy was earnestness and softness, honesty and compassion, a kind of sadness and deep, heart-deep, care. She knew, instinctively, that he believed in what he did: made them safe, spared them pain, decided when they could not. He handled what they didn't need to see, kept out that which might hurt them, harm them.

Then Noa remembered Annabelle.

She grasped her hand from his shoulder, drawing back. "And if we do have questions, if we sense the mess, you just kill us like Annabelle?"

He looked stung, even betrayed. Noa bit her lip, fought the pang of guilt that rose inside her. She kept Annabelle in her mind, the terror she'd seen of Annabelle exploding.

"The world is not a safe place, Noa, don't you see?" the boy insisted, growing urgent. "It's dangerous, and ugly, and requires ugly things. I make those choices, do those things, so *you* don't have to. It's my duty; I save you all—" He breathed hard through his nose, eyes fervent, volume rising. "You are safe here, content here, because I keep this place protected! I alone take on that burden, even if it means, if it means—" He broke off, eyes wild around the room, as if the right words might be written there. Finally he met her eyes again, his aflame: "There is a price to stay here. We all must give."

Noa swallowed, throat dry with fear. "What price? What do we give?"

"I call it *Light*."

"Light…"

Her echo made him hopeful, his words tumbling quickly now: "We all give it, like breathing, simply taking refuge here. But when someone gets infected by what's outside, the dark and murk…" His hands pulled through his curls—*Judah's brother*—"At first I thought I'd have to kill the infected to keep us safe"—Noa gasped, and he spoke more quickly, urgently—"but then I discovered a way to heal them! If I bled their Light, fed it to the Dark, oftentimes I could reset, repurify them, help them stay—"

"Jeremy?" Noa whispered. "That's what Review is?"

"I *saved him*, like I saved others. That frame"—he gestured at the empty picture frame, the one in which Annabelle had exploded—"I can bleed more Light, leech out the infected parts, a kind of rehabilitation."

Noa recoiled. "Jeremy came back a zombie, like his *soul* was gone! And what about Annabelle? Or Dr. Chandler? The others who never came back?"

She expected him to deny it, but he didn't; he just squared his shoulders like a soldier. "They'd been here giving Light too long. The Review process took what was left and then…" He clenched his jaw. "We all make the sacrifice eventually. None of us is more important than the safety of the whole. Not you, not me."

"And your brother?" Noa asked.

She didn't know how she expected him to react, what she had hoped to arouse in him, but it was certainly not the utter bafflement, the pained confusion that seemed to knock his whole body off balance.

"I have no family. I yearn for it, wish … but I am alone. It is part of my sacrifice, my burden—"

Something inside Noa flared. This wasn't right. The boy's compassion, his regret, his sense of duty—those felt real to Noa, like they were truly parts of him. But this—the denial of Judah, his confusion—it didn't fit. It jangled wrong, reverberated out of tune, just like the walls of Harlow flickering, like the Girl appearing and disappearing, like finding classmates with no faces—

Noa suddenly knew: this boy was going to kill her.

He was not her enemy; oh, no—an enemy she could have defeated, convinced, won over, even tricked. He was something worse. A fellow victim. A pawn of something darker, larger. The same dark thing that had somehow captured them all, wound its tentacles into their minds. She'd snapped hers with words and poems, questions and fears—and this place, for its own survival, would kill her for it.

This place would kill her using him.

The boy sensed the change in her immediately, but before he could do anything, Noa sprang at him, teeth and nails bared: part girl, part beast, all fight. Heat spiraled from her scar; a feral growl ripped from deep inside her throat. The boy stumbled back, caught her spitting, fighting form—and she lashed out with her only weapon, teeth, biting savagely into his neck.

The boy cried out as she tasted blood. Noa ripped her teeth free, spun toward the door, but he caught her hands, still bound behind her, and pulled her back. She slashed her bound arms up and down to shake his grip, to land a punch, and he released her, tried to regrip higher on her wrists—but the momentum of her moving arms sliced down across his palms, and her bracelet's charm ripped through in his glove, exposing skin. When he finally caught her arm, they touched skin to skin, palm against wrist, silver bracelet in between—

—and the world exploded into rapid, spinning images: Noa and the boy, meeting in the Harlow office; Noa and the boy, kayaking in the sea; Noa kissing him, he kissing her, beneath the giant spreading oak; Noa crying to him as he sat invisible, freeing him from unseen bonds—

The images were too much, too vibrant and too strong. Noa was blasted backward, wrists freed of their ties. She slammed into the examination table, leg contorting in pain beneath her, and she saw the boy also sprawled across the room. He struggled up, turned her way, and she met his eyes—

Eyes she knew by heart.

"Callum."

• • •

NOTHING MADE SENSE. Noa knew his name, the Otec's name. He was Callum, and he was the Otec, she knew him but she'd never met him until now. Her body remembered kissing him, his hands had been tangled in her hair, but now his hands were White Hands that had murdered Annabelle, would murder her as well—

"You know my name," the boy, who was the Otec, who was Callum, panted, stumbling to his feet.

"I don't understand," Noa whispered. "You're here ... but you're not here. We're here but we're not here! *Callum.* Why do I know your name?"

He looked frantic, terrified. "It's you! Your poems! All your questions! You're infecting me!"

"No!" Noa cried. "I know you saw it too! This place isn't right! This isn't who we are—"

"You're wrong!" he shouted, almost like a child. "I'm the protector, the Otec!"

Noa wanted to leap to her feet, to run to him and shake him, but her screaming leg would not obey. He grasped his temples, shook his head, his whole body, as if to make it all go away. "I don't know how you've done this, but I won't let you destroy what I have built!" He finally looked at her, eyes wild, hard, bestial with fear.

"Callum, no," Noa cried, skittering backward. With her injured leg she couldn't flee, could barely fight. She had no way to resist the Man with White Hands—who was the Otec who was Judah's brother who was Callum, Callum, Callum.

Callum grasped her by the shoulders, hauled her toward the picture frame. He faced it, wrapped her struggling body with one arm, held out his other palm, fingers splayed. The wall inside the frame opened into a howling tunnel, shining green, sizzling sparks and hissing like an animal opening its jaws—hungry for Annabelle.

Noa scrabbled against Callum, bit and kicked and wriggled until finally she slipped from his one-armed hold and crashed onto the floor. Knowing she couldn't run, she grabbed the nearest leg of the examination table. The vortex roared to suck her back, pry her from the table bolted to the wall.

"You're too dangerous!" Callum cried. "You must be cleansed!"

"Callum—"

"*Otec!*" Callum tried to pry her loose, to shove her back. Her grip slipped, her fingers on fire—Callum was too strong, the suck too brutal. One of Noa's hands came off, and on impulse, Noa thrust it onto Callum's chest.

"Mermaid hearts," she cried against the howl, finding his eyes, pressing her fingers into his pounding heartbeat. "My mermaid heart to yours!"

Callum froze, words breaking through; the frame roared more loudly, sparks multiplying in anger. Callum fell, skidded toward the tunnel's jaws. He reached and caught the same table leg Noa held, his hands on hers, anchoring them both with his strength.

"Noa..." he said painfully, in torment, "I remember ... loving you?"

Noa nodded numbly, eyes watering in the whipping wind. The metal table groaned against its bolts.

"But ... did you love me? I think ... I hurt you...."

The bolts whined; Noa knew they were sliding free. "Callum, please—"

His face twisted, confused. "I can't, I'm the protector—"

"We're not supposed to be here, Callum, please—"

"Are we supposed to love each other?" He was pleading, so confused, so scared—

"*Noa!*" Judah's voice broke through the noise, followed by repeated slamming against Ms. Jaycee's door.

Noa's mind surged with memories, color on touch on taste: sitting with Judah in the library, lying with him in the sun, his fingers in her hair, her hands in his curls, kissing him kissing him kissing him—but the other memories flooded too, pushing and fighting to be seen: swimming with Callum in the sea, sitting with him in the rain, tangled with him sharing secrets—

Two of the table's wall bolts flew out like machine-gun fire and were sucked into the frame. The vortex roared and spat, voracious now, as the metal table twirled almost into its jaws, hinged on one last bolt.

"Callum!" Noa shrieked. "The table!"

But Callum was somewhere else. "You have feelings for him, too?" he demanded, so lost and so confused.

"Callum, please—"

"You want me to throw it all away when you cry out for someone else?"

"Throw what away? We don't belong—"

"*I* belong! *I* belong!" Callum screamed. "It's my duty—"

"*Noa!*" Judah shouted, shaking the wall, frantic to get through.

"Promise me!" Callum burst in frenzy as the final bolt began to screech. "If I give it up, fail it all, promise at least you will be with me! That I won't be alone!"

"*Noa!*" The door splintered, little chunks finally giving way—

"Promise me we'll be together! The way we saw! Whatever happens!"

The last bolt detached; Noa shrieked as their anchor careened backward into the screaming frame. "I promise! I promise to try to love you!"

Like lightning, Callum had her whole body wrapped inside his; he rolled them both sideways, still skidding back, but he'd pushed them far enough that they slammed into the wall, just adjacent to the opening in the frame—

"Noa..." A wail this time. Close. And hurt.

Noa squinted toward the door, where Judah stood. He had finally broken through, was standing in debris.

"Jaycee!" Callum yelled at him, the vortex now sucking both him and Noa sideways. "Jaycee now! Or Noa dies!"

Judah flew into Jaycee's office, reappeared with the vice head-mistress, bound and bloody.

"Free her! Now!"

Judah hesitated, and one of Noa's shoes was sucked into the void, her legs stretched so hard she knew her tendons would soon snap. "Judah, please!"

Judah ripped Ms. Jaycee's bonds, and Callum called, "Your duty!"

Ms. Jaycee didn't argue, didn't cry. She saluted Callum, brave and even proud—and ran and leapt into the vortex. She hovered there a moment, body flashing and flickering within the frame as every bit of essence drained —and then she exploded into virulent green sparks.

Sated, the vortex growled, then sealed back into white wall.

Noa had seen none of it, felt none of it. Wrapped in Cal-lum's arms, tangled with him on the floor, she could look only at Judah—at Judah's shattered, broken eyes.

Olivia and Miles rushed in.

"Miles rescued me and punched Jeremy out!" Olivia crowed, then gasped. "Ohmygod, Noa, are you okay? Holy crap, Is that the Otec?"

No one answered as Callum jumped to his feet and pulled Noa up. He held her fast; her leg could not support her, but Noa somehow knew his grasp meant more than that. She looked ago-nizingly at Judah, still planted, face and body completely closed—

Callum pulled Noa to the dormant picture frame, held out his spread palm again.

"No!" Noa shrieked. "You said—"

"It's okay," Callum, gritting his teeth in fierce determination. Sweat beaded at his temples as he splayed his fingers wide. "I'm telling them to make it different."

"Telling who?"

"The atoms," Callum groaned harshly. "To send us back to the place we saw—"

"Yoooo ... is the Otec cray?" Olivia murmured. Again, nobody answered.

The picture frame vibrated, and then the wall inside opened once again, this time blue and rippling, a curtain of pure water.

The moment it opened, the floor beneath them all started shaking violently. The walls vibrated, howled and groaned—

"It's angry!" Callum cried. "It's angry I've betrayed my duty! We have to go fast. I don't know how long this exit will last, how many it will take—"

"My friends first," Noa said immediately. "Olivia! Miles!"

"No!" Callum said, cracks exploding in the walls. A crevice started to split the floor. "Us first, before the whole place crumbles!" He shoved her forward toward the plasma-blue. Noa tried helplessly to resist—then felt someone adding his strength to hers.

Judah.

"You heard her! Her friends first!" Judah spat at Callum. He pulled Olivia and Miles with him.

"Uh, what are we doing? Where is this going?" Miles protested weakly. "Surely I get a life vest or—"

"Geronimo!" Olivia shrieked, cutting him off, grabbing Miles and jumping them both through.

When they vanished, the room shook harder. The crack in the floor widened into a chasm, split across the room behind them—

"Us now!" Callum cried to Noa. "Before it's too late!"

"Judah, come on!" Noa cried, reaching for him.

He stepped away from her.

"Judah!"

"Leave him, then! It's safer with two—"

But Noa's eyes were on Judah's. She couldn't look away.

"I heard your promise," he told her.

Their side of the chasm fell several feet; above the picture frame, the wall began to crumble.

"Noa, now!" Callum urged, pushing at her.

But Noa couldn't look away from Judah, wishing for words that did not exist. Suddenly Judah grabbed her, kissed her hard and deep. When they finally broke apart, Noa gasped, and Judah's eyes were hard on hers. Saying nothing, he took her other hand.

A chain of three—Callum, Noa, Judah—they faced the blue, just as the ceiling fell.

And Noa saw it—a glimmer of brown curls in the corner of her eye. The Girl, her Girl, running away from the blue exit, back into the collapsing world.

"Noa, no!" Judah and Callum yelled together as Noa spun after the Girl, shielding her head from falling shrapnel, breaking both their holds. Her leg was somehow steady now, as if healed by her conviction that she must always follow the Girl. That she must always find her, no matter what.

"Noa, no!" the brothers shouted again, as Noa leapt up to the other side of the widening chasm, clambered over the rubble that had once been Ms. Jaycee's door. But the office was gone, completely gone, nothing more than an empty floor being swallowed by a black tidal wave of oblivion. It roared, rose toward Noa from where the rest of the school no longer was.

Judah and Callum stumbled in after Noa, then skittered backward from the wave. "Noa, get away from there!" Judah yelled, pulling back on one arm as Callum grabbed the other.

But Noa didn't hear them, barely felt them; she stood her ground, suddenly serene. She watched the Girl, a toddler really, smile her impish smile, laugh a pealing laugh— and dive into the tidal wave, as easy as slipping into a lake.

Noa walked forward, pulling the boys with her as easily, as lightly, as dandelions to keep for future wishes. She heard nothing but a quiet calm, felt nothing but certainty, saw nothing but the faint sparkling white where the Girl had dipped from sight. Noa smiled, eyes wide open, scar shining the way like a golden beacon—

—and walked them all into the dark.

When they woke up in Aurora, they remembered everything.

PART II: THE TUNNELS

AT FIRST, THERE was only the crash: Noa existed completely within it, her whole existence the reverberation of bones against steel. Or not steel, but something just as cold and hard—something broken and uneven, knots and twists of ... stones and roots? She slammed against them like a human tuning fork, her whole skeleton shuddering into some strange night.

Noa lay in that night, unmoving, as jagged feelings put themselves together. She was outside, the ground was sharp and cold, but the air wrapped her tight with muggy heat. Darkness wound around her like a shroud—sticky, cloying, clogging—suffocating, except for the ice-cold ground. But below her, beneath her, the wood and leaves had bite as well as chill—raised tree roots grooved with sharp-edged bark, leaves ringed with tiny teeth. Noa could feel them, every thorn and every spine. She felt everything, each barbed particle of dirt, each razored mote of dust as it settled, sizzled on her skin. The air here *hurt*.

She didn't want it in her lungs.

"*Sasha.*" The name came out with dirt, with bile, swords, and knives. Noa coughed, lifted her head, and for the first time, opened her eyes. Around her, shapes and shadows lingered in light so pale it was almost silver, almost lavender. She looked up: twin sickles of mirrored moons. The air—so hot—was spicy on her lips. Like raw ginger, but thicker, sharper.

Noa sat up, straining against her still-vibrating limbs. "*Sasha…*" she wailed again, softly, to the eerie night. The night answered with the sound of nearby movement, a sort of scuffling, and the little bits of voices weaving to her ear.

"Need to move…"

"Don't know where we are…"

Noa swallowed, tried to wet her throat. Breathing in this air felt like not getting air at all. She pushed up to her feet.

"Noa?"

Noa blinked, tried to focus. The darkness had opened its eyes, had spoken. The eyes were dark and stormy, like Judah's—

Noa gasped: two different kinds of memories crashed upon her consciousness at once: sitting against Judah in their secret corner of Lamont Library, trading kisses while he tried to braid her hair … and at the same time, but somehow somewhere else, Judah screaming on his knees, deranged, tearing at his curls because she'd said she could never love him—

Judah now stepped into the lavender light, reached out to her, and it was like three Judahs all at once: Judah Before and Judah After and Judah Now, three hands in one. Noa wanted to kiss him and slap him, run from him and to him, take his hand and break his hand and stab him and hold him. Instead, she felt herself wrenched backward and away. Judah's dark eyes flickered in all three faces; three became one, clouded with anger—

"Noa, we have to move. We're too exposed here." It was Callum, Callum turning her around. Taller, lighter, more assured; calm and gentle, kind—but now he was doubling, tripling, too: Callum Before and Callum After and Callum Now. Noa slammed her eyes shut, shook her head.

"What's wrong with her?" Judah's voice.

"She's in shock. She doesn't make Light here like we do; her mind has to recover on its own. If it even can. Mortal minds were not meant for the In Between. Come on, there's a cave over there."

Noa heard angry, stalking footsteps fading fast. But the steadying, guiding hand remained. *Callum's,* she knew, from the gentleness. Judah was the one who'd sped away, crunching leaves into the night.

Callum guided Noa, became her eyes, her mind, until she could slowly lift her lids again. Every step steadied by his hand let Noa's mind focus and recover; her body slowly stretched within his gait. Every muscle ached with soreness, but nothing felt broken or out of joint.

Noa's eyes slowly adjusted to the silver-purple sickle moonlight. Trees and vines coalesced from shadow-clay around her, some familiar and some in spiny-textured shapes Noa had never seen. In the distance, on every side as far as Noa could glimpse, these tangled thickets rose upward in endless towers to the sky. As if at the boundaries of this world, the wilderness somehow swallowed upward and devoured the horizon, yawning wide-toothed and ravenous into the sea of stars.

Callum led Noa into the shelter of a cave, but her mind had begun spinning, firing jumbled memory-pieces into place. No sooner had the stony walls reached out to take them than Noa shook off Callum's hand, recoiled. Judah looked hopeful and reached out, but she cringed from his touch too.

She stumbled backward, tensed to flee like a hissing cat.

"We're in Aurora, aren't we?" she asked, eyes darting from brother to brother.

Callum stepped toward her, pleading: "It wasn't me in there. It wasn't any of us. It was the In Between—" Her flinch made him freeze. Noa watched his every movement but heard Judah chuckle low.

"That place, that Harlow, it was the In Between?" she asked.

Callum nodded slowly, trying not to spook her. "The Portal was devouring our Light, holding us between the worlds while it slowly ... *ate* us all. It made the In Between so we would stay there, so we wouldn't know—"

"You knew!" Judah scoffed. "You ran the place!"

Callum tensed. "I didn't *know*. I thought that world was real, just like you."

"It was a mind trap," Noa realized slowly. "The Portal made us think the In Between world was real, put us there to occupy our minds...."

"So Callum could serve us up on a silver platter," Judah sneered, shoving Callum backward.

"I *didn't know!*" Callum insisted, shoving back as Judah growled.

"Stop it!" Noa commanded. "Just let me figure this out!"

They both stopped, seething, and turned to her, distorted mirror images.

Noa swallowed as anger flushed through her—nebulous, murky anger she knew was for them both. But before she could deal with that, she just needed to understand. "So the Portal created a world where our minds wouldn't protest—the In Between world we thought was Harlow—so that we would let it drain our Light, our life, until we…"

"Died," Callum finished softly, looking down.

"More like until we were murdered, drained, *disintegrated*," Judah sniffed. "If we're being accurate."

Noa ignored him, ignored them both. "So the Portal needed us to accept that the In Between was real, so we wouldn't fight free. That's why the arts—poetry, drawing, dreams, anything that tapped into our subconscious—were forbidden. Because they could stir memory, feeling … awareness."

"I think so," Callum said softly.

"But there was more, wasn't there?" Noa accused, glaring at him, forcing him to meet her eyes. "There was more to it."

Callum looked away. "Seems that way."

"What?" Judah demanded.

Noa waited, but Callum just shook his head, unable or unwilling to explain. She didn't need him to. "It sweetened the pot, Judah. Made the world a place where we *wanted* to stay, don't you see? By giving each of us something we wanted."

Judah's eyes flashed defensively. "What do you mean?"

Some of Noa's anger cooled. "Think about it," she told him more gently, "how it changed everyone's reality. Olivia had freedom. She could do whatever she wanted with her hair, her style, even her tattoos, all with her parents' approval. In real life, she has to hide all that, hide *who she is*, because they'd never support her. And Miles—in the In Between he was popular, a huge lacrosse star, when in real life he rides the bench because of his asthma, and he's not exactly part of the 'in crowd.' Ms. Jaycee was vice headmistress, so she had power without having to make decisions—and she got to feel like she was really *saving* kids while still lording over us. That wall of success stories! Jeremy got to date Olivia, with peer approval"—Noa broke off, swallowed hard— "and I had Isla back, alive…"

"And Judah had you," Callum finished stonily.

Judah met Noa's eyes for the briefest of moments, then scowled quickly, whipping venomously toward Callum. "How do you know my wish wasn't just to be an orphan? To be free of you and Dad? 'Cause I had that too."

Callum scoffed. "Please."

Judah turned red with rage. "Well, if Noa's right, look what the Portal gave *you*! *Your* deepest wish to be some murdering tyrant like our father!" Callum's eyes flared; his jaw clenched.

"Stop it, Judah!" Noa cried, more anger dissipating, more warmth returning, this time for Callum. She went toward them both, stepped in between. "Callum didn't want to hurt anyone! Don't you see? His wish was to take care of everyone! To keep things safe, protected…" Callum looked at her hopefully, so hopefully. She stuttered, continued: "The Portal just … in that world, the only way the Portal could grant that wish was to have him actually *protect* that world."

Noa focused her mind, her heart, on the Callum she had known before—the Callum from Harlow, from Monterey. Callum now was looking at her with such hope, wanting to believe this was how she truly felt—and Noa *did* feel it, the way she'd even felt it in the In Between. The safety of him, the way his face sparked heat and longing and trust and something more, just as

it had since the first time they'd met, when he'd been Callum
Then—

Except that Callum, Noa suddenly remembered clearly, had
lied to her, about almost everything.

Noa's resolve flickered, uncertain.

Judah smirked. "Sounds right to me. Callum *thinking* he
knows best, and in the process hurting and destroying everyone
around him. In the Portal, in real life…"

"Sasha," Noa murmured, with heartbreaking clarity. Her little sister, the Girl she'd searched for in the In Between, her heart
of hearts, her love … except she was not Noa's sister at all. She was
Callum's and Judah's. She was in Noa's life only because Callum
had faked her death, blamed it on Judah, and then secretly hidden her in Noa's world, in Noa's family.

That was the real reason Noa had met Callum. She'd thought
it fate, or love—a special soulmate appearing at exactly the time
she'd needed him after she'd lost her older sister Isla. Noa had
needed someone to help her breathe again, live again, and they'd
bonded over both having "lost" a sister. But that wasn't true. It
wasn't fate; they didn't resonate in loss. She had simply been part
of Callum's elaborate web of lies.

But. Noa's heart beat on the word. It hadn't all been lies. He'd
told her about himself, after all—about being Fae, Blue Fae, and
about his gift to manipulate the elements. He'd told her about his
race, their different gifts, and the story—at least partially—of his
exile and his family. Those were intimacies Callum hadn't had to
share; in fact, sharing them with her had put him in great danger. And he'd literally broken his soul for her, let awful creatures
carve off a piece, to make a talisman-bracelet to protect her when

touching her in the mortal realm without it would have meant draining her spirit, her Light.

"Noa?" Callum asked anxiously.

Noa shook her head. It was too much.

"She's just remembering how much you suck," Judah smiled.

Callum spun on him. "I'm not the one who threw her little sister into the Portal in the first place, Judah—"

"It was an accident!"

"You declared your love for my girlfriend, she rejected you, and you threw her sister into the Portal to punish her!" Callum pressed. "It was no accident at all!" Noa closed her eyes, shuddering at the memory. Judah hadn't known then that Sasha was also his sister, Lily, but it didn't matter, Judah would never have sacrificed an innocent child for revenge.

"*You're* the one who actually killed people, Callum! Putting them on 'Review' in your deranged little fantasy world, Mr. *Otec*. You sucked their Light into oblivion to feed the In Between! That girl, Annabelle, and that teacher, Dr. Chandler, and who knows who else! You let the Portal *murder* them! I'm surprised you didn't also find a way to have me blamed for it, the way you framed me for 'killing' Lily!"

"I was being *brainwashed*, Judah! Unlike you, who chucked Sasha into hell without a second thought!"

"I *didn't*—"

"Stop it! Stop it, both of you!" Noa yelled, suddenly furious. "It doesn't matter!" It was too much—too much to handle, too much to balance, too much to feel. "Who cares who meant what, or who wished for what, or who knew what at what time! None of it matters now! I'm deciding!"

"Ha." Callum couldn't help but gloat, glaring at Judah.

"Goes both ways, bro," Judah snapped back.

"I said *shut up!*" Noa commanded. "I jumped into that hell dimension in the first place because of Sasha. That's what's important here. Finding Sasha. Lily—"

"She's Sasha now, I told you," Callum said. "She's Sasha Sullivan, I'd never take that from you—"

"The way you took Lily from me—" Judah started.

"To protect her! From Darius!"

Noa held up a hand. "Stop! Look. All the people who Thorn and Judah threw into the Portal were in the In Between too." She glared at Callum when he scoffed at the reminder of Judah's myriad other crimes. "Annabelle, Carly Ann, Ms. Jaycee, Dr. Chandler—they were all really there. The other people who weren't, like Ansley, they were just blurs, approximations, because their minds weren't really in the In Between—"

"The faceless people you saw," Judah said.

Noa nodded. "But Sasha, who we *know* went into the Portal—she wasn't there, except as some ghostly hallucination. Why? She should have been there, too."

"Her gifts," Judah offered uncertainly. "Her special powers; she must have used them to go right through, bypass the In Between."

Noa looked at Callum, who nodded slowly.

"It must be. The whole reason I tried to take her from Aurora, protect her, was because I'd never seen powers like hers before." This was true; Callum had confessed as much when Sasha's true identity had been revealed. Unlike the usual races, or Colorlines, of Fae—Blue Fae like Callum, who manipulated the physical world; Red Fae like Judah, who manipulated thoughts; and Green Fae like their mother, Lorelei, who manipulated emotions—Lily had been able to do all three. She was some sort of magical hybrid, different even than the Clear Fae like their father, Darius, who could Channel different Colorline powers but could not produce gifts on their own. Callum had worried that Darius—who ruled Aurora as the king-like Otec—would use Lily's gifts to solidify his tyranny, further oppressing the Colored Fae whose gifts he and other Clears jealously siphoned.

It was to protect both Lily and the Realm, Callum claimed, that he'd faked Lily's death and taken her to Noa's world, the 'prison' world, where he'd hidden her with Noa's family, where he himself would have to live without his gifts.

"She didn't come back out of the Portal in your world, and she wasn't in the In Between, so she must have gone straight through to Aurora," Callum hypothesized.

"She could do that?" Noa asked.

"Her mind would be impossible to trap," Judah put in. "It makes sense that the In Between wouldn't hold her."

"My scar ... where I cut myself to open the Portal again so I could find her," Noa realized. "Every time I saw the Girl in the In Between, it was like my scar was connecting me to her. My scar was what pulled me away from the exit Callum made to take us home, and toward that big black wave that brought us here instead—"

Callum nodded. "Because your blood really is her blood now, bound by a deeper magic than genes."

"What, love?" Judah snorted.

"Exactly that," Callum said evenly. He turned back to Noa. "That bond, that magic, was crystallized in your scar, and so must have guided you on the path she took."

"It led me to follow her here, to Aurora," Noa finished. She closed her eyes, gathered herself, then faced them both. "We have to find her. All of us."

"Of course," Callum said immediately.

Judah scowled.

"We'll need your help, too, Judah. It's *Sasha*—"

"We're not in the In Between anymore. I'm not your boyfriend," Judah said icily.

Noa's chest tightened. "Judah," she said gently, "I felt it too, there—"

Judah stepped backward, held up his hands. "Stop! You said we're not talking about it, right? We're just forgetting what happened?"

"I didn't mean—"

"Who cares, anyway? Even if we didn't forget it, you promised him. I *heard* you. When we got out and we remembered whatever it was we had forgotten, you swore to forgive him and love him and be happy forever!"

"Judah, please—" Hot tears stung Noa's throat.

Judah snorted. "You always choose him anyway. Back in your world and in the stupid In Between too. But don't you worry, I'll help you find Sasha because she's *my* Sasha too. But I don't need your pity, and I don't want it."

Noa swallowed hard. Her throat felt like fire. Callum put a steadying hand on her back; as always, his touch soothed and strengthened her—and she didn't have the energy to question it.

Judah smirked. "It *is* a bit gross though, right? I mean, we're all brothers and sister now. Callum saw to that." With that, he spun on his heel and stalked to the far corner of the cave, where he curled up on the hard ground, his back to them. "I'm getting some sleep."

Noa watched him until she couldn't bear it anymore, then turned and slumped into Callum.

"I am so sorry, Noa," Callum murmured into her hair, voice soft and warm. "You saved us in that Portal. Just like you saved Sasha ... you just keep saving us, saving me. I'm going to prove to you that I'm worth it."

Noa turned slowly to face him. "I meant what I said," she whispered carefully. "I know you wanted to protect us in that Portal world. And even, with Sasha..." She broke off, closed her eyes, not yet able to forgive that lie. "I meant what I promised in that world, the In Between. I'll *try*..." She opened her eyes, made sure her voice firm and clear. "But Callum, it's going to take time."

Callum glanced sadly at Judah's back. "Time?" he echoed.

Noa sighed. "It's complicated now," she admitted. "Can we first please just find Sasha?"

She felt his jaw tighten, but he nodded, head on hers. "I'll find her, Noa," he murmured. "This time I *will* protect us all. I *swear*."

• • •

CALLUM AGREED THAT whatever was to come, they needed sleep. Noa lay beside him, back to back, but could feel he wasn't sleeping either. Judah remained in his corner, still as stone.

Judah.

Noa knew the In Between had not been 'real,' but that didn't mean she remembered it with any less precision. Moments there vibrated like all others: sharp spatial forms inside her mind, hums and textures in her blood. Noa knew Judah's body language even better than she knew Callum's; in a paradoxical way, she and Judah had actually been together longer.

Of course, Portal Judah hadn't had this Judah's history, this Judah's guilt, this Judah's scars. And yet, as much as the 'real' Judah defined himself by his past, the Portal Judah, stripped of that past, had somehow been more *true*. Portal Judah was Judah at his core, not diminished by history or family—he was a Judah who was too strong for that. Noa understood that Judah. She admired that Judah, could feel for him.

Noa looked over at Judah now, lying in the corner: back knit with anger, wrapped with that shell of who he thought he had to be. Capable of things that scared her. Opaque and hard to understand.

Callum moved slightly behind Noa, and reflexively her body fluttered, the way it always did. But there was something new in this flutter too—the smallest bit of fear. If the In Between had shown Judah's truer core, then had it done the same with Callum?

Noa shut her eyes. She would not let the Portal simplify these brothers, make them smaller than they were. Judah was no lover, and Callum was no villain, any more than Miles was a popular jock or Olivia a pointy-haired vixen. The In Between was a mind *trap*.

Noa had already decided. From that point on, she would trust her *real* memories, and the complexity of feelings that came *only* from real life. In real life, she was angry with Callum for how he'd lied, but in real life, deep down, she'd already forgiven him, because his lies had brought her Sasha. No matter how it had happened, no matter how it had taken shape, Noa had Sasha now, and nothing could undo that. Sasha was her Sasha, Sasha her love—because of Callum.

Noa's body calmed. Of course it was Callum; it had always been Callum. Judah was right after all: she had already chosen Callum, would always choose him. Her body had known, even in the In Between, what her mind now saw so clearly.

Callum turned gently in the dark, and Noa tucked herself back against his chest, accepting the warm wrap of his arms.

She closed her eyes, and slept.

• • •

"IT'S LIGHT ENOUGH now. We should be able to figure out where we are," Judah announced. He stood at the mouth of the cave; the world was still dark but lightening with dawn.

Callum rubbed her shoulders. "You okay?" he asked softly. She turned to him, nodded shyly.

Judah walked over, scowling, and pulled her bracelet from her wrist. The bracelet that blocked her from his and Callum's— and anyone in their family's—magic.

"Heal her muscles, you moron," he told Callum.

Callum looked instantly apologetic. "He's right. I'm so sorry, Noa. I didn't even think of it. We're in Aurora, so I can use my gift on you and not have to take your Light." He placed his hands on Noa's arms and focused. Noa closed her eyes as a pod of warmth spun itself like a chrysalis in her chest, then spiraled outward down her arms and legs, healing every bruise. Callum lifted his hands, and Noa exhaled with a little *pop*. She opened her eyes to see Callum's proud, boyish grin.

"I can't tell you how long I've wanted to share my gift with you," he said. "In a way that wasn't torturous."

"That was definitely superior to when you healed me back at Harlow," Noa agreed.

Judah sighed loudly from the mouth of the cave. They turned to see Noa's bracelet flying back at them. Callum barely reached out and caught it before it hit Noa in the face.

"Hey, a little warning," Callum said to Judah.

Judah shrugged. "Put it on so we can go."

"She doesn't need to wear it here," Callum replied sharply. "What is it, you don't think you can stay out of her head?"

Judah rolled his eyes. "Sure. Whatever." He turned back, muttering. "Can't be that she's better off with *some* protection in case our *father* is out there...."

Callum looked at Noa, cheeks pink with angry shame again. "He's right, Noa," he said reluctantly. "I'm sorry, I was just so excited to show you what I could do—but he's right. It's too much of a risk. Whatever protection you can get from Darius—"

"While we look for Sasha. I get it," Noa said, fastening the talisman bracelet back onto her wrist. "Don't worry, finding her will be all the magic I need."

Callum got to his feet, helped her up. "We'd better start by figuring out where we are."

"Bad news: no idea," Judah announced as Callum and Noa joined him at the cave's mouth. Noa squinted. She realized that what she'd thought the night before was wilderness was actually fairly landscaped, as if they were inside a massive Central Park. Thicket-like islands rose from wide seas of flat and hilly grass, and the cave itself was an immense, serpentine stone bridge, casting deep shadows and caverns where it rose and fell.

"We seem to be in a housing center," Callum said, walking out slowly and spinning to look around from every angle, "but I don't recognize any of the buildings. Do you remember Darius planning a city extension like this?"

"Wait, am I blind? What city? What buildings?" Noa asked, bewildered.

Judah sighed impatiently, pointed in a circle all around them. Noa looked where he pointed but still saw nothing, so he walked over and took her by the shoulders, directing her. She jumped a little at his touch, which they both pretended not to notice.

Look closely," he directed.

Noa squinted in the distance—and then gasped.

"See it now?" Judah whispered. Noa heard his smile and nodded as it all took shape before her. The previous night, she'd been sure she'd seen walls of towering vines and trees on every vista, climbing to the sky—now she realized those leaves and trunks were the exteriors of soaring buildings, *skyscrapers*, built of vines and stones and roots. The 'park' where they stood was much smaller than she'd thought—a shared plaza, really, inside a square of towers.

Judah turned to Callum. "This wasn't here when I left. Darius must have built it since. I say we go to the Tunnels. I can find our way from anywhere down there."

Callum scoffed. "But no one else can."

"Yeah, where's that traitorous Hilo when you need her, right?" Judah muttered.

Callum glared at him, clenching his teeth at Judah's reference to yet another of the lies Callum had needed to facilitate Sasha's escape—how he'd turned Judah's best and only friend, Hilo, into his spy.

Noa was grateful that Callum didn't rise to the bait.

"*Anyway*," Callum said instead, "we clearly can't rely on you to give us an accurate report on what's going on here."

"What is *that* supposed to mean?"

"Just that we need to get the lay of the land and obviously a lot of stuff has happened since you left! Calm *down*."

"What do you think we should do?" Noa asked Callum, trying to keep them on track.

"We should go into one of the buildings and talk to someone—"

Judah snorted. "Could you think of a stupider idea? We have no idea who's in there—"

"Well, we're not going to find anything out by going under the city like rats!"

"Stop arguing, both of you! Look," Noa sighed, turning to Judah, "I agree with Callum. We should try the buildings, talk to someone, just to get *some* idea of how things are. If it doesn't work, we'll go to your Tunnels, okay?"

Judah rolled his eyes. "Whatever." But he followed grudgingly, shoulders hunched, as they walked toward one of the buildings.

As they got closer, they passed by a series of poles, almost like power lines.

"Hey, what are these?" Noa asked. Instead of wires, the poles held aloft a network of raised tubes around the complex, a little like miniature aqueducts. The tubes were clear but held fluid of different colors: in some places they were red or green or blue, and in others three were stacked together, one of each. The network stretched all around the plaza and was clearly being extended inside the park, though the project wasn't finished.

"I'm not sure," Callum said, frowning as he looked up to study them. "Don't touch them."

"Thanks, Dad," Judah mumbled, as they finally approached a block of three buildings, one next to another, forming a row. The power lines directed different ducts into each building: one building was fed and lined with blue tubes, the next with red, the last with green.

Judah turned to Noa, smirking. "Lady's choice."

Noa bit her lip and pointed at the middle one, with the red tubes. Judah looked surprised for a second; their eyes caught; he quickly looked away.

"Let's go," Callum said, reassuring hand on Noa's back.

Using his gift, Callum parted the front-facing sliding doors without trouble, and they walked inside. Noa had expected a magnificent lobby, some ornate triumph of Fae magic, but there wasn't one. Just a long, red hallway, lined with identical, shut-tight doors, lined by the red-tube ducts where mortals might have put crown molding. If Noa looked closely, she could see that the walls and floor were, like the facade, built from fire-leaves and red-clay stones, pressed flat, rather than building material and paint.

"Is everything ... made like this?" she whispered, hand hovering by the wall. For some reason she didn't quite want to touch it, didn't want to talk too loudly, even though the hallway was deserted.

Callum nodded, lowering his voice as well. "With our gifts, we tend to manipulate what already exists in nature. We've never had the need to invent things like bricks or mortar. Or ... tools." He shivered at the word *tools*. "Thorn was particularly fascinated with that aspect of the mortal realm, the … *inventiveness* of humans without gifts."

Noa put a steadying hand on Callum's arm, knowing he was back, in that moment, in the shackles of the Clear Fae hunter who'd kidnapped him and tortured him with screwdrivers, electrodes, all manner of 'human' tools.

"Good thing we saved you, eh, Brother?" Judah whispered, eyes glinting darkly.

"Guess so, since you brought Thorn into Noa's world in the first place," Callum replied, acid for acid.

"There are those tubes again," Noa interrupted, pointing at the ducts. "They almost look like fiber optics."

"Maybe we should knock on a door," Callum said, raising his fist toward the nearest door.

"Won't that make too much noise?" Noa asked nervously.

Judah sighed dramatically. "You've *really* spent too much time with mortals. I'll take care of it." He walked up to the nearest door, closed his eyes and prepared to reach in silently with his Red gift—the gift to read and speak to minds—to probe the room.

Instantly—faster than instantly, somehow—a boy in filthy, gray-stained rags flung the door open, lunged at Judah and tackled him to the ground, hissing, "Are you *insane?*"

Judah struggled beneath his attacker, spitting and kicking; Callum yanked the boy off Judah and flung him into the wall. The boy yelped and grabbed his arm, swallowing a scream of pain; he winced backward as both brothers bore down on him.

"*Look, look!*" he whimpered, nodding his head upward. Above them, the red tubing was glowing faintly.

Judah scowled. "What the…"

"You're lucky I stopped you before the alarm," the boy spat, part sneer, part cry, as he rubbed a clearly dislocated shoulder.

"Alarm? Explain!" Callum whispered sharply.

The boy stopped rubbing his shoulder in shock. "The *power* alarm? The one that detects if you use your Red gift without authorization? I just saved your asses from *Review*—"

"Review?" Noa echoed, stomach falling.

"Is this some sort of test?" the boy asked, panicked now, eyes darting among them. Noa suddenly realized how young he was— no more than twelve.

And terrified.

"Please don't report me—"

"Callum, heal him," Noa urged Callum, suddenly desperate not to see someone so young in so much pain. The boy lurched backward into the wall.

"This *is* a test!" he cried. "Get out! You can't be here! No!" he screeched at Callum's outstretched hand. "Don't touch me! No mixing! No mixing! Are there Blue detectors here now, too?" He looked frantically up at the walls, at the red tubes, then back at Callum, Noa, Judah. "I didn't do anything! I didn't do anything!" he pleaded, grasping his hanging shoulder with his good arm, scrambling clumsily through them toward his door. He flung it open, hurled himself inside, and whipped it shut behind him.

Noa, Callum, and Judah stared at the door—which locked— and then at one another.

"What just happened?" Noa finally breathed.

Callum and Judah eyed each other. Callum clenched his jaw. "I have no idea. But I think it's safe to say you shouldn't use your power," he said, studying the red tubes.

Judah's lip curled angrily. He was about to retort, when a blaring alarm suddenly split the air, pulsing so loud Noa could feel it inside her, seizing her heart, shattering it with waves of paralyzing noise.

"*Judah! What did you do?*" Callum accused.

"*Nothing!*" Judah yelled in outrage, covering his ears.

Noa pointed up at the red tubes, which were not glowing. "It's not them! It's *something else!*"

She was right—it wasn't an alarm so much as some sort of signal. All along the hallway, doors were opening, and Fae and pixies—all dressed in variations of the boy's molded, grayish rags—marched out in a perfect single-file line. Judah tried to pull one pixie aside to ask what was going on, but she shook him off, glaring, and darted into place. Just like the boy, these Fae seemed edgy, scared. No one looked up, broke ranks, let alone dared to talk to them.

Judah and Callum looked at each other; Judah shrugged and Callum nodded. They lowered their heads and joined the line of Fae, Callum first. Judah steered Noa into line next and followed, keeping her between them. Their clothes had become so grimy and worn that they blended in, and Noa tried to feel safe bookended by the brothers—but as her feet marched the fearful, precise, percussive marching, deep foreboding melted icily down her bones.

The marching line, in perfect time, filed out of the building. Outside, the day had burst forth bright and glittering—*too* bright. It stung Noa's eyes, blinding her for several moments. The air felt even thicker, warmer, moister, somehow more suffocating than in the dark. When she could see again, identical lines of marching Fae took shape around her, pouring from all the buildings. They were all converging in a central courtyard completely ringed by tube lines of every color.

Then Noa saw them—every few feet, separate from the marchers. Brawny, tall, clothed in shining white uniforms and suspicious eyes. Noa recognized the posture of these Fae, the *feel*. They reminded her of Thorn.

"Clear Guard," Judah breathed behind her, confirming Noa's intuition. These were Hunters, Darius's special squad of Clear Fae enforcers. Noa quickly dropped her eyes to the ground, forced herself to continue marching despite every instinct to flee.

Eyes downward, Noa saw a flicker of movement between the lines: a small hand reaching toward her line from the line beside them. Then a larger hand—but narrow, a woman's, or rather, a pixie's—quickly reached back across the narrow space, caught and squeezed the tiny fingers. Noa didn't need to see their faces to recognize the touch: a mother reaching toward her frightened child. How long had they waited for this moment, this split second of a second, when they might pass each other?

A screech split the air, and the marchers halted. Noa slammed into Callum's back, Judah into hers. A kind of whimpering erupted all around them; Noa looked up to see the green tubes strobing, whistling above the place where the mother and child had touched. Immediately, the mother broke ranks with Noa's line and ran to cover her child with her body, three Clear Guards descending like tornados upon them.

"Unauthorized Green use! Unauthorized Green use!" a tall and whippish Guard was screaming. His voice sliced around the plaza, sharp with clear authority; his fellow Guards were pure brawn, like Thorn, but this man—a Captain clearly—was razor thin, every feature edged and aquiline.

"Fayora's son," Judah hissed behind Noa. Noa's stomach twisted; her mind reeled back through a hundred conversations, real and dreamed, for where she'd heard that name before....

So close, too close, the offending mother was begging the Captain, sobbing. She was barely taller than his waist; she wrung her hands and clutched for her child, a boy no more than eight. "Please have mercy! My son! He was frightened, he only sent me love—please Captain, *Arik*—"

Arik's face didn't even flicker. He twitched a hand, and two Guards pried the woman off him, peeled her back like a rotting skin of fruit. Her hands scratched and scrabbled at the air as they hurled her to the ground. The slam of her body finally shook loose the name Fayora in Noa's mind: the Clear pixie Darius had married after Banishing Callum, disowning Judah, and casting out the Green pixie Lorelei, their mother. Judah had told Noa that Darius, overcome with Clear Fae zealotry, had quickly married Fayora and adopted her Clear son—now Captain Arik—to replace his blood family with one that shared his prized Clear gift. Noa had once thought it kind of cool that Colorlines were random, not genetic, but now she saw how it tore families apart.

Arik kicked the howling mother, who'd crawled to grasp his legs, with his silver boot. She flew back with a sickening crunch, face gushing blood.

"I'll indenture him for life!" he threatened.

"No, take me instead—" the mother wailed thickly, through the blood.

In response, Arik shoved aside the henchman who held the woman's son. The small boy looked surprised for a moment, finding himself suddenly free—but then Arik's own hands were on him, and he was shrieking like he was being electrocuted. The shriek echoed sharply and then went silent as the boy slumped, eyes and mouth wide open, face frozen in a waking trance of terror.

"No!" the mother screamed as Arik spun to face her, whipping her son with him like a rag doll. Arik glared intently, and her crying abruptly stopped. Her eyes blinked sleepily; bits of drool ran into the blood still pouring from her nose. Her body relaxed absurdly: still alive, but paralyzed with a terrible kind of calm.

Noa shivered, realizing what had happened: Clear Fae Arik had Channeled the boy's Green gift with emotions. He'd used the mother's own son as a tool to paralyze her protest. Instead of modulating her emotions carefully, he'd overloaded her emotional system, fried her into numb oblivion.

Unconcerned, Arik left the mother mute and slumped upon the ground. He stepped over her carelessly, dragged her son to a contingent of six or seven Guards, who seemed to swallow him up and usher him away.

"Back in line!" Arik hissed, his beak-like nose sharp in profile. "And let that be a reminder! The Otec has ruled! No mixing! Power only with permission!" His spindly arm sliced toward a sign, one of many shining harshly every few feet of tubing: giant *M*s with lines through them, stating Mixing Punishable by Review, by Order of the Otec.

Noa swallowed hard as the line in front of her resumed its march, stumbling to join in—then shuddered as she realized they were marching right toward Arik. Would he sense that she was flanked by Blue and Red brothers—pretty much the definition of "Mixing"—or worse, that she herself was not Fae at all? She kept her head down, panic swelling. Was being ordinary something you could see? Something someone could kill you for?

In front of Noa, Callum's steps stayed even and steady, but behind her, Noa heard Judah's breath quicken. But what could they do but follow?

Then it was already too late: they were passing Arik. Noa kept her eyes down, saw how his boots were lined with flecks of gold—and also spots of greenish spray. A sickly sweet smell thickened the air, like sweat but cloying. Noa bit her lip to keep from crying out; the four steps it took to pass Arik seemed the longest in the world—

Suddenly Noa was flying up into the air, a bony hand biting into her shoulder. Noa gasped, losing her wind, and looked frantically below her—right into the small, black eyes of Arik, searing into hers.

Up close, Arik's face was even sharper: cheekbones deep and cavernous, stubble like tiny knives. He was so tall that Noa actually got vertigo as he hoisted her up to stare her down.

"What's this, Red whore?" Arik yelled, shaking her so violently that blood rushed into her eyes. As her vision flickered, she saw Callum, trying to hold Judah back.

When Noa didn't answer, Arik wrenched Noa by her arm toward the colored tubes above them. No alarm sounded, but the blue tubes began to glow faintly. Arik shook her by the arm, the wrist—where her talisman bracelet glittered in the sun.

"Blue Magic!" Arik yelled, livid. He whipped Noa to the ground and bent back her arm to rip the bracelet from her wrist.

Noa's shoulder shattered in a sickening, hideous crackle; she screamed as Arik twisted her arm back and tore the bracelet from its dead weight.

The pain was so intense, and it all happened so fast, that Noa barely saw what happened next. Suddenly, Judah and Callum together were knocking Arik forward onto the ground, Noa's body crunched beneath him; the red and blue tubes above screamed in pulsing noise and strobing light; and the ordered lines of Fae erupted into chaos and pandemonium.

Judah, fierce and feral, shoved Arik from Noa and pinned him back, his face an inch from Arik's face.

"*It can't be—*" Arik hissed as Judah slapped his hands to Arik's cheeks, glaring at him hard.

A sudden warmth filled Noa's arm, making her vision rosy so she couldn't see what happened next. She turned her head and saw Callum was beside her, his hands around her shoulder. "It'll be okay," he was murmuring. His words sounded fuzzy, like she was hearing them from underwater.

"We have to move! Now!" Judah cried from somewhere on Noa's other side. "I can't control all their minds at once!"

Callum said something to Judah then turned back to Noa, his face coming thickly into focus. "We have to run," Callum told her, pulling her to her feet. She felt a distant sting of pain needle up her legs, but her muscles started easily, wrapped like her mind in Callum's warm, gooey healing fog. Callum pulled her after Judah, who tore into the crowd, yelling, "Make way!" as the tubes above him screeched and flashed in red. The Fae in front parted easily under his command.

"Stop using your gift!" Callum called up to him. "They'll track us through the crowd!"

With each step, Noa's body sharpened back into itself. But once Judah silenced his gift, she and Callum had to push and shove through the startled Fae in their path. Noa's mind and senses focused with her body, whipping with adrenaline: she saw, from every corner, winks of white and silver closing in. Swarms of Guards were fighting toward them.

From the right, sharp, staccato screams sounded like rapid pops, and suddenly, three Fae right in front of Noa and Callum fell to their knees, sobbing uncontrollably. Noa tripped violently; only Callum's grip on her arm kept her from plowing facefirst into the ground. To their left, another group of Fae collapsed in tears, and Callum zigzagged through them, narrowly avoiding crashing in their wake.

"They're Channeling Greens, trying to flatten us with sadness!" Callum yelled to Noa as they ran. She didn't need to look to know the green tubes on their right were strobing and screeching wildly. "Be ready—"

Suddenly Callum was in the air, flying face-forward over Judah, who had dropped to the ground and rolled into a ball. He wasn't sobbing; he was shaking with a sadness even deeper, too profound for tears. As Callum stumbled back to his feet, Noa fell onto Judah, grasped his shoulders, tried fruitlessly to break through his pain.

"Judah, Judah, it's not real—"

Callum whipped toward the section of the crowd where the green tubes were screaming wildly, the place where they now knew the Green lines were clustered and the Guards were Channeling.

He closed his eyes, crouched and pressed his palms into the ground, facing their way; blue tubes directly above him erupted as a gale-force wind, like a hurricane, rose and swept the Greens and Channeling Guards backward. Callum breathed deeper and conjured spikes of hail within the wind; more Green Fae fell back, flattened, bringing down the Guards with them.

On the ground, Judah blinked and blinked, confused. Callum's wind, it seemed, had knocked out whoever had been Channeling Green to incapacitate him. He stared at Noa, thunderstruck.

"You're alive," he said in shock. "You're not dead?"

Noa squeezed his hands, as Callum groaned with effort: "They're Channeling, Judah. We have to run; I can't hold—"

Judah jerked alert, dropped her hands, sprang to his feet.

"Got it!" He pushed once more into the crowd, tubes above him strobing red as he ordered them telepathically to let them through.

Callum, heaving, stumbled up to follow. The blue tubes silenced; the sun came back out, and the Greens and Guards behind them clamored in confusion. Noa grabbed Callum, urging him this time, and together they took off after Judah.

Immediately, from their left, a new wave of popping screams erupted—screams Noa now recognized as Color Fae being Channeled. The lines of Green Fae had been to their right; Noa barely had time to wonder which Colorline was clustered to their left. Huge spikes suddenly pushed up through the ground in front of them, skewering Fae around them like bloody, hungry spears.

Noa screamed as her foot barely missed a rising spike; red blood splashed across her face from a boy cleaving in two. In fact, red drops infused all the air around them; she choked on blood-mist, squinting through it to see Judah leap and jump between two thrusting razor peaks.

"Callum!" Judah cried over his shoulder. "A little help?"

Callum pivoted and grabbed Noa by both shoulders, lifting her up and over twin bleeding pixies, spiked wetly through. She felt Judah grab her as Callum passed her to him, then slapped his palms to a rising spike instead. He breathed in hard and ahead of them, the ground turned to melting ice. The rush of Fae slipped and fell, crashing through the now blood-and-flesh slopped spikes.

Noa sprinted faster, matching Judah stride for stride, grateful for the suddenly grippy soles Callum had thought to add onto their shoes. Noa looked at Judah, not needing words; they dropped hands and used their bodies, arms, and shoulders to charge through what snowy spikes remained.

"They're fighting back, the Blues! They're rebelling to help us!" Callum called as he ran through the space his gift had cleared, catching up. Noa and Judah looked quickly back to the left, where the Guards had been Channeling the Blues. The Blue lines, superior in number, were now rallying, fighting; the Guards had their hands full trying to crush the outburst. Blue tubes were screaming, and wooden shards flew everywhere, Blues were conjuring shrapnel toward their captors.

Callum pulled alongside his brother; they shared a little grin. "I guess they don't like their relatives being made into shish kebabs," Judah smirked. Energized, they all ran faster, feeding off the chaos. Channeling pops like firecrackers sounded somewhere behind them, but they were running so quickly and so together Noa didn't dare to turn to look.

"Reds," Callum told them, breathing evenly with the increased stride. "They're using Reds to stop the Blues."

Ahead, the crowd was thinning; they were reaching the end of the sea of Colored Fae—and also space to run.

Beyond the crowd, they now saw, was a towering, solid wall.

"Where do we go from here?" Noa asked, panic rising. "Which way do we run?"

"Right or left, we'll have to double back and disappear into one of the buildings," Judah called as he hurdled over a fallen Fae.

"But right or left?" Noa cried.

"Left," Judah and Callum said together, both reaching out to save Noa from slipping on a river of melted ice.

"They're still scrambling there to control the Blues," Callum explained, not slowing down a step. "The Guards will be distracted." They all turned left, and Noa felt herself actually relax a little. They had agreed on something, finally working as a team, just when it really counted. They might actually make it out of this—

"*No!*" Noa cried, yanking back against the brothers' hands, pulling them to a skidding stop.

"What?" Callum cried. "We can't stop, Noa! They'll catch up!"

"No, it's Red, it's a Red compulsion, can't you see it?" She turned desperately to Judah. "Right or left, can't you feel the thought? It doesn't fit! It isn't real!"

"Noa, come on," Callum insisted, dismissing her, but Judah was thinking hard, trying to feel what she was feeling.

Callum yanked on Noa, roughly now, but Noa yanked back. "Judah, you feel it, don't you? We can't go right or left! They want us to!"

Judah scowled, squinting, but didn't answer.

"Judah!" Callum insisted, panicked. "She doesn't know what she's saying, help me—"

"No," Judah said to Callum, putting a firm arm to his brother's chest, spinning to look intently at Noa. "If not right or left, then where?"

Noa swallowed, looked around frantically. "I don't know...." Then she gasped, seeing the only solution: "*Over.*"

Callum shoved Judah aside. "This is ridiculous, we're going left!" he insisted, lifting Noa off her feet, slinging her across his shoulders. Noa yelped, grabbed Judah by the arm. Her wild eyes found his.

"*Do it!*" she cried.

Judah hesitated for a split second, then his hands were on Callum's back and he was using his gift with all his might.

"*Stairs,*" he hissed through clenched teeth. *"Put her down, and go make stairs."*

Callum's face contorted, struggling to disobey, finally slackening into acquiescence. He put Noa down, ran to the massive wall, and laid his palms upon it. Behind them, Noa heard the thunder of an approaching stampede; the Guards were fighting through the Colored Fae resistance. They had moments only, if that.

As Callum did Judah's bidding, his voice came out strangled: "We don't even know ... what's on the other side..." but he didn't stop his work. When the stairs were done, Judah pushed Callum up first, then Noa, then shoved himself up in the rear. The wall was tall, so tall, but they *had* to climb; Noa forced her legs to work, forbade herself from looking down, tried to ignore the growing noise of thunder—

But the thunder was on them. Below, Channeling pops erupted like machine-gun screams, and fireballs began spraying at the wall. Huge scorch marks sizzled beside, below them, as the fireballs torched closer and closer to their mark.

"*Move!*" Judah screamed upward. Against her better judgment, Noa looked down; Judah's foot was on fire.

"Callum, move!" she screamed, shoving his calves from behind.

Callum obeyed and climbed like lightning to the top, still moving jerkily as he bent to haul Noa up. Noa reached down for Judah's hand just as the stairs beneath him smoothed away. The Guards had reached the wall; they'd Channeled Blues to flatten Callum's stairs right out from under Judah's feet. Judah slid down the wall; Noa screamed and barely caught him by the fingertips. But he was too heavy, and she too weak; she slid down too, pulled by his body like an anchor. Callum grabbed her disappearing ankle, falling to his stomach on top of the wall, and with an almighty hurl, wrenched them all up and over.

"They're climbing the wall!" Judah panted as he got to his feet. "They've conjured lines and ballast!" When Noa and Callum didn't answer, Judah turned—they were staring out over the wall's other side, frozen.

Judah looked where they were looking.

It wasn't a wall that they had climbed; it was a dam. A dam that dropped down and down and down, into a sucking riot of rushing, crashing rapids.

Judah didn't wait, didn't stop to worry or to think—

He grabbed Noa and Callum, and jumped them all over the edge.

"What if I was hurt myself?" Callum demanded.

Judah rolled his eyes and looked away, but Noa saw his flinch; adn't had a plan for that.

Callum sighed and shook his head, helped Noa up. "We ld get moving."

"It may have been dangerous," Noa whispered softly, not ing Judah to hear, "but if they think we're dead and they 't be coming after us, it's better for us, isn't it?"

Callum paused a moment, his head on hers. "*If* they believe "

"Hellooooo," Judah called impatiently, arms crossed a few away. "Let's get out of sight just in case."

Callum glared at him, suspicious.

Judah glared back defiantly, then sighed. "The thing is…," h began, pointedly ignoring how Callum closed his eyes in l, "when Arik hurt Noa, and we lunged at him? He kind of ny face."

"So? He doesn't know us."

Noa bit her lip, her stomach sinking. "He knows Judah."

Callum turned back to her, confused. "What?"

Judah told me about him one night, when we sort of d about stuff…," Callum tensed, and Noa continued ly, "It was when we were looking for you, after Thorn had pped you."

Oh." He didn't look reassured.

Arik's the son our father wishes he had," Judah explained iently. "After you left, Darius kicked me and Mom out, ed Arik's Clear mom, Fayora, and adopted that bastard. he's the little Otec-in-training."

• • •

"NOA! ARE YOU okay?"

Noa was coughing too violently to answer, choking on darkness and swirling dust so thick she could barely suck in any air. Through filthy tears she saw the white of her elbow bone—naked, grotesque—poking terribly from her arm, its skin swinging sickeningly in a mottled, filthy swath. Moonlight lit the verminous debris around them—the carcass of the cabin's landing which had disintegrated beneath their feet.

Noa knew they should never have ventured into this rotting, freaky cabin. Why did she let Isla talk her into things like this?

Isla's silver eyes pierced the darkness sharply, alert and tense. She had also fallen through the decayed, insect-eaten floor, but had bounced up easily, in the way she always seemed to do. Now she hovered over her fallen sister, fervent with concern, poised to fight any foe that should appear. Isla was speaking, but her voice echoed thickly in Noa's ears, her words amorphous blobs slowly swelling into shape.

"I'm calling for help, stay still. I won't let anything happen to you, I swear."

Noa collapsed backward, let her body slacken, did as Isla said. She tried not to think of the insects and rodents, the larvae and fungus breeding in the dampish rot beneath her head. Why oh why had she let Isla talk her into going inside this stupid 'haunted' cabin?

Noa shuddered, remembering the fall.

"Stay still, silly."

Noa whipped her head to the right, ignoring the shooting pain up and down her neck. That voice wasn't Isla's—not commanding, not imperial with confidence and strength—but clear and high, like the burble of a laugh. It sliced through the dust, the thick, the fog—and belonged to a little girl with chocolate curls.

"Sasha," Noa murmured, smiling, knowing now it would all be okay. "Isla, Sasha's here—"

"Who's Sasha?" Isla demanded. Noa painfully turned her head back to her older sister.

"Sasha," Noa urged, "Sasha, our sister."

Isla frowned. "What sister?"

Noa opened her mouth to respond—but all that came out was water.

• • •

"NOA!"

Noa heaved and choked as the water roared up and out her lungs, a deluge of everything inside. It was a torrent, a flood, and for some reason tasted spicy, with the tang of mint. It went on and on, until Noa felt herself on the edge of passing out—then suddenly her lungs stuttered and breathed *in*. Her eyes flew open and were blinded instantly, everything too sharp, too bright: the blinding sun, Callum's and Judah's faces, even the air itself.

And she was wet.

"You should have let me conjure a parachute or something!" Callum exclaimed at Judah. "Not just shoved us over like some—"

"There wasn't time! You were dazed from my compulsion—"

"Yeah, that's *another* thing!"

"She's fine!" Judah looked defensively at Noa. "Right? Tell him!"

Noa sat up gingerly, still breathing vora[...] She realized she was on a bank of some kind, [...] from the giant, frothing whirlpool of seethin[...] wasn't far enough for Noa. Not that she could [...] ently to do anything about it.

She breathed and breathed, slowly adju[...] was warm and spongy in her lungs. Surprisi[...] long as she would have thought—even in h[...] ting used to the heaviness of the air.

Noa turned to Callum, wincing, "He [...] Callum. The Guards had you mind-contr[...] compulsion. You wanted to run us into a tr[...]

Callum grimaced, ashamed. "I know. I [...]

"It's okay." Noa stretched shakily. "Yo[...] natural for Judah to be able to sense it bette[...] very comforted, so Noa turned to Judah for [...]

Judah was tense, unreadable. "Right." [...]

Noa stretched again and looked ar[...] dently traveled quite a distance in the w[...] on the horizon.

"Did we lose them?"

Callum nodded grimly. "For now."

Judah smirked. "They probably thin[...] looking for us for a while. Which they [...] had you conjured your little *parachute*."

"You say that like you're proud, but No[...]

"I broke both your falls, Callum. [...] couldn't stay there and let them catch us. [...] we got hurt."

Callum's eyes flared. He spun from Noa, furious: "You let Darius abandon Lorelei? You had *one* job!"

"I didn't *let* the Otec do anything!" Judah fired back. "And in case you weren't listening, he kicked me out too!"

"Stop!" Noa demanded, again getting between them. "This is not the place—"

Callum ripped his hands through his hair. "Where is she? We have to find her! Judah, please—"

The muscle at Judah's jaw pulsed, and he looked away. "I don't know. The last time I saw her..." He broke off, swallowed hard.

Noa bit her lip. Right before they'd gone into the Portal, Judah had revealed what Lorelei had told him in a desperate moment: that she'd wished Judah had been Banished, that Callum was the son she'd wanted with her. It was partly why Judah had run away to Noa's world.

Judah took a deep breath, his voice tight. "The Resistance was helping to take care of her before I left. Moved her from place to place, kept her safe."

"We'll have to find them, then," Callum said immediately, then turned to Noa. "You understand, don't you?"

Noa's hand found his. "She's your mom. We'll find her and Sasha both." She quickly glanced at Judah's back. His face was hidden. She squeezed Callum's hand.

"Judah, you were right before. I was wrong. We should hide in the Tunnels," Callum said sincerely.

Judah shrugged, but turned to face them again, scowling his trademark scowl. "I'll lead, obviously. You suck down there."

He took off in front, leaving them to follow. Noa squeezed Callum's hand in thanks, and he squeezed back.

• • •

JUDAH LED CALLUM and Noa along the bank until the rapids narrowed into a rushing river. They walked in silence for what felt like hours, until the bank itself got thinner, a single-file path, beside a rising, angled wall that Judah and Callum told Noa outlined the border of the city. The wall, like Aurora's buildings, looked like melted wilderness: pressed leaves and dirt and vines, hardened into stone. As if the city literally grew out of the ground.

Noa puffed and pressed her body on, everything made harder by the strangeness of Aurora. The heaviness of the thick, fragrant air, the searing brightness of the sun, even the minty after-tingle of the water. It was overwhelming to Noa's senses, even as it energized the boys.

"How much farther?" she asked no one in particular.

"Looking for an entrance," Judah mumbled in front.

"I think I recognize part of where we are," Callum said from the rear. "Do those look like the Southside plants to you?"

Judah paused to look at the city beyond the sheerness of wall, and Noa put her hands to her hips, trying not to show her relief at the tiny break.

"If you're right," Judah answered, "that would mean that those skyscrapers we just ran from…" He trailed off, eyeing Callum.

Callum exhaled slowly. "The homesteads. Darius replaced the homesteads."

"What do you mean?" Noa asked. "He built that freaky tube-place where people—I mean, Fae—used to live?"

"It was really different before, kind of bohemian," Callum told her, "Families combined their gifts to build in their own style—no two homes ever looked the same. Some were caves or shelters, others big mansions or strange angular tepees…"

Judah's eyes glinted, mouth curling into his half-smile. "And it always changed, even day to day. It was the perfect place to hide out, especially after pulling pranks. Hilo and I—" Judah broke off abruptly, face hardening.

"Hilo was still your friend, Judah. Your memories of her are real," Callum told him gently.

"Until you made her your little spy."

"I explained: I had to keep an eye on you, for your own—"

"*Good*, yeah. I've heard that before, Callum."

"But if Darius got rid of the homesteads," Noa interrupted, "where do Fae live?"

"Those skyscrapers," Judah said. "I guess like dorms."

"No," Callum corrected softly. "They were barracks." His eyes met Judah's.

"Segregated," Judah nodded.

"Segregated … by Color?" Noa asked.

Callum nodded. "That's why the one we entered was only alarmed with red tubes. It only housed Reds. Darius destroyed the homesteads and separated the families by Colorline."

"'*No mixing*,'" Noa murmured. "'*Power only with permission*.'"

Judah glanced at Callum; even Noa could see the fear behind his eyes. "If Darius destroyed the families and basically enlisted into Color-segregated ranks … where is the Resistance?"

The muscle in Callum's jaw flickered. "I don't know."

Judah closed off, turned to study the embankment.

"Well, the good news is I know where we are." He half-walked, half-climbed up the bank to a spot in the outer wall. Noa would never have noticed it among the green and brown camouflage of colors—but there was the faintest tracing of a circle. Judah pulled and pried at the edges of the circle, grunting.

"What's wrong?" Callum called up after a minute. Judah ignored him, continuing to strain, and finally gave up.

"He actually *sealed* this entrance off," he scowled back in disbelief. "Unbelievable."

"Aren't there others?" Noa asked.

"Sure! Inside the city. The heavily populated, highly hostile city."

Noa's stomach twisted. "Aren't there any others outside?"

Judah sighed, squinted into the distance. "The next one's far, we won't get there before dark, and if one wall entrance is sealed…"

"They all probably are," Noa murmured.

She turned to Callum, startled to find him grinning.

"Oh crap, he's demented again," Judah muttered.

Callum actually laughed. He held up his hands. "Not demented, just gifted. I don't see any of those alarm tubes here, do you?"

* * *

THE TUNNELS WERE labyrinthine and uniform, a maze of dark-gray walls, echoing drips and reverberating sameness. Even though Callum had sealed the entrance behind them as easily as an engineer welding a sewer cap shut, the same eerie lavender-gray twilight permeated down through the ceiling, as if carried through the stone-pressed roots. The walls appeared rough and many-textured, made of wound organic matter—but when Noa touched one, it was cool as ice, and just as smooth.

They had walked only a little way, made a few turns, before Noa was sure they were lost. Every step took not only her body, but her mind into deep tangles of confusion—she suddenly felt as if she'd been wandering there forever and would never emerge anywhere else again.

But Judah led on strongly, never hesitating to choose a turn, to select one of the ever-branching paths. While Noa's and even Callum's feet sometimes slipped unsteadily in the thin water pooling at their feet, Judah never made a sound. The underground was a place he knew, mapped like whorls in fingerprints inside his mind. The muscles in his back became Noa's guiding currents, shifting gracefully, fluidly, as he led the way into the dark.

"Who built the Tunnels?" Noa asked after endless steps in silent sameness. She found the Tunnels strangely beautiful, even as they overwhelmed and frightened. She had barely whispered, but her words echoed in sneaking shapes and tones, like a hundred creatures hissing in the shadows.

Callum straightened a little beside her, walked with greater ease. "No one knows. Most believe it was one of the early Fae rulers, before Gwydion, who built the Tunnels. Most likely as a hiding place for leaders, and a way to navigate and control the city in secret."

Ahead of them, Judah snorted; Noa could picture the glitter in his eye. "Too bad most Fae, including the leaders, are way too stupid to find their own feet down here. Idiots."

Callum looked at Judah's back, piqued. "It's not so easy."

Judah shrugged, but Noa saw the smirk in the nuance of his shoulders.

Callum ignored Judah, continued: "Because they are so unnavigable, Gwydion actually tried to get rid of them, but he couldn't, because he couldn't track and map them all. Darius tried too, and failed."

"Something they would have agreed on," Noa mused, earning a chuckle from Callum. She remembered the night he'd told her about Gwydion, the Fae leader before Darius—it was the night Callum had confided in Noa about himself and Aurora. He'd explained how Gwydion, as leader, had magically erased all knowledge of the Clear Fae's dangerous gift to Channel magic— even from the Clear Fae themselves. And how, as a result, Darius—and others of his Colorline—had grown up bullied and tormented for being 'powerless.' When Darius had become Otec and discovered the truth, he'd vowed to undo all that Gwydion had done. And he had—he'd reawakened the Clear gift, and then turned Clears loose for their revenge.

"Well, I guess it's not hard to see why they'd agree on that. Neither Gwydion nor Darius liked the idea of an all-access underground system they couldn't control," Callum replied.

"Why didn't they just use some Blues to, I don't know, blow it all up?"

"They tried," Judah said, turning over his shoulder, unable not to gloat a little. "But the Tunnels are way too complicated. They could never get to them all, and no Blue could visualize them properly. That's why they are a *perfect* hideout."

He stopped in front of them, smug as a cat, and put his hand on the left-side wall, feeling carefully. Slowly, he found and began to pry back a single root with his dexterous fingers. Then he beckoned Noa and Callum forward: Behind the root was a small, hollowed-out compartment, its sides uneven, as if it had been carefully made by hand.

"Hilo and I made these all over the Tunnels. Little hiding places, where we left each other things." He reached into the hole, felt around, and pulled out a smooth, round stone, then smiled a smile Noa had never seen on him before. Not a smirk, but something earnest. The smile of a boy.

"What is it?" Noa whispered.

Judah's fist closed around the stone, and he looked away. "A worry stone," he mumbled, "for me to hold if something happened and she wasn't down here." He pushed the stone back in, closed the wall with the root. "We also hid food and stuff, different supplies. Maybe some of it is still down here."

"We don't need it. My power, remember?" Callum said, putting a genial hand on Judah's shoulder. "Your big brother can be useful!"

Judah tensed. "Well, we know Hilo would have liked that better, right?"

"How do you know where the little hiding places are?" Noa asked, running her hand over the now-smooth wall, trying to feel what Judah had felt.

Judah shrugged. "Same way I know where everything is down here. I just see it." He started walking again, briskly, leaving Callum and Noa stumbling to catch up.

• • •

A TENSE HALF hour later, Judah stopped abruptly, nearly causing Callum and Noa to run into him. He had stopped at a T-shaped lane, studying the dead end in front of them. Noa wondered if he was deciding which side to turn to, but then he walked straight toward the dead-end wall, stretched to his toes, and reached to feel as high as he could. After a moment, his fingers pressed into some hidden groove, then he bent his body like a C and pulled backward with all his might.

A faint vertical crack became visible in the wall above Judah's head, then turned toward him. Judah lunged back, and the heavy, hidden door shifted ever-so-slightly open.

"Let me help you," Callum said, joining him.

"Don't change the door!" Judah snapped. "We need it to close again!"

"I just meant I'd help you pull," Callum told him, reaching up to the top of the door. "Ready?"

Together they pulled backward, bodies like sails taut in the wind. The heavy slab budged. Callum let go, panting with his hands on his knees. Pitch darkness beckoned beyond the door.

"Come on," Judah mumbled, breathing hard himself but striding in.

Noa hesitated. "I'll be right behind you," Callum assured her.

Noa swallowed and nodded, turning sideways to squeeze inside the hidden room. Total blackness made her stumble. Judah caught her before she fell. She inhaled sharply when she felt his face close to hers, his breath near her cheek, even as she couldn't see him.

"You okay?" he murmured.

She nodded, then remembered he couldn't see her. "Yeah."

Callum was squeezing in behind her, and Noa felt Judah take back his hands and move away.

"How do I close this?" Callum asked, suddenly right beside her.

"Hold on a sec," Judah replied. Noa heard him move away from them, deeper into the darkness. Slowly, a little orange glow grew like candlelight from Judah's hands, lighting up the corner of the room where he was standing. It expanded and twinkled, then rose above them and spread out like stars, illuminating the whole cave from its low, uneven ceiling.

Noa gasped in wonder at the little constellations.

Judah's eyes seemed to twinkle in their light. "Stellabugs," he said. "Hilo and I raised a colony in here. You just give them warmth from your hands, and they light up…. Light source for the non–Blue powered."

"They're beautiful," Noa said. "Like fireflies, kind of."

"Very inventive," Callum agreed.

Judah shrugged. "Hilo probably thought of it." He pointed toward the door, which now they could see. "We smoothed a little handle on the back." He walked over to show Callum. "We just pull."

Together, they pulled the handle, sliding the heavy slab closed. Noa expected to feel claustrophobic, but instead she felt safe and warm under the glowing Stellabugs.

Judah lazily gestured around the small room with his hands. "It's not much, but it's hidden. We can rest here safely. Even if they look for us in the Tunnels, they won't find us here."

Callum nodded. "It's perfect, Judah. I should have listened to you earlier."

Judah turned back to the corner where he'd found the Stellabugs. "I have some grains and stuff here to eat if you want. It's pretty basic." He held up what looked like little bowls of nuts and seeds. "Or I guess Callum can transfigure it into a Big Mac or something," he added with a smirk.

Noa smiled. "I'm actually pretty curious about Aurora food."

Callum and Judah looked at each other and laughed. Noa looked between them. "What?"

"Nothing," Callum said. "It's just, I think you may be disappointed. Fae don't really need to eat, but when they do, they favor a more … earthy diet."

"It tastes like crap," Judah told her. "Literally."

Noa looked at Callum, wondering if they were teasing her, but he just laughed and held up his hands.

"Scout's honor. If there was an Aurora saltwater taffy flavor, even *you* could guess it as you spit it out." His eyes twinkled, and she felt that little tingle of warmth she loved.

"Okay, well maybe an apple then?" she said. Callum smiled and went to take some of the mud-food from Judah, transfiguring it in his hands into the round, green fruit.

"It's weird," Noa said as she watched, "I would have thought food here would be crazy-layered with flavor. Since the air is so tangy and the water was all minty."

Judah and Callum looked at each other, surprised.

"What?" She asked.

Callum handed her the apple. "We just didn't know if you would sense that stuff. But then again, we've never had a mortal in Aurora before."

Noa crunched into her apple. "Didn't you know? In my past life, I was an overachiever."

Callum laughed again. Noa grinned, relaxing.

It would have been even better, though, if Judah had joined in.

• • •

AFTER ALL THEY had been through, Noa was sure she would never be able to fall asleep, but the miles of sprinting and falling and hiking and Tunnel-ing got the best of her, and within minutes of finishing her apple, she fell asleep. She was out so fast that she didn't even notice when Callum softened the ground beneath her, wove a blanket from the atoms in the dirt. The last thought she had was of Sasha, *Sasha* ... how when they awakened, they would find a way to get to her....

Noa blinked, and the sun was shining in her eyes. Not the Aurora sun, so bright it hurt and tinged with lavender, but the pale yellow hug that came from the sun at home. She breathed in, the air was light and clear, cool inside her lungs.

"Noa, it's time to pat the dirt."

Noa turned toward the familiar voice. Her mother. She and Noa were in the backyard, in the raised vegetable garden, where Hannah was crouched in her wide-brimmed hat and purple-and-white-flowered gardening gloves. The glove fingertips were black with dirt, and there was a smudge across Hannah's cheek. Hannah's face was round and bright, curved with sunshine.

Noa crouched beside her mother in the vegetable patch, rich dirt moist beneath her knees.

Hannah fondly held the delicate new tomato plant, lowering its roots into the fresh-dug hole.

"Remember to push out all the air," Hannah said. Noa lifted her small blue shovel and began to fill in new, moist soil until Hannah nodded there was enough. Then Noa laid the shovel aside and began to pack the dirt with her fingers, bitten nail-nubs sinking into the velvet damp.

"She would have liked this," Hannah said, smiling up at the little vine.

"Who?"

"Your sister."

"Sasha?"

Hannah cocked her head, confused. "Isla."

"Look, it's starting to blossom."

Noa looked up: her dad was speaking, suddenly standing right beside them as if he'd been there all along. He stood tall, collared shirt unwrinkled, crosshatched green and white with a pocket at the chest.

Noa got to her feet, wiped her hands across her pants. They walked together to the tree with pink blossoms and fire-red maple leaves. He put his hand across her shoulders.

"Soon we'll have blintzes," Christopher told her proudly, fingering a blossom.

"Where?"

Noa looked down: Sasha was clinging to her leg, pulling on her with insistent fingers. Her brown eyes were huge, dirt smudged both her cheeks, like paint. She looked intently into Noa's eyes.

"From the blossoms, Sash," Noa told her, pointing at the tree. "The blintzes grow from the blossoms."

Sasha huffed, cheeks turning red beneath the brown: "But *where?*"

Hannah called out from beside her tomato plant. "Noa, go make your sister macaroni and cheese."

• • •

NOA WOKE WITH a start, forehead slick, heart beating fast. Judah and Callum were asleep in separate corners of the hidden room.

Noa calmed her breathing, reoriented herself to reality. It had been a dream. A *dream*.

Since Isla's death, Noa had gotten used to never dreaming, as if her unconscious mind could no longer bear to face itself. She was out of practice.

Once the cave looked steady again, Noa closed her eyes once more, determined to keep her mind blank and dreamless. She barely felt her head touch the ground before exhaustion overcame her…

And Judah laughed.

He was in the stacks with Noa in their hidden corner of Lamont Library. Or rather, he was with *a* Noa, but Noa herself was somehow apart, watching the pair of them from outside, like watching a couple in a movie.

And in this movie, Judah was laughing because he was trying to braid Movie-Noa's hair, Movie-Noa leaning against his legs. His eyes were focused on her head.

Noa watched as Movie-Noa turned and smiled, so easy and so bright. She put one hand on her own heart and the other on Judah's.

"This won't change," Movie-Noa promised him. "This can't change."

Judah stopped laughing, fear glinting in his eyes. "That's just words."

Movie-Noa smiled, stroked his cheek. "I'm a poet, Judah. Words are sacred."

Suddenly another boy materialized, tall and regal, with white-gloved hands. Movie-Noa stopped stroking Judah's cheek, looked up into his eyes.

Callum held up a bag of saltwater taffy, smiling. "It's time for Review," he murmured.

• • •

NOA GASPED HERSELF awake again, this time strangled for breath, her head hot and pounding.

"Are you okay?" Judah asked, suddenly at her side, though without the Stellabugs she couldn't see him.

Noa laid her palms against the cool floor, willing her heart to calm, her mind to focus. *It was just another dream.* She breathed in and out, tried to push her fingers deep into awakeness. But that dream hadn't felt like the other dream. It had a different texture, a different shape—

Noa looked toward where Judah was, hugged her knees against her chest. "I'm okay."

Judah scooted closer so she could dimly see the features on his face. He was studying her suspiciously.

"I think I'll stay up a little though," she acknowledged, sitting up.

Judah settled back against the wall beside her.

"You don't have to stay up, too," she told him, but she felt grateful anyway. She shifted, wiggling to get comfortable against the uneven rock. She could feel Judah's mouth curl up in amusement.

"What?" Noa said defensively. "It's a little uneven."

Judah suddenly had her hand, was laying it into one of the wall's dips, then laying his own beside it. "Handmade."

Noa bent close to see what she could already feel; their hands fit the dents exactly.

"You dug this out?" she whispered.

"I'm not Blue Fae," he replied softly.

"But my hand fits too, and it's smaller…."

"Hilo's handprint." Judah turned to sit back against the wall, but Noa kept her hand in Hilo's handprint, touching the fine grooves.

"It must have taken a long time," she said softly.

"Better than being up there," Judah murmured. "Or so I thought."

They sat quietly, but Noa couldn't help it. The whisper just came out:

"Hilo helped Callum because she cared about you. She thought it was the right thing and made a mistake. It doesn't mean everything was a lie."

Judah didn't answer.

Noa wasn't sure why it was so important to her that he not write off Hilo, who had betrayed him so terribly and broken his heart. But she'd also been the first to tell Judah he didn't have to be what others thought him. That he could decide for himself. And he'd believed it, however briefly. Something in Noa needed him to forgive her.

"You're forgiving him too quickly," Judah murmured softly.

"Him?"

"Callum," Judah replied. "You're forgiving him too quickly."

"I'm…" Noa swallowed. "He's made mistakes, big ones, but—"

"He lied to us about Lily. Sasha. He's lied ... *so much...*" Judah's whisper trembled. Noa was relieved it was so dark—in the light, she was sure he would have turned away.

"I know he has," Noa whispered, struggling to find the words. "But, Judah ... Callum also *gave* me Sasha. And himself. When I needed them most..." She closed her eyes as she felt him curl away.

But he didn't leave. He paused.

"What about the In Between?" Barely a breath, almost inaudible.

"I ... Judah ... it wasn't real—"

"It was, just in a different way," Judah said.

Noa didn't know what to say. She couldn't open that again; it was too big, too hard—

"Just remember, Noa. You and I? We *fought* it. We fought to remember, to escape ... no matter how much we may have wanted to stay."

Noa swallowed. She couldn't see him, he wasn't touching her, but she was sure he had lifted his fingers toward her hair. She could *feel* the memory of their gentle movement there, trying make braids, could hear his laugh ... but she didn't want to remember. She didn't want to feel it. She wanted him to stop talking, stop prodding. If she spoke now she knew she'd start to cry—

"It burst out of us," Judah continued, "Your poems, my drawings ... even Olivia and Miles, despite having the things we wanted most—"

A tear ran down Noa's cheek; she tasted its salt as it passed her lips.

"*Except Callum*," Judah pressed. "He *didn't* feel it, Noa. He didn't fight."

Noa blinked back her tears, forced herself to answer. "You don't know that."

"But you do. He didn't have any idea when you went to see him, did he?"

"No," Noa admitted. "Not until he touched the talisman."

"A remnant of magic from outside the In Between. His mind didn't fight on his own."

"So what?" Noa said, finally turning toward where she knew he was.

"Because it's him!" Judah hissed in frustration. "It's who he is! He'd rather be in charge, have power, even if it hurts others! We even called him Otec in there, just like Darius! That's the truth of what he wants!" Judah was seething, breathing hard.

"You're *wrong*," she bit back. "You say the talisman did the work for Callum, but you have no idea. The talisman worked because it was something *he* made for me in *sacrifice*. Our *connection* woke him up, Judah, our..." She hesitated, not quite saying *love*. "His mind may not have woken him, but his *heart* did. If that's not proof of who he truly is, how much he *tries*—"

"You promised me you wouldn't forget me—"

"I know what I said, but things are just more complicated—"

Judah muttered something, glaring into the shadows. It sounded like *words are sacred*.

Noa shivered. She hadn't actually said that in the In Between, had she? Hadn't that been in her dream?

Noa shook off the chill, drew up her strength. "He's your *brother*, Judah—"

"And because of him, you've lost another sister—"

"*That's your fault, not mine.*"

Judah and Noa turned: Stellabugs suddenly lit the room, Callum had released them from his hands. Awakened by their war of words, he was now staring daggers at his brother. His face was hard, his voice like ice: "*You* threw Sasha through the Portal, Judah. In your petulance. In your anger. *You* made the decision to take Noa's sister from her, not me."

Judah glared back. "It was an accident," he hissed. "No matter how many times you try to tell another lie."

Callum smiled a small, sad smile. "You know I'm not lying, Judah. Read my mind, Brother. I don't need to read yours."

Judah clenched his teeth, snorted like a bull. The brothers stared each other down, until finally, finally, Judah looked away.

"I'm sick of babysitting. You watch her," he snarled. He got up, stalked to the far wall, and curled up with his back to them.

Callum watched him fiercely, then seemed to sag. He found Noa's face, cocking his head gently to invite her to come sit beside him.

His face was warm; she felt the tingle of reassurance that she always felt from his gentle eyes, but for some reason, she didn't want to go.

"I'm tired," she told him. He nodded in understanding, silently lowered his hands to the ground beneath her to soften the surface. She curled up alone, her back to him and Judah both. Callum dimmed the Stellabugs, and then she heard him shift to lie down behind her. He was careful to leave a space between them, and Noa...

She was relieved.

• • •

NOA COULDN'T SLEEP. Eventually, she slipped softly to the corner, where Judah and Hilo had built the home for Stellabugs. Curious, she reached in to touch them, and to her delight, they glittered into soft, twinkling light.

Noa felt a gentle hand on her back. "They're really beautiful," Callum murmured behind her. "I never would have thought of them because I would have just used my gift... but they're so much more beautiful than anything I could have made." Callum's voice wrapped around her, cocooning her in safety, sureness, warmth.

Which made what she had to say that much harder.

Noa looked where Judah lay; his back rose and fell with even breaths. She hoped he wasn't faking. This was not something she wanted him to hear.

Noa turned to meet Callum's eyes, gasping a little despite herself as she gazed into those rich, pooling velvet eyes. They never failed to mesmerize, even now.

She took a breath, listened to the air. Then spoke:

"This has nothing to do with what Judah was saying, however you much you heard. I want you to know that."

His eyes flickered.

"I mean it," Noa said firmly. "I don't believe what he says, that there's something..."

"Wrong with me."

Noa gently touched his cheek. "I don't believe that. You brought me light when I had none. I remember what that felt like. I feel it still, every time I see you, every time we touch."

Callum nodded sadly. He knew already. She sighed.

"But I can't just go back to how it was. I thought I could, I think I wanted to ... but now ... I just ... need time."

Callum swallowed shakily, closed his eyes. "Is ... is part of it ... because of Judah? Not what he said, but..." his voice became so quiet, she could barely hear it, even in the silent, hidden room, "how it was between you?"

Noa hesitated, but she needed to be honest. For her own sake, as well as his.

"I can't unremember what it was like," she said carefully. She clasped his trembling hands, "but, Callum, that's not why." She held his gaze, willed him to believe her with all her mind and heart. "It's just, right now, all I can think about is Sasha. Everything else..."

Callum nodded bravely. Gently, without consciously deciding to do it, Noa kissed him—not passionately, not deeply, but light and lingering and soft. The familiar, tingling glow spread through her as their lips met.

"It's not the end," Noa promised him breathlessly, knowing he had felt it too, had felt it *with* her. "I will keep my promise."

Movement interrupted them, made them break apart.

"Don't let me interrupt," Judah muttered from his corner, where he'd gotten to his feet.

Noa looked at Callum; he nodded, tired.

"Callum and I ... we're not going to be together right now," Noa told Judah. She hated the way the corner of Judah's mouth quirked up at her words. "It's nothing to do with you," she added harshly. "I just want to focus on finding Sasha."

Despite her tone, Judah slid his gaze to Callum, glinting. Callum stood up straighter, met his brother's dancing eyes with an unwavering and unreadable stare.

"We need to make a plan," Callum said. "We've recovered ourselves down here, but if we want to find Sasha, we're going to have to go back aboveground and try to track her."

The merry glint in Judah's eye was replaced with his familiar cynical scorn.

"And we're gonna do that without showing our faces *how*? Arik saw me. Everyone will be looking for Darius's sons."

Callum frowned. "I'll use my gift to transfigure our appearances—"

Judah threw up his hands. "*Perfect!* We'll just hope no one notices the blue alarm tubes blaring everywhere we go!"

"Well what's your plan, Judah?" Callum replied hotly. "I don't hear any actual suggestions!"

"Actually, I have a suggestion," Noa announced. They turned to her in surprise. She tried not to look smug. "*I* will go above and try to get information. I'm not a famous Forsythe; no one knows my face; I doubt Arik looked at me long enough to see beyond some random pixie who needed punishing. *And* I can't set off any of those tubes."

"Are you insane?" Judah said instantly. "You can't go by yourself!" He turned to Callum, indignant. "Tell her!"

But Callum looked thoughtful. "Actually, it's not a bad idea."

"*What*? Mr. I-Know-What's-Best-to-Protect-Everyone? You're just gonna send her up like a sacrificial lamb into a world she knows *zero* about and where she has absolutely *no* gifts to protect herself?"

Callum remained cool. "Not magical gifts, maybe, but Noa's a quick thinker. Look how she unraveled the In Between—that was some serious magic, and she pulled it apart. *Without* gifts."

"That was different! It was in our *minds*—"

"Which was way more dangerous!" Callum interrupted in frustration. He made visible efforts to keep collected, but his words hissed at Judah through his teeth anyway: "Right now the only thing we have going for us is that they may think we're dead. If there's a chance Darius isn't coming after us, we have to preserve it as long as possible."

"It's the only way," Noa insisted. Judah clenched and unclenched his fists, and Noa hid a smile. She could tell he was seeing the logic of her plan.

"Still," Judah said finally, "Noa will be completely on her own—in *Aurora*. She doesn't know this world. She'll have no safety net."

Callum frowned. He looked at Noa, wavering. He finally sighed, looking at Judah in resignation. "You're right. You should go too. Stick to the shadows, read her mind if she gets in trouble. I don't know, we can dirty up your face somehow, hope they're only looking for us together..."

Judah suppressed a furious, frustrated scream. "It won't work, Callum! Even *if* I could somehow avoid setting off Red alarms, I *can't read her mind*, remember?"

Callum narrowed his eyes. "That's in your head."

"It's *not*," Judah insisted fiercely.

Noa barely breathed: they were standing on a land mine, and they all knew it. They remembered with perfect clarity when Judah had announced he could no longer read Noa's mind, how he'd claimed it was because he was in love with her and she loved him back. According to a powerful Red named Fabian, an ancient magic was evoked when Fae and mortal loved each other—causing the Fae gift to stop working on the one he loved.

But Noa wasn't in love with Judah, and Fabian had been a cruel and sadistic liar.

"I can't read her mind, Callum," Judah insisted through gritted teeth.

"You're just undisciplined, and you always have been," Callum replied coldly. "This is just another excuse. Your gift has always been weak—what, have you been in love with everyone?"

Noa saw Judah's tiny wince, felt the kernel of uncertainty she knew he was desperate not to show. Even Judah had admitted to Noa that he wasn't very skilled.

"Either way," Judah said finally, "I can't read her mind. So for me to go would be pointless—"

"You're both being idiots!" Noa exclaimed. "The whole point is to keep you two from being seen. I don't need a watchdog." She turned to Callum. "You said it yourself. I'm a quick thinker. I can handle this."

"But—" they both protested as one.

Noa huffed, curled her fists into her waist:

"I'm not asking for permission."

• • •

JUDAH LED NOA and Callum in tight silence through the Tunnels toward the hidden exit Noa would use to go aboveground. With every step through the endless, identical roundness and sickly lavender light, she trembled a little more. She knew if she wavered the brothers would stop her from going, so Noa did what she sometimes did at Harlow when she needed to push herself forward: visualized herself as a machine and gave herself simple commands. *Step. Step. Breathe.*

Callum's hand found hers in the dark, squeezed it lightly. To give her strength, no matter how things had changed. Noa thought suddenly of her mother and the secret code of hand-squeezes they'd shared when she was little.

Judah stopped short ahead of them, then backed up, looking around slowly. "Wait—go back to the last turn. I meant to go the other way."

Callum eyed him sharply. "I thought you never make mistakes down here."

Judah scowled and crossed his arms. "I *don't*. But look around, I'm not a robot. You lead the way if you think you can do better." He pushed past Callum roughly with his shoulder.

Callum exhaled harshly. "It's just important that we send her up through the right exit, one that's well-hidden," he said through gritted teeth.

Judah ignored him, turning back into what he now recognized as the correct tunnel. Noa and Callum followed for fifteen more minutes before Judah stopped and looked up.

"We're here. This should let you out into an alleyway in the remnants of the old marketplace. It's the farthest point from the palace, and a complete ruin."

"Plenty of cover," Callum explained. "Where the Resistance used to camp and hide."

Noa nodded. They had gone over the plan already, several times, but hearing it repeated in Callum's calm voice helped to make her brave. "I'm ready," she finally said, voice steadier than her pulse.

"We'll be right here," Callum assured her. "If you get scared, just come right back."

Judah scoffed. "Really useful mission that would be."

Noa glared at him. "I *won't* get scared."

Noa She turned from Judah, took a deep breath, shook her shoulders like a prizefighter warming up. She walked to the wall; Judah showed her almost imperceptible hand- and footholds leading to the ceiling, disguised among the pressed vines and stones.

The first hold was a little high. Noa lunged awkwardly to reach it, and Callum was instantly at her side. "Wait, let me make a ladder—"

"No! There may be alarms up there. I'll be fine."

She finally got purchase on the wall, then lifted up first one foot and then the other. She wobbled but felt Judah's hands suddenly steadying her back.

"*I've got it*," she snapped, trying to ignore the increased pounding in her chest. Not looking down, she slowly, steadily, climbed up the slippery, pockmarked wall. When she reached the ceiling overhead, she felt for the spot that was not as solid as it appeared.

"Feel it? It's kind of murky?" Judah called up from below.

Noa bit her lip as her fingers finally sank into the sticky spot. This was it. Without looking back, she pushed herself up through the dark miasma and out into light.

The first thing Noa realized was that she was *not* in the abandoned, shadowy ruins of a marketplace with plenty of cover. She had popped out into the middle of a wide-open, pristine street, in the dead center of a busy, polished neighborhood.

The second thing she realized was that she'd been seen—

—by someone charging right at her.

• • •

NOA HAD BARELY registered the incoming body before it streaked into her, bowled her backward, and smashed her into the wall of a nearby building. Her head crashed into the smooth, cold surface; her vision blurred; she gasped for air, blinked wildly, and for a split instant saw only the face of her attacker—

It was a girl, just a kid. Younger than Noa. Noa felt a tiny flush of relief—and then the small girl raised her hand…

And slammed a jagged rock hard into Noa's forehead.

• • •

WHEN NOA BLINKED into consciousness, she found herself in an elegant living room, decorated simply but luxuriously with raw silks, plush chairs, clean wood—and all in tones of white. It looked a little like Miles' family's penthouse in Manhattan—too immaculate for normal people. For a moment, Noa wondered if she was somehow still at Miles', waking from the strangest dream—

But then Noa saw her, the girl: dirty-faced and scowling and very, very real.

The *pixie*, Noa corrected herself. The pixie who had attacked her and now glowered at Noa from her perch on a clean, white couch. Noa's head throbbed. She reached up to touch her forehead, felt a bandage there.

"You … *hit* me."

The girl scowled behind messy locks of choppy black hair. It was uneven, some places to her chin, some to her shoulders, like she'd hacked it hurriedly herself with something dull. She couldn't have been than twelve.

"*Saved* you, more like. You trying to get us bagged, popping up like that? Who's your owner?"

"Owner?" Noa's concussed mind was moving like molasses.

The girl snorted. "Please, you're no Clear. You're dirty. And besides, I can sense it." She looked sharply at Noa, as if daring her to lie.

"You're ... Green," Noa realized slowly.

The girl eyed Noa suspiciously. "*Duh.* Usually I can sense Colors without blowing the lines, but I can't quite get yours. I'd use juice to read you, but you know..." She glared at the ceiling, where Noa saw red, green, and blue tubes ringing the room, like crown molding. "So just tell me straight, cullie: Why are you in Clear Province?"

"I ... thought it was the old marketplace," Noa said carefully. If she lied, she knew the Green pixie might sense it in her emotions.

The girl squinted in disbelief. "Your owner a beater? You got some kind of brain damage? This hasn't been the marketplace for years. It's Clear Province now, indentured cullies only."

When Noa still looked confused, she exhaled in frustration. "Don't play all innocent with me. We both know the only way a cullie can *get* into pretty Clear Town is if they've pissed someone off and been pawned to some Clear gob for Channeling. So what'd you do? Use your power? Mix?"

"You first," Noa challenged quickly.

The girl smirked, reminding Noa vividly of Judah. "I made some Clear kid sob like a little baby when he picked on my brother." She laughed at the memory. "Shoulda seen him quavering. Would've been fine but..." She trailed off, sending an evil look at the alarm tubes. "Got nicked."

"Your brother too?"

The girl's face darkened. She crossed her arms. "What do you care?"

A sudden wash of sadness overcame Noa, too quick for her to stop it. "My sister … I-I miss her…."

The girl watched Noa carefully. After a long moment, she spoke, still watching Noa warily: "My little brother was Green too, so we managed to stay together even after Otec Darius wiped out the Homesteads. I'd sneak into his room in the Green Tower, line up with him when we marched. Took care of him, see? Until…" She lifted her chin in defiance. "At least I ran away from the gobs they gave me to. Months ago. Can't risk going past the Guard line, so I've been hiding out in the Province ever since."

Noa looked around at the pristine living room. "Nice hideout."

The small girl shrugged. "Not hard to watch 'em, figure out what Clear's around and what's away. Never stay in one place too long."

Noa nodded. "Smart."

The girl narrowed her eyes. "Your turn, pixie. Tell me what the hell you're doing here, nearly getting me nabbed again."

Noa bit her lip, not knowing what she should say. "Well," she began slowly, "first, I'm Noa. You have a name?"

The girl tensed again, then decided to answer. "Used to be called Marena."

"Used to be?"

"Now I'm just Greenie. Joy Juice. A hit to make them Clears feel good."

Noa shivered.

"You didn't escape an owner, did you?" Marena accused shrewdly. "That's why you don't know any of this stuff."

Noa bit her lip. "No, I didn't. I came..." She hesitated. Marena was shifty, but something in Noa wanted to trust her, though she didn't know quite why. "From the Tunnels."

A strange, awed wonder transformed Marena's face, temporarily wiping away her scowl. For the first time, the pixie looked every bit a girl of twelve. "You're Tunnel Fae?" she breathed, as if Noa had named herself a unicorn. "But ... but they're not real...."

Noa decided to roll with it. "That's how I got into the Province, from below."

Marena seemed to wrestle with herself, with the hope she could not stop from softening her features. Her blue eyes grew vivid, glowing as she leaned in to speak in rapid whispers: "But how do you survive the flushes? How many are there? Are you forming a new Resistance?"

Something thudded in Noa's heart. "Wait—a *new* Resistance?"

Marena clutched Noa's hands with dirty, nail-bitten fingers. "When Otec Darius crushed the rebellion, we all believed what he said, that the rebels were all gone, but there were rumors, and here you are...." She caught her breath, eyes wide and shining. "Queen Lorelei, she's with you, isn't she? I *knew* she wasn't dead. I knew it!"

Noa's stomach spiraled; her vision blurred in panic. "Lorelei's ... dead?"

Before Marena could answer, a strange, low crackling sounded from the foyer. Noa and Marena turned as one to see the surface of the townhouse entrance wavering like a desert mirage.

"They're *back*!" Maren hissed, yanking Noa to her feet. Noa swayed, head still throbbing from her bruise.

Marena quickly surveyed the room and pulled Noa toward what appeared to be a closet. Noa stumbled after her to crouch in the dark compartment, and Marena yanked the closet door as close to closing as she dared. Noa just glimpsed the townhouse entrance dematerializing to reveal a well-groomed man holding a raggedy teenage boy by the shoulder. The last thing Noa saw was that the boy's eyes were glassy but open wide—then the closet door shut him out, and blue light filtered in through the cracks.

"Approved," the man's voice said in the living room, and the blue light—which Noa realized had been coming from the tube alarms—dimmed away.

Lighter, quicker footsteps entered the living room. "You can just use the doorknob, Cyrus," a female voice said, followed by the closing of the door.

"We have him, so I'll use him," the man—Cyrus—replied sharply. "I sure as hell don't keep this cullie for his filth."

Beside Noa, Marena began running her hands carefully against the wall and closet door. Noa squinted in the dark, realizing that this 'closet' was unlike any closet she'd ever seen. Instead of housing shelves or a coat rack, it had two chained cuffs bolted to the floor.

Noa touched one with her finger, shivering.

"Welcome home, cullie," Marena breathed in Noa's ear, still searching intently with her fingertips.

"Yes." Evidently having found what she was searching for, Marena pressed her face against the very bottom of the wall, beckoning Noa to do the same beside her. There were two small, irregular, hand-worn holes—little makeshift windows—hidden near the floor. Noa didn't want to think of how long a "cullie" had spent shackled here, patiently making these secret, tiny openings.

Or why Marena had known to look for such a thing.

Marena and Noa pressed their faces to the wall, cheeks touching, hair intertwining, and looked out into the living room.

Cyrus was now seated on the couch. The 'cullie' boy he had Channeled was slumped in a heap on the floor. The female—a well-coiffed woman with shining strawberry-blond hair—was looking through a purse nearby, swathed in an immaculate white wrap dress made of layers and layers of fluttering fabric.

Cyrus kicked the lump of Blue Fae boy her way.

"Something to eat, will you?" he said. "I need to make an Astral call. Where's the Red?"

The woman took the dirty, drooling Blue teen with distaste. "We need a new one. The old one was so weak I sent her to Review. Half the time her Astral calls flickered out, and she couldn't Suggest a thing to a dog, let alone another Fae."

Cyrus slapped his hands on his thighs. "Amarine! You can't just keep throwing out the cullies! They aren't cheap!"

"Why should we have to deal with incompetence? Are you or are you not on the Otec's new Commission?" Amarine snapped. She disappeared from view for a moment, then returned, holding what looked like a stone. She grasped the teenage boy's shoulder. Noa thought she saw him shudder in his stupor—and the stone transfigured into a bowl of some kind of nuts and grains. Amarine fairly hurled the bowl at Cyrus, who, Noa now assumed, must be her husband.

Cyrus caught Amarine's hand, held it roughly. "We're not supposed to talk of that," he hissed. "The Otec won't hesitate to send us to Review if we're not discreet. No one can know." Amarine tried to pull away, but her husband held her fast. "I mean it.

I've seen the weapon, and none of us stands a chance. Clear or not." He sneered into her eyes. "*Tell me* you understand."

Amarine nodded painfully. "I wish you could just tell me—"

Cyrus vehemently shook her so hard she squealed, but Noa thought she saw fear within his movement. "It came from somewhere else, and it cannot be contained. That's all you need know."

Noa's heart pounded; she could hear her blood rushing in her ears.

Sasha.

Marena slapped a hand over Noa's mouth, frantic; Noa realized she'd murmured the name aloud. Her whole body seized in fear, but after a terrifying moment, Marena eased a little in relief.

Too soon.

"Put the Blue away, will you?" Cyrus told Amarine, and footsteps headed directly toward their hiding place. Noa turned to Marena, and it was like she could read her mind:

Crap.

"What the…," Cyrus cried as the power alarm in the living room began to scream and pulse, flashing red.

Marena grabbed Noa's arm; Amarine's footsteps had paused, distracted, and Noa understood immediately. She nodded once as Marena slammed the door backward from inside, and as one, they leapt out together.

Amarine screamed at the sudden girl-bullets; Cyrus jumped up from the couch, portly face thunderous and red.

"Runaway cullies!" he snarled, coming at them around the coffee table. "Amarine, stop them!"

Amarine shrieked hysterically, quite undone, frozen between them and the front door. Marena took one look at Cyrus's approaching hulk and yanked Noa right at her. The flashing Red alarms were suddenly joined by screeching Green alarms as Amarine crumpled to the floor, sobbing and shaking with overwhelming fear.

Cyrus was faster than he looked, already at their backs. His fingers brushed their backs just as, in perfect synchronicity, Noa and Marena jumped over the cowering, crying Amarine.

"Dammit, Amarine!" Cyrus screamed as he tumbled over his wife's sobbing body. Amarine cried out in pain; Noa turned and saw Cyrus stumbling up, savagely kicking her aside. But he was moving absurdly slowly, face contorted, as he fought through the cloud of fear that now engulfed him too.

Looking backward, Noa slipped on the smooth foyer floor—realizing only now it was made of marble—and slid into the entry banister headfirst. Marena scrabbled to pull Noa to her feet, but she was too small, and the room was spinning. Noa slipped again, this time on something wet and red. She touched her forehead: her bandage was gone, wound gushing.

"Come on!" Marena cried, face twisted with the effort of both pulling Noa and maintaining the cloud of fear behind them. "I can't hold them off!"

"You'll have to do better than this, Greenie!" Cyrus grunted, but gaining speed. "I conquered my fear long ago!"

Adrenaline shot through Noa's veins. Her vision snapped into focus, and she stumbled up, hand pressed into her wound. Marena was frozen toward Cyrus, panting with magical exertion, so Noa grabbed her with her free hand and pulled her at the door. Behind them, Cyrus yelled in triumph just as Noa reached for the doorknob—

—which disappeared right under her hand, along with the door itself.

Noa and Marena collided heavily with the wall. They turned to face Cyrus, world still reverberating.

Cyrus was grimacing, hand pressed firmly to his Blue boy. The Blue alarms had joined the cacophony, but Cyrus lolled toward them, unhurried.

"You have no *idea* what I'm going to do to you," he growled.

"We're not afraid of Review," Marena spat. Noa tried to echo her defiance, failing miserably.

Cyrus laughed harshly. "We shall see."

Noa's eyes flew wildly around the room, landing on the window over Cyrus's shoulder. She squeezed Marena's hand hard, hoping it would communicate what she couldn't say aloud, then in a sudden burst, let Marena go and sprinted straight at Cyrus. His face twisted in confusion as she bowled right into him, plowing him away from the Blue boy.

"The window!" Noa screamed to Marena.

Marena didn't hesitate. Noa latched herself, amoeba-like, onto Cyrus, struggling to keep him pinned. She'd learned the technique from Sasha, whose smaller size never prevented her from achieving some heroic moments in every fight.

Marena sprinted across the room, onto the coffee table, and jumped over the couch right at the window—but her mass wasn't big enough to break it. It bounced her backward like a rag doll and spiderwebbed with cracks. Noa screamed as Marena's little body slammed hard into the back of the couch, then oozed limply to the floor.

"Marena!" Noa cried, just as Cyrus swerved his body sideways to kick her in the stomach. She fell backward, her wind knocked out, and he clambered over to her. She wheezed and choked, unable even to scream as he raised his palm, fingers splayed—

"You're *mine*," he hissed, slamming his hand directly onto Noa's heart.

The air crackled and exploded; Noa's veins sizzled like she'd been electrocuted. She heard herself scream, and for a moment everything turned white. Then her vision blurrily returned: Cyrus's face above hers twisting into focus, his hand still on her heart, pressing, pressing, pressing—

So she pushed back.

Cyrus stuttered in confusion as Noa pushed herself upward, threw him off. He stared at his palm, unable to understand.

"You can't Channel me," Noa whispered with a smirk that would have made Judah proud. She reared back and kneed Cyrus in the groin with everything she had. As he crumpled, gasping, Noa ran over to the window, wiping away blood that was seeping into her eye. She grabbed a cushion from the couch and, turning her face away, elbowed it through the cracked window, which finally gave way in shards.

Noa bent to Marena and, taking a page from Marena's own pragmatic playbook, shook the pixie as hard as she could until Marena's blue eyes fluttered open. Then Noa yanked Marena to her feet, grabbed her hand and met her eyes.

Together, they leapt through the jagged window.

• • •

KNIVES OF GLASS rained absurdly musically against the sidewalk where Noa and Marena landed. They shoved themselves to their feet, and Noa got her first real look at what Judah and Callum had hoped was a crumbling ruin: a sprawling, gleaming cloister of immaculate streets and shining townhouses, each more ostentatious than the last. And everywhere, *everywhere*, were Clears bedecked in silks and robes, glittering in shades of ivories and ice.

And they were staring at Noa and Marena—bloodied, filthy, dressed in rags.

"*Run*," Marena breathed. They took off, hurtling past the startled residents as Cyrus screamed, "Runaways!" somewhere behind them.

"Follow me!" Marena ordered Noa, darting around a corner and speeding down the next street. Noa skidded behind her, trying to match her pixie agility. Aurora's Light had already healed Marena's body, a benefit Noa's mortal body didn't share.

"Crap!" Marena cried as a squad of white-and-silver uniforms flooded the street in front of them. Noa recognized them instantly: the Guard, who took prisoners to Review.

Marena yanked Noa sideways toward one of the townhouses, this one adorned with swirling ridges of ice-like stone. Without hesitation, Marena bounded onto the home's facade and began to claw up the ridges toward the roof—but the ridges were too shallow, too slick for Noa's mortal hands—

"Come on!" Marena screamed down as Noa scrabbled against the wall. Noa could hear the regiment of Guards getting closer, their boots pounding on the ground.

Noa looked around desperately, realizing now how stupid this plan of hers had been, how ill-equipped she was, how she would never see Sasha again—

Sasha.

"Noa!" Marena screamed.

But suddenly Noa wasn't seeing Marena, she was seeing *Sasha*—the way she sometimes saw Isla, there but not there, smiling with a secret. Sasha darted around the corner of the townhouse, eyes lit with mischief, beckoning Noa to follow.

Sasha led Noa to the side of the townhouse, the narrow alleyway between it and its differently styled neighbor. Noa watched as Sasha jumped in between the houses, little limbs spread like a starfish, one hand and foot on each side wall. She then crab-scurried upward, twinkling down at Noa, wanting her sister to come and play.

Noa could hear the shouts of Guards now, almost upon her. Without pausing to doubt herself, she jumped up into the crevice, splaying her hands and feet to crawl up after her starfish sister. She reached the roof just as the patrol descended on the front yard of the ice-house, and Marena's hand was there to pull her up and onto the steep, slippery steeple of the ice-house roof.

"What now?" Noa panted, her arms like jelly as she and Marena crouched against the slick grade of the roof, both breathing hard.

The Guards' chatter below rose up loud and clear: "Bring in the Blues!"

A series of grappling hooks flew over Noa and Marena's heads and slid back to catch within the ridges of the ice.

"They won't wait for Blues to Channel; they're gonna scale the wall," Marena said. "Confuse the climbers so we can run!"

"What?"

"Confuse them! Come on!"

"No, you don't understand—" Noa stuttered.

Marena huffed in frustration, but there was no time to argue. She pulled Noa to her feet and dragged her along as she ran up the steepled grade—then down, before Noa could protest.

"Jump!" Marena cried as they thundered, half-running and half-sliding to the edge. With no time and no choice, Noa leapt with Marena at the last possible second, sailing with her over the alley into the neighboring roof's grade.

There was no way Noa could keep her feet; she clattered against the roof—this one made in slick tiles of pressed flowers, not ridges of ice—and fell backward, falling right off the edge—

—still holding Marena's hand.

Marena skidded down toward the roof's edge too, pulled by Noa's sudden weight dangling off the side. Gripping Noa harder, she shoved her small feet into the border to stop her slide, then heaved back with all her might. Slowly, Noa was dragged up, inch by inch until she could grasp the railing and haul herself back to safety.

Noa slumped for a moment on the roof in order to catch her breath. Aurora's sun reflected hotly from the tiles, but having just almost died, Noa didn't find it nearly so oppressive; even the air felt less cloying-thick in her lungs. She raised her hand to her forehead, relieved to find her wound had finally stopped bleeding.

"What, you wanna stop and get a tan? Come on!" Marena snapped, charging up the new roof as she had the old one. Noa bounced up and followed—up and down and then across—to the next roof in the row.

This time Noa managed her landing better; she wobbled and skidded but didn't fall. Then Marena was on to the next, and Noa matched her stride for stride, sun sizzling on their backs.

They moved in unison until the fifth roof, which shuddered the moment they touched down. They both tumbled toward the edge but caught themselves on the gutter with their feet, the way Marena had done before, and saw that the mansion behind them had exploded into a fiery ball of flame, causing the shock wave that had just knocked them off balance.

"They're Channeling Blues," Marena said, scrambling to her feet. "We have to move faster!"

"Wait!" Noa said, getting up too and snagging Marena's arm. "We can use the smoke as cover!" She ran to the other side of the roof, but instead of leaping across, dropped down between the houses, Sasha-starfish-style, Marena following.

"There," Marena panted when they'd hit the ground. She was pointing down the alleyway toward a small shed attached to the townhouse to their left. At Noa's questioning look, Marena grimaced. "Lotta Clears don't want cullies messin' up the house. Give 'em their own 'houses.'"

"Like dogs," Noa murmured. She and Marena ran to the shed and closed themselves inside. It was damp and dark, and smelled like decomposition.

Noa couldn't have been more thankful.

Boots thundered down the street nearby, punctuated by deafening pops and rapid-fire crackles. Noa didn't want to think of what the Clear Guard were doing with the Blues to try to catch them.

"Is this how they usually go after runaways?" Noa panted, sweating.

Marena shook her head. "That gob, Cyrus, he musta been important."

"He knows we overheard about the Otec's new weapon," Noa realized. "That one he told his wife never to mention."

Marena bit her lip, for a moment as young as Noa had forgotten she really was. "We can't blow Clear Province, the checkpoint gobs'll nail us."

"What about below?"

"The Tunnels?" Marena breathed, eyes widening. "You'd bring me to the Tunnel Fae?"

Noa struggled, not wanting to destroy her dream of some cadre of underground Resistance. "I won't leave you behind," she said finally. "But I don't know where that entrance was that I came out of. Do you?"

Marena nodded uneasily.

"What aren't you telling me?" Noa asked.

"It's in the Main Square. Right in front of the Guard headquarters."

• • •

NOA AND MARENA didn't dare creep from the shed until the commotion had gone quiet for quite some time. When they finally emerged, Noa gulped in Aurora's strange air and light—she'd actually missed both in the stuffy darkness of the shed.

Marena led the way down the alley on tiptoe, copying how the younger girl flattened herself against one wall. Noa realized, somewhat belatedly, that she now completely trusted this girl who'd said hello by knocking her unconscious with a rock. It was more than that actually—somewhere while dodging death, Marena had started feeling, startlingly, like a sister, a fellow girl-beast Noa admired in the way she admired Isla and Sasha.

When they reached the end of the wall, Marena motioned to Noa to pause while she quickly peeked out into the open streets.

"Extra checkpoints," she whispered, voice flickering ever so slightly in a way that made Noa stomach sink.

"So what do we do?" Noa whispered back.

"Dunno. I usually sneak at night, but..." Marena grimaced. "We don't gotta go far, but there's so many gobs, they're gonna notice us."

Noa bit her lip, thinking hard. "What if ... we let them? Notice us?"

"You hit your head again?"

"No, Mar, what if we go through right under their noses? In disguise?"

Marena squinted at Noa, the grinned slowly.

"Do you know where we could get some of those fancy clothes?" Noa asked.

"You've come to the right cullie." Marena rubbed her hands, looked around quickly. She pointed down the alley toward a window, lighting up. "Come on, I'm gonna need a boost."

"Wait, you're going to steal the clothes from this *house*?" Noa asked. "Isn't there like ... a Laundromat that would be safer? Where there are a lot of clothes and no one will notice "

Marena rolled her eyes. "In the Blue work sectors, maybe. Not in the Province." She trotted to the window, turned back impatiently toward Noa, who followed reluctantly.

"Maybe I should be the one to go in," Noa suggested, feeling a surge of sisterly protectiveness, even as she knew she would make a terrible thief.

Marena scoffed. "Please. I'm a pro." She winked at Noa and lifted her foot. "Boost me, pixie."

"How are you going to open the window?" Noa grunted, clasping her hands so Marena could step up. Marena smirked and lifted the glass easily.

"Them gobs alarm our powers but not doors and windows," she snickered, then disappeared inside.

Noa waited anxiously, every second a century. It reminded her of waiting for Isla to return after she'd snuck out at Harlow. Isla had always teased Noa for that because nothing bad ever happened to Isla.

Until it did.

Noa shuddered, silently prayed for Marena to hurry up.

As if in answer, Marena slipped out the window and dropped lightly to the ground, a bundle crushed beneath her arm.

"Good news and bad news," she whispered quickly. "Good news is, I got you some ickle-pretty pixie robes. Bad news is, there weren't any in kid sizes and I heard them gobs in the next room so I didn't wanna hunt around."

Noa did not like the sound of that at all. "Can't you just wear the same size as me?"

Marena snorted. "No Clear kid would wear clothes that didn't fit. That's what them Blue cullies are for."

"Well we can't just break into a bunch of houses until we find your size—"

Marena waved away Noa's panic, smug. "Duh. I'll just be *your* indentured Greenie. Get it?"

Noa studied Marena uncertainly. "You think that'll work?"

Marena grinned. "'Course. Just act like a selfish, lazy, spoiled gob and we'll be slicked!"

. . .

NOA NEEDED MARENA'S help to dress herself properly in the intricate Clear robes. The numerous elaborate ties and criss-crosses—clearly the work of indentured Blue Fae—slipped inexpertly through Noa's fingers. The voluminous robes were deepest ivory but danced in sunlight: thousands of tiny diamonds were interwoven with the stitches.

Marena scrutinized Noa when she was finished. "Your face is ashy and your hair's all fuzzy, but it'll do."

Noa suppressed a laugh. "Thanks."

Marena held up a short cord, attached to two circlets. "Nicked this too." Noa crinkled her face in confusion, and Marena rolled her eyes. "Forgot you been living under rocks. It's your leash. Or mine, I guess. Can't be dirtying your pretty Clear hands unless you need to Channel me."

Grimacing, Noa leaned over and helped fasten the rings around Marena's wrists.

"Cut that out," Marena scolded. "Don't look at me. I'm beneath you."

"Or just really annoying," Noa teased.

Marena huffed, but Noa saw her eyes dance. "C'mon, Clearie."

. . .

NOA TOOK A deep breath and walked into full view of the sidewalk, yanking Marena behind her. She managed not to look back at Marena, who yelped with each step—pretend-yelped,

Noa hoped—but she couldn't help glancing anxiously at bustling passersby.

"Stop lookin' guilty!" Marena hissed behind her.

Noa began to nod but stopped herself. 'Clearies' didn't interact with cullies. She pressed her lips together, made no sign of hearing as Marena whispered, low and even, "Go right here. Left at the crossing. Then we're smack in the Main Square."

Noa walked purposefully to the right but stuttered when she saw the checkpoint directly in her path. Her heart beat so fast she was afraid, for a moment, she might pass out.

You can do this! Noa ordered herself. She reached back through her mind, searching for an inspiration, someone to emulate—and found Ansley, the golden social queen who swanned through Harlow's halls. Privilege was Ansley's native skin. Noa pictured Ansley's face as her face, made Ansley's walk her walk: every stride prettier and fiercer, as if the sidewalk were her own. Before she knew it, she was at the checkpoint, face-to-face with a silver-clad Clear Guard.

Her Ansley-aura vanished. His face swallowed it whole—not his eyes, which were sharp hazel and certainly frightening, but more his *brows*, so inky black and thick that his whole presence became ursine. Growling from every hair.

Ansley, Noa thought feebly, but the strengthening spirit did not come. She reeled, almost turned and fled—and then saw her: *Isla.*

Isla's ghost coalesced just beyond the Guard, blond hair swirling madly like a lion's mane or a mermaid under the sea. Her silver eyes shone like beacons, glinting bright with mischief: Isla, girl-beast, calling out to Noa's girl-beast blood.

Noa inhaled Isla's spirit like breathing fire; she straightened up, flared her eyes, raised her nose into the air.

"Ugh! What's all this?" she demanded before the Guard could speak. She saw instantly that it was the right move; he stepped back, apologetic and deferential, on his heels.

"Sorry, miss. Just some runaway cullies we need to find."

Noa rolled her eyes and tossed her head. "Cullies are like dogs. You practically have to potty-train them." Noa yanked the leash leading to Marena. "*This* one used to try to get away. But we house-broke her good."

The Guard chuckled, nodded. "You headed to the main square?"

"Where else!" Noa snapped snottily, as if offended he'd even ask.

"Runaway cullies can be dangerous. If it's not urgent, I'd advise you go home quickly—"

"I'm not afraid of *vermin*."

The Guard reddened deeply, flushed with shame. "Of course, miss, go on through."

Noa stalked past him, yanking Marena behind her. "Praise Otec," she sneered in the Guard's ear, feeling a savage spark of glee at his flinch.

As soon as Noa was past the checkpoint, she exhaled deeply, shuddering, as if releasing Isla's reckless bravery. A very Noa-like anxiety flooded back, along with shock and hindsight—fear that made her tremble. Her skin felt ripply like jelly.

Behind her, she heard Marena's faintest snicker.

Noa didn't risk turning around, but could picture the pixie's approving smirk. It made her proud instead of scared.

She turned left at the crossing, feeling confident again—

Until she saw another waiting checkpoint, this one larger, and manned by *several* Guards. One held a dazed, gray-shirted cullie at the ready for enhanced interrogation; there was a backup of several Clear Fae waiting to be allowed to go through.

Noa licked her lips. If they had an army, she'd need one too, if only in her mind: *Ansley's walk. Isla's swagger. Marena's smirk. Sasha's mind.* She got in line, girl-beast blood pumping.

But something was wrong. Ahead of Noa, one Clear after another was turned back, denied access to the Main Square.

Noa's fingers tightened on Marena's leash, but Marena could say nothing. But Noa knew what Marena wanted to say: *we have to find a way.*

Noa shook her hair back, picturing Isla's mermaid mane, and stalked to the front of the line as if the Clears in front of her did not exist.

"Square's shut down," the Head Guard said, not bothering to look her in the eye. Noa knew immediately that snotty wouldn't work with this one. He was too arrogant himself.

"I know," Noa said sweetly instead, picturing Sasha's strategic use of snuggles to get her way. "Runaway cullies! Imagine! That's why Daddy Astraled me to come back home right away."

The Guard narrowed his eyes and opened his mouth, but Noa quickly continued. "You know Daddy." Noa smiled, batting her eyes. "Well, of course you do. Everyone does. I'd hate to have to tell him you kept me in danger, but of course you would know best...." Noa dropped her eyes deferentially, then peeked up and saw with satisfaction that the Guard was wavering. She could practically read the thoughts running through his mind: he didn't know who she was, but he definitely didn't want to admit it; Noa's patrician manners proved her story.

Noa knew she was close. She put a kind hand on his arm; he looked at it in surprise, almost awe—the way Noa herself had looked when touched by deities like Ansley at Harlow.

"I know, such a pickle these cullies put us in," Noa leaned in confidingly, as if it were a secret. "But look, you've only just started building the blockade. I'll just slip right through...."

The Guard was still staring at her hand. *Just let me*, Noa pleaded silently. *Just let me go through*. Finally the Guard straightened, the picture of a diligent officer looking her in the eye. "Okay, but go *right* home—"

Noa's heart sank as he broke off midsentence; another Guard—a Captain of some sort—beckoned him to a conference of several huddled patrolmen. "Wait here," Noa's Guard said distractedly. He went to join the conference, and a new Guard, extremely burly and missing a chunk from his nose, came to stand stock-still in Noa's path.

"Um, hi. He was just letting me thr—" Noa began.

The burly Guard slid his eyes chillingly to Noa's, not moving another muscle. Noa shivered. Her spirit army of girl-beasts evaporated in that single look.

Marena suddenly gasped behind Noa. Noa turned, then froze.

Cyrus and Amarine were striding toward the conferencing Guards.

"Um, it's okay, I'll just go back after all," Noa told the burly Guard quickly, spinning fast. But he grabbed her arm with meaty fingers.

"Wait," he growled. Noa swallowed, trying not to shake.

In the conference, Cyrus was gesturing emphatically around the square, back toward Noa. She bit her lip. *Don't look here, please don't look here,* she prayed with every beat of her frantic heart, *Please don't look here, please—*

Cyrus didn't, but Amarine did. Her eyes swept the line of waiting Clears, falling on Noa; she looked confused, then recognition practically screamed from inside her mind—

—and above them all, glass exploded in deafening chains of fireworks that filled the air with shards of translucent, swirling shrapnel. Not just glass but something else, something wet and red—

Noa gagged, realizing she was inhaling flying blood. The Clears in line screamed, white clothes shearing and staining crimson; the burly Guard released Noa's arm in the sudden chaos. Noa looked down at her own robes, drenched in blood; she wondered why she felt no pain, knowing she must be bleeding too. She looked around frantically, glancing up, and realized—it wasn't blood but liquid from the red alarm tubes above them, still shattering and exploding everywhere.

Others pointed, screaming at the tubes. Noa saw Cyrus look up in fury; then in a sudden, terrible instant, his head whipped her way, his eyes meeting hers in total recognition—

Marena's leash suddenly ripped out from Noa's hands, and the Green alarms above erupted in screams and flashes. Noa barely understood the streak of Marena sprinting into the center of the Square, leaving doubled-over Clears sobbing in her wake—

"Get her! She's one of them!" Cyrus screamed fanatically, pointing at Marena. The cloud of Guards fell upon her, descending like a hurricane over her tiny frame—

Noa sprinted after Marena. She could just see Marena's face through the swarm of silver and white, barely found the pixie's small blue eyes—and Marena's look silently said it all:

Run, you dolt. I'm saving you.

Noa's heart broke as her body turned independently of her conscious will. Blinding tears streamed down her cheeks as her legs ran to the hidden entrance to the Tunnels. She keened, bone-deep, as her arms found and twisted open the heavy circular door, as her legs propelled her body inside—

—and she fell down, down, down, into air, into emptiness, the trap door clanging shut above her...

So when she finally crashed, everything—her body, her soul, her self included—was swallowed into darkness.

• • •

IT TOOK NOA a long time for her body to discover it was still alive. Her eyes came first, blinking to adjust to the eerie lavender glow deep within the Tunnels. When they did, she lay still, sure she was dead, sure what she had just seen could not be real.

Marena had not sacrificed herself. Noa had not let her. Marena was not lost. Not dead. It could not be. She stared up into the dark, knowing only grief.

Then Noa turned her head—and remembered fear.

Judah and Callum were there, where they'd promised they would wait for her, but they were backed up against one wall, hands up in clear surrender. Across from them was the most beautiful and frightening girl Noa had ever seen—a girl-beast made real, feral in the flesh. She was lithe but hard, all muscle, and crouched to leap with tearing claws; her ice-white hair, scraped

155

back tight, fell down her back like a blade; her pointed, filed canines were bared and gleaming with the blinding light of fangs. She had a knife aimed at the brothers' throats. The knife blazed with orange fire.

"Noa," Callum strained, not moving his eyes from the flaming knife for even the slightest instant. "Please meet Hilo."

• • •

"DON'T MOVE," HILO growled at Noa, sending her a slicing glare. Hilo's white hair glinted like a long knife when she moved; her eyes were a chillingly light blue, like those of an an arctic wolf.

"She's not a threat, Hilo," Callum said slowly, calmly. "None of us means you any harm."

"Speak for yourself," Judah muttered, though he remained quite still.

"Hilo, please put the Faefyre away," Callum continued calmly, ignoring Judah. "I think we all know it's not something we want to play with."

Noa didn't even want to breathe, the air was so charged and tenuous.

Hilo didn't move, still poised to strike. Callum took a tentative step toward her, then another, and finally put a gentle hand on her outstretched arm.

"Please, Hilo," he urged softly. Hilo reared back; Noa shut her eyes, unable to see another loved one die—but then she heard a tiny sigh. She opened her eyes: Hilo held the blade at Callum's throat, but the flames were gone.

Judah chuckled bitterly under his breath, and in a blur the knife was pressing into his throat, drawing droplets of blood.

"Do it," he challenged.

"You think I won't?"

"I *know* you will."

"Enough!" Callum grabbed Hilo's arm. "Hilo, put it *away*." His eyes were dark, his voice terse and deep, in a tone Noa had never heard him use. A tone that made her shiver.

Hilo snorted but tucked the knife into her tunic. Noa saw her lupine eyes follow Callum warily.

Callum turned his back on them, then knelt to Noa. "Are you okay?" he asked in his different, gentler voice.

"I-I don't know," Noa said. He helped her up; she tried not to flinch from his touch.

"Lean on me," Callum instructed. "Your leg is broken." Noa looked down, surprised, but he was right: her leg was shuddering under her weight. She hesitated, studying his face—but it was again the gentle Callum face she had always trusted. She squashed her misgivings and leaned her weight tiredly against him.

Over Callum's shoulder, Noa saw Hilo watching them. Noa looked down into Callum's collar, flushing and shivering.

As Callum wrapped his arms around her, warmth began to spread from Noa's chest, radiant from her heart. Little flowers of heat bloomed over her injuries as Callum knit her back together: not just her leg, but her arms, her wrist, her back, her knees. All the things she hadn't had time to feel when she was running for her life with Marena.

Marena.

Noa closed her eyes. *Push it away*, she commanded herself. *Turn it off.*

Amazingly, it seemed to work. Her mind shut out everything for a moment, let her live in the feeling of being healed. It cocooned her—no chasing Guards, no confusing brothers, no insane pixie with a Faefyre knife—but then it was over, and Noa felt the chrysalis fall away.

Callum held her for the briefest second, then gently pushed her back to her feet.

"I'm glad you're back," he breathed in her ear.

Noa swallowed hard, avoided looking at Hilo. She'd endured too much to be derailed. "I have a lot to tell you."

"Not here," Judah said curtly, eyes on Hilo.

Hilo glared right back. "Where you go, I go, Judah- Pants," she sneered. "She's not the only one who's gonna talk."

• • •

THE WALK BACK to the hidden Tunnel room was strained. Judah fixated on Hilo, seemingly torn between wanting her in sight at all times and not wanting her to lead the way. Noa and Callum fell behind, trying to stay out of their tension even as it infected everything.

"Where'd she come from?" Noa whispered.

"She came looking for Judah. She'd heard we were sighted in the near the Barracks in the Work Sector, knew if it really was Judah he'd hide down here."

"She *wanted* to find him? After what she did?"

Callum sighed quietly, uneasily. "She says she missed him. Regrets what happened. Wants forgiveness."

"Funny way of showing it."

"Well, you know how receptive Judah can be. Hilo's cut from the same cloth."

Noa didn't know why she felt a tiny pang. "Do you believe her?"

"She's like Judah," Callum said guardedly. "She's ... malleable."

"I guess you would know," Noa replied, more sharply than she intended.

"We were young," Callum said softly. "And without her help, I could never have gotten Sasha safely to your world."

Noa didn't answer. She heard the hurt in Callum's voice and regretted it, but even though she'd defended both Hilo and Callum to Judah, now she felt compelled to take Judah's side.

"I'm not proud of manipulating her feelings, Noa," Callum murmured. "What I don't know is if there isn't someone else now, pulling her strings, the way I did before."

An entirely new chill went down Noa's arms. She glanced ahead at the frightening, stunning pixie, jostling with Judah to take the lead. Even fighting, they moved their bodies the same way.

"That's the wrong way!" Hilo suddenly snapped at Judah.

"It is *not*—"

"Yes! Look!" Hilo pointed at some indecipherable part of the dark expanse neither Noa or Callum could distinguish. But Noa watched Judah see it.

Hilo rolled her glittering eyes. "A little rusty, huh?"

Judah glared at her. "Just don't trust you without proof."

Hilo's hand flew to her knife; Callum tensed; then all at once, Hilo's shoulders sagged. Noa was startled to see how her body seemed to soften, hair rippling in silver waves. Beneath the armor,

Hilo was actually delicate, as if drawn with intricate, fine brush-strokes, like etchings made in glass.

Like Judah, Noa realized.

"You have to forgive me sometime, Judah," Hilo murmured, the words barely reaching Noa and Callum.

Judah's profile looked carved from ice. "It's funny how every-one keeps telling me that." His gaze traveled back toward Callum, toward Noa. It lingered for a moment, then he turned to face the dark instead.

"Come on," he muttered.

Callum pulled her forward; Noa stumbled to walk beside him, fighting the sinking feeling in her heart.

• • •

"I'VE BEEN ON the run ever since the Resistance fell," Hilo told them that night in the cave as they passed around Callum-con-jured grapes and nuts beneath the glow of Stellabugs. It would have been cozy, like a campfire of old friends, if not for the unspo-ken knots and tangles twisting through the dark.

One by one, Hilo handed Callum the rough-hewn cups she and Judah had once made so patiently by hand. Callum filled them using his gift, then they passed them hand to hand around the circle.

When Hilo turned to pass a cup to Noa, Noa hesitated—but in the Stellabug light, Hilo's bestiality had softened, like clay beneath warm hands. Her angled cheekbones—before sharp as knives—became hollows worn slowly back by loss. Noa knew, could *feel*, the fingerprints of grief there. Noa's own face had been re- sculpted by those hands.

Noa met Hilo's eyes, still the lightest blue she'd ever seen. Wolflike, yes, and chilling—but also the first eyes to see Judah's heart for what it was.

Noa smiled tentatively, accepted the cup.

"Careful, Noa," Judah said quietly. He'd taken Hilo's knife—his condition of allowing her to speak—and was flicking it methodically against the ground. Noa tingled uneasily—was Hilo using her Green gift to make Noa feel more at ease?

"Shall we ask the Otec to alarm the Tunnels then?" Hilo asked Judah with a smile.

"If you expect us to trust a word you say," he replied, not smiling back.

"When did that alarm stuff start, anyway?" Callum interrupted.

Hilo sighed, turned away from Judah. "Once the Resistance was dismantled, Darius began rigging the whole city. A Colored power gets used, those things go off unless a Clear gives permission."

"I get that, but how do they work? I mean, they're clearly magical. But magic can't just exist on its own. It has to be *performed* by Fae—"

"Not the talisman," Noa pointed out. "That works on its own."

"What talisman?" Hilo asked immediately. Her face sharpened, eyes flicking from Callum to Noa. Judah snickered softly.

"Nothing," Callum said quickly.

"What talisman, Judah?" Hilo demanded.

Judah smirked. "Your boyfriend made it for Noa in the mortal world. To protect her."

"Callum, *no!*"

"I had to," Callum told her firmly.

Hilo's eyes filled, and she hastily looked away.

Judah scoffed bitterly. "And you claim you came here to make things right with *me*. Another lie. What a shock."

Hilo sprang to her feet, anger burning up her tears. "I *didn't* lie. I *don't* feel that way about Callum anymore, not since it meant losing you. And…" Her voice shook hoarsely, but she forced herself to say it: "*Lily*."

She spun toward the wall in humiliation, wiping the tear streaking down her cheek. But Judah wouldn't give her that. He leapt up too, right at her back, hissed relentlessly into her ear: "*Your Fyre—*"

"She already apologized to you, Judah," Callum said quietly.

Judah snarled but backed off. For the first time since Hilo had appeared, his eyes found Noa's eyes. His were angry, hard. But Noa held his gaze. *Feel it*, Noa tried to tell him. *It's okay to feel it all.*

Behind Noa, Hilo was breathing fiercely. When she finally turned back to face Judah, his eyes left the beam of Noa's gaze.

"I'm not in love with Callum," Hilo repeated at him, calm but even. She turned to Noa, eyes like ice. "But I *know* what a talisman is."

Noa flushed in shame, then anger.

"Don't blame her!" Judah snapped.

Hilo flinched, eyes flicking between Judah and Noa. For a moment, Noa saw the fierce, silver beast—but just as quickly, it was gone.

Hilo turned to Callum, calm.

"You asked how the tubes work. They're actually not unlike a talisman. A talisman works because it has a piece of living soul. The tubes—the liquid in them? Darius harvests it."

Noa closed her eyes.

Hilo smiled bitterly at her. "Yes, little mortal. Those tubes hold liquefied Fae. That's what happens when the Otec calls you to Review."

Noa wanted to scream and fight and cry—but against whom, against what? She'd built walls and borders—Home, Here, and In Between—and her sanity hinged on their separation. More than her sanity, because her sanity was just her mind; this went deeper—to her marrow, to the chambers of her heart.

Hilo kept talking, not knowing how she was breaking Noa's boundaries, cutting the fragile threads that were holding Noa's *being* together: "If you use your powers, or you're caught mixing with other colors—'cullies,' they call us, like dogs—you're first indentured to some Clear family as their personal Channeling slave. But if you really mess up, or repeat-offend ... you're melted down in Review."

Judah snickered quietly, didn't need to speak aloud: *Sounds familiar.*

Callum leapt up, frantic, angry: "He can't ... He's that far gone? Our father? He can't be!"

"Are you really surprised?" Judah demanded.

"But murder, mass *murder*—"

"What did you think would happen when you took Lily away!" They all were standing now, Judah furious in his brother's face. "He snapped! He cast out Mom!"

Callum stumbled backward as if Judah had slapped him. Judah spun on Hilo. "Tell me now and don't *dare* lie! Where's Lorelei? What happened to her when the Resistance fell?"

"Judah—" Hilo stepped back, held up her hands. Noa's body seized, frozen in fear.

"Tell me!"

"I—"

"Please, Hilo—" Callum croaked.

"I-I can't—"

Judah snarled, grabbed her, shook her by the shoulders. Noa had to look away. *"Tell me now!"*

"She's dead! Okay? She's dead!" Hilo cried, breaking.

Judah's face contorted with shock, anger, disbelief. *"Liar!"* He threw her to the ground, held her open knife flush against her throat.

"She's not!" Noa cried, lunging at him, desperate to pull him back. "Judah, stop, please, she's not lying! Please, she's not, she's not!" Noa started sobbing wildly, heaving against him, scrabbling at his hands. He let her pull him from Hilo; they collapsed together to the floor. He didn't cry but she did in torrents, as if it were her mother who had died—because it was, not her mother but Marena, and Isla too, and the fragile, broken strings that no longer kept anything separate or safe—

Judah looked at her, more frightened than any child. He didn't move or speak, poured every plea into his gaze.

"I heard it above," Noa told him, tortured. "They declared her dead when the Resistance fell." She expected him to scream, to wail, to make noise and curse the world—but he didn't. What he did was so much quieter, and so much worse— he crumpled inward.

Something in Noa couldn't bear to watch.

"But the pixie, she also said—" Noa said desperately, recklessly, knowing it was wrong, knowing it was the most wrong thing she could possibly do. "She seemed to think there was a chance, somehow, that it wasn't true—"

Judah froze and stared at her, then slowly rose, a sunrise of terrible, terrible hope. From behind, Callum gripped Noa's shoulders, spun her toward him so hard it hurt. It was blinding there from his face too—this terrible hope she'd conjured when she knew, more than *anyone*, it was magic so dark it could kill them all.

"What do you mean?" Callum begged. "Please, Noa, what do you mean?"

"I-I...," Noa cried painfully. What had she done? What was happening? How could she have betrayed everything she knew most deeply—

"They didn't show her body, they never buried it," Hilo said slowly, softly. "They should have. She had been queen." Hilo glanced at Noa, and Noa braced herself to see that hope there too— but Hilo's eyes weren't hopeful. They were tired, and sad, and kind. Hilo was helping Noa. She was sharing the burden of Noa's mercy.

"Well, she's obviously not dead then!" Judah declared, latching onto certainty with giddy glee. "Darius would have strung her from the rooftops!"

Callum was more measured, but Noa saw him falling too. "If she were dead, there'd be proof," he agreed.

Noa took a shaky breath. Hilo touched her hand. Noa breathed out, so grateful she almost cried.

"We'll find her, save her," Judah was saying.

"Yes, our sister and our mother both," Callum agreed.

Hilo's hand lifted from Noa's. "Your sister?"

"Noa's sister," Judah said quickly.

"What's going on?" Hilo said sharply. "Don't lie to me. I can feel your anxiety bleeding through the room."

Callum looked at Judah, and Judah exploded. "Absolutely not!" he cried. *"No!"*

"Judah—"

Judah turned to Noa. "Tell him no!"

Noa bit her lip, conflicting thoughts and feeling overwhelming her.

Callum stepped in. "Look, she's down here with us, isn't she? And nothing's happened, no one's followed her. We need all the help we can get, especially if we have to find Lorelei too—"

"She can't be trusted! Noa, tell him!"

"I-I don't—"

"She's *alive*, isn't she?" Hilo whispered. "Lily—I didn't ... My Fyre didn't..."

"Of course she's not alive!" Judah said immediately, but Callum hung his head in acquiescence.

Hilo looked shocked, then elated—then furious. "How could you not tell me?" Hilo screeched at Judah. "I thought I killed her! You let me think I killed her!"

"Then I guess we're even!" Judah screamed right back.

Hilo wailed and stumbled back into the wall of the cave, crumpled down against the wall. "You're right," she cried. "You're right. I let you think you started the Faefyre when it was me ... I let you think you killed her too." Hilo was crying now, from anger and shame and regret and so much more. She cried ferally, both girl and beast, both fierce and shaken to her core.

"I deserved it," she cried, ripping at her silver hair, the way Noa had seen Judah do so many times. "I deserved it, I deserved everything I got—"

Judah ran to her, rage pouring from every cell. Hilo's knife was in his hand; his arms were shaking; Noa had never seen his face so cruel—

He screamed, an animal's scream—

—but then he fell to Hilo's side, the knife clattering to the floor.

The look that passed between them then—it broke Noa's heart.

Hilo and Judah fell against each other, shuddering, and Noa had to look away. She felt a light touch on her elbow, looked into Callum's plaintive face, and tentatively, touched his arm.

When someone spoke again, Noa was surprised to find it was she herself.

"She's my sister too," she said clearly, voice steady and strong, standing once more on her own. Judah and Hilo pulled apart to look at her. They looked as if they'd been eviscerated, wrecked— but now put back together right.

Noa focused on her words. "Her name is Sasha now, and when I was above, I think I heard where she is." The room remained so quiet, Noa heard every beat of her own heart. "They say Darius has a new weapon, a secret weapon beyond any power ever seen. As Callum said, powers must be *performed* by Fae, and Sasha ... well, you know what she could do."

Callum began to wheeze. "The very thing ... I failed ... I failed..."

Noa reached out to touch him, or hold him maybe, she didn't know—because before she did, the cave door exploded into a million flying rocks, and jaws of deep black water roared into the room.

• • •

THE FLOOD OF liquid blackness pummeled Noa's body backward and crushed her against the wall. There was no air, no Stellalight, no warmth: only freezing, torrential water swirling and pounding in every inch of the room.

It went everywhere: drumming in Noa's ears, ripping through her hair, swelling in her nostrils, spuming in her mouth. Her tongue bloated with minty salt; her eyes stung and blurred because there'd been no time to blink them. Swirling eddies tossed her and the others like dead rats in tiger jaws: they slammed up to the ceiling, hurled down into the walls, spun and flipped and churned in currents seething angrily out the door.

No amount of flailing could prevent their passage. They tumbled, smashing past jagged rocks and one another's limbs into the stronger tide pelting down the Tunnels' arteries. In these wider, central pathways, the waters moved more fiercely and erratically, as if the extra speed and space bred warring currents like Medusa's hair. Noa was slammed against one wall and then another, then up then down then up, and each impact felt as if it might be her last. Bones were breaking; joints were crunching; and she couldn't even scream.

Noa writhed, eyes bulging, swelling—when out of the rushing dark, Callum's face appeared, wavering and blurry but focused intently on hers. He was tumbling but also trying to direct his motion toward her.

Noa didn't even have time to feel relief; she smashed through stalactites that had hung from the onetime ceiling. The pain forced out what remained of her air; her brain fuzzed up, and a strange, warm calm crept over her. She opened her arms to greet it, wanted nothing more than to fall asleep in its arms—

Callum's hands grabbed onto her ankle. Sharp pain knifed through her body, exploded in her head, rattled her back into agonizing consciousness.

Noa struggled, tried to kick Callum away; she wanted to go back to the warm, the calm—but he held her fast, fingers biting into her leg like a metal vice—

And suddenly, her body gasped. Like her lungs had filled with oxygen. She arched her back, muscles spasming with the rushing feeling of breathing air. The current pushed her into somersaults and raked Callum, still gripping hard onto her ankle, against the floor, the walls.

Noa opened her mouth to breathe again but only choked on water; her lungs had never cleared at all. But Callum was still gripping her, and her *body* gasped again. This time, Noa felt it—the relief wasn't from her chest, but from her back. Her shoulders flexed and arched; Callum struggled to stay attached; and Noa understood:

Callum was giving her gills.

Noa tried to see through the dark translucence, suddenly wanting, *needing* to see Callum's eyes. But his face was contorted with concentration, so much, in fact, that he didn't see the jutting rock until the current slammed him into it, headfirst, tearing him from Noa's leg.

Noa shot forward far past Callum, screaming uselessly into the water, body choking again. She tried to turn back but couldn't make Callum out—he was trapped against the rock, unconscious or even dead. The current whipped her around a turn, and then she could see the rock no more.

Noa swirled and tumbled, eyes stinging with salt from the water and probably tears. Her gills were gone, her lungs exploding, every part of her body swelled and begged her to just *breathe in*, breathe in deeply and finally, finally go to sleep….

Big arms, Noa.

Noa blinked into the dark, harsh flood, and suddenly she was standing on a diving board, the water moving clear and blue beneath her. Her dad was on the pool deck holding up two orange water wings, designed to go around toddler arms to keep them afloat while they learned to swim.

Noa furrowed her brow, confused. She didn't need those anymore. She was past the days of sandwich hands and blowing bubbles.

Those are Sasha's, Noa told Christopher. *I already know how to swim.*

Christopher looked at her quizzically, like she was telling him a joke. *Who's Sasha?*

Noa looked down: beneath the diving board, the water now peaked and crested violently. She could not see clearly beneath the surface. Then through the blur, she caught a flicker, a little hand like a starfish. She heard a small voice, but muffled, as if underwater far away.

Where?

Urgency ignited inside Noa, pushed like fire up through her throat.

Did you see that? she called frantically to Christopher, but her father's face was blank. Noa had no time. She grabbed the water wings from his hands, popped open the plastic filling tube, sucked in air.

Without pausing to explain, she dove into the water, stroking hard.

• • •

NOA'S EYES FLICKERED; her body was still whirling in the current, but the pain in her chest had loosened. Her mind fluttered with growing clarity. She had no energy to fight, to swim, but she somehow knew she had the air to ride it out. Her whole existence shrank to the Tunnel, everything vacuumed away but water, movement, and survival.

Suddenly, harsh, bright light reached around Noa from all sides. Its fingers strangled the flood's throat, squeezed and squeezed until the water broke into thunderous spray. Noa sputtered, gasped in the flood's explosive disintegration. Her arms spun madly, her legs kicked out, and she realized she was falling, shot from the Tunnel's exit as from a blasting cannon of waterfall.

Noa's body processed the change more quickly than her mind. Her arms and legs pulled in, curled pill bug–style, like Sasha in their shared duvet. When Noa finally hit the trench below, the slap of water ripped across her outside skin, but her face was safely guarded, eyes squeezed shut tight. She plunged under and down quickly; her legs unfurled to push against the sandy floor. Then she was shooting upward, hands and arms beating fast, and breaking through the surface like a mermaid. She flipped her hair back, faced the sun, and breathed in deeply.

Then she opened her eyes—and screamed.

Callum and Judah were in the rocky shallows, lolling in the tide. Facedown in the water.

Neither one was moving.

• • •

"CALLUM! JUDAH!" NOA screamed, swimming madly toward the two limp bodies. Her muscles spasmed in their sudden restoration of oxygen, hobbling her stride. She forced through it, half swimming, half doggy-paddling to the horrible, oddly peaceful scene.

When Noa finally reached where she could stand, she stumbled up, crashing through the water at a slogging run. She finally reached the edge of the rocky shore and fell upon their softly drifting bodies. Judah's hand, Noa saw now, was tangled in Callum's shirt. He had pried his brother loose from that snagging rock back in the Tunnel.

"No!" Noa cried, flipping both brothers over. "No, no, no!" Both were stone still, eyes closed; Callum had a deep gash across his forehead; blood ran messily across his face.

Noa looked frantically from one to the other, not knowing what to do. She screamed in desperation and fell to Callum's side, pressing into his chest to give him CPR. She counted the compressions then leaned down to breathe into his mouth, her wet hair tangled and sliding down her face. His lips were cold and tasted bitter, a mix of metallic blood and choking mint. And she didn't get that tingle—that tingle she always felt when they touched.

Noa pressed and pressed, but there was no life; so she pressed harder, as hard as she could and more. Then finally, finally, after moments that were centuries, millennia, eons, Callum coughed and sputtered, hacking up a torrent of black water.

"Noa..." he groaned, blinking toward her.

This was no time for a reunion kiss.

"Heal him!" Noa cried, yanking Callum upward with all the force she had, ignoring how he winced.

Callum squinted as he focused on the body beside him. Judah. Adrenaline spiked him to attention. He put his hands on his fallen brother, eyes intent through blood still pouring down his face.

Nothing happened.

"Why isn't it working!" Noa demanded.

"I don't know," Callum muttered through tense, clenched teeth, straining so much his wound gushed more. "I don't—"

"Oh my God! What is *that*?" Noa shrieked, pointing madly to Judah's face. Black sludge had begun to leak from Judah's nose. Not like the water; thicker, much thicker, like molasses deep and rich.

Callum didn't answer, but his eyes were terrified. He clenched Judah even harder, sending Judah all his Light—

Judah's body suddenly spasmed, contorting in a seizure; Callum was flung backward through the air and slammed into the rocky bank.

"Judah! Judah!" Noa pleaded, trying and failing to grab Judah's flailing, seizing arms. "Judah!" she screamed, as his eyes opened and rolled up into his head, leaving white blanks behind.

"Noa, be careful!" Callum strained from behind her as he tried to pull himself to his feet. But Noa didn't listen, couldn't; she finally caught Judah's arms, tried to pin his body down. But his legs were seizing too, even more rapidly now—his knee smacked hard into her stomach, taking out her wind. She gasped but refused to relinquish her hold upon his arms. With no breath to speak, she could only think her pleas to him instead, though of course he wouldn't hear her.

Judah, wake up!

173

A snap of electricity burst beneath her palms, burning the place where she'd grasped his skin. Noa screamed in pain just as Judah's other leg connected with her ribs and sent her toppling to the side. She landed facefirst, tasted the nutty roundness of the bank, hands sizzling with pain.

Noa groaned, stumbled to her knees. Beside her, Judah's seizing body stilled.

Dead.

Noa watched him, unable to believe it. His face was white, and wet, and cold. And then she believed it, all too well. She knew death. She knew the feeling of death beside her, of her shoulder beneath its hand. Death had become her patron saint.

Then, absurdly, Judah gasped, springing up with wild eyes.

Callum half-ran, half-crawled to Noa, who was stunned, paralyzed. Sure what she saw could not be real.

"Judah?" She doubled over in pain as she tried to touch him; she needed to touch him to know it was the truth.

Judah was panting, trembling, running his hands through his dark, wet curls. He wiped at his nose, smearing away the brackish sludge.

Then Callum's hands were on Noa's arms, trying to help her up, but she struggled to get past him.

"Your rib is broken, Noa, wait!"

But she needed to touch Judah, touch him now. Because he really had been dead. Noa knew it, she had felt it.

But Callum was blocking her; he wouldn't move. A healing warmth shone outward from her rib cage. When the bone had knit, she finally broke free, half-crashing into Judah.

"Are you okay?" she asked, reaching for him, taking his hands. She realized Callum was steadying her from behind, the only thing keeping her from face-planting in the mud.

Judah looked toward Noa with cloudy eyes, relief pouring over him as he found her face.

"Hilo..."

"Stop right there!"

The sudden, slicing voice made them all turn as one: Arik stood above them, above the Tunnel's outspout. An unbroken line of Clear Patrolmen stretched from him in both directions around the shore.

Noa, Judah, and Callum were entirely surrounded.

PART III: PRISON

THE SILVER BOOTS were closing in, a swiftly tightening noose.

"Your *faces*," Noa hissed, digging her nails into Callum's shoulder. He was frozen by Judah, staring, but the pain snapped him into action. He grabbed Judah's forearms and bent his forehead to his brother's, ignoring Judah's confused muttering.

"Separate them!" Arik's voice rang out, and just like that, two rough hands yanked Noa up and away as if she were some irksome weed. More hands grabbed Judah and Callum and twisted them apart. Noa screamed as something like handcuffs burned around her wrists, and whatever hands were holding her spun her so she was facing outward, Callum and Judah in full view.

They no longer looked quite like themselves.

In the split second that he'd had, Callum had managed to slightly alter both their faces: their cheeks were rounder and paler, without the cutting Forsythe cheekbones. Their usually olive skin was pink and splashed with freckles. The shape of their eyes was also different, more almond, though that change was subtle—but that hair, those Forsythe curls, Callum's regal posture and the glint in Judah's eye … Noa still knew them both in the splittest heartbeat.

Would Arik?

The whippish Captain didn't hurry. Arik took his time, sauntered toward his prisoners, the long sword at his belt accenting his height. Each step was even, patient.

To Noa, that made it worse.

"Reward the pixie," Arik told one of his men as he breached their line. "Never liked Greenies much, but her tip was good."

The lieutenant—squatter, broader, more in the mold of his muscle-bound comrades—nodded once and stomped away.

Noa tried not to look at Judah, but couldn't stop herself. He'd clearly regained his faculties; his now-rosy lip was curled, his now-rounded eyes sharp with hate. She could practically hear him seething. *Hilo.*

Arik walked first to Judah, who was pinned between two burly Guards. Not that they needed much strength to hold him; Judah's face was fierce but his body sagged, knees bent, toes dragging on the ground. Arik lifted Judah's new chin, stared at him sharply.

The Captain squinted as he studied Judah's features minutely. He turned Judah's head abruptly from side to side, examining his profile. Then he shoved Judah's face away impatiently. Arik seemed to ponder something intently for a moment, then he looked back at Judah with a rueful smile.

"That expression," he said, as if amused. "It's you I saw in the Work Sector, isn't it? *You* caused all that trouble. For days now I've been haunted, thinking I saw a ghost! But it was only *you.*"

He laughed harshly, and white spittle hit Judah's cheek. Judah's scowl deepened.

Arik leaned in close, his face only a millimeter from Judah's. "But of course, that would have been impossible," he hissed smugly. "Not from that useless mongrel."

Arik straightened up, somehow looking even taller now, as if a great weight had been lifted from his shoulders. He turned to Callum carelessly, raked him up and down. Unlike Judah, Callum was hard for the Guards to hold. It took four patrolmen to immobilize him, and he was heaving and lurching, primed with anger.

"Restrain him," Arik said lazily, and a fifth Guard belted him across the forehead with the blunt end of his sword. Callum's gash reopened, leaking blood down his face.

Callum's eyes met Noa's, resolute.

"Don't even think about it," Arik warned Callum, suddenly not so careless, and with his sword pressed right up against Noa's throat. "Or I'll start with *her*."

Callum froze.

Arik smiled, let the tip of his sword travel slowly down Noa's chest. It was so sharp it cut right through the top of the soaking Clear Fae robes she still was wearing, which were now nothing more than a sopping, dirty blob of heavy rags.

Arik stopped his sword a few inches below Noa's collarbone, revealing her long, lengthwise scar. He leered. "Been caught before, pixie?"

Noa didn't answer, but Callum looked ready to detonate. She glanced pleadingly toward him—Judah was too weak, there were too many Guards, they'd never get away. Callum's eyes were fire, but he nodded minutely.

Arik saw it all, supremely amused. He walked toward Callum, chucked him tauntingly under the chin, then turned to his nearest lieutenant.

"These are the ones who caused the mayhem in the Work Sector. Take them to the prison."

"For Review?" asked Noa's captor immediately, grip tightening in a sickening kind of excitement.

Arik glared at him. "They came out of the Tunnels," he replied, obviously annoyed. "Interrogate them first. Find out what they know. If there's anything *to* know. After that you can have your little ... *show*." Arik's mouth curled in distaste. His patrolmen evidently didn't share his revulsion; they murmured excitedly what Noa knew was a very messy prospect.

Noa's stomach turned. She looked up to see Arik studying her face guardedly.

One of Callum's Guards was also looking her way, watery eyes moving sinuously from her face to scar to...

"We could recycle that one a different way," he suggested, voice oddly higher than Noa would have expected. She shivered beneath his gaze, the way those eyes took their time. The tip of his tongue wet his bottom lip. "If she's Green, I mean, that's some Joy Juice worth a try—"

Arik's icy glare cut off his lieutenant.

"We are the Otec's highest Guard," he said softly. "Remember that."

Callum's Guard bowed his head, and Noa breathed out. She hadn't realized she'd been holding her breath.

Arik gestured to his cadre, and one of the Guards from the back brought forward a limp, bedraggled boy with glassy eyes, no more than nine years old. The boy's tufted brown hair was uneven and fell into his eyes; Noa could tell it had been months since a mother's tender hand had cut it back. One ear was bigger than the other. He was still growing into them. Noa couldn't tear her eyes from the freckles on his arms.

But Arik didn't even look at the boy. He just slapped his hand to his chest as if swatting an irksome fly, and the boy's back spasmed awkwardly as popping noises electrified the air. The shallow water of the bank funneled upward, along with rocks and weeds and sludgy mud, and spiraled toward the bank. It spread, breeding outward into something like an amoeba, then resolved itself into a horse, pawing and snorting onshore. Arik flung the boy down; his knobby adolescent knees made a faint *splat* as his body careened into the shallows. Then Arik strode to the horse and mounted. The Guard who had produced the boy picked him up like a dripping sack of potatoes and flung him over the back of Arik's saddle, tying him down with cargo cables.

Without another word, Arik rode away.

The remaining Guards closed in, the captors all tightening their grip.

Judah's eyes were flickering as he fought to remain conscious. Noa looked at Callum: *Interrogation ... Review ... recycling ...* none of it sounded good.

Not to mention that wherever they were being taken, there would absolutely be alarms. Which meant Callum's disguises were soon going to do more harm than good.

Callum's face was furrowed deeply; Noa knew he'd realized it, too. She barely had time to pray that Callum could work out some amazing plan, some way to save them—

—when green mist fogged around them all, and the world shimmered away.

• • •

NOA CAME TO in the dark. She was lying on something hard, and her hands were still bound behind her. But the hard surface was also moving, jostling from side to side, and the air was pungent and stuffy, a little like it had been in the shed where she and Marena had hidden. It smelled like decomposition, like rotting fruit.

The floor jolted upward, and Noa crashed onto her side and realized she was in some kind of vehicle that had gone over a bump. With her hands bound, she couldn't break her fall, and her shoulder took the impact.

Noa groaned quietly in pain—not wanting to alert any Guards that might be lurking in the dark nearby—and heard a tiny moan echo beside her. She twisted herself around using her legs and blinked rapidly, willing her eyes to try to adjust. Finally she saw the shadow of Judah's shape, also bound and toppled on its side.

Noa strained to look around: they were in an enclosed square, like the back of a loading truck. She didn't see Guards, but behind Judah's lump, Noa saw long, lean legs sprawling, tangled and awkward.

Callum.

"Judah?" Noa whispered. "Are you awake?"

Judah didn't answer; his unconscious body rolled over limply as they jolted up again. Another moan pinged off the compartment walls—and Noa realized the sound wasn't from him; it was coming from behind her. She rolled herself over again, biting back a yelp as she pressed down on her bruised shoulder and looked for the source of the noise.

She saw the source of the smell instead.

There was a pile behind her, a heaping mountain of figments resolving in the dark. It had knobs, and sticks ... Noa bit back a cry of terror: not knobs and sticks, but arms and legs. It was a pile of dirty bodies, skin and bones and rags—all unmoving. All dead.

The little moan sounded again. It seemed to come from the bottom of the pile.

"Is someone alive in there?" Noa whispered.

The buried voice moaned again, but this time it sounded like a word: "*Cuffs...*"

Noa breathed through her mouth, forced herself to squint more closely at the pile of bodies. The truck jolted and Noa slid right into the hanging arms and legs, clammy and damp against her skin. She heaved, gagging, twisting away—and came face-to-back with a pair of handcuffed arms.

The rotting smell invaded her, but she swallowed it to examine what she saw. The cuffs were twined alarm tubes, almost welded to the wrists.

The ground suddenly stopped moving. Noa froze in panic as the back wall of the cargo bay slid up. The sudden light blinded her; she flinched but made out the silhouettes of two Guards outside—

Then green fog clouded all around her again, and everything blurred away.

• • •

THIS TIME, NOA'S ears woke up before her muscles, before she could even lift her eyelids. She could feel that she was being dragged over ragged land, like gravel, but though she couldn't struggle, she could hear voices fading in and out.

"Overcrowding…" one said, annoyed.

A second, squeakier voice chuckled. "Enough to finish the alarms…"

"Serves them right." The first voice again; a woman's. "… treated us before. Watch the gate."

The ground under Noa changed from rocky dirt to something smooth and cold. This lasted for a while, then she felt herself pulled across a little ledge with a metal lip, followed by rougher ground, stony but uneven. Here the dragging stopped, her arms released, followed by a clanging noise.

"Hey, these look different to you?" The woman's voice, this time a few feet farther away.

"Nah. You're just not used to seeing cullies clean," Squeaky laughed, voice fading into the sound of retreating footsteps.

Finally, much fainter, as if from down a long hallway, the woman again: "All unloaded. Tell him we're running out of room."

After that, silence. Just the hard, pockmarked ground, the taste of stale, thick air, and the pain of being heaped on her sore shoulder.

Later—hours or moments, Noa couldn't tell—a tingling of pins and needles spiked through her limbs, followed by a dragging feeling of muscles waking after having been asleep. Noa tried to flex them tenderly, then pushed herself slowly and awkwardly into a sitting position. She blinked her heavy eyes. It was dark again—not pitch black, but dank, lavender-gray, as if outside it was nighttime.

And she was in a cell.

One of a line of cells, facing another line of cells, in what appeared to be a dungeon.

"A pixie, just my luck," a scratchy voice croaked from right behind her.

Noa turned her tingling body painfully. She wasn't alone in her cell: a toothless, wrinkled man smiled from the corner.

His smile shook Noa to her bones.

"Who are you?" she asked, trying to keep her voice even as she moved her hands slowly backward, hoping to feel some kind of makeshift weapon on the floor. Her manacles had been severed, though each wrist was still circled by its own alarm-tube bracelet.

"Free hands won't do you any good," the old man laughed, eyes glinting.

"Who are you?" Noa repeated, more firmly. Dimly she remembered reading that in prison, fear was seen as weakness.

"Cullies have no names," the old man replied. "Trying to trip me up?" His tone was friendly, but Noa flinched. *He's just some geezer*, she told herself, hoping the name would make her brave.

Geezer smiled again, this time showing broken, rotting teeth. "I was alive when those Clears were nobodies, powerless vermin. But this *Otec*." Geezer chuckled. "He'll have the last laugh, won't he."

Geezer leaned toward her, into a pool of moonlight. "Welcome to the Place of No Return, pixie." Noa shuddered despite herself. He slowly hunched his ancient body upward, got creakily to his feet. Noa was reminded unpleasantly of Kells, the curmudgeonly Harlow groundskeeper who'd turned out to be a Banished Fae—and who'd lived so long out of Aurora that he'd rotted from the inside out.

Geezer grinned a chilling Kells-like grin. "I haven't had a cell mate in a while, and certainly not a pixie." He began to limp toward her from his corner. "They must *really* be running out of room. Prince Arik, such an overachiever." Noa scrabbled sideways until she hit a wall behind her, but Geezer had somehow closed in quickly. A jagged birthmark split one cheek; his wrinkles were so black they looked like mold instead of skin. Noa didn't know what he intended, but she could feel his fetid breath, could taste its rot—

—and the wall behind her clanged terribly, startling them both.

"Get back, old man," Judah's voice growled from somewhere across the wall. Noa spun, stumbled to her feet: Judah was in the next cell, alert, seething through the tiny, square barred window in their cells' shared wall.

Something in Judah's face made Geezer back up slowly, hands up, but the old man didn't drop his smile. He shuffled back into his shadowed corner, and Noa had the terrible feeling that he wasn't so much intimidated as willing to bide his time.

In that moment, though, she didn't care.

Noa whirled to clutch at Judah's hands through the small square of bars. She had never been so happy to see his face—

"Oh no—your face!"

Judah put his hands to his face. "What?"

"It's … it's yours again."

"*Noa?*" It was Callum's voice, also from that cell, but from somewhere behind and below. It was very groggy and confused.

Judah glared accusingly behind him toward the ground, where Noa assumed Callum must be lying. "You idiot!" he hissed.

"What?" Callum murmured, clearly dazed.

"We're us again! Put back the disguises!"

"Callum, are you okay?" Noa asked, straining on tiptoe, trying to see around the back of Judah's neck.

"How'd we get here?" Callum muttered, slurring.

Behind Noa, Geezer chuckled throatily.

"Zip it, old man," Judah warned, his fierce face filling the frame again.

Geezer sneered, showing those rotted, hole-filled gums, all pretense of friendliness now gone. "So one of you's a Blue. Be grateful they hit you with the Smoke when they did, boy, or whichever of you is the Mask Master would have set off the prison alarms."

"The Smoke?" Noa asked.

Geezer picked at his fingers, drawling. "This Otec is so *innovative*. The alarms, the Smoke..."

"What's the Smoke?" Judah demanded.

Geezer smiled his Kells smile again. "Powdered Green Fae of course. Knocks your limbic system right out." He moved toward Noa again, eyes glittering. *"Wanna know how they make it, pixie?"*

Noa recoiled instinctively, hitting the wall again. Judah was somewhere in his cell, jostling Callum. "Get up and help and figure this out, Cal—" He cut off, covered quickly. *"Blue."*

Noa heard Callum heave to his feet, then his face wobbled to the small square window. Judah's popped up next to him, shoving him to the side.

"Back off," Judah warned Geezer, who shuffled back again, muttering darkly.

Noa turned back to the brothers and stifled a gasp. She hadn't noticed before, but they were both terribly gray and wan. She hoped it was only a side effect of the Smoke.

She swallowed, whispered through the opening, "I think I heard the Guards who brought us in talking…. I don't think they noticed your faces—"

"But if Arik comes—"

Geezer snorted from the corner: "Arik dirty in the slaughterhouse, that'd be the day."

A high, shrill voice—not one Noa remembered—exploded down the hall. "Stop all that screechy!"

"Here comes Crazy," Geezer muttered, slinking deeper into the shadows.

Noa looked through the sliding door of bars that opened to the cell hallway. Across the aisle, in the first cell facing hers, an almost-deranged pixie prisoner was glaring right at Noa. The pixie wasn't old like Geezer, but her body looked desiccated: her red hair was gnarled and matted into filthy dreadlocks; her cheeks were sunken holes that seemed to swallow light. Her gray ragshirt was torn across the front in five slashes—probably, Noa realized, from her own long, curling yellow fingernails.

"Come back, come back, it's okay," a soothing voice said from behind the pixie. A tired, male Fae stepped from the shadows and put a calming hand on Crazy's shoulder, bowing his forehead tenderly toward hers. This Fae looked like the young man he was: his hair was inky black and thick, luxurious even in the dankness of the dungeon. He was classically handsome, like a silent-movie star.

"Too long, too long, too long," Crazy muttered, fidgeting impatiently from his touch. She curled her spidery fingers— with those nails—around the cell-door bars and rocked herself against them, back and forth. "Puddles and muddles, puddles and muddles, puddles and muddles..." she muttered, each hiss building in hysteria.

"Come back and rest," Movie Star urged her gently, calmly. He put his hands on her shoulders, light and slow, as she rocked and muttered. Finally she turned to him in surprise, as if just realizing he was there; her bony shoulders curled toward him like a little girl's, and she let him guide her back into the darkness.

Noa retreated from the cell door, crossing her arms and her hands up and down her arms.

"Been here a while, those two. Not as long as me, but my mind is strong," Geezer told Noa from the shadows. "Take a peek into your future, sweetness. Ain't no way outta here."

• • •

THE SCARIEST PART of prison, Noa decided, was that there was nothing to do but wait. Wait for sleep, wait for morning, wait for Crazy's shrieks into the night. Wait for Callum and Judah to drift in and out, still not recovered, wait for Geezer to make his move. Wait in silence, in cold, in the whisper of shadows....

Then seamlessly, a new kind of waiting began: wait for the Guard with the mustache to walk down the row at sunrise, dragging his nightstick past the bars. Wait for that staccato thunking to repeat, reverberate, every ten minutes when he made the trip again. Wait for the squeaky-voiced Guard to clean the strange glass room at the top of the Ward—some kind of watching station, Noa assumed—whose windows had to be kept perfectly clear. Wait for the Guard with the tattoo on his eye—a spider, his pupil the fat, black body—to shove a piece of hard bread at every prisoner, cell by cell, six intervals into Mustache's rounds.

Wait for evening, for Crazy to hurl her stone of bread—always uneaten—toward the ward's jaw-like gate. Wait for those metal teeth to sense the movement and crash down, pulverizing the bread to dust.

Wait.

Noa would have given anything for pen and paper. She felt her mind becoming numb, caught between the spokes of prison-pattern, prison-routine, like some relentless metronome. Were the bars what locked her in, or these repeating rituals—precise, perpetual—that wore more deeply with each day? Her spirit strained; she ached for wild freedom—not of her body, but her mind.

"Marena," Noa murmured. The pixie who'd lived among the cages, but somehow never been confined. Noa was slumped against the bars in the late afternoon of her sixth imprisoned day, staring out into the hall; it was one of those endless moments— after Spider-Eye but before the next shift change—when daily monuments were far apart, and only nothingness remained. Noa longed to see the ghost of Marena's face—or Isla's, or Sasha's—but they didn't visit here.

Noa was not being a girl-beast, and they knew it.

Stop whining you dolt! Only a gob would need paper and pen!

Noa closed her eyes. She couldn't see Marena, but she could conjure her voice. And Marena was right. Noa was better than this. Marena hadn't sacrificed herself for Noa to waste away, to become— like her mother had in that home so far away—the moon.

So Noa kept her eyes closed, made her mind a canvas, her thoughts the pen, and wrote herself back to fullness with Marena as her guide:

Mar is the sea
but not this sea
not these predictable currents
not these precise, breaking waves.

Mar is a riptide
the flow under the flow—
she sinks where they rise,
retracts where they push.

Beware swimmers, who use only your eyes
hypnotized by peaks cresting
and neat lines of foam.
Mar's fingers are seaweed, the deep and the dark,
Mar's whirlpools are hidden
spinning down coral shoals.

Seagirl stop stroking
in peak, crest, and fill—
See instead with your skin
with your scales
with your gills.

When Noa opened her eyes, she felt, for the first time since
waking in this place, that she could breathe.

Evening was falling. Like clockwork, Crazy began to moan
with the dark. It had been ten hours since Spider-Eye had
opened the silver supply chute, retrieved the day's sack of dry
bread, and doled out rock-hard lumps with his signature sneer.

Ten hours of Movie Star quietly urging Crazy to eat—and, like every day, failing.

Reaching her coda, Crazy slammed herself into the bars and screeched, hurling her bread toward the ward's front gate. Sensing motion, the gate's teeth raised and smashed down upon it, pulverizing the 'insurgent' instantly to dust. The thundering echo rattled every bar in the row, mixing ominously with Crazy's endless, looping "*Puddles and muddles!*"

As the echo slowly dissipated, Crazy collapsed into a whimpering heap. "*Puddles, muddles, puddles, muddles...*" Movie Star knelt by her side, stroked her tangled red hair, the way he always did.

Noa sighed softly. The inevitability felt like dangerous quicksand. She longed to talk to Judah and Callum, even if only through the tiny cell window, but she could hear the silence in their cell. The brothers had suffered a much more protracted withdrawal from the Smoke. Exhaustion still flattened them unexpectedly, knocking them out cold sometimes even in the middle of a sentence.

Noa cast a wary eye toward Geezer's shadowy corner. He'd been unnervingly silent these days—sleeping too, or so it appeared. But Noa could feel something thrumming beneath all this silence, this lulling routine. She repeated the lines of her poem in her head, willing her mind to remain sharp, but beyond her, Crazy's whimpering was winding down to silence, right on schedule, the pattern concluding, continuing, anesthetizing—

And then it exploded.

"You can't do this to us!"

Noa ran to the bars. The screech hadn't come from Crazy. It was Movie Star, no longer silent. He was howling like an animal, handsome face contorted in rage, fists shaking the bars.

"You're taking her mind! Her *mind!*" Anger seethed through him, obliterated the careful caretaker he had been. Noa couldn't look away, even as every Guard ignored him.

"*You can't do this to her!*" he yelled wildly at their indifferent backs. "She has to get out!"

Not even a glance.

Movie Star's face twisted horribly, became deranged. It was the *ignoring*, Noa knew, the willful *not* hearing, *not* seeing. He was not only imprisoned, he was being *erased*.

She knew what he was going to do before he did it.

Movie Star howled in rage and alarms split the air, screeching from the tube bracelets around his wrists, now strobing virulent green. A pulse of pure hatred blasted down the hall; its shock wave flung Noa back into her cell as Movie Star hurled every bit of violent loathing that he had. The Guards definitely noticed him now; the hatred lashed across their faces like burning whips, leaving sizzling marks across jaws and eyes and cheeks.

Mustache and Squeaky charged Movie Star's cell, flung back the bars to tackle, pummel, destroy him. Spider-Eye joined the fray, dragging two unconscious Color Fae behind him. Movie Star screamed as Spider-Eye first Channeled Red to tear into his mind and fry his brain, then Channeled Blue to snake him with razor-sharp cables, conjured from the floor. Movie Star's body thrashed against the bladed noose tightening around him, slicing off its own flesh to the bone. Chunks slopped messily into blood down around his feet; Movie Star slipped in the marsh of his own matter and juices, writhed on the now-sticky, tacky floor—

And then the woman came.

Noa could tell right away she was a senior officer. She wore the special silver stripe of Captain that Noa had seen on Arik, but far more noticeable was the fact that she was missing an ear. A mottled stump led into an ugly, dark scar that sliced down half her face and pulled her mouth into a twisted, terrible scowl.

The Captain barely glanced at Movie Star's still-alive carcass, writhing and whimpering on the floor. Her eyes wandered past him to *her*—Crazy, the pixie Movie Star was so desperate to protect. The one he clearly loved.

The Captain nodded lightly at the Guards. Spider-Eye hoisted Crazy over his shoulder. For once, she made no sound. Mustache, scowling in disgust, picked up what was left of the dripping, oozing Movie Star, and Squeaky grabbed the feet of the two unconscious Channeling slaves to drag them up the hall. They all followed the Captain to the little glass room at the front of the ward, the one whose windows Squeaky cleaned so religiously. The Guard station visible to every cell, yet for some reason never used.

"Keep him conscious," the Captain said. Noa realized she recognized the Captain's voice—she was the woman who had supervised their imprisonment with Squeaky. Spider-Eye deposited Crazy inside the glass room, then came back out and grabbed Movie Star's squishy, dripping shoulder and one of the unconscious Color-Fae slaves. He Channeled Red once more, and Noa saw the light flare wildly back into Movie Star's eyes. Movie Star's body remained in ruins, but, sickeningly, Noa knew, he could now see and process everything.

Spider-Eye and Mustache hoisted Movie Star right up against the outer window of the glass Guard station, forcing him to watch whatever was to come inside. A sludge of bloody goop dripped from Movie Star's mangled body down the windowpane.

The Captain entered the glass room where Crazy was slumped, shell-shocked. The Captain moved meticulously, like a doctor, and delicately put on a pair of white plastic gloves.

The Woman with White Hands.

Noa bit her lip hard, tasting blood.

The Captain took something from her breast pocket, something delicate and silver, and clasped it around her wrist. Noa squinted, trying to see it better, then recoiled as the woman suddenly throttled Crazy's throat with those clinical white-gloved hands.

Crazy's eyes bulged and swelled as the Captain strangled her; her mouth flew open to scream, but no sound came out. Noa was thankful at least for that, to be spared the screams—and then she realized how much worse that made it.

It wasn't that simple, what the Captain was doing—she wasn't just choking Crazy, taking her breath. As the Guards forced Movie Star to watch—the one who had urged Crazy to eat, who had calmed her night after night—Crazy's face melted like a grotesque candle, eyes and mouth oozing away, her whole head liquefying into jelly. Noa understood then why the Captain had put on those white gloves: the pixie's remains spilled down and through her fingers, thick and viscous and darkest red. It didn't stop at Crazy's head, either: the melting spread downward, rendering arms, legs, and torso like pig fat until the pixie was no more than red slop on the floor.

The one-eared Captain stayed impassive, but Noa saw the tiny glint of triumph in her eye as she nodded briskly outside. It was then that Noa realized she had summoned an entire squad of Guards—twelve, probably any and all on duty from the active wards—and they had gathered eagerly, gleefully, noses practically pressed against the glass for the show.

The Guard the Captain had summoned wasn't one Noa knew. He was broad and hulking, with bunched-up shoulders, and dragged an unconscious Blue behind him. Channeling the Blue, Shoulders made the Red sludge that had been Crazy pool together and then fill a long silver canister in his hand. Still Channeling, he put his palm over the canister's top and neatly sealed it off.

Noa almost vomited as she recognized the fluid in the canister: it was the same fluid that ran in the alarms around the city. The gallons and gallons and gallons of fluid.

The fluid then ran in the tubes around her own wrists.

At the glass wall of the room, the thing that had been Movie Star strangled out a gargled, searing moan. In her horror, Noa had forgotten that he was watching too, that however horrific the scene had been for her, it was so much worse for him.

"Let him bleed there," the Captain said, handing off her soiled gloves to be thrown away. Shoulders handed her the filled canister of Red fluid, and the Captain promptly walked to the supply shaft—where Spider-Eye received the prisoners' daily bread—and pushed it through the swinging silver door. There was a slight *swoosh* as the canister was sucked away.

Finally, carefully, the Captain unclasped the bracelet-type thing from her wrist and gave it to Mustache. She tossed her head toward the trembling carcass of Movie Star. "When he loses consciousness, Review him too. We could use more Green now that we're making the Smoke."

The Captain then turned her twisted face to the ward. Noa shivered. In Aurora, the Captain could easily have had her injury healed by a Blue. She had *chosen* to remain monstrous.

"Let this be a reminder," she said calmly, commanding every prisoner's attention with no need to raise her voice. "Do not resist, do not rebel, and above all, do not *defend*." Her gaze seemed to wander directly to Noa, who shrank back despite herself. "If you try," she continued softly, "you will watch as those you seek to protect are punished for your sins."

Then the Captain turned toward the Guards and said the worst thing of all:

"Interrogations tomorrow. Ready the Reds."

• • •

"SURE YOU DON'T want to enjoy your last night, pixie?" Geezer hissed in Noa's ear that night, waking her from a troubled sleep. He trailed a bent finger, jagged with a broken nail, in a circle around her shoulder where she had been curled against the wall they shared with the brothers' cell. Noa's eyes snapped open and she shoved him back with flailing arms and feet. His lined face became clearer in the darkness: he was laughing at her.

"Come on, Blondie, we're all gonna be oozed.... I may be the last Fae face you see."

"Get back," Noa snarled. Geezer's eyes danced as he glanced at the window above her head, the one that connected to the next cell. It was still empty. "Seems your protectors are weaklings, girlie. That Smoke done did them in."

Noa kicked out at Geezer again; he retreated a little, eyes still glittering.

Noa heard a little *thunk* in the dark beside her. She reached behind her and found a piece of the rock-hard prison bread, stale and gnawed into a sharp, shard-like blade. When Geezer circled closer again, she didn't hesitate; she leapt forward and stabbed him in the stomach. He yelped in surprise, falling backward, looking in confusion at the trickling blood in the center of his shirt.

From the next cell, Judah chuckled. Noa and Geezer looked up at the window; he wasn't there, but his whisper came across clean as ice.

"Guess she protects herself."

Geezer frowned angrily but retreated to his corner, slumping down in a hulk. He faced the wall, muttering, and through his gray rag of a shirt, Noa saw his old ribs curled away from her.

Noa sighed heavily and sat with her back against the wall separating her from Judah. She could feel him now on the other side, his back leaning against the same place as hers.

"How's Cal—I mean, Blue?" she whispered.

"I'm here," Callum whispered back, voice faint and strained.

"He's next to me. I think we're finally coming out of it," Judah said.

"Just in time to be interrogated," Noa murmured, stomach sinking. "Think that's a coincidence?"

There was quiet murmuring from the other side.

Finally, Judah whispered, "Are you sure?"

Noa nodded, then remembered they couldn't see her. "I heard the Captain—not Arik, a woman. She ordered it."

Silence. When Callum finally spoke, his voice was barely audible. "We have to be careful. With what they read in our minds."

"What if they…" Noa looked through the dark at Geezer, who seemed to be lying still, but she barely breathed it all the same: "Find out about … the weapon?"

Another silence. Then Judah: "When we were back in the … your home … Fabian kept trying to break into my mind in the Club, remember? I learned to sort of … block it."

Out of the corner of her eye, Noa thought she saw Geezer twitch. Or maybe it was a shadow.

"Well when Thorn used Fabian on me, he found out nearly everything," Callum replied heavily.

"But not about Sa—the weapon," Noa pointed out.

"True. But I don't know how much longer I could have kept her—it—a secret. Besides, back then I could anchor myself to you, Noa … to your certainty, your belief in me…" He trailed off.

Noa flinched into the dark. "I still believe in you—"

"Well, *Blue*, you'll have to find a way," Judah hissed. "You owe us that."

"*You're* the one who threw Sa—the weapon—here in the first place!"

"*For the last time*, that was an *accident*—"

"*Stop*," Noa interrupted with quiet force. "Blame is not the point! The weapon's here and so are we! And we can't let Otec Darius get it, no matter what your brother issues are!" They grumbled quietly, but Noa didn't even try to hear what they were saying. "And what about me? I'm not *like* you two. Even if you hold up with your gifts, I have no chance!"

The boys answered at the same time.

"We'll protect you," Callum said, just as Judah said, "You'll just have to fight it."

Bickering broke out again.

"She's not like us, *Red*!"

"She'll have to manage!"

"How—" Noa began.

"Yeah, *how?*" Callum demanded.

"Like your plan would work? Just sacrifice ourselves trying to protect her when obviously it would be impossible?"

"No," Noa hissed, interrupting. "I mean, really, *how?* Jud—I mean, Red—how would I do it? Block it out?"

Noa heard Callum sigh, but Judah seemed to press closer to the wall. She could feel it. He began to whisper, low and clear. "Well, I guess you sort of ... see it. When Fabian was trying to invade my thoughts, I could *see* it, the threat coming in. I kind of faced it, saw all its angles, then pushed it away."

Noa frowned, struggling to understand.

"Are you a moron, Judah?" Callum muttered. He whispered urgently across the wall, "The important thing is to shield from the attack, not *look right at it*. Put the things you don't want them to know in a kind of box. Close the lid, seal it up, then push that box down deep and far away. Bury it so deep they can't find it. Then look away, and hope they do too."

"No, that's the *opposite* of what I'm saying," Judah argued.

"What you said made no sense!"

Noa breathed shakily. "I-I'll just have to do my best."

"You're stronger than you think, Noa," Callum whispered urgently, though which of them she was trying to convince, she wasn't sure. "You ransacked the Clear Province all on your own."

"I had help—"

"From a *child*," Judah whispered.

Noa's stomach twisted painfully. "You're *wrong* though, both of you," she whispered in panic, needing to explain, needing them to understand. "Marena really helped me, and it was like ... I don't know, it was like the adrenaline or something made me braver and quicker than I really am. I was able to ignore the injuries and, I don't know, common sense I normally have! It was fight or flight!"

"Well, this is too. Even more," Judah whispered unhelpfully.

"So is staying here, interrogations or not," Callum pointed out. "We need an exit plan."

"Well, we must be in the castle, right? Somewhere in the dungeon?" Judah guessed. "Maybe we can use the interrogations tomorrow to figure out more about where we are. And maybe even where the 'weapon' is being kept—"

"But I don't recognize this ward," Callum replied. "That knife-down gate is something new."

"That's my point. If we can figure out where we are, we can figure out how to break out."

Silence.

"That sounds ... like as good a plan as any, right Blue?" Noa finally whispered tentatively.

Judah scoffed. "Of course not, since I thought of it."

"That's not it," Callum murmured. Something in his voice made Noa's stomach tense. "I'm just thinking..."

"What?" Judah asked derisively.

Callum began whispering so softly, so rapidly, Noa could barely make out the words, though she was pressing as hard as she could against the wall. "Darius's quarters have to be somewhere above us. Maybe, I don't know, maybe we should go to him, maybe there's a chance that we can appeal to him, reach him, he *is* our father—"

"Are you *insane*?" Judah whisper-cried in outrage.

"No listen, he really loved me—"

"*Before!* Before you supposedly killed Lil—the weapon!"

"But if he has the weapon now, then he knows that wasn't what really happened—" Noa pointed out.

"Yeah, and you think he'll be *pleased* Cal—Blue stole it instead?"

Noa bit her lip. "He's right, Blue," she whispered.

"You just don't understand—"

"Let's get out of here first, okay? Then we can debate whether you're still the apple of psycho-Papa's eye."

Noa felt Callum's pain, wanted to soothe him. She put her palm against the wall, as if to reach to him. "We just have to be careful, Blue. Look what Darius has put in motion here. You ran from him once—"

"I know, I just—" Callum broke off. "What if I was wrong? What if I shouldn't have given up on him? I have to *try*—" His words became so soft Noa could barely hear them. "Don't people you love deserve a second chance?"

Judah huffed and Noa closed her eyes, pain fluttering in her heart. In the corner, she heard Geezer shift.

"I think…," she whispered carefully. "I think we should all try to get some rest. We need our strength for tomorrow."

Seemingly in agreement, or maybe just acquiescence, they all lay down in silence.

The next day, they came for Noa.

. . .

THE MORNING STARTED like the others: the familiar ping of the supply chute, Spider-Eye's twelve footsteps toward its silver latch, the creak as he pulled it down, the thump as he removed the sack of bread. Then his footsteps, punctuated by falling stones of staleness, down the ward.

At Noa's cell, Spider-Eye shoved two hard chunks of bread through the bars. She quickly snatched both pieces, smirked at Geezer with a curling lip.

Geezer squinted narrowly, but he made no move to challenge her, slinking back. Noa thrilled a little. Maybe she *was* stronger than she thought.

Then she heard the Captain at the front of the hall. "Intake."

Noa looked through the bars as the Captain and Squeaky dragged a new prisoner toward the cells. Noa couldn't see the prisoner very well, but she could see where the Guards were headed— to the now-empty cell that had been Movie Star and Crazy's. Noa shuddered, remembering what had happened to them—then felt incredibly angry that this place had made her someone who could have forgotten something like that, even for a moment.

Squeaky tossed the new prisoner into the back like a sack of moldy potatoes. "They hit her with a lot of Smoke. Probably be a while—"

A rock of bread suddenly soared past him and the Captain. It hit the ground and bounced toward the front gate, which slammed down and pulverized it instantly. As if the ghost of Crazy had returned.

"Who did that?" the Captain demanded furiously, turning to the ward. It was the first time Noa had heard the Captain raise her voice. Noa looked with her up and down the hall, praying it hadn't been Callum or Judah who had been so foolish. She clenched her fingers around her second piece of bread—and realized her first was gone.

Noa stumbled backward, stunned. *What did I do?*

The Captain stormed down the aisle, and Noa cowered backward, terrified—when suddenly, from every jail cell on every side, rocks of bread soared like grenades into the hall. The front gate slammed down and stretched up again and again, but even it was too slow to keep up with the onslaught. The noise of the smashing, lifting gate, of the skittering stones of bread, of the shouts of Guards and yells of prisoners was thunderous, shaking the very stone beneath their feet.

"Stop!" the Captain demanded, but the hail of bread kept coming until no one had any more to throw. For several beats after the air was clear, the front gate smashed down and up again, still struggling to keep up.

Noa was transfixed at the bars of her cell, her second piece of bread still clutched in her hand in the now-silent hallway. Somehow in this place of desolation, her fellow prisoners had risen up to save her.

"It was her!" Geezer shouted clearly from behind Noa. "I saw her!"

The Captain whirled on Noa, eyes like ice.

Noa heard a body slam into the bars of the cell beside her, heard Callum fuzzily protesting, but all Noa could see were the Captain's eyes, boring into hers.

"Interrogations start today," the Captain smile-leered. "I think you'll go first."

• • •

THE INTERROGATION ROOM was small and windowless and gray. A perfect cube, the walls pressed with flat vines like dead-eyed serpents. They left Noa in there, feet and hands bound to a hard, stark chair, and let her wait alone to imagine what was to come.

Spider-Eye came in first, holding a tray of silver instruments.

"I don't know anything," Noa heard her voice say defiantly as he began to arrange them.

Spider-Eye paused, looked at Noa as if seeing her for the first time. He studied her eyes, her lips so long it made Noa squirm.

"They say you're Tunnel Fae," he said finally, in a rumbling voice Noa realized she'd never actually heard before. He'd become so familiar, and yet, she knew with shocking clarity, he was still an unfathomable enemy. "But I'm not here to ask about that."

"Then why *are* you here?"

Spider-Eye looked at her, again with that odd, open curiosity. Not hostility, but objective fascination. "The Otec wants us to learn, challenge ourselves. Do things on our own." Spider-Eye sorted through his tray, then picked up one silver instrument, a long, sharp needle, examined it carefully and calmly. "So I'm going to experiment with these, before the questions start. Such oddities, these tools."

Then, faster than Noa could have seen or tracked, Spider-Eye whipped the needle down clear through her thigh.

• • •

NOA LIVED IN an endless loop of pain. Spider-Eye had grown old and died; the square room had crumbled away to dust; the universe Before had expanded too far, too fast, had ratcheted back and swallowed itself up. The only thing left was this rawness of flesh—not skin but *flesh* that once had been called a girl, bare flesh now for name and skin were gone. Flesh and nerves exploded to a million shards of light, constellations of a girl unwound. Raw matter for some new universe to await its own destruction. Noa was caught in it, again and again, for the cycle was inexorable: the world destroyed, life erased, eruption of the cosmos to die anew.

Then suddenly there was a face. And something changed.

On its trillionth echo, the cycle slowed and flickered—that face—and resumed, then slowed again. Then it paused and he came fully into focus—the curious man with the strange marks around his eye. Around his face, civilization rebuilt itself in four white walls, a room that was a perfect cube; Noa's cells multiplied, divided, and new limbs stretched into legs, and arms, tied to the hardness of a chair. It all wavered—here, then disappearing like a mirage—and then the face became Noa's father, leaning over her in bed.

Don't scratch, Christopher told her, his hand cool on her fiery skin. She couldn't lift her arm for some reason, not when she was lying down. But she saw it was blurry with tiny red bumps: the painful rash of scarlet fever.

Poor you, Christopher told her. *You've had this before, you know.*

Noa wanted to tell him she knew, but she had no voice; her throat felt sanded dry. She looked into his eyes instead, his calm eyes, and thought how nice it was to have a father—

"The Otec is right," Spider-Eye said, his face crashing like glass through Christopher's calm eyes. "Invention is worth the effort."

Noa tried to cry out, back in her body lashed to the chair; she heard a whimpering, high-pitched gurgle and wondered if it came from her.

"Be still," Spider-Eye told her. His rough hand clamped her shoulder. She tried to scream as again heat seared across her skin, but she couldn't—then suddenly his hand was gone, her vision was clear, and the spots of fire across her skin only throbbed, like old bruises on the bone.

Spider-Eye smiled kindly. "Some things you still need to Channel for. Can't have you bleeding all over the Captain. Now, you answer the nice lady's questions, or I'll come back for you, you hear?"

Noa could barely breathe for the relief, even as every part of her still hurt. Distantly, she could appreciate why the Guards operated this way: she was torn apart, her body rent; her brain screamed, *Tell them everything!* Her body pleaded with her to save it; her lungs sucked in the cool, cool air. She wished she could live inside that air forever.

Then suddenly, so suddenly, the Captain was looking at Noa with her slicing scar, her twisted mouth. Noa gagged to see the Captain's tortured ear-stump up close. Clearly, it had been torn, not sliced. The scars were old but still looked infected, seething, like something rancid was trapped beneath the surface.

"You and I are kindred," the Captain began. Noa looked from the stump to her eyes, startled. The Captain's eyes were soft gray, and gentle. "You're surprised to hear me say I feel kindred to a Color? Perhaps you think all Clears are the same."

The Captain leaned forward and Noa flinched, but the Captain didn't seem to notice. Her fingers gently, tentatively, went to trace the skin beneath Noa's collarbone. Noa's scar.

"You never had this healed?"

Noa swallowed. "Some scars are necessary."

The Captain leaned back slowly. "Yes. Some scars. Some crimes, even."

"H-how did you get yours?"

The Captain looked Noa in the eyes. "Tell me about the Tunnel Fae. How big is the Resistance and when did it reform?"

"I-I have no idea."

The Captain's mouth twisted down in disappointment. "I was hoping we might do this in a civil way." She sighed and gestured to the door, which immediately opened. Spider-Eye came in and deposited a dazed pixie on the ground.

Noa swallowed. A Red Channeling slave. The Captain was going to break into Noa's mind, the way Spider-Eye had bored through Noa's flesh. And Noa knew it completely in that instant: she would never be able to hide Sasha from this woman. Sasha was everywhere in Noa, in every synapse and every cell. Her chocolate curls and glittering eyes shone like beacons across the heartbeat of Noa's brain. There was no box she could lock her in, no way to bury her, no way to keep the secret safe.

Noa looked at the dazed Red pixie on the floor: she had wavy yellow hair, not messy blond variations like Noa's but yellow like the sun, or cornfields in summer light. A sunlight pixie. To bring her doom.

Noa didn't have time even to brace herself; suddenly the Captain's hands were on her and the pixie, and the room ripped apart to blinding white. To Noa's surprise, her body was not in pain—in fact, her body was not there *at all*—everything, skin and bone and flesh itself, vanished, and her whole being became like a living eye. Images flickered so fast she couldn't see one color from another. They blurred into a vibrant smudge, lightning on the ribbon of everything in her mind.

The Tunnels—find the Tunnels. The words were not Noa's; they reverberated from some outside place, some above-place that shook everything from every side. Noa-the-Eye was plastered wide and open, and immediately she saw the winding Tunnels, and Judah's back, the little room lit by Stellabugs. She saw herself fall down a shaft, saw Hilo wielding her fiery knife, saw Callum and Judah backed against the mossy wall. Then inside the cave again, she saw Hilo look longingly at Judah, pleading silently for forgiveness or was she asking something more, the way they fell into one another, embraced each other, two parts of the same whole—

Focus! The Resistance! The Captain's earthshaking voice again. A knifelike pain drilled down into Noa's skull, and the images flickered faster: now they were in marching lines, surrounded by gray-clothed Fae in rags, but the Clear Guard was closing in. The ground was erupting in spikes, alarms were screaming overhead, there was Callum, pulling her, lifting her over and up and around, hands sure and fast— but gloved in white—

And then Noa was suddenly leaning against Judah's chest in Lamont Library, and he was playing with her hair. They were smiling; things felt easy but not quite right. Noa turned, a ghost-girl stared back at her from the shadows—

No … not here … This was Noa's voice, not the Captain's, thin and faint, as she pushed the Girl back into the shadows. With great effort, she built a box around her, a box that turned into a wall—the wall of the room where Callum stood, hands gloved white and raised around Annabelle as she disintegrated into nothing—

Go back! There's something there!

The ground shook as Annabelle swirled away, and Callum spun around in circles, getting smaller. Noa was in the library again, Judah was at her back, but this time Noa refused to look where she had seen the Girl. She looked down a different aisle. Judah reached into his pocket, gave her a jigsaw puzzle he'd made with his own hands. It was beautiful, she hadn't known he could draw—and the puzzle became a book of sketches, hidden beneath his bed. Of a brother, of a father, a little girl—

No, no, not here either, we have to run—Noa-in–the-Memory said to Judah, crumpling the sketches. He looked confused, and the drill bored and rattled inside Noa's head, its gears caught on something uneven. It hadn't happened that way, it hadn't happened that way at all—

But now Noa was running, running and grabbing the shears from the body of the dead Hunter, Thorn, on the floor of Kells' shack; she brought them up and slashed them deep across her chest, opened her arms wide toward the heaving, spitting Portal. *Her blood is my blood*, Noa cried, and then the brothers were holding both her hands—

It cannot be! The Captain's voice was urgent, splintering down into Noa's mind, needles pressing in from every side. Noa tried to run again but where was left—s? She turned and found herself in a great fire, a terrible fire in a club, and everywhere she looked were stars of flame—Noa screamed and heard her real body scream aloud as something pressed upon her chest, a hand splayed harsh and rough upon her scar—

—and the stars of fire became stars of tiny hands, fingers sticky, warm in hers. Then the hands were limbs, starfish splayed, in the cool air of the sleeping night. The starfish moved, scrunched, and turned, its eyelids flickering: Sasha's eyelids, Sasha's face—

No! Noa screamed, with strength this time, and the scream shook the image into a million points of light. They blended together, turned back blinding white, the entire canvas too bright to see—

Then Noa was standing, solitary, black against the white, silhouette in the vision. She planted her feet, stared straight ahead, yoked the world deep into her core. The colors stopped, the noise went blank—

—and Noa saw it all.

She saw them, the ear-scarred Captain and the yellow-haired girl, linked by light and pressing in. Between them, a sort of golden rope—thick and spiral-woven, its ends fraying open to splay their threads. The threads looked alive, like tentacles or searching roots, reaching into Noa's mind. The filaments were fine and bright and quick, so fine you almost couldn't feel them, so bright you almost couldn't see them, so smooth you could mistake their pathways for your own—

But Noa didn't.

Noa saw them. Noa felt them. And with the simplest raising of her hand, Noa found she could control them.

Calm settled over Noa. She flicked her pinky finger, and the searching threads dipped and bent and stilled their advance. Beside Noa, Sasha now stood, backlit too against the white. Sasha looked up at Noa and laughed, tugged on her hand. Noa turned her head: on her other side was Isla. Isla rolled her eyes and smiled.

Noa looked back toward the Captain and the yellow-haired pixie. Their faces were wrinkled with confusion, their reaching tentacles of Red magic no longer obeying their commands. Noa tilted her head, and the tentacles wiggled back to life and moved in toward their keepers.

The Captain's and the Red's faces startled in shock, in fear. Noa let Isla and Sasha vanish as she pressed her wriggling tentacles harder, pushing with everything she had. She forced them into the Captain's face, the Captain's head, and suddenly the white world shook and blasted wide:

Images spun and rushed, images Noa didn't recognize or know quite how to see: a baby's face, downy reddish hair, gurgling up in happiness; another face reflected in the baby's pupil: the Captain's, maybe, but unscarred. Then both faces shattered—woman's and child's—by rocks hurled through a window. Cracks flowered up and split the ceiling, which collapsed into a silver swirl of marching boots. The Captain was there again, her boots among the boots, but she had no epaulets; then she was marching in an empty hallway, all alone, standing at a single door. The door opened to show Arik, angry and yelling: *the Tower ... no clearance ... for this weapon.* Noa's fists, the Captain's fists, curled with rage, and she screamed—not Noa but the Captain—terrible and gargled—

And Noa was slammed backward in her chair, to which she still was tied, and her head smashed into the floor of the square interrogation room.

"Get her back to her cell!" someone was screaming, amidst thunderous commotion somewhere in front of her. Noa was ripped upward and off the chair, flung over a Guard's broad shoulder, whisked roughly from the room.

"Smoke her!" a different voice commanded, and green sparkles exploded in Noa's eyes. Guards massed inside the interrogation room; Noa glimpsed them as her vision faded; they were huddled around a mass of silver on the floor—it was the Captain, eyes huge and wide and frozen, body unmoving.

• • •

THE SMOKE NUMBED Noa's consciousness, or tried to—she dimly felt her body bumping as she was heaved down hallway after hallway, each jostle more and more annoying. She craved rest, oblivion, but sounds niggled at her ears, garbled and indecipherable. By the time she was tossed onto the dirty, stone-cold floor of her cell, her eyes were blinking rapidly, vision already clearing, and mere moments later, she was up and rubbing her elbow. She looked from the red welts on her arms and legs to the bars around her cell.

"Noa!" Callum's urgent, frantic whisper. Noa looked and saw his hands grasping the bars in the window between their cells.

"Move over!" Judah, jostling to get close.

"I'm fine, I'm fine," Noa winced their way. Geezer watched guardedly from his corner. He clearly had not expected her to be returned alive.

"A ton of Guards are massing at the front," Judah said anxiously, and suddenly Noa realized how loud the ward was with noise and arguments and commotion.

"They know, don't they?" Callum asked desperately. "They know everything—"

"No, no—" Noa tried to push her mind to focus. "The Captain didn't—I stopped her—"

"What do you mean, you *stopped* her?"

"I mean I did what you said, I tried to hide her ... and you ... both of you. Make a box, bury it like you said ... But

213

it was coming from all sides. It felt like me, it looked like me, I couldn't tell—"

"I knew it! We never should have let her—" Callum cried.

"Shut up!" Judah hissed.

"I ran, but there were no more places…" Noa gulped down air like water, each second more awake to the panic pounding in her veins. "So I, finally I … stopped running. I stopped. And I … looked at it, and I … pushed it away somehow—" She broke off, not sure why she felt apologetic.

"You pulled apart what wasn't you—" Judah began.

"But were you in time?" Callum interrupted, frantic.

Noa's heart hammered wildly. "I—think she saw us, the Portal. Maybe everything—"

"That's it, we have to—"

"No, but wait!" Noa cried, her mind moving so fast it was like she couldn't see. "I pushed it back on her! I turned it around, I took it away, and I saw—I saw something!" Noa's head was spinning but this was too important, she needed to come back to focus—" She's in the Tower! I saw it! I saw Arik tell the Captain, the weapon's in the Tower—"

Yelling erupted from the Guards' station, cutting her off.

"*Call Arik! I don't know! The Captain's out!*"

"*No report! I say juice 'er and keep it quiet—*"

"*Who the hell put you in charge?*"

"*Someone has to be!*" Wild scuffling, angry fighting.

Callum flung himself to the bars. "That's it then! We go to the Tower. I'll find Darius—"

Judah screamed. "No! Run first, plan a rescue later! We agreed!"

"No!" Noa interjected. "I'm with Callum, we go to the Tower!"

"What?"

"She's there! I know she's there! She's right *here,* we can't leave her!" She heard her desperation but didn't care. Her aching head and limbs swirled with strength and heat and the wildness of hoping. "And the Captain's out! I saw her! She was unconscious!"

That was enough for Callum. "It's now or never! Get ready—"

There was a huge bang against the wall as Judah shoved Callum into it. "*That's* your plan? You can't be the distraction, you idiot!"

"Someone has to set off the—"

Callum's voice was drowned out as the ward alarms screamed and strobed in green. The flashes and noise reverberated so loudly, so chaotically, the ceiling and floor seemed to vibrate.

"What the hell—" Judah began, cut off by the storm of boots and yells, five Guards charging toward the offender. *But who?* It hadn't been Callum or Judah, couldn't have been, because the flashing light was green—

The Guards swirled down like a tornado on Noa's cell. Noa turned in confusion and suddenly understood why the alarms were so shattering and intense: they were screaming not just in the hall, but also from the wrist cuffs of the Fae who stood two feet behind her, the Green Fae with whom she shared a cell, who had set them off:

Geezer.

His eyes were fierce and bright and bold, his mouth a determined, angry sneer. A greenish aura seemed to radiate around him; he stood up tall, feet planted, snarling at what was to come. Noa caught his eye, awash in confusion, not understanding what was going on.

The Guards flung back the bars to their cell with a blistering crash; they muscled Geezer to the floor, bending his arms so far his every joint popped wetly with dislocation—but Geezer didn't even scream. As he was dragged out, he caught Noa's eye—defiant, piercing, sharp—and a wave of courage broke over her, filling every cell.

Geezer suddenly lashed and screamed like a banshee. The Guards tried to subdue him and hauled him away, hurriedly slamming back Noa's gate. As it crashed home, Noa heard him cry, in a strangled, terrible yell, "*Hail harmony*—!" just as the gate bounced back, ending up slightly ajar.

Noa looked at the gate: Geezer had shoved her bread-shiv into the track. Noa's cell was open.

And the Guards hadn't seen it.

Every Guard was racing, crowding eagerly around the clear-glass room to watch Geezer liquefied to Greenish sludge. Geezer had given them their distraction.

Noa didn't pause to wonder why Geezer had done it, didn't let herself feel confusion, fear, or even sympathy. There was only urgency and this moment, and the courage that surged through her pumping veins.

Noa opened her gate and ran to the brothers' cell. She pulled at their gate fruitlessly. Not letting herself think, because to think would be to fear, she left their cell and sprinted to the jostling, jeering crowd of Guards who were now watching Geezer melt. Noa refused to let herself look and, thinking instead of Isla, of Marena, she deftly lifted keys from one of the Guards cheering wildly at the back.

Then she was back at Callum and Judah's cell, forcing the key into the lock, heaving back their door. And they were running, all three of them, for the front entrance gate, the one that slammed down and pulverized anything in motion with its jagged teeth—

"Save me! Save me too!" The hall exploded in a sea of panicked cries and pleas echoing from every cell, reaching arms flailing through the bars. Noa stuttered, the voices finally piercing through her armor of single-minded action. Judah grasped at her—*we can't, there isn't time*—and Noa knew he was right, there wasn't, the Guards had seen them, now alerted by the pleas.

Judah yanked her hard, pulling her after him toward the last jaw-like gate.

"Now!" Callum cried to his brother, and Noa watched as he and Judah both threw pieces of prison bread at the gate, hitting the ground beneath it simultaneously on separate sides. The gate fell and then retracted, hitching in sensory confusion, the way it had the day Noa had incited the bread rebellion with too many targets at one time. In that split-second delay Callum dove and rolled through the gap, Judah pulling Noa to leap with him right behind—

"Noa?"

Noa froze, skidding to a halt. Her fingers slipped from Judah's as he dove beneath the gate and rolled through, right before it smashed its jaws, severing her from the brothers and from freedom.

"Noa!"

The voice was all Noa could think about. No time to realize what she'd just given up. She spun and sprinted directly at the Guards who were rushing up behind her, catching them by surprise. As they tried to halt their forward momentum, she Channeled Sasha and dove through their legs. Her body sprawled and skidded to a stop in front of the cell that had been Movie Star and Crazy's, whose new inhabitant had finally recovered from the Smoke.

"Marena!" Noa cried, leaping to the cell's gate, fumbling with the keys, flinging back the door, pulling the girl free. But then the Guards were on them, everywhere, grasping at Noa's arms, ripping at her hair. Noa spun and kicked and bit and punched, screamed and lashed and struck out with the brass knuckles of the keys. Beside her, Marena slipped and ducked and darted, too sharp and quick to catch. But they were too many, and too strong—

"*Stop!*" Noa suddenly screamed, making the word itself her weapon. The Guards stilled in shock for the splittest of a second—but it was enough. Noa grabbed Marena, alarms still blaring and pulsing chaos in every color, and they sprinted toward the gate. It was on lockdown now, stuck fast—

"Callum!" Noa screamed through the hard, thick stone, not knowing if he could even hope to hear her, not daring to slow her stride. The Guards thundered on their heels; Noa smelled Spider-Eye's breath. Noa looked desperately at Marena, hoped the girl remembered too: running like this before, from roof to roof: "*Callum, now!*"

And with nothing but faith and the wild hope of prayer, Noa and Marena leapt directly into the solid mass of stone—

—and shimmered through its altered atoms, tumbling into the hall beyond.

• • •

LOCKDOWN ALARMS BLARED in the outer hallway, the flashes so bright and fast it was difficult to see. Judah helped Noa and Marena scramble to their feet in staccato, strobing frames of panicked movement.

"I can't hold it!" Callum yelled somewhere behind them, just before they were all blasted backward.

Guards poured through the exploded gate as they struggled to free themselves from concrete chunks and swirling dust. Judah's leg spun into Noa's ribs; she shrieked in pain as he sprang up and pulled her to her feet. His hand was slick with sweat, his body heaving, overwhelmed by the exertion. But there was no time to rest—they were running down the hall through strobe and dust and noise, unable to see, Callum first and Judah right behind, Marena pulling Noa through the pain of her fractured ribs.

"Right!" Callum called, swerving at the hallway's end. Judah turned the wrong way but caught himself, nearly slipping into Marena's stride.

Another hallway just the same, strobing and screaming, but Callum had focused on something: a set of double doors, waiting at the end. Noa tried to focus on them too, to erase everything else from her consciousness and leave no room for fear. She stared those doors down as she sprinted toward them, made them the center of her world—

Which was how she saw the horde first.

"Guards!" she cried, skidding to a clumsy stop. The windows of the doors were filling, as surely as silver boots thundered toward them from behind.

With nowhere else to turn but sideways, Callum flung himself at the hallway wall, spreading his body against it to maximize the points of touch. The section he touched shimmered then liquefied, splashing like boiling water to the floor.

Judah didn't hesitate, leapt through the waterfall and into the darkness behind it. Marena followed immediately on his heels. Noa reached for Callum's hand to pull him after her, but he shook his head.

"I can't let go too soon!" There was no time to argue, but Noa didn't like the look in Callum's eye: resignation and self-sacrifice—and a frightening kind of peace. She jumped through, but at the last moment grabbed his hand hard anyway, startling him, and yanked him into the waterfall. But his connection to the wall was lost, and Noa screamed as the wall began to return to stone around them, forming on all sides.

Marena and Judah yanked Noa free just before she was crushed inside the wall. She tumbled forward in a hail of rock and stone, her left hand tight on Callum's even as she heard the bone in her forearm snap. She screamed in agony and released him as he crashed out behind her. Marena shrieked: Callum was free from the wall, but his whole body sagged beneath his head without any structure, like a bag of shattered sticks and glass.

"Keep running!" Judah ordered Marena and Noa as he ripped off Callum's shirt. He moved his brother's hands for him, onto Callum's own chest, and forced Callum to look into his eyes. Noa knew she should be running, but even though Marena pulled at her, she couldn't move.

Judah glared into Callum's eyes, clearly thinking hard into his brother's mind, Suggesting with all his might. "Dammit, heal!" he finally screamed aloud, full-voiced, and finally Callum's mind started to take the order. His body began to shimmer under his own healing touch. His ribs rebuilt, his legs stretched out. Judah yanked him roughly to his feet.

"Just run!" he yelled. Callum obediently shook himself, pushed his rebuilt legs to move. Noa found her feet again too, and together they tore into the darkness of this new room—the room on the other side of the wall—when the rest of that wall blasted in behind them, bringing Guards and rubble and blinding shards of light.

Noa nearly stumbled as the room took shape in the new illumination. Judah and Callum stuttered too, for it was not a room but a huge indoor arena, two football fields in length and width and several stories high.

"We're in the Training Center!" Judah yelled, sweat pouring down past his wild eyes. Noa felt a burst of panic: the last time Judah and Callum had been in the Training Center, it had been burning to the ground.

Callum's determination vanished; fear and confusion took its place. But Judah growled, sprinted harder, like a beast, roaring to the lead. He veered and jumped, dodging training apparatuses left and right, leaving Noa, Marena, and Callum to do their best to follow in his path.

They ran, but explosions like grenades bit at their heels as the Guards closed in. They were Channeling Blues, but luckily, were clearly wary of destroying too much of the arena around the ducking, dodging fugitives.

Finally Noa saw where Judah was leading them: a section at the far end of the Center hung with ropes from the ceiling, at the very top of which—several stories up—was a line of small windows designed to let in a roof of light.

When they reached the ropes, Judah immediately launched himself onto one, climbing hard; Marena did the same a moment later. Callum had just reached his when he saw Noa, trying and failing to climb hers, unable with her fractured ribs and a broken arm.

Instantly Callum was behind her, bare chest against her back, hands around her grasping the rope.

"There's no time to heal me—" Noa protested, but it seemed that wasn't Callum's plan. Instead, the rope shimmered and became a pulley, whisking them both upward amid a hail of fireballs launched in their direction.

"Learned about these pulley things in your world," Callum breathed into Noa's ear, and Noa could feel his smile in the midst of all this panic and what she knew was the trauma of his worst memories.

With the efficient pulley, they bumped up to the top of the rope ahead of the others, reaching the ceiling first. Callum began to swing their rope, gaining momentum until they crashed their feet against the nearest window, breaking the glass. Glass slivers rained down past Judah and Marena, who were just reaching the top.

"What about the other side?" Noa cried, suddenly realizing just how high up they were, and how far they would fall. In that second, the rope in Judah's hands burst into flame beside them. Judah looked surprised for a moment as he found himself suddenly grasping ash, then his arms began to pinwheel, his body fall. Marena quickly reached and caught him by his fingers, screaming as his sudden weight wrenched down on her tiny frame. She began sliding down her rope, dragged by his body like an anchor, her palms smoking from the rising friction.

Callum immediately swung his rope over and transferred himself and Noa to Marena's. Noa looked down and her mind screamed what there was no time to articulate in words—luckily

Marena's mind had the same thought, and, shrieking with every ounce of strength she had, she released her rope hand and grasped Callum's foot instead. They were all clustered now: Callum's body a comma around Noa's, Marena dangling from his foot, Judah dangling from her other arm. Behind them, their former rope-turned-pulley vanished into ash. Their current rope was next.

Strain snarled from Callum's throat; their rope combusted—but instead of falling, Noa felt them all pulled upward in an odd jerking motion. Noa twisted to look at Callum: he wailed in agony as pain flared across his face, and she gasped—behind him, great white wings burst outward from his spine.

Howling, tortured, Callum flew all four of them clumsily toward the window. A hail of fire arrows, Channeled by Guards from Blues, soared up from below; Judah yelped as one thunked into his thigh, but then they reached the window's opening, Marena and Judah dragging across its jagged edges.

Noa tried not to hear the slicing, ripping, tearing sound as Callum pulled them out into the sun—then suddenly, his body shuddered all around her and fell from them, spinning away, its great white wings—bloody where they had burst from his interweaving scars—utterly, utterly still, like those of a murdered, falling angel.

In that moment of total weightlessness, Noa saw Aurora all around them, horizon to horizon—

—and then she and the others plummeted, stones to the rocks below.

• • •

IN THAT MOMENT, the moment Noa knew she was going to die, she saw her mother. Hannah's head was tilted, eyes soft. *My*

Noa, said her voice, as if to ask a question. *My Noa, who shines the light—*

Then Noa slammed into the ground, and she never heard the rest.

• • •

NOA WAS DEAD.

She was dead, and there was nothing. No color, sound, movement, for there was nothing after death.

The question was asked and answered only with stillness.

Except.

Except the ground was not still. Not entirely.

It was falling, sinking…

And then rising.

Sinking and falling and rising and sinking, a cycle in slowing peaks. And it had texture too, the ground, for it cut upward in patterns, little squares against her skin. Except Noa didn't still have skin that could feel anymore, her skin was still now, without sensation, for in death, everything ended.

So why did her skin feel?

Noa opened her eyes. She was several feet from the stony ground, tangled in a net gently rising and falling from the momentum of its basket catch. Noa was sure it had not been there moments before—she had looked down at Callum's bloody wings, she was sure of it, and there had been only stone beneath them—

Noa craned her head to look around; her neck screamed with pain, but she ignored it until she saw them, Judah and Callum and Marena too, also safely caught inside the webbing. She barely had time for relief when a voice chilled any wonder or gratitude from her heart.

"Hello again," Arik said, fingering the net appreciatively, like a fisherman delighted with his catch.

• • •

ARIK WASTED NO time signaling to his Guards. They immediately pulled the net fast and tight into a bundle, not caring how the prisoners collided. Callum's body rolled without resistance, unconscious, and pinned Judah's against the net. Noa slid on top of them, too stunned to even think to fight, but Marena, on her other side, squirmed and scratched and hissed fruitlessly at the enclosing ropes. She had been farthest out and found herself on a part of the net now near the top; she clung to it with wiry fingers so that she dangled, avoiding squashing Noa.

The Guard nearest Marena—a woman with green eyes and a bored expression—sighed and whacked Marena's head with one strong blow, knocking the small girl out. Marena's thin body toppled onto Noa's, her left hand smacking Noa like a whip against her cheek. With Marena dislodged, the net pulled tighter, smaller. Judah kicked out as best he could; Noa tried to take up the struggle.

"Just Smoke them!" Arik ordered, irritated. Immediately green mist was thick in Noa's lungs again, and once more the world sparkled out.

• • •

NOA WOKE FROM the Smoke first again, but this time she felt groggy, confused, disoriented. She wondered if they had used more Smoke, or if her body was simply wearing down—this time

225

she'd had no interim of sound and dark, only complete oblivion. And now that she was waking, it was an aching kind of wake.

Noa looked blearily around her. They were not back in their cells, but in a room, together. Judah, Callum, and Marena lay unconscious on cots set against the wall. Noa's palms found the surface beneath her, soft and spongy; she was sitting on a cot as well. It was actually comfortable. She pushed her fingers into the plush surface and realized her wrist and arm had been healed. And as far as she could tell, so had all her bruises.

Noa got to her feet, intending to test her legs and ribs, but her leg caught; her ankle was chained and bolted to the floor. The cot was bolted too. Alarm tubes were embedded in the chain and the cot's metal.

Noa looked around the room more closely this time. A chill of misgiving went through her when she realized there were four walls but no door. Every wall was identical, even to the ceiling and the floor—monotone stone without even vine or leaf or pattern.

They *were* in a cell. Just a different kind.

Noa looked at her cot with newfound dread. This semblance of comfort made her fear this prison more.

Marena shifted on her cot, then suddenly broke awake in a torrent of choking coughing. Noa instinctively jumped to help and tripped over her lashed ankle. Noa watched helplessly as Marena coughed and coughed, her face turning purple and then blue—then, like a volcano, the pixie vomited green bile on the ground. Marena slowly raised her head, heaving gulps of air.

"Marena! Are you okay? What happened?"

Marena closed her eyes tight, like the room was spinning.

"The Smoke," she wheezed finally, spitting saliva again. "I'm Green Fae too, so I metabolize it faster. It's made from…"

"Other Green Fae," Noa murmured. "I know."

"My body rejects it, like a foreign organ, since it's Green essence but not mine." She took a few deep breaths, focused on the ceiling. Then she turned to Noa. "I could've sworn you weren't Green."

"I-I'm not."

"But you recovered already. Even before me."

Noa was saved from replying when the wall directly across from their cots began to shimmer. It turned blurry as it dematerialized, and Arik stepped through, flanked by two Guards. One was Channeling a Blue and had clearly created the passage. As soon as the cadre had stepped in, the wall sealed up behind them.

"Well, I guess that answers that," Arik said shrewdly, shaking his head. "Two Greens. Most would say the most dangerous kind of pixie." He turned to Noa, studying her carefully. "How powerless you must feel here, unable to beguile me."

Noa tried her best to show no reaction, only the appropriateness of her fear. Better to have him think her some slutty Green than know the truth of how defenseless she truly was.

Arik looked at the boys, unconscious on their cots. Wearing their true faces. Arik smiled a tiny, rueful smile. "I should have trusted my own eyes in the Square after all. It just seemed so *ridiculous*." He turned to Noa, almost sadly. "Foolish of you, you know, to choose *these* traitors. I bet you have them competing for your *love* … but then Greens are never too discerning with their playthings, are they." He turned back to the boys, though he kept speaking to Noa. "I suppose that makes you my plaything now."

He glanced over at Marena. "Both of you."

Arik turned to the Guard dragging the dazed Blue Fae behind him. "Wake them," he ordered in his much firmer, official voice. The Guard stepped up to Callum, placed his free hand on Callum's chest. Callum's body started to seize, vibrating madly; his eyes sprang open and his torso bolted upright, and then he, too, vomited green bile. Noa cringed and closed her eyes. Callum began panting and heaving, coming back to his senses, and the Guard moved to Judah. He touched Judah the same way, and Judah too began to seize and shake and shiver, limbs rattling and flailing.

"What are you—stop!" Callum cried from his bed, jumping out and falling over his unexpectedly tethered ankle. Judah seized more and more violently, and Noa waited breathlessly but no bile came. Just black foam, bubbling up through Judah's mouth.

"What's wrong? Wake him!" Arik demanded. The Guard bore down harder, leaning his weight into Judah's chest. Noa bit her lip to stop from shrieking, screaming—until finally, finally, Judah's body contorted explosively, flipping him around, and black, black ooze spilled from between his lips.

Arik cringed and stepped backward. "Disgusting."

The Guard looked confused. "I'm not—"

Then Judah slowly rolled himself up, coughing weakly, eyes fluttering awake.

Arik nodded to the Guard, who got up but kept a wary eye on Judah.

"Welcome, *Forsythes*," Arik said, the name clipped and crisp. His tone stayed even, but when Arik looked at Judah, his lip curled just a touch. "I should have known that smirk could only come from you." Arik turned to Callum, lifting his chin almost imperceptibly. "The Blue Son," he said, unreadable. "How very ... unexpected."

Callum pressed his lips together and glared at Arik.

"You were banished from this place," Arik said, with the slightest hint of defiance, "so perhaps you do not know. Your father disowned his Colored ties. Your Green mother, too. I am the Otec's rightful heir."

"You can have him," Judah spat.

"The Otec or your brother?" Noa bit her lip; Arik smiled. "Don't worry, Judah, you don't have to answer."

Arik's head suddenly flicked minutely to the side. "Ah-ah, Blue Son," he warned softly. "This is a special cell. If one of your alarms is triggered, a gas comes in. A variation on the Smoke, but made from Blues. Like you." He smiled a small, cold smile. "Instead of knocking out the limbic system, it denatures your spinal cord. I must say, I'm curious to see it."

Callum's calm rippled into a sneer. Again Arik lifted his chin—just slightly—in defiance. *Or maybe*, Noa realized, *fear*.

"Just kill us and get it over with, Arik," Judah snarled. "Your slutty mommy always wanted that anyway."

Arik turned toward Judah. "You really are the poster boy for all the bad the Colors can become."

"Tell us why you're keeping us here," Callum demanded quietly. Noa thought she saw that flicker again, that nervousness in Arik's eye. But just as quickly, it was gone.

"Your ... disturbance ... caught my attention," he replied carefully.

Very carefully.

"You're in trouble," Noa realized. "For not knowing who they were, and for letting us escape—"

"You didn't escape!" Arik spat, then quickly mastered himself. "And I'm not in trouble. I simply choose now to make this an opportunity." He looked at the brothers. "Yes, I could simply deliver you as prisoners to the Otec now and let him deal with you, but I've decided to do better. Take some initiative, as it were."

"Need to impwess Daddy Otec?" Judah simpered.

Arik ignored him, addressing Callum instead. "I'm going to deliver you as soldiers, dedicated to the Otec's cause." He smiled, smug.

"Good luck with that," Judah snorted. "We hate Darius."

Arik only grinned more gleefully. "Oh, but dear Red Son," he said to Judah, as if Judah were simply an amusing little child, "the Otec *loves* for us to innovate these days." He leaned in close to Judah's ear, *"I have such great things in mind for you."*

• • •

AFTER DELIVERING HIS threat, Arik used his Blue slave to slip through the atoms in the wall like a frightening paper doll. Noa's eyes went instinctively to Callum's, but he was staring pensively at where Arik had vanished.

"How'd he know you?" Judah demanded, eyes fastened on his brother. "Darius didn't adopt him until after you were gone!"

"You're really them, then? The gobbin' Otec's banished *sons*?" Marena cried in disbelief. She looked so defiant, so like Judah in fact, that Noa almost laughed aloud. Marena wasn't amused, however. She glared accusingly at Noa. "Think you left a little out, cullie?"

"Would you have believed her?" Callum snapped.

"I didn't think it was my secret to tell," Noa said, more gently.

Marena screwed up her face. "I'm not *mad*. I mean, I knew you was risky business being some mad Tunnel Fae." Marena's face suddenly flashed bright with hope. "So you *do* have Queen Lorelei then! You got the gobbin' princes and the new rebels in the Tunnels!"

"What new rebels?" Callum said sharply, as Judah demanded, "Who has our mother?"

Marena looked from Judah to Callum, faltering. "*Your* rebels … I thought. Don't you have her? Don't you run the new Resistance?"

Noa's heart seized. She couldn't bear to look any of them in the eye, even as she felt both brothers' eyes burning into her.

"What do you mean, *new* Resistance?" Callum asked Marena evenly.

"Well, you know how Otec Darius said he drowned all the rebels with the Flushes, but people always was whispering how some escaped, and you're here so that means it's true…." Noa felt tears spring her eyes as Marena feebly persisted, "And with Queen Lorelei too. Because that was another gobbin' lie, they didn't kill her like they didn't kill the rebels, and you lot wasn't really Banished…."

As she trailed off, Noa closed her eyes, cursing herself. She'd given them fruitless hope in a moment of weakness, and now they'd have to repay her debt. She forced herself to look at them, to at least watch the pain she had inflicted. She, who knew so well the desperate hollowness of hoping for what could not be.

Judah's face alone was enough to break her heart.

It was Callum who found, somehow, the ability to answer Marena. Who found the bravery to say what Noa had not been able to, and now made so much worse. "No, Marena," he said softly. "We haven't been in the Tunnels all this time. We were Banished, both of us. And when we were down in the Tunnels … I'm sorry. There was no one there."

"Hilo," Judah whispered angrily, swiping at his nose.

Callum nodded. "A pixie came and found us. Before they … 'flushed' the Tunnels."

Marena studied her feet. Noa cringed to see her, Marena, the tough one, look so upset. "They send scouts down there. Good way to get out of Indenturing, be a spy for them Clears. The Scouts tell 'em if they need to flood those Tunnels again, so no one can gather there again…." Her voice grew smaller and smaller. "That's why my brother always told me not to believe. And I didn't, but then…" She wiped her nose roughly with her arm, nodded her head in Noa's direction.

Callum sighed. He looked so tired, but his face was filled with compassion for Marena. It was so like him. Even in the moment he learned the truth of his mother's death, he was concerned for someone else in pain.

Or maybe, Noa realized, he had not been so foolish as she or Judah. Callum was stronger than they were in that way. He knew always to prepare, use his *mind*, not just his heart.

Noa gasped as a sharp pain suddenly split across her head.

"Noa?" Callum cried. "Are you okay?"

"I-I just have a headache," Noa said, blinking rapidly. Thankfully, the pain began to lessen to a background buzz. "I think it's been a long day, and…" She wanted to apologize for what she'd done, but she couldn't even give it words. They didn't seem to blame or accuse her, which, in a terrible way, made it even worse.

"I guess we all should try to rest," Callum said. "Then we'll start to figure a way out of here."

Judah was already lying on his cot, rolled toward the wall. "Don't you get it, Brother? It's over. It's all over."

"Maybe you think so. But I can't." Callum answered. "We'll all feel better once we rest."

Callum and Marena lay down, but Noa remained sitting, unable to look away from Judah's back. She wanted to believe with Callum. She owed them that. Both of them.

When they woke up, Callum was gone.

• • •

NOA HAD NEVER known panic like the panic she felt when she opened her eyes and saw Callum was missing.

"He probably found a way out and took it," Judah said bitterly. "We would have slowed him down."

"He wouldn't do that!" Marena cried, indignant.

"You don't even know him, shrimp!"

"I know he's the Blue Son, who lost his freedom for the rebellion—"

Judah laughed fiercely. *"Like I said."*

"Enough! Enough!" Noa pleaded. "Judah, you *do* know Callum and you know he wouldn't do that."

"Are you serious?" Judah cried in utter disbelief. "Are you forgetting he's abandoned me before?"

"That was different, it was—t … to rescue someone—"

Judah looked at her pointedly. Noa bit her lip. Sasha needed rescuing now too, just like then.

"Point is, he's *poof*!" Marena interjected. "Arik will probably blame us!"

Noa tried to keep calm; she didn't like how Marena's voice had trembled on Arik's name. Without Callum, she would have to step up and be the leader, the voice of reason—even if inside she felt like anything but. "We can't panic. If he did somehow escape, we truly didn't know anything, so we can't be held accountable. *But*"—she eyed Judah—"he wouldn't leave us anyway. When we were running before, he could have let us get caught and saved himself at any time. But he *didn't*. He almost killed himself trying to fly all of us to safety!"

"*Big hero*—"

"Judah! You have history with him, but so do I. When my world shut down and I was broken, he saved me. He didn't run. He helped me heal."

Judah seemed to struggle. But when he spoke, it wasn't what she expected at all:

"You think he fixed you because he acts as if he did. But Noa, you were never broken in the first place." With that, he turned from her, lay down again. Noa's headache sliced through her again, the pain so strong she had to lie down and close her eyes, find the relief of blackness—

When she finally opened her eyes again a long time later, Marena was catatonic with shock and fear...

And Judah had vanished too.

• • •

NOA LURCHED TOWARD Marena, her ankle catching where it was chained. Spitfire Marena, who had introduced herself with a brick to the forehead, was rocking in terror on her cot, arms wrapped tight around her knees.

"Marena, please stop, please—" Noa pleaded desperately, flailing for any way to reach her. Finally, helpless, she slid down and sat on the floor, put her throbbing head against the cot. It still ached dully, as if it weren't enough that her migraine had clearly knocked her out.

Noa gave herself five seconds.

Five.

She took a deep breath, pushed her fear down deep. She wrapped it tight, caged it in her ribs, and left it there.

She turned to Marena, whose knobby knees were tucked under her scraped-up chin.

"Marena," Noa began, but she couldn't find the right words to bring Marena back. Instead, Marena surprised her by speaking first, voice strangely tinny:

"The Blue Son's a warrior, we all know that. Rose high. We all know that."

"You mean Callum?" Noa asked, but Marena didn't look at her, as if she wasn't talking to her at all.

"Otec's boy, but then he turned. Rebelled for us. We all know that."

"Marena—"

"But not at first, no not at first." She began to tremble, and a tear trickled down her cheek. "A good son, the Blue Son, a very good son. A very good son…"

Deep fear tingled in Noa's stomach; she pushed it down. "I

know, Marena, he told me already," she soothed. "He served in the Blue regiments when his father asked, as a healer—"

Marena shook her head vehemently, eyes wide. "Heal and hurt! The Blues! Heal and hurt!"

Noa bit her lip. *Healers and torturers, the selfsame gift.* Where had she heard that before?

"Maybe the others did, Marena, but not Callum, he couldn't—"

The pixie shut her eyes. "Yes, yes, yes! We all know that!"

"Marena, listen to me!" Noa said urgently. "You *know* Callum now. He helped you to escape—"

"A good son! A very good son!" Tears streamed thick down Marena's face but she wouldn't unwrap her arms to wipe them. They spattered from her chin, her nose, sopped messily down her knees.

Noa's fear broke free. "What happened, Marena?" she cried. "Where's Judah?"

"He came! He came!" Marena sobbed, loudly now. "They made me watch!"

"Who came? Who? Where was I?"

"They tried to wake you! To make you watch too!"

"I don't understand!" Noa cried, tears flooding her throat.

"He came! The Blue Son came!"

"Mar—"

"And *he ripped his brother's soul apart.*"

Noa's body slammed her backward against her cot; the air in her chest was gone. She was a vacuum, gasping to stay alive.

"Not Callum, it couldn't have been Callum—"

"A very good son! A very good son!" Marena shrieked.

"No, Marena! It's something else! He must be pretending, as a way to get us out—"

Marena's eyes met Noa's for the first time, and they were wild. *"He says he's coming back for me."*

•   •   •

MARENA DIDN'T SPEAK again, and neither did Noa. The night stretched out before them, somehow endless, even as neither could bear for it to end. Noa didn't know what to make of Marena's words. Callum couldn't, wouldn't, do to Judah what he had done for her—maim his soul. He had done that only to protect Noa, because it had been the only way to make a talisman to keep her safe. He would never inflict that on his brother. On anyone.

Not the Callum Noa knew, the Callum Noa *felt* in her heart.

He had lied before, it was true. But Noa had already made peace with Callum's dishonesty about Sasha. And she had memories like touchstones to remind her of who Callum really was. Like the way Sasha had instinctively trusted him and curled into him while Noa read to her class. Though of course now, Noa knew that trust had been memory as well as instinct.

But there was also the kiss beneath the tree, his tree, when the world swirled and flew around them as arms and lips intertwined. Except … he'd also taken her Light in that moment, unable to stop himself. And that had happened again, when she'd rescued him from Kells' shed—

Noa bit a scream. It was like each memory she had of Callum had turned to soapstone, worn into some new shape. This world, this room—they were taking things from her.

"Stop!" Noa cried aloud, pressing her palms against her aching, throbbing temples, head pounding like it might explode. She squeezed her eyes shut, reached back for something, anything steady to hold on to, something deep inside her core, but all she wanted was to run far away as far as she could go—

"They *ran*," Noa gasped, eyes flying open. She turned to Marena urgently, wildly. "They *ran*, Marena! Before! They both ran from this world, because it was the only way to fight! Don't you see—"

"You don't know—"

"I *do* know," Noa interrupted. "I do know, because *they ran to me*."

Marena became quite, quite still. For the first time, her eyes sharpened, became once again the fierce eyes Noa had come to know. "What do you mean?"

Noa knew it was dangerous, but she had to say it; she had to build something in stones too strong and clean to change their shape.

"I'm from the mortal realm, Marena," Noa said, this truth a golden bridge, "and when they ran, they ran to me. *I'm* the reason they came back, not to rejoin their father. *That's* real."

Marena's eyes grew wide, but she wasn't afraid.

They held each other eyelocked, even as they felt the storm around them picking up. Even as the wall across from them began to shimmer,

and Arik came inside.

• • •

ARIK'S EYES IMMEDIATELY went to Noa.

"Good, you're awake." He turned behind him, where what-ever Guard had opened the door was following him through the opening. "Not needed, thank you." The Guard turned and left so quickly Noa barely caught a glimpse of him—just a swirl of silver and dark hair as it vanished.

Dark *curls*.

Arik let the wall seal up behind him.

"Where are they? What have you done to them?" Noa demanded, shocked at the force of her own words.

Arik didn't answer right away, but calmly walked to what had been Judah's cot, smoothed its cover sheet, and sat carefully upon it.

"You passed out before. Probably a side effect of the Smoke—I apologize. We've really only just started using it." He paused, as if he were actually waiting for her to accept his apology. When she was quiet, he played a little with the corner of the cot's cover sheet, caught himself, and folded his hands. "I'm told when you were interrogated, Captain Lia passed out as well. Improper Channeling technique. Again, not your fault."

"Where are Callum and Judah?" Noa repeated, more nervously.

Arik sat back, sighed a little, Then he leaned toward her plaintively, hands on his knees.

"Is it so difficult to imagine that Callum and Judah see the wisdom of this movement? Our father started it, after all."

Noa pressed her lips together.

"I get it. You think I'm evil. That this movement is something terrible, and cruel."

Out of the corner of her eye, Noa saw Marena clutch her knees once more.

"My cell mate was melted into ooze," Noa replied stonily. "Tell me that's not evil."

Arik bowed his head. "Captain Lia has a difficult job, but remaking the world takes change, and sacrifice. I thank the Otec every day for not giving me her post, essential as it may unfortunately be."

Noa frowned.

Arik nodded. "I suspected as much. Lia didn't pass out in your interrogation because of her technique, did she. You did something to her." Something about his tone—conversational, frank, even … respectful—made Noa feel uncertain.

Noa bit her lip. "If so, I don't know what," she answered honestly.

"You think she's a demon, too. But you don't know her, just like you don't know me."

"I think I've seen enough."

Arik leaned back, smiling sadly. "The world before was very unkind too. Surely you remember? Or maybe you don't, because you're not Clear, and so were not the one being hurt?"

"Clears weren't slaves, Channeled like lifeless tools," Marena said from her cot, eyes angry.

Noa felt a pang of pride.

Arik considered her, as if actually thinking about her opinion. "Not slaves in law, perhaps," he acknowledged, "but certainly in practice. In a million ways that went unsaid."

"It's not the same," Marena whispered, holding her knees even more tightly.

"No," Arik agreed solemnly. "It was unregulated and so boundless, depthless. An insidious kind of hate, left to the hater alone. We had no powers, so they made us powerless. And abuse was governed by no laws."

"It's the same, isn't it?" Marena asked.

"No," Noa answered, surprising even herself. "No ... it's not."

Arik was watching her. "Captain Lia, whom you so dislike ... would it surprise you to learn she feels the same? That she knows that difference?" Noa bit her lip, and Arik continued: "Before Otec Darius Awakened the Clears, Lia's husband was a Blue politico. To curry favor, he made a practice of renting her—his powerless Clear wife—to useful friends. She was quite a beauty, before."

"She agreed to that?" Noa breathed.

"She was never asked," Arik replied simply, "and had no say. Clears were useless, and Blues, you know, the unofficial elite ... such an impressive power." For the first time, strain flickered at Arik's jaw. He suppressed it, continued: "When Lia learned she was with child, her husband suspected it was not his and punished her, though his doubts were his own fault. He threw her through a window so hard she cracked the wall and split open the ceiling, which crashed down on top of her. The glass and rubble massacred her face and ear, and when Blue medics arrived, her husband explained she was just a Clear in need of a lesson." He looked at Noa. "They left. Standard procedure." To Marena. "Powerless, you see? Not simply without gifts."

Noa couldn't help it; sympathy's tiny jaws yawped and cried inside her. *Sympathy*, for Captain Lia. Memories began to play through Noa's mind—not hers, but those she'd seen in Lia during the interrogation.

Arik's story was the truth.

"It's a terrible story," Noa murmured.

"But still you think us monsters."

Noa closed her eyes. Just as when she had tried to think of her memories of Callum, her mind was betraying itself, throwing into question things she had known to be the truth.

Judah once told me about the Hunter who followed him through the Portal," Noa began, grasping onto a strong, solid memory.

"Thorn," Arik nodded. "I knew him well."

"He was cruel for the sake of being cruel."

"Like every Clear," Marena mumbled.

Arik nodded at Noa grimly. "Thorn did enjoy the distasteful things, it's true. I met him in the Clear Province, before it was such a place. When it was the burned-out market shantytown where Clears went to starve in safety."

Noa bit her lip. Another truth from Arik, she knew. Judah and Callum themselves had told her about the old, ruined market-place—just not that it had been the last refuge of persecuted Clears.

"I lived in that place with my mother and several other abused Clear women," Arik continued, "The smell, the air..." he shivered. "It's where we met Lia actually, after she'd fled her husband. Thorn arrived there too one day, alone and badly beaten— he was seventeen, skinny and starving, had been caught faking his Colorline to stay in school. Thorn had known the risks, but he was so curious, had such an appetite to learn..."

Noa shut down her sympathy, refused to feel it. She remembered Thorn's 'curiosity' well—he had tortured Callum for sport.

Arik didn't seem to notice her sudden anger. "We were rotting in that ruin, living decomposing lives. Otec Darius saved us. He changed everything." Arik's eyes shone. "Imagine! A Clear who was not powerless at all, despite having no gifts. He had his own power that came from inside him. No one could deny it, not even the Colors; even they knew he was born to lead."

"Exactly," Noa pointed out. "He was a powerless Clear, and yet he rose to lead. Because at least in that society, he had the freedom to try."

Arik didn't seem to hear her, lost in his memory. "I remember seeing Thorn at the Otec's rallies. Skinny Thorn! Those hollow eyes, round and bright with *worthiness*! He grew strong with it, we all did. Like tasting sun for the first time...." Arik looked into Noa's eyes, reverent. "The Otec rebuilt us, he made us *real*."

"And melted some people along the way," Noa replied.

Arik's eyes turned cold and hard for the first time. "Do you know what that prisoner did? That old cell mate you grieve for? He ran a service disposing of Clear babies! So parents could try again until they got the Colored children they desired!"

Noa flinched. She had not loved Geezer, but he had sacrificed himself to set her free. She had come to consider him at least a fellow victim.

Arik laughed harshly. "Such a nasty cosmic joke, Colorline being random for every child. They couldn't just breed us out. At least it gave Fae like your cell mate a lucrative trade!"

Arik made a visible effort to regain control. "Can you even *imagine* how Darius must have felt when he learned of Gwydion's hideous crime? Not only to suppress all Clear powers, but to erase the *knowledge* that Clears ever had them at all? To make us, *everyone*, believe we were intrinsically worthless?" Noa had to look away from the blaze in Arik's eyes. "*That* is why there was no Otec until Darius, because he is father to all Fae. The only one who loved us enough to right something too evil to let stand, no matter what it cost!"

"Why … why are you telling me this?"

"Because I need you to understand what happens next."

"What … happens next? I don't understand."

Arik met her eyes with no hint of apology: "Your sacrifice."

• • •

ARIK LEFT, HIS final word uncurling like a serpent. Noa and Marena locked eyes, tasting the same dread.

That night, under the cover of darkness, they talked—not about what was to come, or how they might evade it, but simply to connect. In careful, whispered words, fragile daisies chained together, Noa told Marena about her world, her family. About Isla who'd been lost, but whose spirit lived; about Sasha, beloved, bestial and brave.

Marena told Noa about her younger brother, Gerard, whom she'd tried to protect after the Segregation, clinging fast to him in the Barracks in violation of the law. Gerard was wrapped inside Marena's spirit, the way Sasha and Isla beat through Noa's heart.

"He's dead now," Marena said finally, without tears.

"How do you know?"

"I feel it."

Noa nodded. She had felt it, too, when Isla died.

"What?" Noa asked. Marena was studying her.

"It's just—you're no pixie, and as a Greenie I can feel that's true. You feel different. It's small, but it's there."

"But … ?"

Marena's mouth had furrowed a little. "But when I talk about how I know my brother's dead? I feel you *feel* it with me. Not just listen, but *feel*. But that's Green. That's Fae. Our gift."

"Or empathy," Noa replied softly, "which is human, too."

Marena nodded, but her eyes remained uncertain. They dropped off into silence for a time.

Finally, just when Noa was sure the pixie had fallen asleep, Marena asked, "Why'd you come back for me, in the cell? When you and the boys were escaping?"

"I heard you call my name. I knew it was you in there."

"That's just it," Marena murmured. "I didn't say anything. I never said anything at all."

• • •

WHEN ARIK RETURNED, Callum followed him inside.

"Callum!" Noa shrieked, surging awkwardly against the chains.

Callum didn't answer. He was standing ramrod straight, curls shorn short and tamed, jaw square and face erect. He wore a silver uniform, perfectly pressed, and scuff-free, polished boots. He looked at her, and Noa trembled. There was no recognition in his eyes. They were hard. Dark. Callum, always tall, suddenly seemed to loom. And worst—the very worst—was his *stillness*. The stillness of purpose.

And certainty.

Arik took in Noa's horror. "It's what's right," he told her gently.

"What have you done?" Noa wailed, whirling on him. "What have you done to Callum?"

"Nothing, pixie!" Callum spat.

"Pixie?" Noa repeated, wondering if this was some secret message, some way of Callum telling her he was simply playing along—

Callum turned to Arik. "Is this the prisoner?"

Noa suddenly knew with terrible certainty that this was no act. "Callum! It's me! It's Noa."

Callum's face only flickered in annoyance.

Arik answered Callum, ignoring Noa. "No, you'll do the other." He tilted his head toward Marena, who screamed in terror and hurled herself in the only direction she could: against the wall.

"Callum! No! That's Marena!" Noa cried. "Marena!"

But they weren't listening, neither of them; they were turning to greet the third Guard who'd just arrived. Another Guard perfectly erect in a shining silver uniform, but slighter, darker—

"Judah!" Noa screamed. But Judah's eyes were cold too.

"Judah! Judah, please! Don't let Callum hurt her!"

But Judah didn't stop Callum; he simply moved aside, blank-faced, as Callum grabbed Marena's arm. Marena howled, squirmed, kicked, bit, but Callum was too strong, too calm. He unlocked Marena's chains, held her easily by a single, skinny arm, dangling her like a broken doll.

Noa didn't know how to think, how to react; her mind had become too feral in its incarceration. Something important was pulsing urgently through her brain. She had to listen, she had to listen more than she ever had before—

Noa shook her head, trying to clear it: she had seen this before, this Callum-But-Not-Callum, this impostor in her beloved's skin. But where had that been, what place, what time, and hadn't she found a way to wake him? To uncover what was buried, find a touchstone to call him back, a talisman against the madness—

Noa flung her left hand to her wrist, remembering. In the In Between, freeing Callum from the Man with White Hands, she'd needed the talisman—but her wrist was bare now, Arik had taken the talisman when they were marching through the square—

She looked desperately at Arik, opened her mouth—

"Judah, that one's yours," Arik ordered immediately, and Judah grabbed Noa's arm. But Arik's gaze had flickered, Noa had seen it. She squirmed, twisted to look where Arik had looked in that split instant: at Callum's wrist. There, encased in a thin red tube, her own talisman was clasped.

"Callum! Callum! It's the bracelet—" Noa screamed, but Callum didn't even turn her way. "It's the bracelet—it's controlling you!"

Callum ignored her, shoving Marena, still kicking, screaming, biting, out through a passage he conjured in the wall. Judah yanked Noa along behind them.

"No! Callum!" Noa spun and flailed in Judah's grip, fighting with all she had. She was bigger than Marena, and Judah had always been slighter than Callum; Judah had to haul Noa in front of him, grasping her basket-style to hold fast her wild limbs. She wanted to scream at the absurdity of it, this hero's hold now when he was not him and she was not her. Judah—always the mockery of a hero, posture right and conviction wrong.

Noa struggled to keep fighting, humiliating tears streaming in torrents down her cheeks. Because through their blur she'd seen it—the bracelet on Judah's wrist which meant Marena had been right about it all. For though it was a bracelet Noa had never seen, she recognized it by heart: another talisman, housing a broken soul. Like Callum's, it was encased in a red tube, and fastened around the wrist of the one whose spirit had been torn.

"Judah," Noa shuddered with terrible tears. "No, no, Judah—" She choked on her sobs, gasped so hard she couldn't see. Something about this bracelet, Judah's bracelet, was the worst thing, the very worst thing. She melted, sliding down through his hands, the hands cradling her like the dear one she never now could be. Because now she could never tell him the important thing, the only thing, the thing that she hadn't known she'd known and only now knew was important.

That was why it almost didn't register when Arik motioned for Judah to face Noa to the glass; why she almost didn't hear Arik's words, "Be brave," or realize where Arik and the brothers had taken them.

The glass cube room. Where Geezer and Crazy had been turned to ooze.

It wasn't until Callum's back came into focus within the room, his strong, broad arms holding Marena's screaming, flailing form directly in front of Noa's eyes, that Noa understood what was about to happen.

"No! No! Callum, no!"

But it was too late, Callum's hands were on Marena's skinny, fighting body, and then Marena's skin was glowing Green and sizzling, dripping off her bones. Noa screamed and struggled, insanity making her strong—and for the briefest instant, Judah's grip faltered. Noa's arm flew back wildly and crashed into Arik's nose, shattering the bone.

Arik yelled, grabbed his bloody face as Judah regained control of Noa's arms. Marena's voice howled and also gurgled; she had no legs now, no hands, her arms were melting into sludge…

"It's necessary!" Arik yelled at Noa, desperate for her to understand. "The final test!" But Noa wouldn't understand, couldn't understand, never would; nor would she stop screaming. She wailed and wept until she wasn't even human, until she was just a beast, an animal, a thing. And like an animal, she couldn't look away because she had no Reason, so she stared into Marena's wide and mink-fringed eyes—the eyes of Isla, of Sasha, of Noa herself—until they became islands, the only islands left, and then they too dissolved into the sludge beneath his hands, Callum's hands, those white, white hands.

A horrible keen tore itself from Noa's throat, from that place that was pure instinct, pain. She knew she was next and didn't care, and then she realized that if they were tests, as Arik said, she was supposed to be *Judah's*—

Judah's hands—

—and suddenly she had to say it, even though she knew he couldn't hear it anymore.

"You were never broken, Judah!" she told him with force and focus. "You were never an impostor!"

"Judah, bring her in!" Arik ordered. Callum filed out of the room, holding the tube of Green goo that once had been Marena. Judah's hold tightened on Noa's arms, but his step hesitated, just minutely. His eyes found hers, and something flashed in them, so distant and so brief—

"Judah!" Arik demanded.

But Judah was looking at Noa, searching, listening, hearing—

"*Impostor…*," he echoed, or maybe he just mouthed it, and maybe Noa mouthed it too, and whispered, "I'm sorry."

"Judah! Now!"

Judah looked at Arik, nodded once, took a step forward in obedience—but then his body turned and ran, crashed toward the wall, thrust Noa into the supply chute and slammed the cover tight.

The last thing Noa saw was his confused, conflicted face. Then the door crashed closed and the thunderous screams grew faint as she plummeted backward in total darkness.

PART IV: ISLANDS

CALLUM COULDN'T SEE it happen clearly because the other soldier—the one who looked like him, who wasn't quite a stranger but felt better, worse, and *more*—was smudged and fuzzy around the edges. Even though it happened quickly (so said the shouts and leaping-into-action), it still happened the way everything happened now: smoothly, like pirouettes in ice. The other soldier (Judah who remember is my brother, though I do not think I love him) had been holding the blond girl tight, waiting his turn to come and do his duty. But then he was hoisting her up (like a mermaid) and running and pushing her into the delivery chute. She disappeared, blond hair last (or maybe the tail, the long green tail, something that glittered).

Except the girl was not a mermaid. Her hair was many colors of yellow, that was true, and that meant something except it didn't. Because she was a prisoner, and she was not diving down some towered tree of kelp, she was escaping down that chute like the garbage that she was.

And the other soldier (my brother Judah, remember, but maybe it's that he does not love me) let her escape instead of going into the room of glass and doing his duty, doing what was right. The room of glass was the place where the things that did not make sense—the feelings like who loved who, and who was what, and what was good or bad or lies—were purified, melted down to smooth, clean color, poured neatly into thin tubes that went on to serve an ordered function. Because order was the most important thing. Order, which was neat and clean—and safe.

There was no room for mermaids—half-Fae, half-fish, half-fable—in a world of order.

So after it happened, Callum strode over to the chute, where the other soldier (my brother, remember, who needs my love because look at how he makes mistakes) was now blocking the silver door with his body. Judah was tall and strong but not so tall and strong as Callum. Judah could fight the others and even Captain Arik but not his brother who knew all the ways he flailed. Callum couldn't place the memory exactly, but his muscles knew just how Judah would pretend he had six arms and legs. His body knew the ways to work around it (my brother thinks he is an octopus, but he is not, it is the trick of that tricky mermaid).

Callum pinned Judah in front of him, the way Judah had so recently pinned the girl. Callum used his gift to block the air from Judah's brain to make Judah fall asleep. Then Callum calmed. He was surprised, for he had not realized he was so agitated—that his muscles had been pulsing, seething, until Judah was immobilized, safe from making the wrong choice.

Warmth spread through Callum—thick, pleasing in a numbing sort of way—to know Judah now was protected. Callum had done his job. Callum was, after all, the one who could see, and who wanted to be good. Callum knew to make things quiet when they were noisy, bad, and bright.

"Good work, Callum," Captain Arik told Callum brusquely as he got back to his feet from the place Judah had kicked him down (Octopus legs, Judah has, but not the eyes to see). Callum felt another swell of pride because he liked to please this gaunt, stretched-out man (whose face is like an eagle). But it was strange how Captain Arik never met Callum's eye, and even though his words of praise—like all words and voices, and ordered noise— came to Callum slightly fuzzy with round edges, they still sounded sharp. Like Captain Arik didn't want to say them, or was biting off their perfect, rounded ends.

Things like this sometimes made Callum wonder if Captain Arik really *saw* the way that Callum did. If he really understood the importance of order.

Callum closed his eyes a moment, let the pleasant warmth expand and blur away that thought. He had discovered it was very good for that. Callum didn't like to think badly of Captain Arik: Captain Arik had rescued Callum, after all, and reminded Callum of what he'd used to know so well: the certainty, the blissful certainty, of helping his Great Otec father. For even though Callum's other memories crumbled like dry sand, his memory of helping Otec Darius remake the world was crystal clear, and clean.

Callum remembered every detail with the fineness of a photograph: how he had learned to use the finest aspects of his gift, sometimes to knit broken skin and bones, and other times, to convince the ones who did not understand about the stillness (and the order) that, for their own protection, they should speak the things they thought were secrets. Many times, those Fae (confused Fae, named Rebels) thought things were true that were really lies they didn't even know would hurt them.

It made sense, perfect logical sense, then, what Callum had performed as his duty in those days: he'd shown these misguided Fae, in a way they could feel (since they could not see), how their messiness was hurting them. It was not enough to reorder things from the top, to Awaken the real, clear truth—you also had to make it stick for those too confused to see it. That was why hard things were necessary then, and why they were necessary now.

The small girl, Callum thought, was a good example. She had flailed and bit like Judah in Callum's arms but was light as a paper doll. She'd been in the cell with the mermaid (not a mermaid, remember, even if she has a mermaid heart), and Callum hadn't wanted to pick her up because she was a child. But he had to, because seeing the small girl, and especially the other not-a-mermaid (the one who is gone now, remember, because Judah let her escape), had caused that unpleasant chaos to race across Callum's skin. The small girl (and more, the other) disturbed the warmth of Callum's inside order.

So the hard thing had to happen.

And so Callum had done it, just as Captain Arik had commanded. He'd picked up the small girl and taken her to the glass room and done his duty (even though inside I screamed! Where is my voice! Whose are these hands!) and hadn't stopped till it was done (her little limbs dissolving into pure, pure Green, but it does not feel clean, oh no, not clean at all—). Callum had successfully transformed the girl's messy noise into a still and silent tube of purpose, ready for the preciseness of its job.

(But sick, nauseated, inside-out, and the bottle feels so cold.)

Now Callum held Judah pinned in front of him unconscious, because Judah's mistake had made a mess and let the mermaid girl escape. Callum closed his eyes again, waited for the numbing salve of fuzzy warmth. It worked, the way it always did when everything was finally in its place.

"He must be fighting the collar somehow, that's how he disobeyed," Captain Arik said to Callum. Callum opened his eyes and saw Captain Arik fling down Judah's wrist, the one with the red tube that held the special charm. Callum had made that charm, another hard thing needed to keep the order (but it hurts for some reason to remember this, it does not feel warm and safe, even though Arik says it is ...).

"What about the prisoner who escaped?" Callum asked in that voice that wasn't his but always knew just what to do. Relief poured over him to hear it; it was so much easier when that voice took charge.

"Forget her, she's not important. But we'll have to put *him* into a cell again until I can find a more permanent way of swaying him."

Callum's warm numbness hitched unpleasantly. Captain Arik looked upset. His plan for Callum's brother had not brought order.

"No, I don't want to do that," Callum's strong voice said.

Captain Arik glared at Callum. "It's not up to you to decide."

Callum's ears twitched, hearing something funny in Arik's voice. Callum squinted: Arik was not glaring into Callum's eyes, but at a spot between them.

Captain Arik was *afraid*.

255

There was no room for fear in order. Not with hard things to be done.

Callum, Strong Callum, stood up straight and turned to the Guard on Arik's left. This Guard had a spider tattoo around his eye and admired Callum—he had followed Callum around the compound and asked about those memories, the sharp ones, of when Callum had served in the Otec's regiments.

"We are not going to put him in a cell," Callum's strong voice told Spider-Eye directly. Spider-Eye glanced at Arik, and Callum's shoulders squared. The warmth came again, but sharper, stronger, in a way that was different than before.

"Don't look at him. You look at me," he ordered Spider-Eye.

"You're out of line—" Arik began, but Callum caught his spindly arm as it made a move to grab the bracelet on Callum's wrist. Callum twisted the arm back, told the elbow joint to break. Arik screamed, but Callum didn't listen. Arik knew how pain had to be used to teach what was right.

It was not right that Arik touch Callum's bracelet, not anymore.

"You are not his son!" Arik cried, voice strangled and piercing and slurpy with pain. Messy.

Callum told Arik's mouth to seal itself and turned away because Arik's face was messy too.

"Put him somewhere until he calms down," Callum told the Guard beside Spider-Eye, the one with the squeaky voice. With each order, Callum felt more robust with purpose. Still and calm and clean.

Callum turned to Spider-Eye, knowing just what was supposed to happen next. "Take my brother and me to see the Otec; it's time to join our father."

. . .

NOA TUMBLED AND tumbled down the chute, sliding and careening down the cold silver walls. It felt like being swallowed— the slippery, slipping darkness, the gurgle clang and rub—but Noa didn't care. Anything was better than what she had just seen, still saw, could never now unsee: Marena melting, *Marena melting*, right through Callum's white, white hands.

So it was too soon, much too soon, when the dark throat expelled Noa into the stomach of the palace—the heat and steam and sweat of the grinding, belowground laundry. Gray-shirted Colored Fae rushed, ironed, wrung, and hauled in a constant state of siege and sweat. The pile of sodden Colored Fae rags that broke Noa's fall was sopped with the heavy air.

No one noticed Noa's entrance amid the chaos and the heat, which was just as well since Noa's eyes still only saw Marena, Callum, and not what was in front of her. Fortunately, her body didn't need her eyes to help; it reacted on its own. Her arms reached down into the moist, hot rags, pulled some on over her bruises, limbs, and scar. Her feet walked to the stove, her hands picked up a bubbling pot of boiling water, her head bowed itself over the steam, and her legs scurried across the fray.

"What the hell are you doing?" a fat pixie yelled when Noa slopped hot water on her rag-wrapped foot. Noa tried to focus on her face, but instead of lines and jowls she saw Marena, only Marena—

"Watch *out*, you gobbin' cul! What's wrong with you?"

Noa clumsily dropped the pot, pushed past the pixie to the center of the Laundry. Mounds of silver uniforms were being sprayed and steamed; sizzling liquid swirled down a huge grated drain. Noa walked directly into the seething steam, heard but did not feel its sizzle on her skin. She took a white-hot uniform, used it to pry up the scalding grate.

Somewhere distantly behind her, Noa heard the fat pixie's anger turn to fear and swell with other voices, mixing with the hiss and spray, but Noa didn't listen and didn't care. It was so hot, so hot, so hot, but Marena had melted so what did it matter if Noa melted too, and anyway, Noa couldn't see so she couldn't see to be afraid—and she jumped directly into the hole of boiling heat and burning air.

Down, down, down Noa fell inside the scalding drainpipe, down, down, down, burning and searing off her skin. But it didn't matter how hot it was, how much flesh she lost, because at least it was dark and away and so who cared—

—and then she hit the hard, tepid wet where hot droplets met a stagnant, shallow pool.

Noa's body curled, then rolled. She looked up, but any sign of the opening from which she'd fallen had been lost, along with light. The only light now was weak and sickly. Lavender.

Noa had been here before, in this sandpaper place.

Her legs stood, her body walked. Forward then left then right then right then left until she was so deep into the Tunnels, so far gone into the endless maze, that finally, *finally* no one could ever touch her.

• • •

BUMP, BUMP, BUMP. Bump, bump, bump.

Judah's head was hitting, jolting, against something hard that rose and fell—something hard, but breathing. He tried to see what it was, but it was difficult, because whatever it was was moving—and so was he.

He was being carried. Up stairs.

Judah felt shocky, disjointed. Like his mind had been disconnected then put back too loosely, with the wires all wrong. So when he turned the switch, his fuses blew.

Bump, bump, bump.

Judah tried to glimpse the breathing mass of white against which his head kept hitting. He saw the shine of a silver button, the crisp neatness of the fabric—a soldier's uniform. He cringed, and as he cringed he caught that scent: trees, sea, a little bit of lavender.

His brother.

In uniform.

Panic and pain exploded in Judah's head, wild and indecipherable; he cursed the faulty wiring that was so slow to translate. Something bad had happened, really bad, they'd both been lost and a pixie—

No, not a pixie, *Noa*—

Had vanished into a hole—

"Callum," Judah crackled, knowing the name only as he spoke it. "Where are you taking me? What happened? Where's Noa?"

"Don't worry, Brother," Callum replied. "I'm going to help you. I'm going to make sure you are all right."

But Callum's certainty didn't calm Judah; it did the opposite, the way Judah guessed it was not supposed to. Things were mixed up, backwards, inside out. *Impostor.* But who was the impostor? Was it Callum? Noa? Him?

Fear exploded in Judah's throat. "Who am I? Who am I, Callum!"

"You're my brother. Don't worry. Our father will fix you."

"Callum, no!" Judah cried, not sure of anything except that he was terrified. He wanted to struggle, to get away, but his body would not obey, as if his veins were filled with tar. Panic bloomed atop the terror, another horrific certainty: "Something's wrong! Something's wrong with me! Something's happened!"

"Shh," Callum soothed, neither missing stride nor slowing. "You made a mistake, but that's what you do and then I help you, and so will Otec Darius—"

"He'll kill us, Callum!" Judah screamed, again discovering the truth only as he screamed it.

"Shh, Brother," Callum cooed.

"No! No!" Desperation made Judah's words slurred and messy, impossible to control with sharpness. "No!" he whimpered, then sobbed. *"No!"* But Callum wouldn't hear, and somewhere Judah had known he'd never hear. Now they were at the top of those endless stairs and a Guard with a spider on his eye was opening the door.

"Callum!" Judah screamed.

"Hail, Otec!" Spider-Eye proclaimed, opening the door.

The boys walked in together; the Otec, their father, turned—

—but it wasn't their father, wasn't Darius at all.

It was the Gatekeeper.

It was Kells.

• • •

DEEP WITHIN THE labyrinth, Noa's legs finally gave out beneath her. Her body sprawled on the wet ground, cheek in some unknown, stagnant runoff. It was probably crawling with disease. It was probably infecting all her burns. She didn't care.

Marena was dead.

Marena was dead, Callum was lost, and Judah was … something. And Sasha—

No.

Noa could not bear to think of Sasha, of the hole where Sasha was supposed to be, on top of everything else. Better, safer, to think of this filthy puddle and try to sleep. Even sleep forever, if it meant oblivion now.

"Nose, *hello*, Nose! Don't *make* me poke you, girl. I just painted these bad boys."

Olivia's neon-yellow fingernails wiggled in front of Noa's eyes. The fourth fingernail on each hand was painted Day-Glo pink.

"Nose! I am in the middle of telling you about my Jeremy drama! And yo, did you get dressed in the dark this morning?"

Noa looked down. Her wrinkled Harlow oxford had definitely seen better days.

"Your mom the moon again?" Olivia asked gently.

Noa looked into Olivia's soft, concerned dark eyes.

"It's gonna take time. At least your aunt's helping now, right? Here, wear mine." Olivia went to her closet. "I keep it ironed on the hanger. I swear, my parents *trained* me to be OCD."

For some reason, Noa felt tears come to her eyes. "What were you saying about Jeremy?" she asked, the way she knew a good friend was supposed to.

"Oh, just I get the feeling he's gonna ask me to the Alumni Ball, and I need a good excuse. Not the 'it's-not-me-it's-you,' because duh, it's totally him."

"Wait, I thought you and Jeremy were dating—"

"Um, what are you smoking, and can I have some?"

"No," Noa remembered, confused. "No, you're right, he just *wanted* to be with you, that was his wish, what kept him happy in the In Between, but none of that was real...."

Olivia put the shirt down, sat down slowly next to Noa. "Are you okay, Noa?"

Noa shook her head, tried to smile. "Yeah, yeah, I'm just ... dream hangover. You know me and my weird artist brain."

Olivia smiled. "True dat. The imagination can be a dangerous thing. But then again..." she wiggled her eyebrows mischievously, "so can sleeplessness resulting from all-night rendezvous with jolly green strangers. Don't think you don't owe me deets, lady. I gave good alibi last night."

Noa furrowed her brow, trying to understand.

"I know, I know, you don't like me to call Callum that. But I have to find *some* way to make fun of that guy, otherwise he's too Adonis-y for his own good. So how was the date? The whole Noa-in-Charge deal?"

"I ... I took him to Monterey," Noa said slowly. "We kayaked and ... ate saltwater taffy. There was an otter...."

Olivia rolled her eyes. "Get to the good stuff. Any smoochies?"

"No," Noa said, remembering more clearly. "Not then, but later. Under the tree. And it was..." *His face, the light, the electricity between them, hands upon hands upon leaves upon lips, something hers, only hers, always hers ...* "It changed the world."

"Whoa, Noa—"

"I don't mean to be melodramatic, it really felt—"

"No, Noa!" Olivia leapt up, pointed to Noa's chest. Across her white, wrinkled Oxford, a line of red was bleeding. "Did you cut yourself? What happened?"

"It's my scar—"

"It's bleeding everywhere!"

Noa looked up. Red droplets were raining down from everywhere, now turning green—she looked at Olivia, at the green spots on her Harlow vest, but now it wasn't Olivia, it was Marena, trying to look tough but failing, scared, and she was melting into greenest rain.

"*No!*" Noa screamed. She didn't want to be here, didn't want to see this. She closed her eyes but still the vision lingered—

Change the nightmare, Noa.

Noa gasped. Her mother's voice, not her mother-the-moon, but Hannah in full light, robust and round.

Noa opened her eyes, and Hannah was standing beside the silently screaming Marena, the green rain making circles on her hair, her shoulders. Hannah was younger, the way she'd been when Noa had been small. When Noa had run into her mother's room, night after night, unable to sleep without fear.

"Go back in and change the nightmare, Noa," Hannah soothed her. "That's the way it can't get you. Make it someplace safe."

Hannah's eyes held Noa's, sure and calm. Noa nodded. *Someplace safe.* She concentrated, and around them the green rain turned to swirling leaves, to grassy ground. And Noa was leaning against Callum beneath his tree, encircled and so safe. She wore the bracelet, the one that let them be and breathe together, the gift, the talisman….

Noa lifted her wrist, let the tiny charm glitter in the sun. She laughed; it was so fragile, so frail, to have given her so much. A world of her own. A place that was hers, unbreachable by chaos, chance, even invisible things she didn't know yet to fear. She turned to Callum, looking to see this happiness mirrored in his eyes—and lurched away. Because Callum had no face, his face was blank, and the talisman burned around her wrist.

The talisman that was bad, not good, that had maimed his soul, let dark things in, let him be controlled—

Change the nightmare, Noa. Make it someplace safe.

Noa strained and made the grass, the leaves, grow tall and flat and lined with books. Lamont Library, a cocoon of words, but she looked around and saw she was alone. Cold, alone, afraid. Where was Judah? Noa remembered: he wasn't here and neither was this place, it did not exist, it existed only in the Portal that had devoured them alive. The world that was meant to feel right but never had, not to Noa, never right and never safe. Not for her or Judah or anyone at all.

She screamed.

Change the nightmare! Make it safe!

The room and colored book covers flickered, flashed, became a whirlwind of light and roaring sound. Noa went home, but waiting there was Isla's loss, the cavern inside the cavern.

She went to school, but she was inside the box, the commuter locker where she no longer fit.

She searched frantically for Callum, because Callum had helped her breathe, had shown her air, had given her gills and wings. And she hadn't had to take care of him, not like her parents or like Judah; even Callum's lies had given her the gift of Sasha, her someone round and whole—

—but Callum was nowhere, nowhere, nowhere. Not at the dock in Monterey, not in the bicycle surrey on the coast, not holding the taffies on the Salinas bus. He wasn't next to her building the Neverland float, or enduring extra help with her in history. He wasn't in the tree outside her window, watching over her to make sure she was okay. Those places were there, but Callum wasn't; he was unraveling from the fabric of her mind—or maybe he was in the glass room, only in the glass room, his hands ever on Marena's shoulders, melting her to green—

Someplace safe!

The Tunnels! Damp and dark, lost and alone, safe where nobody could touch her, where nothing could sneak in and change her mind. No touch, no loss, no change or love or lies. Aloneness. Perfect aloneness.

Sasha.

Not alone. Not even here.

Noa would never be alone, could never be alone because Sasha was her heart. Sasha's blood was Noa's blood. Noa breathed because Sasha breathed. Sasha's mess was Noa's life.

Sasha's form shimmered, wavered, coalesced in Noa's dream.

"No, please, not here—it isn't safe for you here—" Noa told her. Sasha could not know this deep, this dark. Noa would not let it learn the taste of Sasha's sweat. *"Go."*

The ghostly image faded away, obeying Noa's command before it even fully formed. Noa's cheek fell back into the puddle—or maybe it was her dream-cheek, into an echo puddle in her mind.

Noa turned her head, let her other cheek rest against the wet. The silence of the Tunnels filled down around her, and she saw Hilo, arm in arm with Judah, hiding something in one of their special places in the wall. Judah looked lighter, younger; Hilo looked at him with that special something budding

265

deeper. Noa recoiled sharply, gasping, and Hilo turned toward her, glared directly into Noa's face. Hilo's face twisted in anger, confusion, disbelief—then the whole tunnel, the real tunnel, popped back empty, damp, and black. She was awake.

She was alone.

Noa closed her eyes again, prayed for dreamless oblivion— and finally she got her wish. She slept and slept, dreaming nothing, lying still in the puddle until her body chilled and her clothes were sodden. She didn't dare to think, to move, until a hand grabbed and shook her roughly, forcing her to open her eyes.

"Why," Hilo hissed, eyes fierce in the dark, "were you walking in my dream?"

• • •

FOR A MOMENT, Noa was paralyzed.

"Answer me, Dreamwalker! How and why and *now*!" Hilo demanded, hair shock-white in anger like some alabaster demoness.

"I-I don't know," Noa stuttered. Her palms slipped clumsily in the stagnant water.

Water.

"What about *you*?" Noa remembered angrily, emboldened by rage. "You tricked us, and we were captured! They took us to—they made us—because of *you*—" Noa didn't want to remember it, couldn't contain it, wanted only to punish the person, pixie, *siren* who had caused it all. She lunged at Hilo, claws out, hissing; she wasn't Noa anymore, she was Isla, Sasha—no, *Marena*!—and she was biting and scratching and screaming like the girl-beast she knew she was.

"Stop it! Stop!" Hilo cried, trying to cover her face with her hands.

Noa felt a wave of something try to get at her, a cloud of helplessness and fear pressing its fingers toward her mind. She laughed aloud, ignored it; its thumbs were tentative and weak and blew away like so much smoke.

Gift failing, Hilo hurdled into Noa instead and bowled her backward. She pinned Noa with her knees and talon-hands, eyes fierce and canines bared. Earthy and lethal, just like Callum had said—except Noa couldn't quite remember how he'd said it, couldn't quite hear the timbre of his voice—

"What's with you!" Hilo shook Noa hard, slapped her across the face. "Where did you go just now?"

"My head…," Noa said slowly, skull suddenly thundering painfully. "My head hurts so much…."

Hilo's ferocity wavered; she pulled herself off Noa, eyeing her warily. Noa knew vaguely this was an opening to lunge back, but all she could do was put her hands to her hammering temples.

Her suffering made Hilo look uncomfortable. "Here, I'll make your limbic system relax, ease the pai—"

"Don't!" Noa spat. "No help from you, you traitor!"

"I suppose letting someone explain isn't something mortals do," Hilo replied icily.

"Not when honesty clearly isn't something *you* do." Noa's headache suddenly eased again, as rapidly as it had come. She straightened up. "We could have drowned for all you cared!"

"You don't know anything about me."

"I know plenty, and Judah—"

"And you *really* don't know Judah," Hilo snorted.

Noa resisted an urge to snarl.

"Oh, you think I'm wrong?" Hilo laughed. "You think you have some special window into his soul?"

Noa narrowed her eyes. "We've been through quite a bit together."

The humor vanished from Hilo's eyes. "Oh, really? Have you 'been through' hearing him say he wants to die? Have you 'been through' listening to him plan the ways, *and asking for your help*, because somewhere, somehow, he was taught he wasn't worth his life?"

Noa looked down, but Hilo didn't stop: "Were *you* there when he made the hollow cave to be his tomb? Were they *your* hands that had to help him dig it out, so he wouldn't actually grave-dig himself to death? Were *you* there, Noa?" She wiped angrily at her eyes, her cheeks. "And when he explained there was no hope? Because what was wrong with him was so insidious and so invisible, it was deeper than any marrow, more basic than any genes, and would poison any way he tried to grow?"

Noa trembled. "I wasn't there, no, but Callum told me, and Judah—"

"But you didn't *see* it. You weren't here, *below*. Not like I was."

"Yes," Noa finally acknowledged, "you kept him safe—"

"No! Don't you see?" Hilo cried. "I tried, I failed! I helped Callum because I *couldn't* ... I couldn't do it alone—" Hilo broke off, swallowed hard.

"And your feelings for Callum?" Noa asked quietly.

Hilo shrugged. "I was dazzled by him, we all were. *The Blue Son*. Even if you didn't support Darius, it was impossible not to—" Hilo steeled herself. "But what I did, I did for Judah.

I knew he would hate me for it but at least he'd be *alive*—"

"What about *now*, Hilo," Noa replied. "You informed on us, delivered us right to Arik."

"It wasn't me," Hilo said plainly, looking right into Noa's eyes. "I would never cross over to Darius after what he's done."

"You mean his oppression of the Colors?"

"I mean the oppression of his *son*."

Despite herself, Noa bit her lip. Hilo was not trustworthy, she knew that, so why did she find herself wanting to believe?

"The worst," Hilo continued softly, shivering, "were the things Darius *didn't* say. The subtext, the silence—Judah breathed it all in with the air. It got inside him, and he didn't even know it…"

Noa steeled herself. "But your silence hurt him too. You started the Fyre in the Training Center and never told him it was you. You let him believe he might have done it, killed his own sister. You could have spared him that but you said *nothing*."

Hilo looked away, wiped hard at her cheek. She stayed silent so long Noa thought she had finally done it, won this argument, proven Hilo was the villain—and for some reason, that made Noa want to cry.

But then Hilo spoke, a whisper, her entire body trembling: "I couldn't tell him. I couldn't say it. I-I loved Lily, too. And even more"—a little sob broke up her words, but Hilo pushed herself through it—"I loved that she made Judah feel loved too." Slowly, painfully, Hilo turned back to meet Noa's eyes, face wet with tears. "I couldn't tell him I'd ruined that, taken that away. So I put it in a box—all of it—and I sealed it up and stuffed it down as deep as it would go, because there was no other way that I could live and breathe past it."

Noa's hand found itself touching Hilo's arm.

"Lily didn't die, Hilo," she said gently. "You didn't kill her. And even more important, what you did helped save her life."

Hilo buried her face in her hands, surrendered to her tears. Somehow, Noa's arms fell around her and Noa was crying, too. They cried together, held each other, there in the damp dark. When the tears finished, they looked at each other, clean.

As if they'd been baptized by truth and sorrow, tears and tunnels. As if they were united now, and the world had been washed new.

• • •

AFTER THAT, AND without saying anything explicitly, Noa and Hilo were no longer enemies.

"How did you find me?" Noa asked as they began to walk together.

"You found *me*," Hilo replied. "You Dreamwalked in my dream—"

"No you were in *my* dream," Noa insisted. "I saw you laughing with Judah at the wall—"

"That was *my* dream, Noa. You Dreamwalked into it. I saw you watching us, and I recognized where you were so I came to find you. I know these Tunnels just as well as Judah, don't forget."

"Is 'dreamwalking' an Aurora thing?"

"No," Hilo said. She stopped, looked unhappy. "It's a Red thing."

"A Red—wait, you mean a gift?"

"An extension of the Red gift—reading minds, reading dreams—but it's a really advanced skill."

"Then that's not what happened. I'm mortal."

"I *know*," Hilo snapped.

Noa hesitated, but she was tired, so tired, of having to carry all her worries around alone.

"I … I've also been having really bad headaches. At first they were just annoying, but now … they're getting overwhelming. But they come and go really fast, like spasms."

Hilo's face was guarded. "What else?"

"My … memories," Noa admitted, fears tumbling out too fast to stop them. "Especially when I try to think of Callum—it's like I can't quite see him or grasp onto him, or the way I remember him is unraveling—and the air here is too thick, and even the water has a taste, and the sun is so bright…"

Something flashed in Hilo's eyes, almost too quick for Noa to see.

But she did see.

Fear uncurled in Noa's stomach. "Please, Hilo, just tell me."

"I…" Hilo gritted her teeth, as if not wanting to have to say it. "I think Aurora might be … killing you."

Noa exhaled slowly, her panic giving way, startlingly, to acceptance. Her heart had broken, after all. Why not her body too?

She was surprised to feel Hilo's hand on her arm. "You need to go back to your world," Hilo said gently.

Hilo's gentleness, more than anything, made Noa know it was all true.

Noa's head fell. "I can't. Not without Sasha. And … I can't abandon the brothers. Not the way they are right now."

Hilo's fingers tightened. "What do you mean, *the way they are?*"

Noa sighed, so tired, so very tired … too tired to hold it back. She explained what had passed within the prison in monotone, barely registered how Hilo's face drained even whiter than before.

"So they not only have the Green and Blue Smoke now, they've found a way to harness Red."

Noa nodded, blinking away the vision of Marena, melting…. "They encased the talismans in red tubes. It must work the mind control."

Hilo closed her eyes, gritted her teeth. "That's it then. It's over." She fell back against the wall, every inch of her lithe body giving up. "Just say goodbye and seek the Seer."

"What is that, some kind of slang?" Noa asked.

Hilo smiled bitterly. "It's what Fae say when there's no hope left, just death. You 'seek the Seer' and never come back." Her eyes glittered a little in some last gasp of amusement. "It means you go into the Tunnels as deep as you can go with no intention of coming back."

"Like a dog going off to die?"

"Yes."

That single-syllable *yes* rebounded around the tunnel walls, pinging them with its final taunt.

Many moments later—seconds maybe, maybe hours—Hilo spoke again, idle musings of the damned.

"You're a poet right?"

Noa sighed, almost too tired to reply. "I guess. I was. Why?"

Hilo shrugged, but there was something in her shrug—a spark. "I don't know. Just that … you believe stories could be true?"

Noa narrowed her eyes. "You mean that story about secret Tunnel Fae?"

Hilo scoffed. "No. Even you aren't dumb enough to believe that trash. Hidden heroes waiting secretly to save the day? That was something parents told their kids during the Segregation so they wouldn't lose hope. No one lived in the Tunnels."

"Not until two confused brothers, a liar, and a helpless poet," Noa replied, earning Hilo's appreciative little laugh. "So what story then? The one you obviously want me to say could be real?"

Hilo scowled. "Forget it. We'll come up with something else."

"*Hilo*—"

"It's nothing! Happy thinking for hapless idiots!"

"If it means a chance to save my sister, to get home—"

Hilo growled a little, fighting herself, clearly regretting having begun this conversation in the first place. "Look," she said finally, exasperated, "the expression 'seeking the Seer' came from a story, an old story. A whisper, a whisper of a whisper a really long time ago about someone maybe hiding really deep within the Tunnels."

"Who?" Noa demanded.

Hilo sighed. "An Attendant from our Sacred Temple, back from around the time Darius ascended to power. There was a story—just a stupid story!—that the pixie who was next in line to be the Mystic ran away. Supposedly she chose to disappear and live completely alone in the bowels of the Tunnels instead."

"Why?" Noa breathed, her poet's imagination piqued despite herself.

"Exactly!" Hilo huffed. "No one would just run off instead of becoming a *god*. It probably started as some gobbed-up morality tale for kids. In the story she didn't even have a gobbin' name! I mean, please."

"But why would this Attendant even be important?"

"If she *exists*."

"Okay, yes, Hilo, on the very very very remote chance she exists."

Hilo looked affronted at Noa's sass, but Noa didn't care and stared right back. Even raised an expectant eyebrow. Hilo held Noa's stare, challenging her, then finally looked away with a little *hmph*. Noa fought a victorious smile.

"She'd be important," Hilo answered, "because if she trained to be Mystic—even though she never took power—it means she would have studied our sacred Scrolls. And *that* means she'd have a greater understanding of our magic than any other Fae, even Otec Darius. She wouldn't be the Mystic, but she would be a—"

"*Seer.*"

Hilo squirmed uncomfortably. "But it has to be another lie. I mean, she would have popped up to help in the Rebellion, right? If she really did run away as some sort of nutso protest against Darius? But the Rebellion *died* and she never showed her face. *And* tons of stupid Fae went desperately in search of her, hoping she'd save them, and came back as bodies washed out of the Tunnels!"

"So … 'seeking the Seer' now means giving up and going off to die," Noa realized.

Hilo rolled her eyes. *Duh.*

"But…" Noa said, foolish poet to the end, "but no one knows for *sure*…." She couldn't help it, her heart began to thrum. "And she could do it, it's what made you think of this in the first place—"

"Lost my gobbin' mind—"

"She could help set the brothers free, save my sister."

"Going mad—"

Noa glared. "Look, I'm not an idiot. I know this is the longest of long shots. But this is my sister, Hilo. I have to try. And I understand you won't come with me. It's okay."

Hilo rolled her eyes, exasperated. "I'm *coming* with you."

"Why?"

"Would you believe I want to save your damn life?"

Noa studied her. "No."

Hilo threw up her hands. "Would you believe I really want Judah back, then? And saving you—it would be helping him?"

Noa bit her lip.

"I know he loves you," Hilo added softly. "That's my gift, remember? They both do. And you—"

Noa held up her hand. "Stop," she interrupted. "Please, just … let me figure that part out."

Hilo frowned. "Look, if this Seer does exist? You're gonna need me. Because the only way she could have survived all this time—through all the flushes, the searches, the raids—means she's somewhere deep."

"How deep?"

"Deeper than anyone's gone and ever come back alive."

"You don't have to help me," Noa reminded Hilo again.

Hilo's hand shot out, and Noa recoiled, thinking the pixie was going to hit her—but Hilo touched the scar beneath Noa's collarbone instead. Met her eyes. Resolute.

"Yes. I do."

• • •

WHEN THE BROTHERS saw Kells, Callum stumbled so jarringly he dropped Judah. Not that Judah cared, because whatever else was mixed up in Judah's brain, he knew Kells was not his father, was not *Darius*.

Sprawled on the floor, Judah felt only relief.

"*Hail Otec!*" Spider-Eye announced emphatically from the doorway.

Judah wobbled to his feet, watched as Callum bowed jerkily in confusion to the sneering Fae seated in the Otec's throne.

"Hail Otec."

Kells' eyes—the Otec's eyes which were not Darius's—traveled to the bracelet around Callum's wrist. A slow smile gnarled onto his lips.

Kells turned expectantly to Judah, and Judah had the slow feeling he, too, should have bowed and hailed. But since the bumpy ride up in Callum's arms—no, since before that even, since the swirling chaos with that prisoner girl, her name, what was it—Judah was acting on impulse only. The sudden, explosive ones like *Free the girl! This is Callum! Run from Darius!* that broke like shells through this strange and numbing fog.

Bow, hail the Otec—those ideas just wafted lazily. Judah was far too tired to do any of that. To be frank, he felt like shit.

There was no way in hell he was bending to the floor.

Kells glared at Judah. Another shell of remembrance exploded. "You look different, Gatekeeper," Judah croaked, realizing he knew this man, this Otec who was not Darius. The Kells in Judah's memory had been the prisoner of Darius, a shriveled, sneering gargoyle forced to guard the Portal in the prison world. That Kells had lived so long without Light he'd withered to a crusty, gnarled husk.

This Kells was no husk. This Kells, Kells the Otec, was handsome. Youthful. As if he had traveled back in time.

276

Handsome Kells turned briefly to Spider-Eye. "The Blue Son is clearly loyal. Find him a suitable post. The Red Son," Kells said, turning back to Judah with a faint curl to his lip, "remains *as ever*. But you all have clearly done good work with him, he's basically decomposing before my eyes," Kells laughed. "He's no threat. You may leave us."

Spider-Eye led Callum from the room.

"What the hell, Kells?" Judah asked, cringing as he tried to smirk. Kells was right about him, he realized—his body felt like it was dying. Irritation exploded inside his brain, making his thinking sharper.

A chair would be nice, you ass, Judah thought internally.

"Are you really so dense, Red Son? We're in Aurora. Light is plentiful. Of course my body rejoices."

Judah squinted painfully, almost gagged. Partly from the pain, and partly because of what he saw when he looked closer at the ex-Gatekeeper's body. Kells' hair was dark and lush, his face unlined, his stature straight—but it all looked weirdly grotesque. As if beneath the pristine skin, something dirty had been buried.

"Maybe I should be asking what happened to *you*, Red Son. But I'm guessing it's that new trinket 'round your wrist."

Judah looked down at his wrist and was surprised to see the little chain, entubed in red, clasped there. Like Callum's. *Since when do I wear jewelry?*

"Arik's been having all the fun experimenting these days," Kells sighed. "I suppose it's my fault. My directive after all, to innovate. After I killed your vile father."

Sharpness exploded in Judah's head again. "I saw Thorn kill *you* and feed you to your Portal."

Kells roared with laughter. "That's your reply! No scorn for your father's murderer? No anguish? Anger? Tears?"

Judah clenched his jaw—*crap that hurts*—as Kells wiped away a mirthful tear. "Well I suppose I did you a favor too, eh? As for *Thorn*, that Clear brute actually did me a favor. *Many* favors, truth be told, for someone so unmannered. Not least of which was 'feeding me to my Portal.'"

Judah struggled to pay attention. His mind kept wondering about the girl—Noa?—he'd pushed into the chute.

"*My* Portal, Judah," Kells continued emphatically. "I was that Portal's *keeper*. It loved me like a caged lion comes to love its captor. Its cage became its universe, and in that universe I was *God*."

"That's why you weren't there with us, in the Portal mind-trap thing," Judah managed, wincing. "The In Between." Even thinking hurt, but luckily, this section of his memory—the time he had spent together with Noa, yes that was her name—seemed more solid.

"Of course not. My lion would never devour *me*." Another flicker of irritation resurrected Harlow's gnarled groundskeeper, just for a moment. "How did *you* escape?"

"Thought my way out," Judah smirked, fully worth the pain.

Kells raked Judah carefully with his eyes. "Lying to me despite the bracelet. *You.* How very … unexpected."

Judah smirked again, this time more sharply. He didn't know what Kells was talking about with the whole bracelet thing and didn't really care. He began to flex his fingers, see how far his sharpness could go.

The answer, he realized, wincing terribly, was not far.

Kells was muttering on, mostly to himself. "He's never had skill, maybe the fact that he's Red too … We've seen that with the

Smoke sometimes, doesn't work as well on Greens. Invention is a process, after all—"

"Invention?" Judah interrupted, ears pricking at the word.

Kells smiled. "Another of Thorn's unexpected gifts. He saw it first, that human need to rise, create, empower. To make strength even without magic. *Invention*." Pride crept over Kells' face, like an oily sheen: "I've started quite the revolution since I killed your worthless father. I'm getting Fae to *think*. Experiment. Push past any limits of the gifts."

"Wait—" Judah muttered, "those alarms? That ... Smoke? And, and *Review...*" Judah broke off, squeezed his eyes shut; a young pixie's face had suddenly appeared inside his mind along with the words, the memories rapidly exploding. The girl was tough but young and *melting* within cold white hands—Judah shook his head, ignored the pain, shoved the face away as far as it would go.

"All my inventions, inspired by my directive," Kells said proudly, "and we're finding new ways to distill Fae magic every day." His eye fell again on Judah's bracelet. "Though I must give Callum credit for this latest beauty, kinks though it may have."

Judah's skin prickled. "What do you mean?"

"Callum's talisman!" Kells said scornfully. "The one he made for that little mortal wench! Arik has it encased in Red serum. It's actually quite genius—submerging a piece of the target's soul in the essence of mind control."

Judah looked at his own bracelet with dread. He was forgetting something important, or else hadn't remembered it yet—then suddenly, like a pile driver, the memory flushed through him with such force it actually knocked him over. He bowed over his knees, slapped his hands to his temples and screamed in agony.

Kells crowed in delight. "Remember now, do you? Who made yours? Was it Arik?"

But Judah barely heard him over the roaring in his ears, fire razing his skin. White hands, pale white hands, were touching his chest everywhere; one of them wore a bracelet, encased in red—

"*Callum, no!*" Judah wailed, for he was seeing and feeling it again, would always see it and feel it, over and over forever. "*Callum!*"

Kells shrieked and clapped his hands. "Callum, of course! A good son to the last!"

Judah twisted onto his side, began to writhe and seize madly on the floor. Kells could barely breathe for laughing. Finally, as if it were just too much—too much joy or too much justice—Kells took a small green vial from his pocket and crushed it against Judah's back.

Judah's body stopped seizing, and for the first time in since what felt like forever, his body became calm, controlled. His heart stopped its erratic, pulsing fling, and the terrible memory blurred and blurred until he no longer had to see its details. It pulled itself into a nice round bubble, tied at the end, and floated gently out of view.

Judah sat up slowly, sore and tired but sedated. Bits of glass from the vial tinkled from his back to the ground.

"My brother ... cut my soul...," Judah murmured, looking at his wrist in awful wonder.

"What there was left of it, anyway."

"What does *that* mean?" Judah demanded, wincing again. *Crap bastard, the physical relief is only temporary.*

"Just that maybe your bracelet not working doesn't have to

do with a defect in the invention. Maybe it's just a defect in *your soul.*" Judah tried to growl in indignation but whimpered instead. "Oh come on, Red Son. You've never had any loyalty! No sense of duty! You burn things down, you run away, and you make the mess! Always have! *Callum's* the one who cleaned it up, who did his duty, who actually *desired* to be a useful person. No wonder we can't tap into anything useful inside you!

"Look at you even now!" Kells pressed. "All this time, conversing with your father's killer! Not shedding a tear, not asking a single question about what happened! Who knows if there was even any soul in you to cut!"

Judah growled into a stumbling, clumsy lunge at Kells. Kells stepped easily out of the way, then ripped the bracelet from Judah's wrist.

"But I think I'll take this anyway, just in case," he hissed over Judah, sprawled again on the floor. "See what my people can do." With that, he crushed another bottle on Judah's back, this one muddy-colored.

Judah's physical pain vanished—along with any feeling at all below his neck. His mind and face became intensely alert, however, sharp without pain, and even sharper without the bracelet.

Kells cocked his head. "Interesting."

"What did you do!" Judah demanded, feeling, finally, his voice as his own again, even as he could not move any part of his body.

"A mix of Green and Blue serum, to paralyze the body but not the mind. Blue essence is tricky. Until now we've been trying it as Smoke, Blue Smoke; but it tends to … undo the spinal cord."

Judah grimaced. "Arik mentioned it."

"Unlike you, Arik was quite bereft at Darius's passing, you know."

Judah scowled. "He would be." He narrowed his eyes at Kells. "You hated Darius just as much as I did. More, even. So why are you trying so hard to be him now? I mean, you're running his Clear society! Did you forget you're Green?"

Kells glared at Judah, voice low. "Darius took *everything* from me—my love, my freedom, and my Light. So now I will take everything Darius had and more."

"Greedy much?" Judah sniped. "You're back in Aurora and pretty again, you don't have to go all psycho. You're healed!"

"Healed!" Kells' face contorted. He picked up a sliver of broken vial glass and dug it into his forearm right under Judah's face. Dark, black sludge began to bleed from the wound. "My body, yes, but not my gift! Because of Darius! He Banished me to that place so long, no amount of Light will ever return my blood to Green!" Kells swung his arm away, disgusted, let the blackness ooze. "I'm *not* Green! Not anymore! I'm nothing! So *I don't care* who's in what caste or how the vermin squabble! I will have my revenge, I will have everything he wanted! I refuse to be powerless, do you understand?"

"*That's* why you're inventing ways to distill the gifts—Smoke, serum, relics. Fae magic, without the Fae—"

"I told you, *everything* that was his. His Realm, its magic," Kells said bitterly, "and his family too." He looked away, muttered something Judah couldn't hear.

"Darius never had me, and neither will you," Judah spat at his back.

"Oh, little one," Kells whispered, coming back to kneel at

Judah's paralyzed side, to stroke Judah's curls. "I don't need to have you. I have something better, something I found in the Portal. I'm going to unleash it soon, and when I do, I'll start with you."

. . .

CALLUM WAS UNCERTAIN, and it was unpleasant. He didn't like the roiling he felt inside as he followed Spider-Eye down the hall and left his brother (because I now know without a doubt he is my brother, and I can feel it too) with the Otec who was not Darius. The Otec who was like a man from a dream from a long time ago, except in that dream, Callum had been small, just a boy, and the Otec who was not Darius had not been Otec yet, and had been young. He'd been a young man, and with the woman Callum loved, the woman with the long, long hair so black it was almost blue and smelled like nightshades.

Lorelei.

The name cut across the roiling, across the uncertainty, the twisty-turvy back-and-forth.

Lorelei. My mother.

Callum remembered how he had been only as tall as the new Otec's waist—the Otec who wasn't Darius—and the new Otec (who wasn't Darius) was laughing, but he wasn't Otec yet. He was Kells. Uncle Kells. Lorelei's friend.

Callum remembered like remembering a movie: how Kells and Lorelei had walked hand in hand through the gardens. How Kells had lifted Callum in his strong arms, high into the way-up-sky. How Kells had let Callum touch a budding rose (with my small fingers, and it felt like silk) and then had made the rose so happy its petals burst into bloom, right inside Callum's hand.

How no matter how many times Kells did this trick, how many times the scene replayed, Callum shrieked with surprised laughter, and Lorelei (my mother, my mother Lorelei, with blue-black hair), would laugh at Callum's laugh, and laugh at Kells' touch which was rough and leathery (and crispy tan, from so much sun and dirt and making things grow.).

They started to come back faster, faster and flush, movies on movies and memories on memories: the many afternoons Callum spent with Kells piling higher and higher, but each one bursting green and fresh. Kells' broad, strong frame bent over his as they dug holes together (their backs in curling Cs), as they planted seeds and pebbles, buttons, little toys. Always four hands: two crisp and rough, two small and soft, digging, digging, nails dirt-deep, tucking secrets into silt. Then Callum's round face would turn up to find Kells' eyes (gentle eyes with little sun-lines, *kisses* my mother called them); Callum would clap his hands and shout *Now! Now!* until Kells would grin and wink at Lorelei and make those seeds burst up with joy. Little green shoots exploding out to stalks and leaves, and then it was Callum's turn: to squeeze shut his eyes and dig in his hands and make the buttons and pebbles grow up too, into plants with threads for petals and woven stalks, pollen of bumpy yellow sandstone.

Those times were different, Callum now remembered clearly, from the times he'd spent with Darius, his father, who had been Otec then but wasn't now. Callum had also transfigured for Darius, who was Otec then, but things with exact corners, precise lines; clean and strong and stable; upright and built to last. Callum remembered puffing up his own small chest to show the crispness he'd woven atoms-deep into his clothes: the shine of silver buttons he'd hummed outward from their core. They'd shone so much that Darius could be seen in their reflection (his mouth-lines smoothed in the halo of my button). Darius had not said words of praise, but had made this style the official uniform, and so everywhere, on every chest, Callum could always see his father's pleasure inside his buttons.

Darius's pleasure had been crisp and still like that. An inside kind of pleasure. Immaculate. For a prince, growing up straight like the straightest stalk.

But with Kells, oh with Kells and Lorelei out of doors, Callum wasn't the stalk because leaves and buds were everywhere, rolling, teeming, bursting. Even weeds, uninvited but yawping too, hot with sunshine and the squishy sink and stink of mud.

Callum furrowed his brow, confused again. Something had happened, hadn't it? Because at some point, the green-time ended, and Kells—that Kells who was not Otec, that Kells not from now but from before—had disappeared. Callum searched and looked in his mind, but they were no more: no hand-in-hand Kells and Lorelei, no two heads bowed, no laughing in the dark of thistle-wild black-blue hair.

It had happened when Darius had adopted Callum's uniform, hadn't it? Callum couldn't see it clearly: the thrusting green, the smears of dirt swirled up into a silver spiral. Callum tried to see more closely, but like so many things these days, it blurred into sea and fog. The fog was thick, and squinting made Callum feel quite tired. Easier, and less exhausting, simply to turn around.

Except.

Except Kells was here. The same Kells, but older now and also Otec. Somehow Kells belonged here—but somehow he didn't too. Things were supposed to be neat, and fit precisely. Messy made Callum feel uncomfortable.

Callum huffed. He did not like to feel unsettled.

He sighed, resigned. He had no choice. He grimaced and searched his mind for Kells again, starting with the scenes he had already found and watched. The memories, round and clear through his boyhood eyes: Kells in the garden, making things grow, rough crisp hands and Lorelei's laugh—

Fog. Road block. Callum gritted his teeth but his muscles slagged and whimpered. *Can't go through.*

Callum forced his mind sluggishly to think. Perhaps he could go around?

Kells again, but later. Still not Otec Kells, still Kells back then, but older, grayer, than those first memories. On the other side, Callum assumed, of the block of fog. Kells' hair and body were the same, but something in his face maybe, the kiss-lines at his eyes, looked different. More like cracks. His leathered hands seemed scaly.

Kells was with Lorelei in the garden, but the garden was no longer riotous but grey. Callum was on a bench, a little taller than before the fog, and gangly. There was another boy now too, sitting at Callum's side. He was smaller (Judah, my brother, who is difficult to love). Judah was scowling, fidgeting, kicking at the ground, impatient to be elsewhere (but wait, Judah, I can't leave yet, I'm trying now to see).

Callum in this memory was like Callum now, watching Lorelei and Kells, heads bent close, whispering rapidly in agitation. A pang echoed in Callum—then and now—for Lorelei was wearing a dark cloak, hood up, covering her hair. And her face was sad, dragged down, as she held tight to Kells' scaly hand.

Callum leaned closer—then and now—straining to hear what they were saying. But then the smaller boy (Judah, remember, my younger brother, who I had to learn how to love), kicked Callum's shin as hard as he could. Callum flushed with pain and fury and whirled to Judah, who was smirking. Callum wanted to scream but turned his rage inward instead (Be patient, Callum! Grown and patient! He does not know better and you do!).

By the time Callum—then and now—remembered to look back and listen, they were gone, Kells and Lorelei, and only fog was in their place (Judah! Why can't you see!). Callum now did not want to look away, but again, the fog was too thick, too hard. Callum tried but his body turned to jelly and he began to fall asleep.

Callum fought this time, fought harder, refused to close his eyes—but then he became afraid. For in the fog now were phantoms howling in warning. Old, shriveled hunchbacks with Kells' eyes, but angry and cruel, as if the Kells from Callum's memory had been vacuumed up and spit out twisted.

Callum stopped following Spider-Eye in the hallway. He closed his eyes, bent to brace himself on his knees, willed the phantoms to leave and go away. He trembled, knew it was all his own fault. He knew better than to question, to try to see inside the fog. He knew better than to use what *felt* like a horizon; he needed instead to trust his instruments, calibrated by the rules and laws outside.

"What are you *doing?*"

Callum barely registered the voice of Spider-Eye as he turned and walked away from him. One thing, at least, Callum now knew clearly: Callum needed someone to lead him. Spider-Eye was a fellow soldier, just like Arik. Callum needed someone to recalibrate his horizon line, realign his levels, make sure he refound an even keel. Someone to decide, to take the burden, to draw the map and show Callum where and how to make … whoever … proud.

When Callum reached the door, it was open, and the man inside was alone.

"Do you have a moment?" Callum asked politely.

The Otec smiled kindly.

"Of course, my son."

• • •

WITH EVERY STEP into the Tunnels' deepest netherworld, Noa and Hilo knew they likely would not rise again. Not unless they found the Seer, who more likely than not, had never existed at all.

Each turn grew darker, deeper, the air heavy beneath its own building weight. Soon Noa could not see even the bright beacon of Hilo's hair, even though it had been blinding before, even though Hilo was right beside her, barely half a step ahead to guide the way.

Then the light swallowed itself entirely, licking syrup-covered chops.

Noa gasped in the moist, thick dark. It felt like drowning.

"It's okay, hold on." Hilo's words made tiny, calm, clear spaces, inside which Noa breathed.

Then, in the place where Hilo's hands were hidden, small sparkling lights began to dance and warm like candle tips, or fireflies.

"Stellabugs," Noa murmured, drinking in the halo of the tiny suns. "Did Judah train those too?"

Hilo's sudden laugh made Noa jump. Her face looked soft in the Stella-light. "Judah claims he *trained* all the Stellabugs," Hilo chuckled, "but they just follow warmth. Anyone can breathe on them to wake them up, and then they'll follow you. Especially down here, where everything else is so cold."

Noa shivered, realizing only now how icy it had become beneath the darkness and the air.

"Oh sorry, got distracted," Hilo said, and Noa's body warmed again.

"Wait, are you warming me up?"

"Both of us. I thought it would be okay—"

"No. Thank you, it helps," Noa said quickly and, she hoped, gratefully, "but your gift is with emotions. Are you ... changing mine?"

In the Stella-light, Hilo's eyes slid sideways in embarrassment. "Stoking a little bravery. It kind of lights a fire inside. I figured we both could use it...."

"Oh," Noa bit her lip. "Um, I guess that's okay. But..." Noa didn't want to offend Hilo, or set her off—she wanted Hilo there, no matter what she'd said before. "But it's important to me to know what feelings are really mine. So maybe just give me a heads-up or—"

"The feelings *are* yours," Hilo snapped defensively. "I can't manufacture anything, just amplify or reduce what's there."

"Still," Noa insisted more firmly, "it's hard enough for me to figure out for myself how I feel." She thought of Callum and Judah. "Really hard sometimes. So let me know. Cool?"

Hilo eyed her, making Noa nervous, then she cracked a grin and said, "Cool," trying out the word with amusement. "I think it's *cool*."

Noa nodded, tried not to show her deep relief.

Hilo took a breath and stood up straight and formal. "Noa, will it be cool to stoke some of your bravery, as I am stoking mine, both to embolden us and to keep our bones from freezing into icicles?"

Noa smiled. "That will be cool, Hilo. Thank you. Good luck finding some bravery in me though."

Hilo looked at Noa in disbelief. "You have a lot of bravery, Noa. More than most Fae."

Noa was shocked. She didn't know what to say.

Hilo laughed again. "I guess you *do* have trouble reading your own emotions." Noa found herself laughing too, and the combined chorus made her suddenly think, with a pang, of Olivia. She had avoided thinking of Olivia and Miles since arriving in Aurora—had they made it home okay? What did they remember? Did Miles remember anything at all?

Noa's laugh faded in the effort it took to shut away her best friend's face.

"You okay there?" Hilo asked.

"Yeah," Noa demurred, knowing full well Hilo could sense her heartsickness.

Hilo nodded, looked ahead. They walked onward in silence.

After a while, their twin steps fell into unison.

"Noa?" Hilo asked, oddly tentative.

"Yeah?"

"Usually I'd just look for myself, but … I really do want you to trust me. So I'm gonna ask, and if you don't want to answer, I won't cheat."

Noa's stomach fluttered uneasily. "Okay."

"The brothers. I already felt before that you love them, but … are you *in love* with one of them?"

Noa's heart began to thrum. She exhaled slowly.

"Forget it," Hilo said, embarrassed, step quickening.

"No," Noa said softly, "it's not that. I'm not ashamed or anything, it's just ... hard."

"You could ... talk to me about it. If you want. I mean, most likely the Seer's a bust and we're dead anyway," Hilo smiled; Noa tried not to see the pleading in her eyes.

Noa hesitated, but Hilo was right: she didn't want to go to the grave carrying all this around with her. And with what they were risking...

Before she could stop herself, Noa was speaking: "I guess I'd have to begin by saying, I definitely fell *in love* with Callum. It happened right away, and I'm sure that's what it was. Before that, I never believed that you could just meet someone and *know*. It seemed like the stuff of books, movies—not real, not for real people. But I felt it, the *certainty* of it. I don't know how else to explain it." She took a deep breath. "It was like he freed me when I was suffocating, like he gave me back the world. So even with his lies, it's like I can see past them because I *know* his heart is good, I *feel* it. And of course, he gave me Sasha."

Hilo watched Noa carefully. "But."

Noa sighed, nodded. "But here in Aurora, and in the In Between world inside the Portal? The things I knew with that incredible certainty at home feel ... strange. And I can't tell, is it my mind or heart or memory that's unsettled? Am I remembering it different than it was, or am I seeing it now for the truth I missed? Is some part of *me* undoing what I once just *knew* I believed?"

Hilo chewed her lip. "If there is a Seer—"

"For the sake of both our sanities, Hilo, let's just start talking as if she *is* real. What with not being able to turn back now and everything."

Hilo nodded, chuckling a little. "Well, then. The Seer will help with that. The confusion is probably not even you—just being out of your proper world and away from what you know."

"But it feels ... *inside* ... somehow."

Hilo shrugged, smiled a little. "For your sanity, then, maybe that's another thing not to think too much about."

Noa nodded, laughing a little. "Okay, I'll hope you're right then. The Seer will fix my memories of Callum. Just like she'll help Callum survive the mind control, and"—Marena's face flashed in Noa's mind, making her voice shake—"that when she does, I won't see this other Callum every time I see his face ... because if I do, if I see this terrible Callum and what he's done, then..." Noa's voice broke, angry tears choking off the words.

"Then what?" Hilo breathed.

"I might hate him."

Hilo didn't comment. They walked in silence a few steps as Noa collected herself.

"And Judah?" Hilo asked.

Noa closed her eyes, felt herself smile a little. "Judah. I have no idea. God, he reminds me of Sasha. His tantrums and his—"

"To protect himself," Hilo interrupted defensively, not meeting Noa's eyes.

Noa bit her lip, flushed a little. "I guess Judah always surprises me, and sometimes that's good but sometimes it's not. Most of the time I just want him to grow up. Like, not just dump out his feelings and expect that to be the end, and get pissed when all it does is make a mess."

Hilo snorted appreciatively.

Noa sighed, smiling. "I didn't feel the same rush when I met Judah, not like with Callum. Actually he freaked me out and then was an arrogant ass I frankly would have been happier not to know. But Callum got in trouble and we had to work together, and I don't know, we became ... friends, I guess. But during that time, I always knew it was Callum for me. I never doubted it. Callum was my revelation. Judah—"

"Didn't change your world," Hilo smirked.

"No," Noa nodded. "Just kind of ... sent it careening." She and Hilo laughed together. "It wasn't even until he said, out of the clear blue sky, that he..." Noa bit her lip again, not wanting to hurt Hilo's feelings.

"That he had feelings for you," she supplied softly.

Noa nodded, suddenly shy. "It wasn't until then that I looked around and realized, it's all a mess, and maybe the world's changed after all." She paused. "But then again who knows with Judah? That's the thing. He tells the truth—sometimes too much—but he also tells it slant. So it sounds like one thing but means another, even if it's not really a lie."

"So..." Hilo met Noa's eyes nervously. "You're not sure about Judah?"

"I-I'm not sure he's sure about me." Noa was surprised to hear herself say it, having not realized until that moment it was something she feared.

"But *you*," Hilo pressed.

Noa furrowed her brow, tried to be honest. "I-I don't have that feeling of safety, of a kind of otherworldly magic like I do with Callum. Everything with Judah's all … messed up. Muddy. But still…" She hesitated. Hilo was studying her carefully.

"You really *don't* know," Hilo said, disappointed. "I'm not looking, it's just wafting off your aura."

"You're disappointed."

Hilo sighed. "The thing is, Noa?" she said plainly, openly. "I *do* know. It took me a long time, but when they were gone, and I thought they weren't coming back … I knew it was Judah." Her voice wavered, and Noa looked away, sensing Hilo would not like Noa to watch her cry. Noa heard the pixie swipe at her cheek as she continued. "Callum had dazzled me, to be sure, but once I had lost them both? None of that mattered. It was Judah. It was always Judah. He's like my other half."

Noa nodded, feeling tears of her own burning behind her eyes.

Hilo continued, and Noa felt how much she wanted Noa to understand. "His face—every day it grew finer, sharper, in my memory, like I was remembering in my heart and not my mind, and my heart kept adding strokes. It wasn't long before I couldn't even picture Callum, but Judah—he burned brighter and brighter, and without him … I hollowed out."

Noa wiped at a falling tear, unable to hold it back.

"So I guess," Hilo continued shakily, "I … I know he says he loves you now. And it's what I deserve, right? For abandoning him, not telling him about the Faefyre. He rebuilt himself without me, and I'm happy for it"—Hilo didn't even try to stop the tears now, falling through her words—"because I want him to be happy, more than I want him for myself. So if that means that he's with you, that's what I want." Hilo broke off, took several deep breaths. When she spoke again, her voice was small and thin, and so un-Hilo it hurt Noa's heart. "But Noa? Please ... if you don't want him, don't lead him on, okay? He seems so strong sometimes, but he gets hurt. He *really* gets hurt. And if you don't want him"—she took another breath—"let me try? Let me and Judah try to find our way back to each other?"

Every breath was painful; Noa didn't know what to say or do. Should she hug Hilo or try to comfort her? Because in that moment, with Hilo's tear-streaked, plaintive plea, Noa found she could not say what Hilo needed most to hear: that she would step away from Judah, that she would give him up if it meant his happiness; that her heart, her blood was not screaming, screaming, screaming:

Do not ever, ever let him go.

• • •

AFTER A TIME, the whisper of Hilo's tears dried beside Noa, chafed raw by the sandpaper of what Noa did not do, what Noa did not say. As they walked in silence, Noa wrapped her arms across her chest and shoulders, squeezing herself tight, as if suddenly afraid her body might come apart. The chill of the darkness raised goose bumps across her skin, and she thought ungenerously that Hilo wanted her to freeze—though deep down, Noa knew it was the stalactites of their words and non-words, icy and dripping, dripping, dripping, that really chilled them both. Just like their footsteps, whose syncopation now was quicksand, sucking Noa under no matter how she tried to change the beat.

Hilo stopped suddenly in the dark, causing Noa to stumble ungracefully beside her.

"Why are we stopping?" Noa asked nervously.

Hilo's blue eyes flared like matches in the dark, raking Noa's face with all the fierceness the pixie had.

"Because this," Hilo said, sharp teeth glinting, "is where I'm leaving you."

• • •

CALLUM TOOK THE proffered seat in Otec Kells' royal quarters, which had once belonged to Otec Darius. They looked the same now as they had then, everything just as Callum had last seen it (though to be fair, with the fuzziness, he was not quite sure how long ago that was). The walls were still white stone, overhung by those rippling silver tapestries.

Delicate and imposing, like Darius.

The furniture was all there too, the bureau standing majestically on one side. No ordinary bureau, Callum remembered with a familiar shiver of boyhood awe: shaped from the softest, reddest timber, so intricately carved it actually seemed to move. But it wasn't special for its beauty; it had been a gift from Lorelei.

Who had made the bureau, Callum could not remember (do I even, did I ever, know?). Surely someone with the gift to speak with nature, to deserve from her a work so precious.

Seeing the bureau again, Callum remembered a scene like an almost-painting, in blurry light: he had sat before the bureau when he was five. The seeming-movement of it had entranced him; he'd reached out to feel its atoms (they are liquid, must be liquid)—when Darius had caught him.

Callum froze now, as he had then, reinhabiting the shame. Until Darius surprised him—then and now—by simply sitting down beside his son, smiling a rare and fragile smile.

"Does it feel different? Can you feel the magic?" Darius had asked, thirsted to know. Callum had done his best to describe it, but only a Blue could know because only a Blue could feel the atoms. And though Darius had nodded, the fragile smile had evaporated in the moments five-year-old Callum had taken to form his words.

Darius had nodded softly, sadly, then reminded his dearest son never to actually change the bureau's atoms. *Touch, but stay within your limits. Touch, but do not change.*

Now Callum looked over at the bureau, still in motion in this room that was and was not his father's. His eyes remembered before his mind, tumbling down the bureau's right leg, the one he'd touched that day.

Even though he knew it would be there, Callum's chest constricted to see the scratch, long and deep and ugly like a scar.

The scar had not been Callum's doing (touch, but do not change). Judah (Judah my brother) had made it with a Faefyre knife for any reason, for no reason at all. Judah never needed reasons. He did things because was bored (that's the kind of thing that Judah does).

Callum had tried to fix the damage, but even he could not fix Faefyre. And so Darius had seen and flown into a rage. Callum still remembered Judah's smirk. He'd known Callum would take the blame, and so Callum had (because I must love Judah, for Darius cannot.).

Judah had forgotten all as soon as Callum had confessed, the way Judah always did. But Callum never forgot. Even in these blurry painting memories, in the warm halo of this candlelight,

LAUREN BIRD HOROWITZ

Callum could see the sharpness of Darius's cheekbones, the sheerness of their hollows, the disappointment as Callum told he'd done the damage, misused his gift, and did not know how to fix it.

Darius's face had hardened. He'd told Callum the leg would not be replaced. It would stand ugly for all time, as a reminder of Callum's disobedience, and even more, of his inability to set it right.

Callum Now shrank in shame alongside the boy he was Then, curling inward beneath his heavy secret: knowing he'd acted nobly, capably, but everyone would see the opposite. And that this wrong gaze, over time, would become even his own too, worn in by habit and reflection (because one gaze is not enough, even if it's the true one. Real things change to fit the shape that others see.).

(And they lose the shape that's really there, as if it never was.)

"Beautiful bureau," Kells commented, waking Callum from his swirl of impressionist memories. Kells was watching Callum curiously.

"My father loved it, until the leg," Callum murmured, pointing.

Kells tilted his head. "I never noticed." He walked over, bent and ran his hand over the leg. The color of his skin had red accents like the wood.

"It's a terrible shame," Callum said sadly.

"It's a mark of life. Everything gets them. Everything and everyone." Kells laid his palm on the face of the bureau with a sigh, a tired smile.

Callum saw him then—the Kells from Before—as if in this room, time had collapsed. Kells Before was looking quietly, fondly at the bureau, the Kells who'd made Lorelei smile, who'd held

298

Callum's hand (small again) in the palace garden, who'd made Callum's fingers warm to make things grow.

Callum now looked at Kells' hands in wonder—they were the same, still rough and worn, dyed brown by dirt and calluses. In fact, everything about Kells' body looked the same once Kells touched the bureau, and Callum saw that face, those hands, that first Kells inside him again.

"I remember you taking me into the gardens with my mother."

"I remember," Otec Kells answered softly, turning slowly. "You could make the buttons grow."

Callum smiled proudly. "I was copying you, in the only way I knew how."

Kells smiled sadly, sat on the ground, leaned against the bureau. He raised a hand to invite Callum to come sit beside him.

"Your mother used to love to watch you," Kells told Callum as he settled back against the precious wood.

"From the redwood bench?"

"That's right. She loved that bench. Took me months to find just its twin in the forest for this bureau. Of course I could have had a Blue change some other wood to match, but it wouldn't have been the same. Your mother would have felt it." He smiled, wistful. "Did you know even wood has a spirit to be felt?"

"You made this bureau for her. I should have remembered—"

Otec Kells waved his hand. "I didn't let her tell anyone. And anyway, he wouldn't have kept it if he'd known."

Callum swallowed. When Kells talked about Darius, he looked less like the man Callum remembered in the garden, and more like the specter of the twisted troll that haunted the bad-memory place, the fuzzy place Callum was supposed to stay well away from because of specters just like that.

But Callum heard himself ask anyway. "My father wouldn't have kept it, you mean," he said uncertainly. "He was the Otec, but now you are."

Kells studied Callum shrewdly. "Yes."

"I-I love my father. But, I think, I *feel* like, I have memories of loving you. I know my mother loved you both, but I ... I can't—" Callum broke off in frustration. His feelings were blurring and diluting.

"That's all right, son," Kells said, putting a hand on Callum's shoulder. "It's okay to be confused."

"That's why I came to talk to you," Callum said, relieved.

"Don't worry. We're on the same side."

Callum met Kells' eyes and shivered. That specter of the twisted, gnarled man had blinked back—but only for an instant. Then Otec Kells was reassuring, kind again.

Callum relaxed. "My dad is ... good. He tries to be. But sometimes, I think I am afraid of him too."

Kells nodded. "I'm sure you have memories of both."

"I know I love him," Callum said with certainty.

Kells considered Callum curiously. "What about your brother?"

"My br—you mean Judah?"

"Yes, Judah. Do you love him?"

Callum felt his mouth twist. "Yes."

"But he is difficult sometimes."

"*Yes*," Callum agreed. "But it's my job to protect him, Lorelei told me—" When Kells winced, Callum felt a sharp pang. "Wait, have you seen her?"

Kells sighed heavily, closed his eyes. "She's dead."

Callum nodded; he knew that, but he hadn't known he knew it until Kells had said the words again. They echoed in his ears, an unpleasant buzz.

Otec Kells got to his feet, gestured they should return to their chairs. He sat in the chair that once had been Darius's, sat up straight. "What if I told you that I am Otec now because I am trying to take care of your father the way you try to care for Judah?"

"What do you mean?"

"Your mother loved us both, so in a way, we are brothers, too, your dad and me. Darius is like Judah: he means well but has his limits. He doesn't understand some things that I understand. Like Judah doesn't see the things you see."

"So you took over to ... protect him? The way I have to decide things for Judah sometimes."

"Yes," Kells said, with an unfamiliar little smile (the specter's smile, he's back again, except this is Kells and Kells is helping, the specter isn't real).

"It makes sense," Callum said slowly, thinking hard about Kells' words. It did make sense: when Callum thought of Darius, he felt a twisty mix of feelings, just like the knot when he thought of Judah. "But can I see my father? I think I would like to see him."

"Oh, I don't think that's wise just yet," Kells advised, leaning across his desk—Darius's desk—to squeeze Callum's shoulder. "You have to trust me, remember, if we're going to save him."

Callum felt uneasy, but Kells seemed so certain. The moment he accepted Kells' guidance, relief pumped warmness through him, that blissful relief of finally knowing what was true and whom to follow.

Except.

"We have to save Judah too, though," Callum added suddenly, urgently. "We can't leave him behind."

Kells smiled warmly again. "Oh, we won't. And you have a very important part to play in Judah's salvation." He stood up, and helped Callum stand beside him. He put his golden hand on Callum's back as he walked him to the door.

"And Callum? That bracelet on your wrist, the one Arik gave you? I'd like to hold on to it."

Callum hesitated, putting a hand to the bracelet, another sudden shard of cold unease. "It ... protects me."

"It's okay, son. It will still do its special job if I have it. You don't need to actually wear it for it to work. I just want to make sure it stays nice and safe."

Callum nodded, pushed away the shard. He offered up his arm to Kells, who carefully rolled off the tight red tube with the silver-and-blue circlet inside. Otec Kells clasped it in his hands.

Callum tried not to shudder at the look that came over Kells as he looked at his closed fist.

The specter isn't real.

• • •

JUDAH SAT IN his new cell—back against the wall, staring through the bars—and listened to the endless, torturous, incessant dripping he couldn't locate no matter how much he searched the Tower room. It wasn't like the room was huge: it was circular and narrow and held only his cell. And a single window, across from his bars of course, the better to taunt with its hint of hazy sky. Judah had named this room the Birdcage on his first day, even though he had no perch to swing on, nor rodent bones shoved through the bars.

Not that Judah deserved them. Not after what he'd done to her, or what he'd almost done and maybe done then let be done, and what the hell was the difference anyway? Because as he'd sat here, things had gotten clearer, and he'd realized how immensely he'd betrayed her—he could not bear to even think her name— sure he hadn't made her into ooze, but he'd let Callum do Marena, *had made her watch*, and then had probably killed her by stuffing her in that chute. It went hell-knew-where to incinerate garbage, and given how unreliable his mind was, who was to say killing her hadn't been precisely his intention? The work of his very legendary impatience to hurry up and get the task done?

The point was, whether he'd melted her or incinerated her, whether he'd killed her friend himself or forced her up against the glass to watch it done, Judah would never see her again and so he'd never see himself again.

For that, a birdcage was as good a place as any.

In a way it was freeing, actually. It reminded him a little of when he'd been younger, running to the safe, small place. It might look like a cell to outsiders, but really it was a Tunnel, mapped by heart, where no one could ever find him because only he knew it from inside.

There was no regret, no heartbreak, no painful hope in this Tower Tunnel of Aloneness. The only downside, in fact, was silence—because it made the dripping worse.

Judah tried to distract himself and ignore it. The only other movement was the parade of Guards, like clockwork: Spider-Eye followed by the Mustache followed by Spider-Eye, each replacing the other in the single, ramrod-straight chair beneath the taunt-ing window. They watched Judah but never spoke. Just silence, silence, silence.

Drip, drip, drip.

Finally, when Judah was sure the drip had actually killed him and trapped his mind in some hellish Portal dimension of unend-ing, eternal days, the door unexpectedly opened in the middle of Spider-Eye's shift and Kells came in.

Despite his best efforts, Judah cringed back—not because of Kells, that bastard, but because of the threat the "Otec" had cursed at Judah before imprisoning him: to subject Judah to "the weapon." Judah hated being afraid, but if Kells had turned Sasha the way he'd turned Callum ... Kells' terrible promise had grown and stretched in the hours of silence in this cell, uncurling into a living, writhing centipede of nightmares stretching tentacled legs through Judah's mind. The very sight of Kells now made Judah shudder against his will, as if Demon Sasha might be steps behind. She wasn't, but Kells smiled an infuriatingly self-satisfied smile at Judah's cowering reaction.

Judah wanted to scream in frustration, but then Kells would take that as a victory too. Besides, no matter how much time had passed, Judah's body was, for some reason, stubbornly refusing to recharge. Even the idea of screaming now made him weary with exhaustion. Which was also infuriating.

Kells rubbed his hands and nodded at Spider-Eye. "Go, and tell Kalen you're both off this rotation."

Spider-Eye looked curious but of course didn't ask, like the mindless drone he was. He walked out, subservient and sniveling as usual.

Coward.

Kells turned to Judah, amused. Judah seethed. If this was the end, he'd be damned if he went out without having the last smirk, no matter how tired he was.

"*Finally,*" Judah drawled, giving Kells his own smug little sneer. "Took you long enough. Off getting more Aurora plastic surgery?"

Kells' eyes glittered. "Don't you even want to know what happened to the girl? Whether your hasty move killed her instantly?"

Judah scowled. *Do not be baited.* "Let's just get to why you're interrupting my 'me' time."

"So surly!" Kells chided happily. "And to think, I brought you a present!"

"You mean besides dismissing Tweedledee and Tweedledumb?"

"Oh, I've done more than dismiss them, child. I've *replaced* them." Kells went delightedly to the door, which Spider-Eye had closed, and gave a taunting little bow. "Your Grace, the Red Son, may I present"—he flung the door open with a flourish—"*your new keeper.*"

Despite himself, Judah gasped in shock. The new Guard was stronger than Mustache, more imposing than Spider-Eye, more commanding than Arik. His uniform shone brilliant white and silver and was outfitted with special extra weapons, tools, restraints of every possible, sadistic invention. His face was fiery, almost mad with intensity and purpose and single-minded, absolute determination—

Judah sagged, all smirk lost.

"Hello, Callum."

• • •

NOA FROZE, WANTING to believe this was only a dream, a manifestation of the unkind thoughts and jealousies she'd harbored for her would-be betrayer. But Hilo's terrible words bounced around the dark wet walls, slapping back against her cheek again and again.

This is where I'm leaving you.

The anger on Hilo's face was obvious. Grotesque, even, lit now by Stella-light from below, like some kind of demon jack-o'-lantern.

"What do you mean, leaving me?" Noa asked, trying to sound strong but sounding weak, terribly weak, at the thought of being left alone, all alone, *down here.*

"I mean—" Hilo cut off, growling and pulling her fingers through her hair. Something prickly broke through Noa's panic: she knew that gesture. Very well. Had Judah learned it from her, or Hilo from him?

"Did you hear me, Noa? I said I've lost my way! I've lost us! I've failed, I've completely—" She turned to the wall, slammed her palms against it. Hilo leaned forward against her arms, head down, as if she couldn't bear to stand back up.

Noa realized she'd been wrong, completely wrong. Hilo was angry, yes, and wanted to punish someone—*herself.*

"We knew it was a risk," Noa whispered uncertainly, as Hilo leaned harder into the wall. "But you can't just—"

Hilo yelled in frustration, spun toward Noa. Her palms were scraped bloody from where she'd hit the hall. "I have to leave you here while I go back. I have to figure out where it got tangled up, then I can come back for you—"

"No frickin' way!" Noa exclaimed. "I'm not waiting here alone!"

Hilo roared. "When you're here Noa, I can't see my way!"

"Hilo—"

"You—You—!" Hilo threw up her hands, looked away, cheeks burning. "It's not your fault, okay? But you make me think about other stuff, remember things I don't want to—and I can't focus, I just—"

Noa tried to master her anger—and her panic. "I understand that. But we have to stick together, like it or not, we're all we've got now."

Hilo turned back to Noa, face crumpled and pleading. She was fighting hard not to cry, Noa could tell—and then Hilo sank, head in her hands, leaving streaks of blood on her cheeks. Noa stood awkwardly, not knowing what to do, and then Hilo began to rock, back and forth, muttering softly to herself.

It was too much for Noa—too much like Marena, in that terrible cell, where Noa couldn't go to reach her, where Noa had to watch and witness. This time she fell to Hilo's side, tried to put an arm around the rocking shoulders.

"Lost and dead, lost and dead…"

But instead of pulling Hilo free, it was Noa who was pulled under. Into the black place, the despair place of collapsing currents, the place with Marena and Hilo and…

Isla?

Isla stood tall across from Noa, stared into Noa with her imperial gray eyes. Isla's eyes were darker than Hilo's and fiercer too. *Pallas Isla.* Those eyes yanked Noa up until she broke the surface, breathed again. This was not Noa's world, these Tunnels were deadly, dark, and deep—but Isla's ghost was *Noa's.* Isla was inside and outside her, magic no other place or time could ever swallow, ever claim.

Noa pulled Hilo and herself up, shook Hilo by the shoulders. "So we can't go back anymore. That's not what's important, it never was. Retreat was never our goal. It was never even an option." Hilo's face rippled under Noa's forcefulness. Noa pressed harder. "Forward, Hilo. *Only forward.* We find the Seer. Then, and only then, do we worry about getting out."

Hilo's eyes were wary but she nodded minutely. Noa released her and stepped into the lead. Isla's ghost shimmered away, and Noa felt a little flutter—like she did every time Isla left—but she knew she had to do this on her own.

Hilo mumbled something behind Noa, but Noa couldn't quite hear it. It sounded like:

Told you. Brave.

• • •

THE FIRST NIGHT, Judah tried to talk to Callum. Something about seeing him there but not there, happy in his delusions, made Judah suddenly unable to tolerate his own. This place was not some safe cocoon. It was not even the network of damp, dark Tunnels. This was prison. They both were in prison.

And they both had to get out.

"Wake up, Callum, come on! You just have to try—a prat like you can do anything if you try!" Judah urged, the effort painful with his stupid slackened muscles. "Look, I know it's all happy times and pretty rainbows to stay asleep. Simple and easy and all that boring crap you love. But we can't anymore, neither of us, we have to remember what's important—"

"I *know* what's important."

"Callum! The stupid Clear movement is not important!

Politics is not important!"

"I'm not talking about the movement. I'm talking about *you*. My family. Rescuing you, saving our father—" Callum cut off, smiled, catching himself.

"Our father is dead! Corpse! Kells killed him!" Judah shouted in exasperation.

"It's okay, Judah. Kells told me you'd say that. I know you lie when you're scared. You've always done it."

"That is *not*—"

"I can't let you pull me into your cave, Brother," Callum continued patiently. "I have to pull you back up into the world. I have to be brave for you, and see for you what your eyes can't."

Judah screamed behind his gritted teeth, ignoring how it burned the muscles in his throat. *"I don't need you to save me—"*

"I know it looks like that to you," Callum nodded, infinitely understanding. "It's not your fault. You were born that way. But that's why it's my job to protect you."

Judah grasped the bars so tightly his knuckles turned white, every bone in his hand protesting. He swallowed another scream. "Okay Callum, you want to save me?" He nodded, squinted his eyes, ignored the pain that exploded everywhere. "Then save me, Brother. You're right, I want you to. And I want you to start by *saving … me … from this cage!*" Judah's scream escaped; he rattled the bars with all the pathetically weak strength he had. "You say you love me, right? Then free me!"

Callum smiled again, that infuriating, knowing smile. "I *am* freeing you, Brother. You just can't see it yet." His eyes became so light they almost looked saintly. "But soon, Brother, with my help, I think you will."

• • •

NOW IN THE lead, Noa made turn after turn, not knowing why she chose the ones she did, just knowing that when she got to the branching end of a pathway, she knew which direction she wanted to go. It was almost eerie; she wasn't sure if she was listening to some inspiration or simply *had to* feel that way in order to keep them moving forward. She had a feeling—she wasn't sure if Hilo felt it too—that if they stopped, the fear would slip back in. And she would not allow it to, not again.

So they kept moving, and Noa kept leading, until they found themselves in one particular Tunnel that slowly began to shrink around them. The ceiling grew so low, the walls so close that Hilo and Noa had to crouch to continue—then crawl. Noa had to use every ounce of discipline she had to avoid a flashback to the MRI machine after her and Isla's accident.

I will not go back to the sandpaper place.

They crawled and crawled in silence—a whisper, like a pause, might let fear free—until their knees were achy, filthy, bloody. But the Tunnel finally leveled, small as it was. It didn't squeeze them to oblivion, even if it did not exhale them either. As Noa had decreed, forward was the only option, apparently on hands and knees.

The Tunnel didn't shrink again, but after a time it did start to tilt upward. It soon became so steep, they had to use the small struts on the floor as handles to keep from sliding backward.

Noa closed her eyes—it was dark anyway—and pulled herself up, rung by rung. It was easier by feel. But as Noa climbed blind, she slowed.

Hilo sensed it. "Only forward," she reminded Noa from behind, her voice stronger again. Noa gritted her teeth: Hilo wasn't Isla, but she was right.

Finally the Tunnel leveled again. She spoke over her shoulder: "Hilo, I think the incline end—"

Noa's last word, and her whole body, plummeted suddenly down, sliding through the suddenly sharply-declining Tunnel. Apparently the small Tunnel had traced a kind of peak, and now she slid and sped and tumbled down the grade on the other side. It was very steep—much steeper than the incline—and slick, slick, slick, with no struts to slow her down. Even Hilo, who knew the drop was coming, could not help but crash down it wildly, limbs banging off the tubular walls.

The slide went on and on until Noa was sure they'd hit the core of Aurora itself—she even had time to wonder if the core would be molten and volcanic or icy like the air—when quite suddenly she slammed into the ground, Hilo bowling over on top of her.

Hilo bounced up quickly on light Fae feet. "You okay?"

Noa groaned and rolled over. "I'll live." She rolled up and looked around. The Stellabugs flew down the passage after them, just in time to reveal that they had landed on some sort of rocky island, surrounded by an enormous, seemingly bottomless underground chasm.

Hilo looked up to where they'd been spit out. She pointed to what looked like a tiny tunnel opening, a long way away in the distant ceiling. "It almost looks like a garbage chute. It emptied us here."

Noa grimaced. "I hate chutes."

Hilo looked strange. "There's really no going back now. Not the way we came at least. But I think … I think this may actually be good."

Noa squinted at her as she tested out her bruised muscles.

"Look around," Hilo urged her. The Stellabugs had continued down the path of Noa and Hilo's fall, drawn by their warmth, and as more gathered, their glow spread more widely around the chasm. Noa saw that the rocky island that had broken their fall was not the only island; several others were dotted around the sea of apparent emptiness. "That's one way to survive the flushes."

Noa frowned. "But how do we get across? It's way too far to jump to the next rock, even for you...."

"If we're even supposed to go across. Think about it. If this is how the Seer escaped...," Hilo said, growing excited. Noa looked around, tried to imagine the most logical path.

Her stomach fell. "We're ... supposed to go down?"

Hilo looked happily at Noa. "I *know* we are."

"How?"

"Down's the scariest way," Hilo said gleefully. Her eyes were shining. "Noa, for the first time ... *I think the Seer might actually be real!*"

Not nearly so excited by how Hilo had landed on this conclusion, Noa followed her to peer over the edge of their island. Islands, Noa remembered from elementary school, rose from mountains beneath the sea; they did not simply float flat on the surface of the ocean. The rocky area that held them was like the summit of a mountain peak. Theirs must have a base somewhere far, far below them.

But when Hilo and Noa looked over, they both gasped from vertigo, clutching at each other's hands. They exchanged a look. The decline from their landing summit fell so sharply, it nearly looked sheer.

Nearly.

There was the tiniest, most-unhelpful-in-history, basically-meaningless, grade widening outward as it descended. But that was it. The base of this island would not be much wider than the peak. They were in for a straight-down climb—or fall, most likely. The surface wasn't smooth as glass—but there didn't seem to be many handholds either.

"I really wish I was a Blue right now. Sticky palms would be so useful," Hilo said.

"Too bad fear sweat is slick, not sticky."

Hilo looked at Noa. "Forward only, Noa." Noa nodded, but inwardly rolled her eyes at how quickly Hilo had recovered her usual bossiness. Granted, they were Noa's words, but still.

"I'll go down first since my Fae reflexes will make me steadier. Then if you fall, I may be able to stop your slide."

Or get taken down with me. Noa shook the thought away. *Forward only.*

Hilo was already hoisting herself over, much more eager than Noa to begin climbing/falling into an unknown abyss. Hilo spread her body like a spider and moved down the first few feet of wall carefully but steadily, searching out makeshift hand- and footholds. Each inch took careful consideration.

When there was enough room for Noa, she took a deep breath, swallowed hard—*forward!*—and lowered herself over the edge. The wall was black—deep, deep black—and so cold it almost hurt to touch it for too long. Even breathing with her face so close seemed to chill her breath and gust it back at her, so that as Noa clung to the obsidian face, it enveloped her in icy mist laced with stalactites from her own lungs.

As black and cold as the wall was, it was not quite as slippery as ice—there were faint variations in the surface, though nothing Noa, with her mortal eyes, could ever have picked out easily. She said a silent prayer of thanks for Hilo's willingness to descend first—the pixie had left smudges of crusted blood from her palms as she'd navigated carefully downward, searching out the handholds. They also—so faintly—were warmer to the touch from Hilo's recent holds, and Noa's shivering fingers gratefully grasped for them. The Stellabugs followed her and Hilo's body heat down the rock face, but Noa didn't dare look around, knowing that whatever they illuminated would be something far more frightening than she wanted to see.

Noa slid slowly down the wall, handhold to handhold, breathing icy shards of her own breath, and her heart began to pound—from the cold, from the dark ... and mostly, she knew, from fear. *I'm there*, she tried desperately not to admit, though it beat with her heart, *I'm back in the sandpaper place ...* Aurora was full of them, it seemed, starting with her cell....

Piercing tears welled in Noa's eyes as she kept moving slowly down the wall with shaking, labored breathing. She couldn't stop, though her mind was reeling; she needed to stoke a fire inside herself, or she knew her mind would overtake her body, her limbs would give up, and she would have nothing left but to fall.

It was the sandpaper place. But Noa knew how to get out of those places, and she would do it now, even as she climbed down blackest ice, into the unknown. She wrote herself a poem. She made the words her kindling, and fired herself onward from within:

I have been here before, in this Sandpaper Place,
I know these stones by chilling heart.
Sometimes they are ragged, slicing my palms,
Sometimes smooth,
or bars,
bright clear windows,
locked doors.

There were times I curled under, away
From the Sandpaper place.
Built my nautilus outward,
spun from bone.
Fingertips in, pill-bug snug, soft worm skin
Chrysalis'd tight—
But it's been long since my wings broke that skin.

Cocoons cannot fit me
(nor this Sandpaper Place),
pinkened palms can't survive in the sun.
I grow suction cups now, inside hands, down both wrists,
Reach out wide, splay myself to cold:

Starfish-to-starfish,
Sister-limbs fuse as one
Girl-beast chain, sister-strong, woven tight:
Isla and Sasha, Marena, Hilo's siren song:
No fear, be brave, *Forward* fight!

Noa repeated the words to herself, becoming the starfish, linked to Isla and Sasha, to Marena, even—she realized—to Hilo, and her panic eased. She continued, handhold to handhold, even as her arms ached, even as she could hear Hilo panting below her.

"I'm afraid to look down to see how much farther," Hilo gasped upward after what felt like hours. Emboldened by her inner mantra, Noa impulsively decided to look up instead, to see how far they'd come—and immediately regretted it.

The summit they had landed on after the tunnel chute had been completely swallowed by blackness. There was no longer any sign of surface—or light—at all. The sight was so startling that Noa's hand slipped off its hold. She swung outward, suspended by one arm only, and her shoulder strained under her weight. She bit back her wails and fought to swing herself back into the wall, kicking and scrabbling, wishing she really *did* have suction cups on her limbs. Just as her stomach slammed into the freezing rock and her other hand caught a hold again, her foot broke through a loose rock—which tumbled down at Hilo.

"Hilo!" Noa cried into the wall as she clung to it for dear life, her momentum still vibrating up her spine, the surface burning her with its cold.

"Don't worry, it missed me!" Hilo called up. "But one inch closer and Judah's choice would have become much simpler."

Noa flushed even though Hilo couldn't see her. "Hilo!"

"You ready? Come on!" Hilo cried from below. Noa heard her climbing again.

Noa took a breath, tried to calm her heart, and began to climb again. *Sasha's arms. Starfish arms.* Her arms strained so hard, her brain absurdly conjured the idea of a massage. She could almost feel the vibrations now....

"Uh, do you feel that?" Hilo's voice called up.

"Wait, that's real? That vibrating?" Noa held herself against the wall. "I thought I was imagining it." Noa turned her head and pressed her ear against the rock: it was buzzing. Before she could stop herself, she looked up again and screamed—though this time for a different reason.

"Avalanche!"

"What?"

But there was no time to explain, no time to describe the falling rocks plummeting like giant boulder hail from above them.

Some massage.

"Slide!" Noa screamed, letting go of the wall, letting herself fall down the rock face. She smashed into Hilo, who screamed and tangled with her into a human tumbleweed of flesh and bone. They crashed faster and faster down the grade; Hilo started to squeeze and push roughly at Noa's body, and Noa realized she was forcing Noa into a ball, trying to wrap her own body around Noa's more fragile limbs. As best as she could, Noa stopped resisting and let Hilo become her pixie shell. They flew down like that, bumping against the grade, Hilo wrapped around Noa. Each jolt made Noa yell, but Hilo never loosened her grip.

Finally, Noa and Hilo felt themselves slide out onto some kind of floor—they had reached the base of the island, but thunderous rumbling told them there was no time to look up or back. Noa got gingerly to her feet and saw Hilo dazed with pain—her shoulder clearly broken, hanging absurdly from her side—but the rumble was too loud, too fast; it shook the floor, the air. Noa grabbed Hilo's other arm and stumble-sprinted them away from the imminent blast zone as best she could— in what direction and toward what she did not know or care. Isla didn't appear to guide her, no Stellabugs had made the fall; there was only one word: *Run.*

Noa heard the first crashes smash the ground behind her just as they dashed from it, the impact so massive it lifted the stone floor itself into a rocky tidal wave. Noa pressed her legs harder, praying for something, *anything* to run to—

—and there it was, the anything, winking from the blackness: another circular entrance to a tunnel, glinting with white, set a few feet off the ground.

Noa sprinted Hilo toward it, skidding to a stop just before they smashed into the sheer black wall around the tunnel entrance. Hilo read Noa's body and swung forward, leaping up and into the tunnel without missing a stride, then reached back to pull Noa in too with her good hand. Noa squirmed and struggled to get up over the heightened ledge. Hilo heaved, and Noa's foot slipped in just as the rock tsunami crashed into the wall, obliterating everything behind them and blowing them backward with a blast of dust and wind and rock and black.

• • •

THE SECOND NIGHT under Callum's guard, Judah tried evoking Noa to wake his brother. Even as his mind—or heart—urged him not to name her. Even though it meant remembering what he'd done, and risked giving her away.

But what good was Noa to Judah, really, if he could only keep her in a place no one—not even he—could reach?

Protection could be a prison. Judah was sick of prison.

"What about Noa then, Big Brother?" he said, dropping the name like one might a bomb: anticipating detonation.

Callum's face furrowed. His 'being-grown-up-is-so-difficult' face. Judah knew it well from when they had been kids. It was even more annoying now.

"You remember her, don't you? I guess you should, since you say you *love* her."

Callum looked annoyed. Which was something. "What is your point?"

"Well, just wondering how she fits into this nice, happy-go-lucky, Kells-worshipping religion of yours. Kells wanted Noa killed. And he wanted *me* to do it. And who the hell knows—" Judah's breath caught but he didn't relent or lose his determined nonchalance. "Maybe I even did, when I pushed her into that stupid chute."

Callum's face wavered. "Those were Arik's orders, not Kells'. And no body was recovered."

"You don't *know*, though. And, what, if she comes back, you think Kells will welcome her with open arms?"

The muscles in Callum's face worked and knotted. He got up, paced to the tiny, taunting window. "She's ... not *family*."

Judah's eyes widened. "You *chose* her, Callum—"

"I have a duty!" Callum snapped. "I don't have a choice! I ran once from my family and that was wrong, and now I owe them! Noa, love, the mortal realm—it was selfish!" His hands went angrily to his curls.

"But you remember, you remember it?" Judah replied quickly, clinging the bars.

Callum shook his head violently. "Stop! You're sucking me in! You're warping my eyes to see like yours! You always do that!" He hurled himself at Judah's cell, shoving Judah's pathetic body from the bars into a ragged heap. "We can't all be selfish like you! You need to *grow up*, Judah—"

"Cal—"

"You're a child! We have responsibilities in *this* world, the one that made us! Those are bonds we cannot break! We both used Noa as an excuse to act like children, run away—maybe we *need* to leave her behind!"

"So you … you don't love her anymore?" Judah whispered in shock.

"*You're* my brother, Judah!" Callum ripped his hands through his curls, erupted into angry, rapid muttering, almost to himself. "I had hoped you would see this, that I could help you see, but I think now you may be too far gone, that Kells is right—"

Judah could see him shutting down, welding himself closed, pushing out things that didn't fit into boxes and straight lines.

"And Lily?" Judah cried desperately. "Have you forgotten our *sister*?"

Callum whirled on Judah. "How could I forget! You killed her! I knew you were dangerous and I let it happen anyway! Now I must atone! I must atone!" Callum's face broke open, completely tortured and distraught, and he began to wail and beat himself.

Judah fell back against the floor, stunned. "Callum, she's not dead—don't you remember?"

Callum pressed his hands to his head, shook it harder and harder. "I remember—I remember—" he wailed, "Lorelei, when she saw me carry Lily's body from the flames—because of you, because of you—"

"But she wasn't dead then Callum," Judah repeated more urgently, crawling and pulling himself toward the bars. "You took her to Noa, to protect her, make her Sasha—"

Callum growled and flung Judah back again with an almost primal force. "And then you killed her! You threw her into the Portal and you took her from me, from Noa, from everyone!"

"Callum—"

Callum's eyes were fire. "One more word, and I don't care, I will kill you where you stand!"

Judah closed his mouth. He felt himself trembling.

He didn't know this Callum, not really, but he knew his brother. And he knew his brother well enough to know that in that moment, Callum meant every single word.

• • •

NOA AND HILO lay crumpled partway inside the tunnel, blown back among rubble, too hurt for tears and too tired for words. The opening was completely gone, sealed and plugged deep with crumbled rock.

Noa was on her stomach in something wet, Hilo on her back.

There was only one thing to say.

"Forward," Noa croaked without moving.

"Forward," Hilo croaked in agreement.

Noa counted to five in her head—five seconds to gather her courage—then pushed herself up. To her surprise, Hilo moved at exactly the same moment.

"What?" Hilo asked.

Noa shook her head. Hilo moved gingerly, wincing and trying not to use her bad shoulder. It still hung at a gruesome angle.

"I wish we had Callum," Noa murmured.

Hilo one-shoulder shrugged. "Eh, he'd have got in the way of all this fun anyway. Telling us to be careful."

Noa smiled, even though it hurt. "True."

"I'll be okay. My Light will heal it a little as we go. Not all, but enough to make it not-so-gross and only partly excruciating."

Noa bit her lip. "Thank you for protecting me when we fell. How you kind of … shielded me."

"Well you don't have Light. Made sense," Hilo replied. "You coulda gobbin' killed us though, letting go like that."

Noa flushed. "We wouldn't have made it—"

Hilo smirked. "No, I'm saying it was smart. Risky. But smart."

Noa smiled back. She still wasn't sure she really liked Hilo, let alone trusted her, but it was nice to have her now. That much was true.

Noa and Hilo turned together to the only way that lay ahead. The only 'forward' left.

"It's a good thing this tunnel's lit, or I wouldn't have seen it," Noa said, as they began to trudge together toward the pale white light she had glimpsed inside the cavern.

"Mm-hmm."

"What?" Noa demanded, hands on hips. "Me reckless and smart, remember? Speak."

Hilo sighed. "Just … the light? Why light all of a sudden? And where did all those gobbin' rocks come from? The whole mountain didn't just suddenly collapse." They started to walk again, and Noa felt that twistiness again. The same twistiness she'd felt when she'd realized they had to go down into the chasm, not across it.

"They're tests, aren't they."

Hilo nodded. "Or security protocols."

"That's a pretty important difference."

Hilo rolled her eyes. "Do we have a choice?"

Noa thought of starfish sisters and *forward!*, but her anxiety grew stronger anyway. She thought of Sasha, of Callum and Judah who needed her help—then locked their faces away tight, sensing for some reason that they needed protection.

"No. We don't have a choice," she agreed.

They soldiered on silently.

"Something…," Hilo murmured, squinting uncertainly ahead. Noa felt it too: they'd been walking farther and farther toward the white source of light, but with every step it seemed to be receding. It was leading them somewhere.

"Another test?" Noa murmured.

"I guess we'll find out," Hilo said with a bitter smile. Noa closed her eyes briefly, thankful at least that she wasn't alone.

The light continued to lead them around several turns, winding deeper and deeper into the dripping, dank dark, until it finally brought them to a wider room. Their tunnel opened into a narrow but towering space, bordered on the far side by a rushing river of black, opaque water. Across the river was another tunnel entrance, embedded in another wall, from which the hallway seemed to continue on.

Noa and Hilo, however, were looking up, mesmerized. They could see, finally, the light source: a white ball of iridescent flame, which had come to rest high above them like a mini-sun. It was absolutely breathtaking.

Hilo murmured, awestruck, "That has to be made from Blue magic. Just like the avalanche. But it would take way more than just one Fae..."

"But who—"

"Noser! Thank *God*! I told Miles you would come for us!"

Noa spun, flabbergasted, at the sound of that sardonic, beloved voice.

"Oh shut up, Livi! You're the one who's been freaking out! Seriously Noa, I've been the one mopping up the tears—"

"Lies, Mr. Kessler! Such lies!"

Noa blinked, heart beating so fast she was dizzy. She didn't know how, or why, but it was true: Olivia and Miles, *her* Olivia and Miles whom she'd pushed from the In Between Portal world through some crazy door, were here, *here*, standing in front of this underground black river deep in the Tunnels beneath Aurora. And they were *themselves*—real, not Portal-y: Olivia with her blunt black hair and tattoos hidden; Miles scruffy in his uniform, golden-retriever smile slightly confused—

"Miles! O!" Noa cried, sprinting to them, grabbing them in desperate hugs. Solid, so solid, and smelling just like them, like her mint gum and his flannel sheets—

"Noa!" Hilo called from somewhere behind her, but Noa didn't listen. She didn't have time for her, for Hilo, because she wasn't alone here, not anymore, she had her best friends who were mortal too and now everything would be okay—

"But, you guys, why are you here? When I freed you from the In Between, I thought I was sending you home—"

Olivia made her 'crazy eyes' face. "Nose, I don't know what kind of paint we've been huffing, but I swear you just spoke gibberish, and this trip is making me seriously wish I'd listened to Nancy Reagan and 'just-said-no'."

"Yeah, you're here so let's just wake up now!" Miles said with evident relief.

"Noa!" Hilo said from behind her, pulling on her shoulder. Noa shook her off.

"Who's Grabby?" Olivia asked.

"Did she huff the paint too?" Miles wondered.

"They were pills, weren't they, Nose. Is this bitch the pill-pusher?"

Miles reached for Noa's hand. "Let's just wake up, okay? Forget her."

Noa nodded, letting the warmth of Miles' familiar touch soothe all the places she was hurt. Olivia took her other hand, and the warmth swelled, magnified outward, washing away all the running and the crying and the seeing—

"I want to wake up," Noa said, and she found her eyes were blurred with tears. "Yes, please let's all wake up!"

"Don't cry, Nose," Olivia cooed, squeezing her hand. "Don't cry when it's almost over."

"I d-don't know how to—"

"It's okay," Miles said reassuringly. "We've been down here a long time, and we figured it all out. We were just waiting for you."

"Noa! *Noa!*" Hilo again, somewhere behind Noa, trying to pull her back from her friends. Annoying Hilo, horrible Hilo, so jealous of Noa and everything she had, how could Noa have ever thought she liked her, even for a second—"*it's Green, it's Green, there's no one there*—Noa shook her head, refused to hear Hilo's petty, jealous words. She turned to Miles instead, drinking in his chocolate-brown eyes. "How do we wake up?"

Miles grinned his retriever grin. "Easy silly. Jump in the water. Water always wakes people up."

"Duh," Olivia agreed, punching Miles playfully. "Guess he's good for something after all."

"I try."

"Not real ... Green..." Hilo again, hammering with fists and words, hammering on this shell of peace and warmth of calm, just—

"Stop!" Noa pushed hard, shoved Hilo's mass somewhere away. Then she let Olivia and Miles take her hands and guide her to the rushing black river. It was so black and opaque. And moving very, very fast.

"Okay Noa? We get to wake up, on the count of—"

"Noa!"

A tiny doubt, a single drop, dripped into Noa's happy gaze. "Not yet."

Olivia frowned. "Girl, we've been waiting."

"I need to get my sister."

Miles squeezed her hand. "She's at daycare. We'll pick her up when we get home."

The drip again. A flash. Was that ... Isla? "No, not just Sasha, Isla too. She's here I think. I can't leave without her."

Olivia and Miles exchanged a look. "We can't wait for her," Olivia said.

Noa hesitated—*this could end, I could go home*—but finally, took a step back from the creek. "Go without me."

Olivia and Miles looked worriedly at her. "We can't go without you."

"Come on, Noa, let's wake up—"

"I want to, I do, but I can't leave her, I need her—"

"Green, Green…"

Isla was coming, Noa couldn't see her but she could feel her, somewhere behind her, where Hilo was yelling.

Olivia and Miles exchanged another look, and then they looked at Noa with terrible, crushing sadness. Their forms became wavy, blurry, then disintegrated into nothing. The sudden coldness in Noa's palms crumpled her to her knees, took her wind; she felt bereft.

Hilo collapsed at Noa's side on the ground, grasped Noa's shoulder and shook her as hard as she could. "Listen to me! It's not real! I can sense the Green magic! You're not feeling anything real—"

Noa couldn't stop herself; she began bawling, fell onto her side, curled into a shaking, helpless ball.

Hilo hesitated, then wrapped her body around Noa's, the way she had when they'd been crashing down the rock face. She let her warmth push away Noa's chill, murmured close into Noa's ear. "It's okay Noa. You're in Green withdrawal, I can make it better—"

"Noooo," Noa wailed. "No more, no more. I was going home, I was going to see Sasha—"

"No, Noa, no you weren't. It was a lie," Hilo soothed, holding Noa like a child. "Please, please, Noa, please hold on."

And finally, finally, because she could not fight it any longer, Noa sank into Hilo, imagining Hilo's arms were Hannah's arms and she was Sasha's age, in a place that was warm and safe.

Finally, slowly, Noa stopped sobbing, and Hilo helped her to sit up.

"It was Green?" Noa murmured wetly.

Hilo nodded. "Very advanced Green. A hallucination pulled from your own heart … it woulda got me too, but being Green, I felt it…"

Noa wiped her nose. "Makes sense."

Hilo smiled encouragingly. "But you finally heard me. You finally broke through."

Noa frowned. "Isla helped."

"Isla?"

"My dead sister. Her ghost. I see her sometimes, even here in Aurora. That's what stopped me from jumping in the river. I suddenly didn't want to leave here without her."

"A touchstone," Hilo guessed. "Something real."

They both got to their feet, looked doubtfully at the river.

"I'm guessing we should avoid that."

Hilo frowned. "Agreed. But how else can we get across? That's obviously the right way. The tunnel continues on the other side."

Noa looked to either side of the rushing river; it was too wide to jump across from any angle.

Noa frowned. It felt like forever since she'd been anywhere dry and warm, since there hadn't been this wetness, coldness, dankness always and everywhere—even under her feet, sinking and sucking at her every step.

Noa crouched, pushing a finger into the sucky mouth of the riverbank sludge. It was some sort of clay.

Noa turned to Hilo, suddenly not caring at all about the wetness. She grinned.

"How do you feel about making a bridge?"

Hilo looked at her like she'd finally lost her mind. "Out of *that*?"

Noa scooped up some of the clay. It was dense but oozing, and made a slopping, kissing noise when she squeezed a chunk free. She held it up excitedly, and Hilo watched askance as it began slowly melting through her fingers.

"Um, Noa, I'm not Callum. What am I supposed to do with that? Make it *feel* like a bridge?"

Noa rolled her eyes in an excellent imitation of the pixie. "Faefyre, Hilo. That's *Green*. If you flashfyre this clay stuff, it'll be like firing it in a kiln. We just need to make a long enough plank to walk across."

Hilo slowly began to smile with this possibility for mischief. It lit her up, sizzled inside her. This was the Hilo, Noa knew, whom Judah had come to love.

Hilo and Noa sprang into action immediately, buzzing with excited energy as they worked together to shape the plank. They moved in and by and around each other with effortless cooperation, two needles looping complex, four-handed stitches.

As soon as they had the shape they wanted, Hilo raised her hands over her head, closed her eyes, and let out a wail like a banshee. Taloned flames flew from her mouth along with her scream, glittering with the fire eyes of a Faefyre serpent. It was a sight Noa had seen before—from Pearl, in the sex club back in the mortal realm, when the pixie had sent Faefyre to kill her. Just like Pearl's, Hilo's serpent uncoiled as soon as it hit air, stretching its long, lizard body, aiming its tentacle arms. Its eyes became dragon eyes, and the mouth roared wide—but instead of diving down on Noa, as Pearl's viper had, Hilo's soared over their plank, roaring flames before it could lose its shape. When the serpent reached the end of the plank, Hilo pulled her body inward, as if choking herself on her own air, and the Faefyre spat into smoke.

As Hilo caught her breath, Noa ran forward: the Fyred plank was hard and dry, still steamy to the touch. Perfect. Noa caught Hilo's eye as the pixie panted. They shared twin grins.

Once recovered, Hilo almost seemed to dance to Noa as they worked together to maneuver the plank to the rushing river. It reminded Noa a little bit of Isla, the way she used to dance around their kitchen when they would make blintzes with their father.

Will I ever see my dad again?

"Ready?" Hilo said, bringing Noa back to the here and now. Noa nodded, and together, they lifted the plank from one end. It took both of them, straining hard—Hilo's pixie strength, even, was stretched to its limit—to get the plank across without letting the far side dip into the ominous, swirling water. With a final shove, they heaved, and the far edge clattered to the narrow bank on the other side. Noa stumbled forward with the effort, but Hilo caught her by the back of the shirt before she fell into the rushing river. Hilo hurled them backward; they sprawled on the bank, Noa's heart hammering wildly at how close she'd come to falling in.

"Thanks," she panted, stunned.

"'Course," Hilo panted back, just as stunned.

Hilo got to her feet quickly, pulling Noa up. "Forward," she reminded Noa. Noa nodded. There was no time to wait.

They approached their plank bridge. The banks of the river were not very high, so there was precious little distance between the plank and the black water rushing beneath it. The banks were also uneven, and the plank wobbled terribly. But it was their only way across.

They'd just have to be careful.

"Mortals have any balance?" Hilo asked, grinning.

Noa bit her lip but forced a smile. "If you can do it, I can do it." She tried not to think of the many, many times she'd tripped doing absolutely nothing. Hadn't she also managed to keep up with Callum and Judah when they were dodging Guards and magic, running from the Barracks? And what about jumping between buildings with Marena—

Marena. Noa pushed the pixie's memory—her face, her grin—back painfully. No time for mourning. Not now.

Hilo was already stepping eagerly onto their makeshift bridge.

"Wait!" Noa said suddenly. "I need to go first!" She didn't know why, but she wanted to be in motion, or she knew, *she knew,* she'd start thinking not only of Marena, but of everyone she'd left behind—

Hilo stepped back, and Noa marched onto the board. It wobbled dangerously, almost tilting into the water.

"Easy! Grace!" Hilo cried.

Noa's heart spun wildly as she swung and swayed her hips for balance. When the board finally settled beneath her, she forced her next step to be slow and gentle. The board stayed steadier this time; unfortunately, that didn't help her nerves.

"Forward," Hilo murmured.

Forward, Noa thought firmly.

Noa began to move slowly and methodically over the dark, forbidding water, one step at a time. She focused on the plank alone. She knew if she looked to either side, if she even glimpsed that plunging opacity that was so unlike any water she'd ever seen—

The board wobbled violently.

"Noa!" Hilo screamed, grabbing the board from her side to try to stabilize it. Hilo knelt on it, holding it as best she could, anchoring it under her weight.

Noa swallowed. *The board. Only the board. Forward!*

Noa took a deep, rattling breath, then started moving slowly again. She didn't look at the water, that strange black water like dark matter from space whose tractor beam could pull you in from your gaze alone. Noa shuddered to think what might have happened if she had followed the fake Olivia and Miles and let the water swallow her whole—

"Noa!" Hilo screamed as Noa rocked again, one side of the board dipping into the water. Noa pinwheeled her arms frantically, finally falling to a crouch. Knuckles white, she breathed in and out in frozen terror as she narrowly missed falling in.

She was halfway across.

Noa gave herself five shaking breaths. Only five, after which she would not, under any circumstances, think again of the watery doom under and beside her—

Noa cried out from her crouch as her balance wavered *again*. She was better than this. She was stronger than this. Or if she wasn't, Isla was. *Sasha* was. And their blood was hers.

Noa forced herself up, and in sudden Sasha-impulse, sprinted down the rest of the plank, letting it rock in wider, more violent arcs, and finally sprang from it to the bank in a tumble just as the board upended.

"Noa, the board!" Hilo cried. Noa had landed on her stomach; she spun and scrambled back through the sludge on all fours to catch her end of the board before it fell back into the water. She grasped it, fully outstretched, and heaved it back, flinging her body on top of it to force it down.

Board beneath her ribs, Noa finally sank in relief into the mud.

"Holy Otec, Noa, what the gobbin' hell was that?"

Noa didn't even look up. She knew her hair would be a matted clump, her face caked with dripping brown and didn't care. "*That* was mortal grace."

Hilo barked a short laugh from the other side, and Noa smiled tiredly into the mud, tasting mint and oddly, sweetness. Then she scrunched up her butt, still channeling Sasha, and got to her brown-slop hands and knees.

She braced herself over the board with her hands and held it steady. "Your turn."

"No problem," Hilo said, twinkling a little with smugness. Noa couldn't see Hilo precisely against the expanse of water, but she could practically hear the smirk.

With the grace only a pixie could have, Hilo danced out onto the plank soundlessly, as if she weighed nothing, each step a graceful flourish. Noa eased her hold on the board a little, rolling her eyes.

When Hilo reached dead center, she paused, body like a ballet dancer midpirouette. She looked around slowly.

"Come on, Hilo, we don't have all day, remember? Enough with the showboating."

But Hilo didn't appear to hear her. She bent lithely, gracefully, to look more closely at the water.

"What are you *doing*?"

"It's so pretty Noa. I've never seen anything like it," Hilo's voice sounded strange—soft, and full of awe.

"Probably because you've never seen death water before. Come on."

But Hilo didn't move another step, instead leaning even closer toward the water. "It's so dark and rich…." She began to stretch an arm toward it.

"Hilo! Stop!" Noa cried urgently.

Hilo looked up briefly in annoyance. "Why?"

"Because it will kill you or something worse, remember?"

Hilo's face became petulant. "But I want to. I want to touch it, I want to *drink* it—it's all I can think about—"

Noa felt her face drain as the pieces fell into place. She, too, had been unbalanced, pulled toward that horrible water when she'd tried to cross the plank. It was so obvious now; she saw it so clearly in Hilo—

"Hilo, you have to trust me! Stop! Stop! Please freeze!"

Hilo's fingers froze a millimeter from the water; she turned her head in mild curiosity at Noa's obvious distress.

Noa tried to say it as clearly as she could. "It's *Red*, Hilo. It isn't your thought to touch the water. It's *Red*."

Hilo's face wrinkled in confusion, but her hand at least remained frozen. "But it'll be fun, like making the bridge. I thought you were brave." She scowled at Noa, then turned back to the water, arm outstretched.

Noa had no choice. She rattled the board, hard. Hilo's pixie reflexes made her stand back up to catch her balance.

"Hey!" Hilo called. "Don't be a gobbin' brat!"

Noa racked her brain. If Hilo couldn't feel the foreignness of implanted Red thought, Noa would to outsmart it.

"Just wait for me then! Don't leave me out!" Noa called desperately. "I want to have fun too!"

Hilo glared skeptically.

"Judah wouldn't want you to leave me out, Hilo! You know he wouldn't!"

Hilo put her hands on her hips, sighing. "Fine, but hurry it up!"

Cringing, Noa slowly made her way back to the one place she really didn't want to go: back onto the board over the death-river.

And this time with no one on either side to hold it steady.

The board immediately began rocking, but at least this time Noa knew to be on her guard for Red fascination with the water. When it came—and it did, pulling her mind and eyes downward—she could see the thought's foreign shape so clearly, she couldn't believe she hadn't spotted it before.

But whoever was doing this—whatever hidden Reds—didn't know Noa could spot it now.

"Ooh, I see what you mean," Noa cooed, trying to match Hilo's strange tone, hoping to keep their assailants' attention divided. If the Reds had to focus on Suggesting the fascination to her, they would have to lessen their focus on Hilo. Noa saw the amoeba-like thoughts in her mind, coming from all sides, at the same time as Hilo's certainty seemed to flicker.

It was working.

"What?" Hilo asked, blinking. "Oh —oh yes. I told you so, didn't I?"

"But first," Noa said quickly, tauntingly, remembering Hilo's mischief smile, "I'll race you to the other bank. Go!"

Sending up a prayer, Noa spun and ran back down the board. It tipped and turned so high she had to jump off the end to make the bank and knew there would be no saving it. She heard the board splash into the water as she belly-flopped into mud and prayed Hilo had made it too, but she didn't dare to look.

At first there was only silence. Then Noa felt something. Someone. She looked up to see Hilo, beaming down at her.

"I *won*," the pixie gloated.

A sizzling sound split the air, and Hilo and Noa turned to see the board bubbling into seething nothing, like flesh melted by acid. The sight of it shook Hilo free from the Red compulsion; Noa saw the fierce wariness return to her face.

She looked at Noa in disbelief. "You could have been killed, saving me like that!"

"And now you *both* will be."

Noa and Hilo turned—a gnarled, filthy mass, a creature of hair and cloak and spit and mist, opened its maw and roared back. The blue ball of light that exploded outward with the sound blinded them to everything else. The orb thundered directly for Noa.

Noa froze. This was it. The end. The orb was on her—

But someone—*Hilo*—leapt on top of her, shoved her over, fell into her place—

And took the blast herself.

Noa screamed, skittered out from under Hilo's gangling body as it slumped into the mud. Noa's eyes took a snapshot her brain refused to develop—the ice that had been Hilo's eyes, the crystal that had been Hilo's skin, still and lifeless and completely, utterly dead—

And the monster that had done it was coming for Noa.

It wasn't that Noa couldn't run; it was that the slowness of the wraith descending upon her was paralyzing, inexorable, inevitable—as deadly as anticipation itself. It limped and scratched toward her, taking its time because it knew, like she knew, there was nowhere to run, nowhere to hide, and no one left alive to save her.

As the creature approached, Noa realized, to her shock, it was an ancient, twisted *woman*—or once had been a woman—hair like sand struck clear by lightning, skin stained to scales by green-brown grime. A woman gone mad, gone rotten, if any woman was left—her blackened rip-like mouth open wide to screech.

The woman's reptilian hands raised upward, lizard-pupils swallowing her eyes, and Noa knew it was over. She couldn't move, couldn't run, and the only words that came to her were from a memory that echoed now like a premonition. The words of another about to die pointlessly and cruelly before monsters in the darkness.

Noa and Geezer opened their bitter mouths together, spoke the words again now in their defeat:

"Hail harmony."

. . .

NOTHING.

Noa opened her eyes—she still had eyes, just as she still had limbs—and saw the old woman poised to strike but still. Her lizard eyes flickered wide.

"How," she hissed, not moving a muscle, "did you know my name?"

• • •

"GO GET HIM, go get him," Judah whimpered on the third night, unable to fight anymore. He hated that his voice was small, that his body was again a little boy's bent from shame and dirty with secrets. He couldn't bear now to look at Callum's eyes—still so calm, so proud with blinded purpose. Judah and Callum were matryoshka dolls, both of them—who they were, who they'd been, what they'd done and who they'd never be—all nested one inside the other inside the other, painted smiles and unseeing eyes. Judah knew each buried doll, each smaller cast, but he couldn't bear to see them anymore. If Callum wouldn't see with him, Judah could not bear the burden alone. It hurt too much to be the only one who saw.

Judah was done.

Judah sagged against his birdcage, didn't look up even when he heard the door open, the footsteps. He waited until he heard Kells dismiss Callum.

Kells was smiling. Waiting.

"Just take him away," Judah croaked, broken. "Send me back alone to the mortal realm, or to my own In Between prison, whatever you want. Just get me away from him. I can't … I can't look at him anymore. Please."

Kells' eyes twinkled. He cocked his head. "Do you really think it is that easy? To just open a Portal, an In Between?"

"Isn't it? You're still the Gatekeeper, aren't you?" Judah wanted to yell. Wasn't stupid Kells good for *anything*?

"Even *I* don't have that power, boy. Portals *rip* worlds! That requires blood bonds of the greatest sacrifice. Did your father never tell you that? The price he paid?" Kells shook his head with a sneer, continuing, "I'm just one Fae. I could maybe, *maybe* make a temporary window, and that"—he shook his head again at the ridiculousness of the idea—"would be so unstable, and last so little time, it would surely destroy anything and anyone who went inside—"

"Then Banish me somewhere else! I don't need a stupid magic lesson, I just need to be *away*! Don't leave him alone with me! You wanted me to beg and you've won, okay? I'm begging!"

"And much as that delights me, that isn't *quite* what I wanted. I didn't want your *allegiance*. I wanted your *love*."

Judah swallowed a scream. "Fine! It's yours!"

Kells laughed. "My powers may be gone, but even I know that lacked the proper feeling. Or maybe you never learned. Letting someone break you isn't the same as letting someone love you. I want the *real* victory."

"Jailing me won't win my love," Judah spat.

"And hugs and kisses will? Ha!" Kells growled. "I gave up on the sentiment route long ago, when my Light was crusted out of me by your dear old dad. But you already know that. You already know I have another way in store for you."

Even broken, even without any strength left at all, Judah found he could still shudder.

Kells smiled a smile that, had it reached his eyes, would have actually looked sincere.

"Ready for my weapon?"

• • •

"HOW DO YOU know my name? Tell me!" the woman repeated, lizard eyes seething, lizard-tongue darting, but making no move to strike.

Noa didn't understand; the words sounded like nonsense, gibberish, and there was Hilo beside her, absurdly like Isla in her coffin. Same blond hair, same fair skin, the ethereal sparkle gone and just a girl, a dead young girl lying still. (Their eyes were different colors but then Isla's eyes had been closed in her coffin, hadn't they, not open like Hilo's now, open and frozen and blue. Isla's eyes had been more gray than blue, imperial, like the sea in storm—)

"Girl! Get out of the way!" Crinkly hands like both slime and sandpaper shoved Noa off her fallen friend. She hadn't realized she'd fallen weeping on top of Hilo, barely felt it now as her body slid back, unresisting, a rag doll in the mud. She let the mud suckle at her skin. She couldn't stop the tears and didn't want to—not even when she felt a familiar presence at her shoulder, not even when she knew that if she looked, she might see Isla's ghost—because the real Isla was gone, and that was who she cried for now, and also Hilo, the real Hilo whom a part of Noa hated, because there had been times she'd hated Isla, even though she loved her—

"N-Noa?"

Noa looked up from her slop, her sobs, her mud, her hands. Hilo was blinking, sitting up, wincing in pain in a bluish haze. The woman—the wraith who had killed Hilo—was now somehow reviving her. Except right now she didn't look so monstrous—more short and crumpled, and old.

But Noa didn't care about her right now.

"Hilo!" Noa crashed across the mud to tackle Hilo in a hug. Hilo fell back with a wince, then they locked eyes and laughed, both surprised at the intensity of their delight. Then the crinkly, slimy hands—now talon-sharp and strong—shoved them apart and pinned them down.

"I'll kill you both and leave you dead unless you tell me now—*who told you my name?*"

Hilo looked in bewildered fear at Noa; Noa struggled to search her shell-shocked brain. "H-Harmony?" Noa asked finally. "Your *name* is Harmony. 'Hail Harmony.' It was a name."

"An unspeakable name."

"You're the Seer," Hilo breathed. "It's true, you're real."

Harmony glared at Hilo and shoved her backward with one hand at the throat. She raised her other claw to Noa. Its nails were pointed, like she'd evolved that way. *"Speak."*

The words tumbled clumsily, rapidly. "An old man, a cell mate, I was in prison … He sacrificed himself for me, I don't know why, gave his life to help me escape even though he hated me—when they were dragging him out, when he knew he was about to die, he looked at me and said, 'Hail Harmony.' I thought he meant something about the revolution, that's why he wanted me to escape—"

"Petty revolutions are of no concern to me."

"Are you the Seer, or aren't you?" Hilo demanded.

The woman squeezed Hilo's throat in punishment, cutting off her breath. "Stop saying *Seer*. Only children believe in Seers. All I *see* is the past."

"But you're the Attendant who ran from the Temple?" Noa pleaded, watching Hilo's face turn red then blue. "You've read the Scrolls and studied the gifts. We need your help—please, she didn't mean it. Please—"

The woman snarled but relaxed her grip a fraction, eyeing Hilo in warning. Noa fought the urge to gag as a small snake slithered out of the woman's knot of hair and then back in, its skin clear too, showing its knobby spine.

The woman didn't notice or didn't care. She looked at Noa. "The name found you, so to *you* I will listen."

Noa swallowed, tried to speak carefully. "You're ... her? The Attendant from the temple?"

The woman nodded once.

"H-how come no one's found you?"

"I've killed the others."

Noa shivered; she couldn't help it.

"What about the others helping you?" Hilo interjected. "You couldn't have laid all those little traps on your own. You bamboozle an army of Fae too, make them your guards?"

The Seer's tone was ice as she turned slowly to Hilo. "I have no Guards."

Noa and Hilo looked at each other. Hilo tried to scoff. "But Blues had to make that avalanche and the white guiding light—"

"And Greens made me see my friends—"

"And Reds tried to make us drink the water! It would take two of each at *least* to do all those skills," Hilo accused. "You're trading on an old legend, and we don't have time to waste. Bring out the minions and let's get real."

The Seer's upper lip curled in Hilo's direction. "You did not have the name. I do not have to tolerate you."

"She doesn't mean to be rude," Noa said quickly, as Hilo's eyes narrowed dangerously, so like Judah's. "We've just been searching, hoping—"

"If you're the Seer, and not just some old hag," Hilo interrupted, overemphasizing the word *Seer*, "tell us why you left the Temple. You could have been the Mystic."

The Seer's lip curled again. "Knowledge comes with a price."

"What price?" Hilo snorted.

Harmony hissed, and Noa put a hand on Hilo's shoulder. "Hilo, I believe her. Who else set all those traps? She must have learned it from studying Fae magic."

"The girl who ran from the Temple was young, Noa! Look at her, this crone's thousands of years old!"

"Silence!" the Seer boomed, flinging her voice and hand at Hilo. Hilo's entire mouth vanished with a little *pop*. Her eyes looked so surprised Noa could have laughed, if it had not been so repulsive.

The Seer looked at Noa. "You wept when you thought *she* was lost?"

"You get used to her," Noa admitted. "And besides, I couldn't have gotten here without her. Your traps were pretty impressive."

"They usually suffice. But two together have a greater chance."

"I guess."

"Not guess. *Fact.*" The Seer nodded back toward Hilo's lip-less, furious face. "She helped you with the Green trap because you do not know your heart. You freed her from the Red one, because she does not know her mind. Be careful of that—one who does not know her mind makes for a shifty ally."

Hilo's eyes bugged with a retort she could not give voice.

Noa bit her lip. "I trust her."

"So be it."

"Do you mind ... telling her why you are so..." Noa trailed off, not sure how to put it. "Much older, I guess, than she thinks you should be?"

"Bodies wear for many reasons. She is lucky not to have learned that yet."

Noa turned to Hilo. "Okay? Please Hilo, this is our chance. It's *her*. Who else would be down here? *Believe* with me. Forward, right?"

Hilo's eyes flared, but then she nodded. The Seer flicked her wrist at Hilo, and her mouth returned with a *pop*. She rubbed it with her hand and looked at the Seer sideways, as if suspicious Harmony had given her back an inferior smile.

The Seer's lizard eyes held Hilo icily. "You will not speak unless I invite you to. I will help the one who knew my name because someone died to give it to her. I will tolerate you only until I no longer wish to do so."

Hilo looked down, an angry child, but nodded. The loss of her mouth had allayed her doubts, but it had badly hurt her pride.

"Ahhh!" Noa groaned, suddenly falling to her knees and pressing her palms against her temples. She'd been feeling the spasms in her head while they were climbing down before the avalanche and crossing the river, but the adrenaline of falling and then fleeing and nearly drowning had helped her to push the headaches away. Now that things were somewhat calmer, the pain knifed through her brain as if her neurons were on fire, and she realized the headaches had never actually stopped.

"What's wrong with her?" the Seer demanded as Hilo flew to kneel by Noa. Hilo looked up, hesitated. "I allow you to speak! Tell me!"

"She's been getting headaches, it's part of why we came to seek your help—"

"I thought I sensed something, magic out of order—"

"Ahhhh!"

"She's not magic! She's mortal!"

The Seer's lizard eyes widened, her entire body completely still. "Are you going to help her or not?" Hilo demanded.

Noa fell to all fours, panting, but the worst had passed. "I-I'm okay now."

The Seer flicked Hilo away and yanked Noa to her knees so she could look into her eyes. "*Mortal.* From the mortal realm. Of course."

"We thought…," Hilo began tentatively. "We worried Aurora might…"

"Be killing me," Noa croaked.

The Seer raked her eyes over Noa, laid her hands on her cheeks. They now felt rough and sure.

"What else?" she demanded tersely.

"M-my memories here. Some of them, they're changing, or fading, I can't really explain it—"

"Any in particular?"

Noa swallowed. "Callum."

"Blue Fae," Hilo supplied quietly.

The Seer blinked, just once. "He's the reason you're here, is he."

Noa looked at Hilo. "Sort of. We used to … be together. In the mortal world. It's a long, weird story."

The Seer's face betrayed nothing. "It will be faster if I read it in your mind. Lean forward."

Hilo sprang into action. "Whoa, whoa, whoa, who said you could just go in there and poke around?"

"You want my help or not?" the Seer replied stonily.

Hilo faltered, turned to Noa. "Think about it first, Noa. She'll see everything. *Everything.*"

Noa bit her lip. "Forward, right?" she whispered, not at all certain, and absolutely afraid. "For the boys and Sasha."

Hilo clenched her jaw; Noa saw the muscles pulse in her cheeks. "It's a risk. For everyone."

Noa took Hilo's hand. "We've come this far...."

Hilo looked unhappy, but squeezed Noa's hand and nodded. "Forward."

"Good," the Seer said tersely. "Step back."

Hilo obliged, not breaking Noa's eye line. Noa nodded at her, then leaned her forehead into the Seer's claws.

It was unlike anything Noa had ever experienced. She had thought it was going to be like the prison interrogation, when Captain Lia had Channeled a Red to look into her mind. Then, Noa had walked the memories with Lia, had seen what she'd seen, had even been able to propel the intrusion out. But this time it was a blur; it was everything moving lightning-fast and white, all at the same time. No way to hold back, no way to shut a door, no way to even see or hear, just lie exposed, open, raw—

And then it was over.

Noa fell forward with the force of it, breathless and strangely bereft. The Seer stumbled back a few steps, scrambling a little for her own balance.

Hilo was instantly at Noa's side, holding her up.

The Seer's voice was uncharacteristically shaky. "Many secrets, Noa. *Many.*"

Noa looked nervously at Hilo. She squeezed Noa's shoulders.

The Seer mastered herself and looked at Noa, terse again. "Your headaches and your memory shifts are the results of two very different things, both equally dangerous. A Mindworm and a curse."

Noa lost her footing against Hilo; roaring shook inside her ears. Somewhere next to her, Hilo asked, "What's a Mindworm?"

The Seer looked at Noa. Of course she knew that Noa already knew the answer, because she now knew everything.

Noa found her thready voice. "Combination magic. In the mortal realm, a Red Fae and a Green pixie put a Mindworm into my friend Miles to change his feelings, erase his memories..." She couldn't go on. It was too terrible to remember what the twins, Fabian and Pearl, had done to her best friend, how, despite the fantasy of the Portal world, in real life he had not recovered and probably never would.

"It works even after the Fae are not present. It takes on a life of its own. A magic that's *alive*," the Seer finished for Noa. A sick bit of awe had crept into her guarded voice.

"The twins got me too?" Noa asked. "Is that what happened?"

For the first time, the Seer looked surprised—and something slipped in and softened her features, just for a moment. Something like ... sympathy.

That made Noa's heart beat even faster. "Not the twins? Someone else?"

The Seer actually hesitated. "Callum," she finally said. "Callum gave you the Mindworm."

Noa clutched her stomach, fell forward; Hilo caught her before she hit the ground. Noa turned to the side, thought she might be sick except there was nothing inside her to vomit up. Nothing inside but the bile of selves exploding into pieces she never knew—

"How is that possible?" Hilo demanded, trying to keep Noa from disintegrating in her hands. "He would never hurt her! And you said it was combination magic! He's one Fae! Blue! Who helped him?"

Noa curled on her side, fireworks razing her beneath her skin.

"Lily, his sister," the Seer answered.

The name rang absurdly through the room; Noa breathed it in; its tang forced her back up, and fighting.

"Never," she cried angrily. "My sister would never hurt me! And her name is *Sasha*. You're a *liar*."

"They didn't do it to hurt you," the Seer replied patiently, "or even on purpose. Callum told you how he and Lily—"

"*Sasha!*"

The Seer bowed her head minutely. "Fine. Callum told you how he and Sasha worked together to insinuate her into your world, edit her into the timeline, specifically into your family and their love."

"But now we really love her, no magic needed," Noa insisted.

"I believe you. And I feel that. Cleanly."

Noa wanted to lunge at her but didn't.

The Seer raised a brow.

"Go on," Noa allowed, through gritted teeth. "Tell me."

The Seer sighed. "But the magic Callum used, the Mindworm of that scale and breadth, was far beyond what he could handle or do with precision. And Lily—Sasha—was so young then, she of course had no control. Her love for Callum, her relief at his rescue, her understanding of him as her protector, her hero—all that went into the Mindworm that went into you."

"Only me?"

"You, Noa, are Sasha's protector now. You are bound most tightly to her, and she to you. The way she was bound to Callum before. So she shared those feelings, that love for him, with you."

Noa felt her anger going out of her, hollowing her out, filling her with tears. She couldn't look at Hilo, couldn't look at the Seer, couldn't speak.

The Seer tilted her head; again—so lightly—her face grew softer, almost maternal. "I know it's hard to hear, Noa. But do you remember? How instant your attraction to him was? How deeply connected you felt immediately? I felt it with you, in your memories—"

"So none of it was true?" Noa asked, wiping angrily at a tear. "It was all a lie? My own heart … my own feelings… never mine and never true?"

As if unable to stop herself, the Seer crouched at Noa's other side, stroked her back with gentle, scaly fingers. "It started that way, but Noa"—the Seer broke off, overcome by some emotion—"who's to say what happened next? Love is tricky, and love is strong. Not some flower but a warrior weed, growing in any condition, through any obstacle, surviving frozen tundras, pushing up through cracks in stone! Who's to say now what came from you and what from him? Your love for Sasha—it began as a Worm too."

"But I *know* that's real—"

"Because it's a different kind of bond," Hilo whispered. "Romantic love … is always more confusing."

"Now who can tell?" the Seer offered. "All the feelings—yours, the illusion's—are too intertwined, growing up together…"

Noa wiped harshly at her cheeks. "How could he *do* that to me?"

"I doubt he knows," the Seer said. "Just as Sasha certainly did not."

Noa bit her salty lip until she tasted metal. "So my memories of him, how they feel as if they're changing…"

The Seer got to her gnarled feet, hunching inward, her motherly moment evidently ended. "The Mindworm was made in the mortal world and is unstable here. As the Worm changes in this atmosphere, it is affecting what and how you remember."

"Well, good," Hilo said. "So the Worm will die off here, and then she'll know for sure exactly how she feels."

"No," the Seer said bluntly. "Eventually the magic will reacclimatize to these surroundings."

"So take it out!" Noa cried. "I want it out!"

The Seer frowned. "I could do that. But the magic is complex, and if I kill the Worm in you, it dies everywhere, taking everything it created with it."

"So?" Hilo cried in exasperation.

"Sasha's life at home, her history, her place…," Noa murmured.

"Shall I do it, Noa?" the Seer asked evenly, emotionless, reptilian again. Noa knew she would do it if Noa asked.

"Of course not," Noa said, a tear falling down her cheek. "I could never do that to my sister."

The Seer nodded.

Hilo touched Noa's arm. "You can still figure it out for yourself. What's yours and what isn't."

"There *is* love for him in you, real love," the Seer added. "I do know that."

"How can it be?" Noa asked, to no one. "He set me free, he gave me wings, and gills, he helped me breathe … and yet he has taken me from me?"

"Not on purpose," Hilo reminded her. "And *he* loves *you*, with no Worm in his mind at all." Noa didn't really hear her, couldn't. Maybe didn't even want to.

The Seer cleared her throat. "There is more, when you are ready."

"Hasn't she had enough?" Hilo snarled.

The Seer didn't flicker. "I told you at the outset there are two problems. The Mindworm is one, and explains Noa's changing memories. The other problem was her headaches, and the cause is the true-love curse."

Hilo frowned. "You just said the love with Callum's not real—"

Noa looked at the Seer. "The true-love curse? You mean that thing Judah was talking about, that makes his powers not work with me? That's not real! Callum said it was because Judah never trained, his gifts were weak. That's why his gift doesn't work on me. That love thing is just some excuse!"

"I'm afraid not."

"So what, I love Judah?" Noa demanded, suddenly angry for some reason. "Is that what's been decided?"

"It may be so," the Seer replied icily, "but not necessarily. He loves *you*, however, truly and deeply, and so he shares the curse with you."

"*Hello!* What is everyone talking about? What curse?" Hilo interrupted.

Noa sighed in irritation. "Something like when a Fae loves a mortal, his gifts stop working on her—"

"Close," the Seer sneered, "but incomplete. The curse was put in place to stop Fae and mortals from intermingling, mostly because the mortal realm is meant to be a prison, not a place of happiness."

"But the curse actually makes things simpler, since it protects the mortal from Fae magic, including being drained of Light," Noa pointed out. "It would have made things a whole lot easier with Callum."

"In the immediate effect, yes," the Seer said, "but what's actually happening is not that the Faeness—the magic—is being blocked; it's being *transferred*, Fae to mortal."

"Transferred to *Noa*?" Hilo said in disbelief.

"You tell me, Noa." The Seer eyed her levelly. "Have you noticed anything odd? I did, in your mind."

Noa wanted to spit some rude retort, but then her eyes widened, a hundred moments coming suddenly into focus:

When she'd been with Marena, hiding in the closet—the Red alarm in the house had gone off, even though Marena was Green. And it had happened after she'd *seemed* to read Amarine's thoughts.

The way Noa, so many times, had felt she could read what Marena, or Callum, or even Hilo was thinking, even though they didn't speak aloud: when Marena had told her to run when she'd been captured in the square, or later, when Noa had heard Marena call her name from the jail cell, when Marena swore she hadn't said anything at all.

And the interrogation, when she'd fought off Captain Lia, seen the Red attack and pushed it back on her interrogator, even knocked her out, in the way Callum had said would be impossible—

"You Dreamwalked," Hilo added, remembering things of her own. "I told you that was a Red skill. You've … you've taken Judah's power."

"But that's not true. He still has his power—" Noa protested, but even as she said it, she could see how she was wrong. "Except ... except it's fading," she realized. "He got lost sometimes in the Tunnels, like he couldn't see them in his mind anymore; he didn't recover as quickly when we were flushed out; and his blood, it wasn't Red, it was black..."

"Black?" the Seer asked sharply. "I must have skimmed over that detail."

"Black and sludgy ... and meanwhile, I've been doing greater and greater feats, things I could never do at home. And when I'm hurt or tired, I'm recovering more quickly. Even the sun here feels less heavy than it did when I arrived, sometimes it even feels like it's healing—like on the rooftops, when I was leaping across them..." Noa looked up pleadingly into the Seer's eyes.

"Pretty stupid curse," Hilo said. "Seems to only suck for Judah."

The Seer frowned, but Noa was already there. "No, no, Hilo, don't you see? Don't you understand? It turns Judah mortal, but it turns me *Fae*! That would mean I lose everything! I would be a danger to everyone I know, everyone I love—"

"Including Judah," the Seer put in. "Fae cannot live stripped of their core magic. Once he turns fully mortal, he will die. That's why his blood's turning black: it's been poisoned by forbidden love."

Horror struck Noa and Hilo both.

Hilo whirled on Noa. "Stop! You have to stop loving him right *now*!"

Noa fell away from her. "I didn't even know I did love him! How can I stop what I can't control?"

Hilo spun to the Seer, mad with fear. "What if Noa dies? Would that stop the curse?"

"Hilo!" Noa cried.

"It would not," the Seer said curtly, "even if you could do it, which I doubt." Hilo growled at the Seer, tore at her hair in despair. The Seer ignored her histrionics. "Judah loves Noa, and if she dies, his love for her memory will continue forever and probably even strengthen—and, along with it, the curse." The Seer turned to Noa. "As for you. I'm afraid one more time I must complicate your feelings." She paused, choosing her words carefully. "It is tempting for me to at least let you have this certainty. To say, this proves it, you *are* in love with Judah, simply and clearly. But ... I cannot give you that."

"W-why?"

"The true-love curse is ... tricky. A very ancient magic. Judah's obviously in love with you; that's why his powers are going to you. But your vulnerability to his curse may be coming from your love for a different Fae. A love we *know* is true."

"Sasha," Noa breathed.

The Seer nodded. "The love between you and Sasha alone would not trigger the curse because it is a different kind of love, but its presence does leave you open, vulnerable, to being cursed by Judah's love, even if you do not love him back the way he loves you. Especially because they share blood.

"In either case," the Seer sighed, "the only way to end this curse, Judah's curse, is to make Judah fall out of love with you. Then the transfer will reverse, and both of you will be saved."

"But I can go on loving Sasha, and she me, without hurting her."

"Yes. Though it will always leave you vulnerable."

"That's a chance I'll take," Noa said. "Living without her

is not." Noa took a deep breath, turned heavily to Hilo. "And it's not a chance we can take with Judah. I don't know how I feel about him, I told you that before. And it's something"—she broke off, realized she tasted tears—"something I wanted to figure out, especially now, with Callum. You understand?"

Hilo nodded slowly. "But—"

Noa hung her head. "But. *Yes*, Hilo. Even if I do love him in that way, even if … I have, I-I will give him to you, Hilo. I will make him fall out of love with me." She wiped her cheeks. "But Hilo—you *must* catch him." She pressed her eyes closed, unable to look at Hilo's face, at the solemn, reassuring softness, the glowing pixie beauty, that she knew would be there. "You must promise me you won't abandon him again. Not ever."

"I promise," Hilo whispered. "I promise. On my life."

"No," Noa murmured, forcing her eyes open, forcing herself to stare hard at Hilo. "On *his*."

Hilo clutched Noa's hands, and nodded.

After a moment, the Seer cleared her throat. "Now, about your other mission to free the boys from mind control."

Noa barely heard her, but Hilo turned, startled back into the reality that there was more they had yet to cover, even beyond this.

"I'm afraid this new technology—which distills Fae gifts into tubes and bracelets, divorcing magic from the humanity that tempers it—it is something I never studied, and therefore I cannot advise you. The Scrolls never anticipated such a perversion. However, if you wish to infiltrate the Palace Tower to try to save them, and perhaps free Sasha if she is there, I may be able to guide you in that part. But your time is running out."

"Noa," Hilo said gently, getting up.

"I can't, I need a moment," Noa whispered, shaking her head, unable to stand or take in any more. She was Marena, rocking in their cell. She was her mother the fingernail moon, swallowed by the dark.

The Seer looked from Noa—unreachable—to Hilo. "I will relay the information to you, Hilo, and then our business is at a close."

Hilo looked at Noa, then walked over toward the Seer, leaving Noa to recover in a modicum of privacy.

Noa lay on her side, curled up in the damp, the dank, the darkness, and let it all fall down on her.

Everything she'd lost.

• • •

HILO WENT TO wake Noa gently. She had fallen fitfully asleep on the ground, but even in sleep, Noa's face remained stricken, tensing, as if she were in no place of rest. Grief rose from Noa's skin like steam, seeping into Hilo until she too sagged with it. Hilo could have blocked it with her gift, but instead she let it happen; she didn't want to forget Noa's suffering, not then or later. She wanted it written on her bones. A touchstone. To remember.

So though time was of the essence, Hilo took a moment to curl beside Noa, stomach to back, nesting Cs again, pixie around mortal. The expanse of skin widened between them, one landscape, two hearts, to spread more thinly Noa's pain.

Harmony watched for only a moment or two, allowing again that small stirring she had once thought dead forever. She'd felt it earlier, when she'd found herself at Noa's side. It had frightened

Harmony; she'd pushed it away, named it transference from Noa's feelings and memories. But here it was again. Warmth, a rhythm beating from her heart.

Motherly.

Harmony felt moisture on her cheek, put up a stunned hand to touch it. It was black, as she'd known it would be. She turned back into the dark.

When she reached the subtle crack between the walls, Harmony wove a light sleeping spell behind her. Hilo joined Noa in her sleep, and Harmony turned to the pixie hidden in the crevice.

Her sister.

"Why did you help them at all?" There was little light in this hidden place, but the scar across her sister's face would have been visible even in the bleakest dark. Harmony could have fixed it, but Lia—or Captain Lia, as she was known above—had wanted to keep it to remember. Harmony too had scars, but she wore them where they could not be seen. They'd robbed her of far more than just a pretty face.

"An apostle hidden in the jail sent her to me, gave her my name. He must have heard something from her in there, and he was right. He'd been waiting there for quite some time, watching, listening. He did well."

"That old man? He was part of your circle? You should have told me, I would have protected him—"

"We are few, but every one who serves me is willing to die for me. He died for a good reason." Harmony looked Lia in the eyes. "She's the one. She will reset the balance. She who shines the light..."

"You sound as if you now believe in prophecy."

"Not *prophecy*," Harmony sneered. "I believe in *balance*! Everything I studied, everything we are, everything that was taken from me in this world comes from one thing: *balance*. A sacrifice was made to open that Portal. But Darius did not want to pay the price. So I had to."

"*We* had to," Lia corrected quietly. "They were mine too. You said that once."

Harmony nodded. "Losing them..." Another black tear, wiped away quickly, angrily. "But this girl can bring them back. This girl will reset the balance. She will reopen the pathway from the other side, with the sacrifice originally intended. She will set my children free."

"Surely they will die...."

Harmony spun to her sister, lizard eyes flashing. "And a long wrong will be righted, the balance set anew."

Lia said nothing, bowing to her sister's passion. She knew what it was to lose a child forever, to see him stop breathing before your eyes. She understood why they must do anything, everything, to bring them home again.

"So what now? You cannot know she will do it. You always say you do not See the future. No one can." Lia asked.

Harmony drew herself inward, pushed out her armored lizard skin.

"I have seen her heart. And I know what endures. Balance, and the inevitability of love."

"That's why you help her now?"

Harmony nodded, grim. "Her love will die, but not just yet."

• • •

THE SEER STOOD with Noa and Hilo on the underground bank one last time. Noa was tired but determined; she'd sealed everything up—the whole messy, twisted, excruciating jumble—inside a mammoth, duct-taped box and locked it in a closet far in the back of her mind. So she could focus on the task at hand. So she could accomplish the goal. Rescue.

For their sake, and her own.

In the back of Noa's mind, she suspected Hilo might be helping her, gift-wise, with this enormous emotional denial, but if so, she was okay with that.

"I can create a small window to right outside the Tower, where you thought your sister might be concealed," the Seer told them. "That's as close as I dare to drop you. You will need stealth on your side."

"A window? Like a Portal?" Hilo asked.

The Seer tensed. "Portals require deeper ritual, and open between worlds. Not even I could do that. Even a temporary rip between worlds would require blending all colored magic—and then it would be so brief and so unstable—"

"But you *do* have all the gifts," Hilo interrupted.

"No, I have *knowledge* of the gifts," the Seer snarled. "It is not the same as possessing them entire, inside."

Hilo looked confused and tired.

So was Noa. "So you'll drop us outside the Tower. Then we can get Sasha, and then figure out how to get the boys."

"We should get the brothers first," Hilo argued.

"No," Noa said sharply. "My sister first."

Hilo clenched her teeth and narrowed her eyes.

Noa frowned, frustrated. "Trust me, you want her with us. Especially if their minds are still messed up."

The Seer smiled a tiny smile while Hilo threw up her hands.

"Ready?" the Seer prompted.

Noa looked at Hilo and nodded. The Seer lifted her weathered hands, and the air in front of her coalesced into a kind of looking glass, but instead of the Seer's face, it showed grass, dirt, the exterior of a vine-covered stone wall.

"Not a Portal, just a window inside Aurora. Nothing to be afraid of."

Noa took a deep breath, and with Hilo at her side, stepped out of the darkness.

• • •

THE SEER WAS right: stepping through was just like sneaking out a window. Harmony had also chosen a good place—they were shaded by nearby trees, hidden in the dappled light.

"Which side is the room where you saw your sister in Captain Lia's mind?" Hilo asked, looking up at the many-windowed Tower.

"I didn't actually *see* her—"

"Whatever."

"I just saw a room up in the Tower that Arik was guarding. Where they keep 'the weapon.'"

"Okay, so where was it?"

"I-I don't know," Noa realized. "I only saw the hall from the inside."

Hilo rolled her eyes. "Well we can't go in the front door so what do we do?"

Noa tiptoed to the Tower wall and ran her hands along it. The vines here were not only part of the stone; actual vines had grown up along the side.

Noa smiled. She knew all about going out windows and up and down trees. She did it all the time.

"We climb."

Noa jumped up into the vine's twists and turns, climbing quick as a cat, her energy rising. It felt good to be doing something she knew and did well. Handhold, foothold, lift; handhold, foothold, squeeze, hop, lift. Higher and higher.

"Slow down!" Hilo hissed from below her. "Damn, you must be draining Judah's juice."

Noa froze. She hadn't even considered that—did her exertion speed up the transfer process?

"Relax, Noa, I'm just teasing you," Hilo said with a smirk as she came up even with Noa. "I'm sure it doesn't work like that, and it's not like we're out for fun here."

Noa wanted to slap Hilo, but didn't. She was right. This wasn't a fun run. But she made a mental note to maybe slap her later.

They continued up the wall several more feet until they began to reach rows of windows.

"Whoa, there are a lot of rooms," Noa said.

"But only two levels, see?"

"Yeah but once we start to look, it's only a matter of time before someone catches us. We need enough time to find her—"

"Relax, Noa. We've got this," Hilo said confidently. "We'll just split up."

Noa almost lost her grip. "*What?*" she hissed.

"Come on, it makes the most sense. I'll start at the top level, and you take this level, and hopefully one of us finds her before we get caught."

"Some plan," Noa said uneasily. "But I guess if one of us does find her, we'll be okay."

"Why do you keep saying that? Is there something I don't know?" Hilo replied suspiciously. "I mean, Lily's a Clear as far as I remember, so she doesn't really have a lot to add on her own."

"Just trust me," Noa says. "She's stronger than you think."

"O-kay. Well let's do this then."

"Forward," Noa nodded.

"See you in a bit." With that, Hilo scurried up higher.

Noa turned to the window above her head, murmuring, "I really hope you're here, Sasha my love." She climbed up beside the bottom of the window well and found, to her relief, it was cracked for air. She considered trying to look through the window first but worried it might make her visible to someone on the inside. Besides, the glare would work against her.

No peeking then. All or nothing.

Noa pulled herself up flush alongside the window, then in one motion, leapt to the well, bent, grabbed, and thrust the window up and somersaulted inside—

—and fell several feet through empty air until a hard iron chair painfully broke her fall. She sprang to her feet immediately, ignoring the pain, poised to fight and bite and kick—and froze.

Callum was standing open-mouthed six inches from her, in a Captain's uniform, and Judah was slumped and filthy in a cage.

"I know you," Callum said softly, confused. "You're in the blurry place, the mermaid, you won't go away...."

Judah struggled to his feet behind bars. "Noa?" he coughed, squinting and blinking. "You're alive? And you … you came back for us? After everything…"

"I came to get you out of here," Noa said tersely, not able to meet his eyes. "I'll explain later." She looked at Callum instead. *You betrayed me.* There was no time for that now either. "Let him out, Callum, we have to go find my sister."

Callum struggled, frowned. "No, he has to stay."

"It's no use," Judah muttered bitterly, breathily. "I've tried, he's just too brainwashed—"

"But you're not."

"Because you woke me up."

Noa's stomach twisted. Judah sounded sick, weak. She ordered herself not to look at him, to focus. "Callum!" she demanded instead, grabbing Callum's uniformed shoulders, staring at him hard in the eyes. "You need to wake up now! Like Judah did!" It did not even occur to her to be frightened. She was much too angry for that. And this Callum was not so sure as the Guard who'd killed Marena. This Callum, she could see, was wavering.

"Noa, no," this Callum whimpered. "You're not clear, you're all mixed up, I'm not supposed to go there, you're the mermaid—" He shook her off, flinging her arms away with sudden strength. "I have to take care of my brother!"

"It's no use. You can't break through," Judah moaned.

Rage flared inside Noa. She steeled herself, shoved away how much she knew this was going to hurt. She grabbed Callum's face, pulled it toward hers and kissed it, hard and angry. Callum fought her at first, then kissed her back, confused and then with hunger, then voracious—

Callum ripped himself from her. "No! No! Take it away!" he cried.

Noa tried to grab his forearms, angry and desperate. "Callum! You know who I am! You know who Judah is! Stop with the lies and just *wake up*!"

"I can't," he cried, frenetic. "I can't, I can't! Take it away!"

"Please Callum—" She fell to her knees, burying her face in her hands, too desperate even to stand. Almost automatically, Callum found himself kneeling beside her, wanting, *needing* to help.

"Callum," Noa whimpered into him, "you breathed for me once, when I was underwater you gave me gills. No matter what else—or what…" He was touching her cheek so gently. She took his wrist, looked into his frightened eyes. Forced her voice to strengthen, steady. "Now you have to let me breathe for you. Come back to us. If Judah can do it, so can you."

Callum held her gaze, wanting, *trying*; he started rocking on the floor with the pain of it, backward and forward. Noa found her arms around him, her voice soothing, whispering. She almost forgot for a moment how his skin burned against her skin, how her heart pounded with what she could not now unlearn.

"Noa…," Callum began. He leaned back to look into her eyes; his were clearing, becoming vulnerable and open—

—and then suddenly, he was screaming. *"Intruder! Intruder!"*

Noa sprawled backward where he had thrown her, slid with a crash into Judah's bars. Her vision blackened for a second as she heard the door flung open, the sound of him racing out into the hall.

"He's going to get the others," Judah said hurriedly.

But Noa didn't panic. She got up tiredly, turned to Judah's cell, and put Callum's keys into the lock. The ones she had lifted from him when she'd embraced him.

"You didn't … that wasn't real? You didn't trust him? You did it to steal the keys?"

Noa looked past him at the wall. "I've learned."

Quickly, Noa slid open the door to Judah's cage and helped him out.

"I'm okay, I can do it," Judah insisted, moving jerkily but with slowly increasing steadiness. He paused to tentatively touch her arm. "Just knowing you forgive me, forgive us both, for what happened, that you don't hate us—"

Noa snapped her arm away. "I do hate you!" she said, looking anywhere but at his face. "When are you going to get that?"

"Callum killed Marena, not me!"

"And you let it happen! And now I hate him too, is that what you want? Is that what this is all about?"

Judah lurched back, stung and angry. "I've told you before how I feel, Noa—"

"How you *think* you feel, Judah! But I never loved you, I've told you that over and over! And now I never could. So *get over it.*"

"Why did you even come back for me at all then!" Judah demanded, flinging her arm away. "Just go and leave me here to rot!"

"Because I *need* you now! To help me find Sasha and get her home! You owe me that." She spun from him because she did not want to see his face twisting back into its scowl. "You must know where the weapon room is, they must have talked about it. Take me there *now.*"

"That's stupid, Noa—"

Tears stung Noa's eyes as she whirled on him. "Do it or I will kill you now, I swear it!"

"No Noa—" he yelled back, stronger with his hurt, his anger.

"Now!" Noa ordered.

"Fine!"

Judah pushed past her, flung open the door. She followed him out into the hall and quickly down the corridor just as the alarms began to blare.

• • •

THEY RAN, AND Noa watched the ropey muscles jerk in Judah's back. He moved quickly but unsteadily, tripping and stumbling as he careened down the hall. She did not offer a steadying hand, however, and he did not turn to make sure she could follow.

In truth, Noa was somewhere else entirely. Her heart pounded with each step, her blood rushed and blurred her eyes—she was going to see Sasha, Sasha at last, Sasha her sister, her love, that crown of curls, her sticky hands, Sasha, Sasha, Sasha .... Noa pictured her, just how she'd look inside the room up in this Tower, how when they flung the door open, there she'd be, down to that sparkle in her eye; the way she'd fly to Noa's arms like she'd been waiting and knowing all along.... Again and again, each step the beat of Noa's prophecy: exactly what she would see, how Sasha would look, how then they would just fly away—

Noa and Judah turned one last corridor and saw the room. Two grim-faced Guards blocked the door: Spider-Eye and Mustache. Judah skidded to a halt just before he completed the turn and became visible.

Judah glared at Noa, coming up behind him—*I tried to tell you*, which felt a lot like *I told you so*—but Noa didn't even miss a step. Her body flew around the corner, thundered down the hall so fast that by the time the two Guards turned, she was already bowling into Spider-Eye and knocking him into Mustache like rickety pins. Mustache's head cracked on the ground; his body fell limp; but Spider-Eye stumbled to his knees, the pupil within the spider contorting wildly in confusion.

Noa didn't see it; she didn't see either of the Guards. She saw only Sasha's face, Sasha's hands, the silkiness of those dewy curls. How they would be bouncing as her little legs hurtled toward her long-lost big sister, in her awkward, urgent gate. How Sasha would smile, then laugh, her laugh a shriek, how it would split the air with joy and finally break through Aurora's heaviness; how Sasha would leap into Noa's arms, cling to her, then squirm to go back down so she could lead the way—

Mind dancing somewhere with Sasha's, Noa felt her body move on its own, with its new and fluid instincts. Her hands went to Spider-Eye's temples and he fell limp without a scream or even a whimper, his mind suddenly made silent.

"What the hell?" Judah panted, limping and gasping as he caught up to where she was. "What the hell was that?"

"They'll be fine when they wake up," Noa's voice said, there but not there. She reached for the door, flung it open—

"Sasha ... "

"Noa, listen, wait."

But she didn't listen, she wouldn't wait, because all she wanted was Sasha's face and Sasha's voice and Sasha here and in this room, the moment as she had imagined it, coming finally to life—

The room was empty, so very empty. No one. Nothing. A lonely bookcase holding test tubes. A bubbling vat shoved in a corner.

Noa looked into the emptiness, mind and body stunned. Neither could register what her eyes told her to see.

"Sasha? Sasha!" Noa cried, suddenly knowing only panic. Her body flailed in chaos, frenzy; she tried to run every direction, all directions all at once, flung herself wildly about the room. But no matter where she looked or where she ran it was the same: empty empty empty, a shelf of stupid tubes, a metal vat!

"I tried to tell you," Judah said weakly behind her, voice cracking from exertion. "She's not here, she was never here. Only this." She turned to him, desperate; scowling, he'd raised his wrist. She hadn't noticed it before, in the place of the talisman—a tube bracelet filled with black. She looked from it to the tubes on the bookcase, the heating liquid in the vat: the same. Black and viscous, liquid tar.

"I don't understand..." Noa began.

"It's Kells' blood. His blood is black, not Green now, and he's learned to use it like the other Colorline bloods. Except it's *not* the same." Judah wiped at his cheek angrily, though no tear had fallen. He spoke louder, more defiantly. "It's the opposite. It blocks magic, Noa, it blocks all gifts. Makes you powerless for real...." He swallowed. "None of my gifts will work, I'm nothing now—"

"Kells? Wait, Mr. Green? The Gatekeeper Thorn fed to the Portal?" Noa cried in confusion. "What does he have to do with this? He's dead!"

Judah sagged, in exhaustion or defeat, Noa couldn't tell. "No, he's not dead. He traveled right through the Portal when Thorn threw him in, it didn't even try to hold its master. He came out in Aurora and killed my father. He's been the Otec all along—"

"And this … *this* blood is his weapon?" Noa whispered, falling to her knees. It was too much to process; the floor was spinning, falling.

"Kells used me to test it." Judah broke her gaze, face hot with shame. "He thought if I were powerless, I might follow him, too, like Callum. He wants everything Darius had and more—"

"No, but this can't be!" Noa shrieked in anger. "The weapon was supposed to be Sasha, I picked it out of Captain Lia's head. It had to be her!"

"No, Noa," Judah said tiredly. "But we'll keep trying."

"*How?*" Noa wailed, as Sasha's face swam before her eyes.

"Together!" Judah snapped.

"We will never be together, Judah!" Noa didn't even need to look away as her anger slapped his face; she could not see him now at all. How was this possible? She had been so sure, Sasha had been here, she'd seen it, they were to be reunited, this was the end of this nightmare, this horrid dream, she'd *seen* it!

Noa began to sob. It was a dream, only a dream, that's all this had ever been. A false hope, her own denial. Sasha was not here, was never here, was only in her mind.

Noa's brain told her to push Sasha's face away, to put the image back into its box with all the things that hurt too much, wind the reel of their reunion back into its canister. Lock it all up, bury it deep and somewhere else, somewhere safe; stop being Noa and become animal alone. Focus on getting out alive.

Except this time she couldn't do it. The box wasn't big enough, her arms weren't strong enough, and her mind, her mind was too fractured now to care.

So she thought of Sasha, Sasha's face, the loop of the reunion that now would never be; she watched it over and over, gave it form the way she often conjured Isla's ghost, and she let Dream-Sasha settle into the corner of this wretched, empty room.

That was when the door slammed open, and Callum, Kells, and another ally thundered in. Noa watched in shock from her place on the floor, discovered she yet had room for one more loss: Kells' and Callum's ally, wearing white, was Hilo.

• • •

"HILO," NOA MURMURED from the ground, not believing at the same time as she believed it all too well. Hilo had the grace to look at least a bit ashamed: she stood by Kells' side, clearly by choice, but she averted her light-blue eyes.

On Kells' other side, Callum stood erect, face steady but body on edge. His eyes flicked warily to Noa; he stood half a step behind his leader.

Hilo turned deferentially to Kells, who nodded, and Hilo ran to Judah's side. Noa realized, with shock, that he'd collapsed into the wall. Hilo knelt tenderly beside him and held him, soothed him as his eyes fluttered weakly.

Feeling sick, Noa turned to Kells. "Mr. Green," she said, though calling him by that name here felt absurd.

"Ms. Sullivan, you recognize me."

Noa suddenly registered the great change in Kells' body: somehow she had not noticed until this moment that his body had untwisted and now stood strong and virile. As if his essence had met her first, and that was still wasted rotten.

"How did you—"

"Light, my dear," Kells answered, but his face turned bitter. "But alas, some things do not come back. Thanks to Darius, the physical is all I get. My gift is gone. Lucky for me, I have found a way to use my predicament."

His eyes wandered proudly to the vat, the tubes of black.

Rage flared in Noa as she thought instantly of Marena. "So the liquefying thing is just because you like to kill people? Because there's your blood, but you're not some murdered puddle."

Kells chuckled, as at an impertinent puppy. "My blood is the opposite of magical now, so it is useful without my essence. Not like the Colors, I'm afraid, though the product works in a remarkably similar way." His eyes twinkled at her. "Very lucky for me, don't you think?"

"Noa, I'm sorry, please—" Hilo suddenly burst out from where she cradled Judah. "I had to—"

"That's enough," Kells said as he reached into his pocket. Hilo screamed and grabbed her head. When Kells brought his hand back out, he was holding three bracelets—all encased in red tubes. Talismans. He smiled at Noa as Hilo moaned.

"I suppose I have you to thank for these, my dear. You don't even know the revolution you started, all because Callum couldn't control himself around you and made you that bracelet. *Young love.* Generation after generation, we never learn." Noa flushed as Kells picked out one bracelet and held it up gingerly, as if it were a rodent, then flung it away into the far corner of the room. "Though that one's useless, clearly," he said disdainfully, eyeing the lump of Judah on the floor. Hilo's face reddened but she said nothing, holding him closer protectively.

"It's okay, Hilo," Noa said, not taking her eyes from Kells. "I get it now. He's controlling you with a talisman, like Callum."

Kells let out a loud, sharp laugh. Callum looked at him nervously, meeting Noa's eyes for a split second and then looking quickly away. Kells held up one of his two remaining red-tubed talismans.

"You think I need this with *that* little turncoat?" Kells laughed, nodding at Hilo. *"Please."* Without warning, Kells threw Hilo's talisman into the bubbling vat of black blood. Hilo screamed as if she'd been shot by a cannon; her chest began to gush with blood as the vat sizzled and boiled and hissed.

Kells nodded tersely to Callum, who went over to knit the flesh of Hilo's wound and stop the pain. Hilo stopped screaming, but her eyes remained frantic, terrified. Noa knew she could still feel the injury and always would: a piece of her soul had just been destroyed forever.

"I doubt you'll miss it after too long, my dear," Kells called to Hilo. "You don't strike me as the wholesome sort to begin with."

Noa locked eyes with Hilo's—they were scared, and *beaten.* Still ashamed, still apologetic, and even sadder now than before. She didn't move. And then Noa knew Kells was right—Hilo had *chosen* Kells' side. She was a survivor; this was the bargain she'd made to survive with Judah at her side, talisman or no talisman controlling her.

Noa turned away and retched.

"That's not very pleasant," Kells commented distastefully. "At Harlow, I would have had to clean that up. Mortals can be so filthy."

"You realize what you're doing? What all this is leading to?"

Noa coughed, flinging her arm toward the black vat. "You'll destroy this world—"

"Yes. And then I'll come for yours."

"*Why?*"

Kells' eyes grew hard. "Because Darius took everything from me, even my gift, and revenge is all I have left." He took a breath, pushed away his emotion. "And now, my dear, as helpful as you've been in getting the whole thing started, I'm afraid you've outgrown your usefulness. I simply can't have you pulling at my puppets' strings and making them go off-book, the way you did with *that* one." He glared briefly at Judah. "Don't worry, the ending comes full circle."

Kells nodded at Callum. Callum swallowed hard—his body twitched a little, clearly uneasy—but he began to walk toward her, looking anywhere but at her eyes. Noa couldn't breathe.

Callum was going to kill her.

So Noa did the only thing she could. She refused to look away. She looked at him unflinchingly, and willed him to wake and see her. And then she realized that even if he didn't see, even if he couldn't, *she* was revealed, just as she was, all that she was—and she was not afraid.

"It wasn't Darius, you know, who took away your gift," she said to Kells, suddenly realizing he too should know, even if he was a villain, maybe because he was a villain, even if it was the last thing she ever did. "Your black blood wasn't Darius."

Kells face creased in frustration, misgiving. He wanted to ignore her, she could tell—but he couldn't. "*Wait,*" he commanded Callum. Callum paused with a little heave of relief. "Look at me." Kells focused on Noa with hard black eyes. "*You're lying.*"

Noa smiled at him as serenity filled her. Sasha was next to her, holding her hand, where she would always be from now on, where Noa could never lose her. Noa met his eyes calmly, an oracle, her words ringing with the peaceful clarity of truth: "Only love is powerful enough to change blood. Darius didn't do it to you, he couldn't. You didn't love Darius. You loved Lorelei, truly, and Lorelei loved you—but she didn't *choose* you. Your blood was poisoned by a love that couldn't be. Your love, for her."

Kells' face flared in anger—then crumpled, his body sagging under itself into the husk it once had been. His lips, dry now and chapped, parted, let out a whispered moan, a keen: "*Lorelei…*"

The name made Callum turn from Noa, body vibrating like a tuning fork.

Kells keened again, again—then filled with rage.

Kells didn't need Callum at all, wouldn't wait for him to do it. Kells wanted to kill Noa himself and kill her now, for shattering the only thing that mattered. Kells' hand flew to his other pocket, brought out a vial of Blue Smoke—the Smoke that denatured spines and atoms, that ripped the body's world apart—and hurled it at Noa with everything he had. It happened in a flash, an instant, but once the vial was in the air, time seemed to slow as every head watched its graceful arc: Callum, Kells, Hilo, Noa, like some bizarre serve in a tennis match of death—and then in a flash, time exploded again as the vial hit and shattered on the floor in front of Noa, as the Smoke unleashed like a roaring, seething lion, uncoiling huge and leaping, jaws wide open, for Noa's kneeling frame—Noa closed her eyes, chin high, the dream of Sasha hand in hand beside her, and she felt unafraid—

And everything went silent.

Noa breathed.

Her body felt cold.

She opened her eyes slowly and gasped: the devouring Blue Smoke cloud was frozen in a massive wave of ice. Callum, Kells, and Hilo were encased too, glacial, turned to sparkling crystalline statues absurdly caught in time—their mouths open midword, midscream, their hands up, outstretched, reaching, turning, leaping. And all around the frozen, ice-filled room, glittering snow-flakes of ice shimmered down, leaving cool, brief kisses on Noa's arms, in her hair, soft as brief brushes of butterfly wings.

"Noa … ?" Judah said weakly from somewhere behind her. His voice broke the isolation of her wonder, and Noa turned to find him. The glacial ice had sucked itself around Hilo's figure and left Judah untouched. He was slumped on the floor, blinking into consciousness in confusion at this fragile fantasy of ice-and-prism. Noa took a step toward him, just as confused and mesmerized—

—and then she heard it.

"*My* Noa."

Tears sprang to Noa's eyes, her body spun, her world became a lightbox filled with sound. That voice, that piercing, joyful voice, and now those quick and stumbling footsteps, half-dance half-flee half-fall—all notes pinging off the crystal ice, blending into the made-up, shrieking song Noa had tried so hard to remember. And then Sasha, her Sasha, in full and living color, burst through the bright reverberations, gave the bells and music form as she ran under a cresting frozen wave—an archway, really, though Noa hadn't noticed it before, because it opened up the world again even as it held their enemies at bay. Sasha ran beneath and then broke upward, leaping into Noa's arms.

Noa fell back, laughing, crying, hugging, as Sasha climbed all over her, covered her cheeks and nose with kisses and with spit, with sweat and stick and warm. Noa heard herself sobbing, shrieking, shouting as Sasha pulled her hair, hugged her head, yanked on Noa's shoulders to urge her to sit up.

Noa did but kept Sasha wrapped up tight. "You came for me, my love," she cried into her curls, gulping that beloved Sasha smell. "I wanted to come for you, but you came for me."

Sasha scrambled backward in Noa's arms so she could look her sister in the eyes, her small face screwed up and annoyed. "I wait and I wait and I wait, I ask, I ask, I ask, and you never show me! Finally you show me!" she scolded. "Next time, show me faster!"

Noa bit her lip, tried not to laugh, but she couldn't help it. There were the furious apple cheeks, the stern bow lips, right here in this room where Noa had dreamed and dreamed and dreamed her—

"Oh my God!" Noa cried in sudden revelation, staring Sasha in the eyes. "All this time—in the cave, in the Tunnels, in the White Province—all those times I saw you in my mind or dreams or remembered you and then made myself think of other things—I wasn't remembering or imagining, was I? I was *Dreamwalking*—to you! And I kept chasing you away!"

Sasha nodded emphatically. *Finally* her big sister understood. Noa couldn't believe how clear it all seemed now. "You kept me asking me *where*, and I kept pushing you back, putting you far away inside a box to keep you safe—until now, until here in this room when I couldn't bear *not* to think of you, not to imagine, no matter how it hurt. So I pictured you here, over and over, you here with me—"

"And so I come!" Sasha squealed in delight. "I come to fix it!"

"And you did," Noa cried, burying her head in Sasha's hair again, that smell. "You did!"

Noa suddenly remembered Judah. This was his sister too. and this joy was huge, so huge it should be shared. She turned to him, heart bursting warm—and her stomach cratered.

Judah was watching, had been watching their reunion. Noa had never seen him look so lonely, broken-down, and lost. He saw her eyes and scowled, flushed, looked away.

"Do you remember Judah, Sasha?" Noa asked her sister gently, turning back to her because she could not bear to see Judah's face that way. Sasha slid her eyes to Judah carefully, then looked back at Noa, burying her face in Noa's neck, the way she sometimes did with strangers.

A cracking sound made them all turn to Sasha's crystal wave of ice—panic flew through Noa as she saw, within their ice cocoon, blue light warming around Callum and Kells, causing tiny fractures to come up to the surface.

"They're breaking through!" Noa realized, jumping to her feet. "Callum must be working his gift to set them free." She spun to Hilo. It was happening for Hilo too, and Judah, who was scrabbling backward on his hands.

And then Noa knew. She *knew.*

Her plan would not work, could never work. And she could not have borne it if it did.

Noa let Sasha slide down her side to stand on the ground, though she kept Sasha's fingers fast in hers. She turned to Judah, held out her other free hand kindly. "We have to go, Judah. Come on."

Judah had slid away from Hilo and gotten to his feet, but he didn't come toward her. He scowled at her outstretched arm. "You have Sasha. You don't need me anymore."

"But you have to come with us! Come on!"

"You hate me, remember? You always have. I accept it, it's what you wanted."

Noa's heart sped in growing panic. "I know I said those things, but they were lies! It was all a lie!" More cracks sounded from the ice, and Sasha squeezed her hand, clearly eager to get moving. But Noa couldn't wait either; she had to do this now, when the whole world was suddenly encased in ice and just as clear. Who knew how long that would last? As if an echo of her thought, chunks of ice began to fall from Kells, Callum, and Hilo.

"I was scared, Judah, I was scared and lost and I wanted to protect you, but you were right, you were right all along and I didn't see it." The words tumbled, jumbled together, inadequate to describe it right. "It's you and me, together, I get it now, I can't leave without you—" She was smiling, grinning, because finally she knew, she knew and she felt and she trusted! "We'll figure the rest out, the rest I can't even begin to tell you, but we'll do it and we'll find it and we just have to go right now—"

But he wasn't smiling back; he wasn't coming toward her; he wasn't reaching for her hand. He was scowling harder, as if she were hurting him, making everything worse. His eyes filled with disbelief and suspicion, pain and angry unshed tears. Sasha yanked on Noa's hand, urging her away, but Noa couldn't leave, not yet—she had to speak until the words were right, until they were the poem that she needed:

"Judah, don't you get it? *We wake each other up.* In the Portal we woke together, and in prison you woke for me, even when they had your soul and it meant pain! And at home"—tears of her own now, streaming messily on all the words—"at home after Isla died and I had nothing, not even dreams, *you woke me*. I thought it was Callum, but it was *you*—not to some fairy tale that wasn't real, but to everything, every feeling, good *and* bad! Anger and happiness and frustration, confidence and daring, fear and I don't know! Everything! Things that hurt, things that were messy, things that were hard—you woke me up! We wake each other, don't you see? So you can't stay here, I don't care about the rest, come with me, let's go somewhere else, let's figure the rest out later—"

Ice was raining fast from Callum, Hilo, Kells—Hilo's arms were free, and Kells' legs up to the knees, and Callum's entire torso, neck to waist. Sasha screamed in anger, yanking Noa so hard she stumbled in the direction away from Judah. Noa pulled back against her sister to reach again, desperately, toward the boy who would not reach back. He looked at her hand, face crumpling now, childlike, wanting so much to believe—

"*Home!*" Sasha yelled, voice booming so loud and strong it shook the room. Noa yelped as a blinding light stung her eyes and a thunderous crack shook the room and split the floor. Noa looked behind her: Sasha had ripped a vertical, wailing chasm in the air, bleeding radiant, blinding light like some trapped, exploding star—

"A Rip in the worlds," Noa murmured in awe, in terror, as everything in the room heaved and shook. The Seer had warned her such a thing could be conjured only if one had all the powers intrinsically, like Sasha—but that it would last for moments only, then devour anything within—

Alarms were blaring in the hallway; shouts and footsteps thundered. Noa turned back to Judah, now on the other side of the cracking floor, the cavern between them growing wider by the moment.

"Come on!" she screamed, arm outstretched, above the roar and blare. "Jump!"

He called back against the noise, the rush, the air, "No time! … Have to go … without me!"

Noa turned to Sasha, desperate. "He's your brother, help him, Sash!"

But Sasha was looking past Noa and glaring right at Judah. She made a little growl at him and yanked Noa hard away and toward the Rip—

Noa resisted, not understanding, whipping back to Judah one last time. He looked stricken, frozen, ashamed, was no longer trying to reach her. Ice kept falling; the thunder of boots descending the hall—

"Judah!" Noa screamed in terror, in panic. "Come on!"

"You were right to hate me!" Judah cried, face crumpling in tears. "Sasha knows, she knows and she's afraid—"

"Judah, stop it—"

"*I threw her through the Portal on purpose! Back in your world! To hurt you!*" The confession tore him apart, loud within the noise with its terrible, terrible clarity. "I did it on purpose! Because I knew that it would hurt you! Because you said you didn't love me! She knows, she knows!" Judah fell to his knees, burying his face as the last ice fell from Callum, Kells, and Hilo and they sprang forward with battle cries, as Arik and a swarm of Guards blasted in the door. "I did it on purpose! I didn't care! I didn't care and I wanted to hurt you!"

Noa didn't see them, didn't see anything. She was so shocked, so devastated, hearing every word and knowing, terribly, terribly knowing, that every word was truth. She was paralyzed, struck dumb, and Sasha had to *make* her move.

Noa let Sasha pull her rag-doll body toward the Rip, but her button eyes remained on Judah, this Judah who was not her Judah at all, who was someone she had never imagined, never seen, but who had been there all along—someone so broken, so terribly broken all he could do was hurt you, someone who could be fixed and didn't want to be. And Judah watched them go, his face so lost it would have broken Noa's heart if she'd still had a heart to break. She thought maybe he mouthed something, threw something as Aurora swirled away to black, but all she could do was close her eyes,

and let Sasha guide her home.

PART V: HOME, AGAIN

THEY WALKED OUT to calm and peaceful quiet. Evening. The cool clear crispness of Salinas. Noa breathed it in, drank the sharp, light air. *Home.*

Behind them, Sasha's Rip simply swallowed itself away, sucking out with the faintest *pop.*

If only everything that had happened in Aurora could be sealed away so neatly.

Noa looked down at Sasha, helpless; Sasha looked back up at Noa and squeezed Noa's hand three times. She smiled her rarest, secret Sasha smile—the shy one, just between them—and then started leading Noa forward, down the hill toward the cul-de-sac where they lived. The moon was full and round; it lit the air in concert with the stars. The road ahead was deserted, peaceful with all in bed.

Home.

Where Judah had not confessed, where Callum had not deceived her, where everything that lay undone was winked out behind her.

Noa's body suddenly seized; her heart pounded. The silence suddenly felt empty, the calm lonely and narrow and alone.

Sasha squeezed her hand, three times. And then Noa saw them.

They had come to walk beside them in the dark. Noa and Sasha were not alone, for here was Isla's ghost holding out her hand, and at her side, a glint of mischief in her eye and a cheeky smile on her lips, was Marena, whole and healthy, holding her spirit-sister's hand. Noa took Isla's other hand, and the four of them—Sasha, Noa, Isla, Marena—continued united, bound, girl-beasts too strong for fear.

When they reached Noa's familiar house, Isla and Marena nodded goodbye and, with linked arms, faded into the night. Noa knelt by Sasha and hugged her tight. When she let go, Sasha handed Noa something from her pocket—something she had caught and kept just as they'd left Aurora. Something Judah had thrown into the Rip after them, that he'd wanted Noa to have, even after everything:

A silver chain, with a tiny silver charm, faintly glowing red, freed from its red tube. Judah's talisman, part of his soul, which Kells had thrown away.

Noa's heart tightened, but Sasha smiled, closed Noa's hand around it. Sasha wanted her to keep it. So Noa tucked it away safe.

They were almost at the door when someone, two someones, hissed at them from behind Isla's tree in their front yard.

"*Noser!*"

"*Don't freak her out!*"

Olivia and Miles, hiding in the shrubbery.

Noa ran over with Sasha in tow, so tired and confused but overwhelmed with relief to see them alive and here and well, but knowing from Sasha's squeeze that they were them and this was real. Noa hugged Olivia first, then Miles, unable to find the words.

"Jeez Louise, Noa, it hasn't been that long. We saw you at school this morning," Olivia laughed.

"What?" Noa asked.

Miles turned red. "We kind of followed you. To that gardening shack with Callum's brother? Judah, right, Olivia? I'm a little sketchy on the details. My memory's still kinda *Memento*-ing on me."

"Wait ... you followed me and Judah, when we went to see K—Mr. Green? In his shack? And that was ... today?"

"This afternoon," Olivia said, squinting at her. "We're sorry for spying, but we were worried. We had to watch from kinda far away and didn't see what happened inside, but then there was this huge exploding light, and, well..." She looked at Miles, who shrugged back at her. "Well, I think his memory thing might be contagious or something because then I had this really weird daydream, except we were all in it and Harlow was super bizarro, and neither of us remembers anything until like, a couple hours later."

"Uh ... wow," Noa said carefully.

"But the point is," Olivia barreled on, in her usual Olivia way, "when we did wake up in the field again, you guys were gone and that shack was like, demolished, so we came here and have been waiting for you to come home to make sure you're okay. Which, clearly, you are." She turned to Miles. "As I *said* she would be, didn't I? I told you Noa's a tough broad."

Miles shrugged and smiled at Noa. "I worry about you. Hazard of my friendship. That I know, no matter how wonky my short-term memory may be."

Noa looked at his earnest, eager face, that golden-retriever smile, his adorably rumpled hair. Miles was always looking out for her, he was always on her side, and he never stopped supporting her even when she let him down, again and again…. He was her Miles, her easy, adorable, loving Miles, he was someone she could be sure of, someone she could always trust, she had never appreciated that so clearly before—

"Uh, hello, Noa?" Olivia snapped her fingers in front of Noa, who was staring at Miles a little moonily.

Miles cocked his head. "You okay, Noa?"

Noa shook herself, blushing for some reason. "Yes, yes, I'm just so glad to have you guys in my corner." She hugged Olivia again, then went to hug Miles, but they did a little awkward dance and Noa blushed again when they finally worked it out.

Olivia pulled Miles away, apparently noticing nothing. "We gotta hightail it back to school, or we'll have a hard time sneaking back in, and I so do not need a curfew infraction to start next term. Good to see you're fine and Miles is still nuts. See you tomorrow, chica!"

"Bye, guys." Noa smiled and gave them a little wave as they ran off, no doubt to cross to the main road where they would call a cab to take them back to Harlow.

Once Olivia was out of sight, Sasha pulled Noa toward the door. She reached up to turn the doorknob, not letting Noa's hand go, and together, they walked inside the house.

Noa paused in the foyer to let the familiar smell and air envelop her like a favorite threadbare blanket. She heard voices, and her mother laughing—*laughing*—in the kitchen; light shone beneath the door. Noa went toward the cozy, unexpected sound like a moth to warmth. It was manna after a long and terrible journey, a sound to dissolve all other sounds remembered and unwanted.

Noa and Sasha together pushed the swinging door into the kitchen and walked into the warm glow. There were Christopher and Hannah, smiling and laughing by candlelight around the worn circle breakfast table—the table of Noa's childhood—and with them, joining in like oldest friends, were two people who cut the warmth like a knife down to the bone:

Lorelei, and Darius.

COLLECT ALL THREE COVERS OF
RENEGADE RED

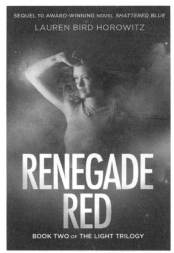

Poet Edition

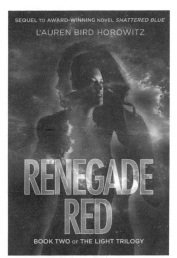

Warrior Edition

Traveler Edition

JOIN FAE NATION

Add YOUR pin to
THE LIGHT TRILOGY Map
and join FAE NATION!

Send in your pictures of *Shattered Blue* and
Renegade Red around the world!

laurenbirdhorowitz.com/book-destinations

THE LIGHT TRILOGY
Jewelry Capsule Collections

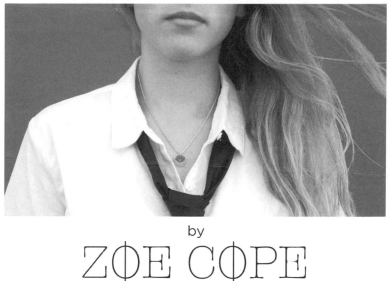

by

ZOE COPE
jewelry

featuring Noa's talisman and other pieces from the exciting trilogy...

www.ZOECOPEJEWELRY.com

POETRY APPENDIX

GIRL

my lids close and your eyes open:
silt-rich and promise-thick,
chocolate pools for wildflowers
if I could only
stay
and
watch.
I blink—you ringlet up,
snail-curled inside your shell. A spiral
I can't pick from
endless, shapeless sands.

But when I write—I *feel* you,
fingers small and fat in mine,
we ink each word together
we make sticky prints in sap.

Who are we, are we starfish?
Hand-cups sucked together fast?
I taste your salt
I smell your tang
Why
do
you
never
last?

TATTOO

Girl-Beast wake and wail with me
Pack your wounds with rocks and mud
Let growls rip betwixt your teeth
Be killer, hunter, fighter, thief,
Give no mercy, no relief,
Spill truth with flesh and blood!

MARENA

Mar is the sea
but not this sea
not these predictable currents
not these precise, breaking waves.

Mar is a riptide
the flow under the flow—
she sinks where they rise,
retracts where they push.

Beware swimmers, who use only your eyes
hypnotized by peaks cresting
and neat lines of foam.
Mar's fingers are seaweed, the deep and the dark,
Mar's whirlpools are hidden
spinning down coral shoals.

Seagirl stop stroking
in peak, crest, and fill—
See instead with your skin
with your scales
with your gills.

SANDPAPER PLACE, AURORA

I have been here before, in this Sandpaper Place,
I know these stones by chilling heart.
Sometimes they are ragged, slicing my palms,
Sometimes smooth,
or bars,
bright clear windows,
locked doors.

There were times I curled under, away
From the Sandpaper place.
Built my nautilus outward,
spun from bone.
Fingertips in, pill-bug snug, soft worm skin
Chrysalis'd tight—
But it's been long since my wings broke that skin.

Cocoons cannot fit me
(nor this Sandpaper Place),
pinkened palms can't survive in the sun.
I grow suction cups now, inside hands, down both wrists,
Reach out wide, splay myself to cold:

Starfish-to-starfish,
Sister-limbs fuse as one
Girl-beast chain, sister-strong, woven tight:
Isla and Sasha, Marena, Hilo's siren song:
No fear, be brave, *Forward* fight!

ACKNOWLEDGMENTS

FIRST TO MARK Pedowitz, who started this crazy adventure.

Leslie, who makes the magic *real*.

Bill Haber, unseen hand behind every victory.

Bruce Vinokour, fighting so hard for me on every front (love you, CAA).

T, the amazing Tricia Ballard: you are Wonder Woman. Nothing—not a word—could have happened without you.

Zoe Cope: artistic genius, crafter of Fae-ness you can actually touch, visual visionary, and most bad-ass chick around—not to mention cover-mastermind, pirate jeweler, geode tour-mate, and girl-beast to the bone.

Mar, namesake of Marena, person to my person, mermaid-warrior brave enough even to read early, wordy, rife-with-mistakes drafts (even on tight, tight deadlines!).

Gil Cope: photographer savant, who made these covers epic beyond my imagination (and Kara, for being Noa, you graceful, fierce woman!).

Ash & Shelbs (and Mar and T): Ninja Otter Sox shout out!

Ash, Neko forever! Shelbs, so glad we share the same "terrible" taste in music!

Andy, Kristen & Ethan: Team Book Tour! Team Ninja! Team Words Against Humanity!

Tanaz Masaba, Jaime Kramer, Anne Bollman, Jhoanne Ayen Jimenez, Abbie San Juan, Bashayer Hakami, Barbara Hunt, and all the T-Birds: You have no idea how much your support has meant to me. You make this all worth it. I promise to keep torturing and tugging your hearts.

Eric, Susan, Elena, and everyone at PGW, for taking on *The Light Trilogy* and getting it out there! You guys are the best!

Brad and Liquis, for making the online face of *The Light Trilogy* so awesome.

BookSparks, for launching my books (and me!) to the world.

Papaloa Press: so happy to bring *The Light Trilogy* home (literally!).

LW: editor-partner for life!

And, forever:

A: always. For bringing me back.

Kauai, my most special, special home, and my Kauai ohana: Aloha nui loa; you are the happiness of my happy place. Shaka!

Tara (& Favor): Kauai sister, shared devotee of the magical floaty (and Mama Sharon: kukui oil forever!).

Jamaica: my teacher.

Janet, Jaime, Da, David, Ryan, Anne, Angela, Team Terrace: still the best friends Noa could have.

Mirah: rescuer of lost creatures—and my dearest, dearest Ninja. Can never repay you, not ever.

Mom & Dad: for giving me my siblings & for first taking me to Kauai, my spiritual center and the birthplace of *The Light Trilogy*.

Jeremy: twin Kauaian, island-heart soul mate, inspiring big brother I will always adore.

Mikey & Michelle: for giving me the gift of the Sasha cover! Michelle, for sharing your amazing, so moving photos. Both of you, for always making me such a special part of your MOMA.

Avi: for always letting me build roads with you outside, and cities inside, and worlds in the everywhere we imagine together.

Livi: for being Sasha for me—on the cover and beyond!

… and my Ninja. Woof!

THE AUTHOR

LAUREN BIRD HOROWITZ, screenwriter and novelist, has won an enthusiastic following for her innovative, lyrical poetic voice. Her debut novel, *Shattered Blue: Book One of The Light Trilogy*, won the 2016 Independent Publishers' (IPPY) Silver Medal for Young Adult Fiction, as well as Finalist honors in the 2016 USA Book Awards for Best New Fiction and Best New Fantasy, the 2016 Next Generation Indie Book Awards for Best Young Adult Fiction, and the 2016 International Book Award for Best Fantasy. It was also listed as one of *USA Today's* top romances of 2015, and selected as a notable book by Buzzfeed, POPSUGAR, Hypable, San Francisco Book Review, Glitter, Culturalist, Teen Reads, MariaShriver.com, Bustle, and others.

Bird studied writing at Harvard University with novelist Jamaica Kincaid and won several prizes, including the Edward

Eager Memorial Prize for fiction and the Winthrop-Sargent Prize for writing. She is a proud member of the Writers Guild of America.

CONNECT

 www.LaurenBirdHorowitz.com
@birdaileen
@birdaileen
Lauren "Birdaileen" Horowitz